Fiona J. Watson is a medieval historian and writer specialising in medieval warfare in particular and Scottish history more generally. Her many publications include *Macbeth: A True Story* (2010), *A History of Scotland's Landscapes* (2018), *Traitor, Outlaw, King: Part One. The Making of Robert Bruce* (2018) and *Scotland's History* (2020). A former senior lecturer in History at the University of Stirling and presenter of the BBC TV series, *In Search of Scotland*, Fiona is now venturing into historical fiction to make the most of the limited evidence for medieval Scotland. Her first novel, *Dark Hunter*, was published by Polygon in 2022.

Lies of the Flesh

Fiona Watson

Polygon

First published in 2024 by Polygon,
an imprint of Birlinn Ltd.

Birlinn Ltd
West Newington House
10 Newington Road
Edinburgh
EH9 1QS

www.polygonbooks.co.uk

1

ISBN 978 1 84697 674 2
eBook ISBN 978 1 78885 671 3

British Library Cataloguing-in-Publication Data
A catalogue record for this book is available on request
from the British Library.

Typeset by Initial Typesetting Services, Edinburgh

Printed and bound by CPI Group (UK) Ltd, Croydon CR0 4YY

To Margaret Elizabeth Watson
1940-2024

And Nick and Finn, as always

For a list of characters, real and imagined, a glossary of terms that might be unfamiliar to some readers and the author's historical notes, please turn to page 337.

Part One

Chapter 1

August 1314

His father wanted only boys. So a boy was what his father got. For twenty years Francis Hilton has done as Andrew Hilton told him to do, acting out in deed and word what a son should be. In outward form he looks the part. If he is naturally short of stature, he has worked hard at manly pursuits to become broad of shoulder and thigh, skin stretched tight over the muscular flesh beneath. For as long as he can remember, he has wrestled boys his own age into the ground, disarmed them of sword or spear with nimble skill, rode longer and faster when they were taken out to hunt. He has been intent on mastering them, certainly, but it is his own nature he fights hardest.

And yet his father watches him still, eyes murky. Andrew Hilton always looks away quickly enough, so Fran can't return his glance with one of his own that might act upon him as a gauntlet thrown full in the face. *This is your fault. Everything about me, everything I am, you chose to shape. If I disappoint you, it's not for want of practice or effort.*

And now his father is dying, fallen from his horse and clutching his side when he returned from Warcop. He was carried into the main chamber where he lies now, as if under an enchantment intent on draining the life out of him. Or so says Jack, the kitchen boy, sent to find Fran up among their cattle on the high pasture because he is fleet of foot. He delivers his message in one shrill torrent of words, shivering as the rain rushes over the hilltops and throws itself at them. Fran turns away from Jack and Harry Sowerby, the bailiff, to gaze upwards at the great fells. But they have nothing to say to him, with their heads hanging in the clouds. His dog, Dolfyn – a restless greyhound with a sleek blue-grey coat – nuzzles his hand, but for once Fran doesn't notice.

He begins to run, his mind pelted with all the things he never said, all the questions he never asked. Of course, his father is no longer a young man; the days when he is up before the first glimmer of dawn are a rarity now, the nights when he sits close to the fire, complaining of this ailment or that ache, grown ever more numerous, even though he is only in his middling years. But what does any of that matter? Fran finds it impossible to imagine himself without his father.

Turning abruptly into the courtyard, his feet scarcely touch the ground. He charges through the front door, leaps at the staircase, shaking off mud like a dog. Some of the outdoor servants stand in the way like abandoned furniture, shrinking back to let him past. He calls out to them to cease their lamenting, for his mind is disordered enough without having to listen to them.

In truth, they have enough to worry about already. These past weeks they've all been sniffing the air, scanning the horizon, interrogating strangers at every opportunity, eager for news of the Scots coming this way (if by 'eager', we mean desperately hoping there will be no such news). Many from Westmorland left their homes to join the king's army more than two months ago. Everyone was so sure the great campaign would bring victory to the English and a halt to Scottish raiding. Instead, it ended with disaster in a fearful battle somewhere far to the north on the feast day of St John the Baptist. King Edward himself was forced to ride like a demon for the border, leaving his men to find their own way home, if they could. There will be no help for the people of northern England this year.

And Fran knows, as almost no one else does, that those lamenting now have even more reason to raise up their voices. And he understands then it is true what Jack said. The old man is going. Has perhaps already gone. And probably no time for a priest to minister to him, though surely Will – Father Warcop – has been sent for.

He throws open the great oak door, strides in so forcefully that the wall hangings are set a-flutter, Dolfyn at his side. All round the room candles blink and dance and he wonders who thinks them so well supplied with coin that they might waste it while daylight lingers, however lightly clad. He feels the eyes turn upon him, the taut figures gathered there, watching, waiting. But he desires only to see *him*, to know for certain if all is undone.

His father lies on the long table, a blanket pulled over him up to his chin, pillow beneath his head. Fran walks slowly now, seeing himself move through the horrified gathering. He does not need to seek out any last flicker of life. The sound his father makes grips the room, each hoarse breath proclaiming that Death has Andrew Hilton firmly in his grasp.

As Fran reaches the table, he feels a hand on his arm and knows it is his mother. Shaking her away, he moves to the other side and gazes down upon a face so familiar that he has scarcely looked at it these many years. For his father is a feeling within him, a constant presence, his moods as knowable as the weather written in the sky.

But now his eye traces those imprints upon the flesh that define Andrew Hilton for everyone else. Fran wants to stretch out his hand, to trace the sharp ridge and bulging tip of his nose, so opposed to each other they seem to have been married together in error or perhaps for divine amusement; to stroke the pale line of knotted skin that stretches from the hollow of his left cheek down beneath his lips, a wound sustained – so says Harry, the bailiff – not in the heat of battle, but from a glass bottle thrown by Andrew's own father; to feel the innocent smoothness of his right eyelid that has always hung unnaturally over the eye itself, obscuring its piercing glitter. But Fran feels so completely unmoored he dares do nothing to expose his thoughts and feelings. Not yet. Not until he knows what he should do.

His father's skin is the colour of old rope, but clammy, as if he lies beneath the heat of a violent summer sun. And always that terrible rattle. Fran feels his heart gallop. Reaching for his father's hand beneath the sheet, he grasps fingers that weigh upon his own not with their usual strength but from an absence of will. He cannot bear the pity of it, and yet he would not have any of it cease, for that would surely be forever.

For a moment, his father's eyelids seem to settle further, but slowly they are raised like insecure drawbridges, though his gaze cannot find Fran's. Alas, if Andrew Hilton wishes to speak, he has not the means to breathe and talk. Fran forces himself to keep hold of that ethereal hand even as the pressure of words lodging in his heart clamours to be let out. And yet what does he wish to say? His father can no more guide him now than he can impose his will.

The hand in Fran's feels cold. But that is not what distresses him, for suddenly the rattle ceases. He listens hard, but his father takes no breath as one second drags into the next. A terror rises in him, chilling Fran's bones until his father rasps again quickly two, three times. Then all falls quiet, only the stuttering of a candle breaking that terrible silence. Fran does not move, keeping his head bowed so he need not meet anyone else's gaze. Once more the rattle comes and is stilled. Outside, Harry Sowerby's dog barks, ardent, commanding. Fran closes his eyes, thoughts rising and spinning like drifting snow. *Anyone else in my place might mourn the death of a father but rejoice that all they might wish done – or undone – is now theirs to command. I know what I want and certainly what is right.*

But how to do it? And what will my life be then? On and
on, these pitiful, thoughts assail him, never settling long
enough to find an unencumbered pathway through. For
surely there is none.

Someone coughs. Fran jerks up his head without
thinking to find his mother looking at him from her
seat opposite. Christian Kirkbride seems composed, if a
little pale, still wearing the old blue tunic she uses when
she's in the garden, a smear of dirt darkening her cheek.
A curl of red hair – faded now to autumn gold – has
slipped out of her coif to hang disobediently over one
shoulder. Lowering her head with the least extravagant of
movements, she directs his gaze back to his father. And
Fran sees that Andrew Hilton's soul has been stolen away
even as he grips his hand, that he holds on to an earthly
substance devoid of meaning and already, no doubt, falling
into decay. He sinks down into his father's great chair,
Dolfyn coming from under the table to rest his long, sleek
head on Fran's knee.

He knows he should rise, address his household and
bring direction, if not comfort. And yet he cannot bring
himself to let go of those fingers, gentle now, to begin the
dismantling of his father's hand upon his life.

'My son . . .' It is a fragile, quivering cry. He turns his
head to find his mother now in a state of some disorder,
leaning heavily on Hawise, her maid. But her eyes gleam
like a cat's. 'I would ask you to help me to my chamber.'

That she dissembles is not in doubt. But to what
purpose? If she had not kept silent all these years – face
immobile, hands clasped tight on her lap – Fran might

imagine she has an opinion on his next steps. He certainly wishes she has some words of wisdom, for the abyss once filled by his father's constant barks of instruction, the smothering solidity of his judgement, has already taken away so much of the ground beneath his feet. Until this moment he has thought of his mother only as the gloomy fount of songs and stories about her native land just north of the border. But Scotland is an unknown country now, thanks to the war.

He sits on for several moments, trying to arrange his thoughts, but the whispering has already begun across the room, his mother's harsh breathing trumpeting her apparent distress. He forces himself to get up, to go and stand over her. 'Are you unwell? Would you like something to drink?' He tries to keep the annoyance out of his voice, off his face. He doubts he succeeds.

And anyway his mother shakes her head, draws a faltering hand across her brow before stretching it out to grasp his firmly. She will have no problem getting into Heaven, whatever her sins, with an act like that. He glances at Hawise, whose gaze mixes tenderness with grave misgiving. There is no help there. Next to her, Sarah giggles, rocking her body quickly from side to side. He places a finger gently to his lips and Sarah smiles at him as if he is the most pleasing thing she's ever seen.

All four of them gather themselves to leave the room. But though Fran is the one in front, still holding his mother's hand, she is the one steering. They pass through those familiar faces, some tearful, others entirely still, as if the enchantment has spread beyond his father to overwhelm them all. Only his mother remains untouched. And then it strikes him that, for her, some other enchantment must have been broken.

As soon as the solar door is closed, his mother bolts it quickly, gesturing to Hawise to stay close by, bidding her listen carefully for someone coming. Pushing a hand into Fran's back, she brings him to the cushioned seats set opposite each other in the recess beneath the window.

Fran clings to the view outside. Turning away from his mother, he lets his eyes drift over Murton Pike dappled with a sudden thrust of sunlight, thinks on the bilberries that carpet the moorland slopes, imagines cramming a handful into his mouth, tasting their sweet tang, juice oozing over his lips and staining them blue. And then his mind turns to the cattle up there now, well away from their small patch of barley hard-won from the hillside.

A great heat tears through him as it hits him that now he is responsible for keeping the shaggy beasts safe, not to mention the crops that will help to feed them through the winter. He buries his hands beneath his thighs, kneading the cushion below. His thoughts gallop hither and thither, resting for a moment on Sir Robert Clifford, who owns their land and led many knights of this country to Scotland in the great army. But Clifford was struck down in the battle near a place called Stirling, his vast wealth and great name counting for nothing among those savages.

'You're not listening.' His mother is leaning forward, tugging at his tunic.

'Hush, woman.' He throws off her hand and sits as far back as he can, as if he is once more a child pouting and moping because his misdemeanours have brought him a beating. Dolfyn stands up, turns round, looks up at him as if desiring they go somewhere else. 'I shouldn't be here anyway. They'll talk if I'm gone so long among women.'

She blinks and they stare at each other as if each speaks a language the other doesn't understand. 'I'm glad to hear you say it.' She speaks slowly, cautiously, settles back on her cushions again.

He sighs. 'You have dirt on your face.' Leaning forward, he rubs at her cheek with the sleeve of his tunic.

She catches his arm, shakes it. 'You need to understand—'

'I understand perfectly. How could I not?' Leaping up, he begins to pace around, kicking up the rushes laid upon the flagstones. 'And since when have you cared? You've always been perfectly happy . . .'

She throws him a savage look, eyes darkening to cool green. 'You know nothing.' It is a low growl. 'But it cannot be cured now.'

He studies her face, the pale skin adorned with a galaxy of freckles, the vulnerable flesh at her neck and the plump softness that has settled there, across her belly, swelling her hands. She was very young when she married, but now she seems to be settling into her middling years as if it were her vocation. It confuses him that his resemblance to her even beyond the colour of his hair or the angular prominence of his bones has long been accepted by friends and strangers, though his father never commented on it.

He wonders how much he would look like her younger self if he had spent his days out of reach of sun and wind, his hands never sullied by the daily grind of metal or leather.

She settles herself back, hands on her lap, a picture of good manners. 'Let's not dance around any longer. What do you intend to do?'

There is nothing simple about the question, even as he has known these past minutes that she was bound to ask it in her newly determined state. He sits down again, licks dry lips. 'There's only one thing to be done.' Throwing this at her, he hopes it might bring some relief. That he could grow comfortable inside his skin is unimaginable. But these words whisper of possibility, of another future. He feels the tranquillity of it, still out of reach but now in sight.

Her hands jump in her lap. 'Don't be ridiculous. You still have a choice. For pity's sake, you shouldn't rush into anything that might . . . You want to be utterly sure before you—'

'Do you know what it's like to offend God?'

'Don't bring God into this. It was your father's decision. And now it must be yours.'

'You're telling me nothing should change?'

She shifts in her seat, draws a thumb across her lips, stretching them into something wildly deformed. 'I'm telling you to think carefully before you do anything. You're far too quick to judgement. Don't forget you won't be the only one—'

The slap across her cheek leaps across the room. As Dolfyn gives a little yelp, Hawise gasps, almost leaves her place at the door to rush to her mistress but thinks better of it. In the sharp silence that follows, the only sound is Sarah babbling away at her own conversation.

But, quick as lightning, his mother slaps him back. Now it is his turn to gasp, to finger the place where he still feels her hand. 'You dare to strike me.' He is shaking so violently that he can scarcely get the words out.

She settles her skirts, sits back again as if nothing of consequence has happened, the mark on her own face still showing raw and red. 'You'd better get used to it' – she raises her gaze to look him full in the face, trying to direct him as she has not been able to do since even before his childish curls were lopped off – 'if you're thinking of giving up that which gives you freedom and honour.'

He curls in on himself, arms clasped around his body, rocking back and forth. 'It is impossible.'

'What is?' She is sharp, impatient.

'I can't go on and I can't go back.'

'Stop feeling sorry for yourself. I would tear out my womb if I could have what you take for granted.'

'You jest?' He stops rocking, looks at her as if for the first time.

'Do I?' Now her hands cut and thrust at the air. 'How hard do you think it is to offer an opinion and have someone else decide whether to even hear it, however much merit it might contain? How much of my life is my own, do you think?'

'I ...'

She leans forward, takes his hand. 'It is a gift. Do not throw it away.'

Fran feels as if he sits behind a great wall of glass, unable to reach out to anyone. 'So, I must pretend to something that should be the most natural ... the most essential part of myself.' Ashamed of the tears threatening to overflow, he crushes his lips together so harshly he tastes blood. 'I'm sure everyone watches me. They know, and I will be unmasked.'

She shakes her head.

He bites on a knuckle. 'I'm so ugly.'

She frowns. 'Don't be ridiculous. You're a fine man. I could not have asked for better, and neither could your father.'

He grunts. 'He found me wanting, I can assure you.'

'Every father does. But you never lacked ... You were everything he could have expected where it mattered.' She pats his hand, withdraws.

He taps his nose, undecided. 'He wouldn't tell me, you know.'

'Tell you what?'

'Why.' He watches her keenly now, sees the surprise leap into her eyes, polishing them.

'What reason did he give to deny you that?'

Fran turns his head towards the window, wishes he could climb out of it and leap on to his horse's back, ride away from this conversation, this life. But only if he could then disappear into nothingness, become a wraith wandering the hills without anyone to tell him what he was or was not. 'He said if he told me, I would think of something to contradict him. That he would not waste time arguing with me, for what was done was done and should not be undone.'

'How like him!' His mother gives a short laugh. 'Do you want to know?'

'Of course.'

'I doubt it will make it easier for you now.'

'Just tell me.' He has long found this knowledge important, fascinating even.

'Very well. You will not remember, but your father had more than one sister.'

'Surely—'

'Don't interrupt. She was his twin. I scarcely met her, for we were only just married, and she lived with her husband in Northumberland, near the Scottish border. But to hear him talk, you would think her the loveliest, kindest, the most . . .' She curls a hand through the air, her mouth a thin, hard line. 'He adored her, is the truth of it.'

He smiles despite himself, imagining her jealousy. 'I'll wager you would have adored her too, on longer acquaintance.'

She lowers her chin, spears him with a look. 'I told you not to interrupt. I won't dwell on such a sad story, but she was killed by brigands. They stole her away from her house, took cattle and other goods, defiled her and slit her throat. It seems there was a quarrel between their leader and her husband. A debt of some kind.' She speaks with calm precision, but he sees her eyes flitting around the room, fingers worrying at her gown.

He is sorry for jesting. But in truth he is none the wiser. 'I can see why father would be distressed. Would want revenge, even. But why would he . . .?'

'The brigand was caught and hanged. But that wasn't

enough.' She sends out a puff of breath so violent it lifts a curl of hair. 'It wasn't enough, by half. Your father locked himself away for days on end, wouldn't speak to me or share my bed.' She tugs at the ornament around her neck. 'I thought he'd gone mad with grief, that I would be widowed by the time I was fifteen. And then one day he came to me and laid his head on my lap. We sat like that for some time, and I didn't dare speak or move, though I grew sore. It was such a precious thing, I remember that so clearly, to have my husband returned to me.' She pauses, stares out into that vivid memory. 'Then he spoke, and he . . .' She stops, turns her eyes inward, towards her heart.

'Tell me!' He wants to shake her till the words fall out, wonders if she is trifling with him.

She sees him again, blinks away tears. 'The madness had not left him. He was himself and not himself. I think he stayed like that until this very day. He believed it was his fault, you see, that he wasn't there to protect her, though what business it was of his . . .' She shook her head. 'He never spoke of her again.'

'But I still don't understand.'

She draws in a long breath. 'For pity's sake, have patience! He told me then he had decided all his children would be boys. I did not understand his meaning, to begin with. It is quite usual for a man to wish only for sons.' She lifts her chin, gives him a nod. 'But when it was time for me to give birth, he flapped around like a hen, told me my mother could not come to look after me, took Hawise to one side and scared her half to death. And at last I understood.'

'Well, *I* don't.'

She takes both his hands in hers, speaks slowly as if he were a child. 'Only men can defend themselves. He would not have any of his children left defenceless. So . . .'

He shakes her hands away, tugs at the abrupt ends of his hair. 'So, when I was born . . .'

She nods.

'. . . he turned a girl into a boy.'

Chapter 2

Fran wakes with a start, as if he has fallen from a great height. He tries to remember, still wrapped in the fog of sleep, why he tossed and turned most of the night, twisting his sheets into tight knots before finally sinking into wary oblivion as the birds began to sing. And, like a flood, yesterday comes back to him.

In truth, he is used to waking heavy with regret, for it is always with him, the hope that God loves him enough to work a miracle in the night. And every morning he finds himself unloved, still monstrous in form and disturbed in mind.

But as dawn creeps through the small-paned window, Fran is moved by a great curiosity about the body into which he was born, the one now compressed beneath strips of cloth and augmented with a small pouch full of rags. His father had decreed that he should not remove these false enhancements at night, but only for a moment every three or four days. Then Sarah would rise very early and unwrap him, cooing quietly to herself, before her stubby fingers worked deftly to restore his manhood in fresh bindings in the flickering candlelight.

Now he need not wait. Jumping out of bed, he bolts the door before scuttling over to the fire and stirring its embers until he can see a glowing glint. Getting down on his knees, he blows hard until a flame leaps out and kindles the small twigs he has carefully arranged on top. Dolfyn watches him for a moment before rising from his place below the end of the bed and padding over to lick Fran on the cheek. Smiling, he pulls the creature towards him, arms reaching around the dog's neck. They stay like that for a few moments, Fran with his eyes closed, enjoying the devotion, the impossibility of any questions being asked of him. But then he leaps up, turning to study the lie of the land beyond the window, fearful that someone somewhere might be able to see him. He knows it's not possible, not in any detail, at least. But he can't proceed without being sure.

No one stirs.

Lifting his shirt over his head, he lets the chill settle before beginning his struggle with knots and fabric grown stiff around the contours of his body. First, he unwraps the cloth constraining his chest, the removal of each layer releasing more of the agitation flowing through him. Keeping his eyes firmly shut, he fights his way through to the skin, a powerful smell of mould running riot as soon as the cloth pulls free. His fingers skim clammy flesh, not yet willing to own what's there. Far more urgent is the pain across his shoulders, around his ribs, that is as much a part of him as his hair or teeth. Twisting and kneading at warped muscles, wincing at the bruised skin, he thinks yet again how plain it is to see he is being punished for transgressing nature and how insensible his father had been to it.

But he does not have all day. Letting his braies fall to his feet, he quickly steps out of them, tugging in a growing frenzy at the last knot nestled in the small of his back. The pouch falls to the floor with a dull thump. As he stands naked in the middle of the room, eyes still closed, small licks of heat bring comfort. Breathing deeply for a few moments, Fran clasps his hands lightly to his throat and slowly traces a line down to the middle of his chest, intensely aware of the swell of flesh on either side, though he has not yet laid a finger there. Dolfyn sits up, scratches his neck, lies down again.

Breath ragged, she unclasps her hands and draws her fingertips slowly over the soft slope of her breasts, exploring the heavy swell beneath, the supple protrusions at their heart. She wishes she could wash away the stale smell of their confinement, drench them in rosewater. Feeling her nipples grow hard beneath her fingers, she wonders at the miracle of it, imagining the insistent suck of a child, its tender, precious weight made safe in her arms. Her eyes spring open, hands dropping away, a harsh dryness in her throat.

She shuts her eyes again, head bowed. Slowly, carefully, she lets her fingers pass over the flat tautness of her belly, moves her hands out again so they embrace the smooth curve of her hips, feeling the insistent strength of the muscles in her thighs.

But it is the unknown terrain within reach of her fingers that calls to her, becoming ever more insistent. She is not ready to listen. Turning her attention on the sounds of scurrying mice, an owl announcing the end of its nocturnal wanderings, the first distant stirrings in the kitchen below, she hovers between two states, at home in neither. Wanting both.

The ends of her fingers tingle, daring her to go on. She wonders at herself, that she should think nothing of a challenge requiring physical strength but has not the courage to know her own body. The knots in her belly tighten. She feels so bound to this moment, this place, she can't imagine being permitted to leave it until she has finished what she's begun. But is it God who holds her hand?

Drawing in a long breath, she reaches across her thigh, the roughness of her fingers assaulting the alien smoothness she finds there. Breath quickening, she moves on, barely touching the skin below but aware of nothing else. She has imagined only a void leading deep within her that is both an absence and the source of her disgust. But now she finds on the surface an intricate topography of ridges and furrows, outer defences protecting a tiny, supple heart that also becomes firm beneath her touch.

Snatching back his hand, he understands for certain what he has known in his heart for long enough: that women are not the simple creatures, deficient in mind and matter, his friend Will has long warned him about. But that knowledge also dismays him, for he knows he wants the impossible, that no one on Earth or in Heaven will give him what he truly desires: to be her natural self but still living his life to the full without forfeiting the good opinion of his peers. All he can see ahead of him is shame or loss.

The door handle rattles. He spins around, diving for his shirt. A sharp knock follows, his mother calling to him. Yelling at her to wait, he struggles into his shirt, throwing his braies on the bed. The door handle rattles again. He strides over and slides back the bolt, nursing a frown. He does not open the door to let her in but goes to stand by the fire.

The door creaks, and she stands for a moment on the threshold. 'Why did you lock it?'

'What business is it of yours?'

Christian's lips tighten, hand tapping at her side. 'I came to see how you were.'

'I am perfectly well.' He feels her gaze heavy upon his person, fears it.

But she merely nods, picks up her skirts and steps further into the room without looking at him.

'If you want to know what I've decided, then I haven't.' He realises his arms are tightly wrapped around himself, releases them, folds them again across his belly.

She comes to rest by the window, staring out for a moment. Turning, she appraises him until a question emerges on her face. 'Are you ...?' In three steps she is almost on top of him, ready to pounce, to reveal him.

'Don't you dare!' He slips out of her reach.

Thwarted, she is already looking around, poking her gaze into every corner of the room, plucking at her mouth with thumb and forefinger.

'It hurts.' He says it quietly, almost as if it doesn't matter.

She falls still, eager to put her mind to something that might have an answer to it. 'What does?'

He hesitates, tears gathering, wondering what he's fighting. 'Everything. All round here. The binding.' He circles the entirety of his upper body. He wants her to know, half for the pity of it, half to punish her, for there is no one else to blame apart from himself.

She comes to stand in front of him, places a hand briefly on his arm. 'Perhaps Sarah might bring you something to heal the skin.'

He nods. 'I'm going to speak with Wi ... with Father Warcop.'

'Today?' She frowns.

He prefers not to think about how she becomes a shadow in Will's presence, finds an excuse to leave the room altogether. There's no doubt the priest has a low opinion of women, which he has taught Fran is entirely supported by scripture and other learned texts. Fran's own opinion is that, while this might be true in general, it can surely be opposed in the particular. But since he cannot gainsay his friend's learning, he prefers to ignore a matter that would only throw up discord between them. ''Tis best I decide what to do soon, I suppose. And I need to tell him about Father.' How long ago yesterday seems already. He feels cold, for all that the day is already warm and the fire vigorous.

'I think ...' She has turned her head away. 'I don't want to be a burden to you. But I don't know what will happen if you ...'

He pats her hand. 'No one will blame you. I will make sure of it.'

She gives a quick, mocking laugh, and he knows with a sharp stab of irritation that she's reminding him again there will be nothing he can do if he decides to ... And, in truth, he cannot begin to imagine what it would be like to live as his mother does, and what would be said about him if he were to admit such a grievous deception even to those he counts as his friends. But he knows that in itself is a deception, albeit of himself. He has no friends, apart from Will. His father made certain of that.

Christian begins to twist the diamond ring on her left hand, face held tight. He sees she is afraid, which only serves to deprive him of courage, of resolution.

He wants to tell her he is afraid too, that he longs now for the certainty Andrew Hilton insisted upon, forgetting how vexatious it was, for at least he was spared this anguish. And yet now he wonders why he never thought to oppose his father. There had never been anything to stop him taking off the bindings and the ridiculous pouch, to end this pretence ... He blinks, appalled.

'Francis?' His mother puts a hand on his shoulder, a tender look on her face.

He feels an intense rage boil up from the pit of his stomach, that she should so stir up the tears already burning his eyes. 'I don't know what to do.' It is a croak, and true, but scarcely helpful.

She sighs, pats his shoulder. With a sweep of her skirts, she is at the door. She turns her head slightly towards him. 'Would you like me to tell Sarah to ... attend to you?'

The first decision. He nods, lacking the strength to
choose anything else. Not yet. And he wants her to leave
so he can think. Or, rather, so he might go and talk with
Will, who will surely know what to say to bring him peace.

Sarah comes, shuffling and chattering like an ungainly
bird with much on her mind. At least she does not chide
or lament when she sees him undone but bustles around
as if nothing is amiss. He has already retrieved the pouch
and tied it back on. Giving him the end of the long strip
of cloth, she swiftly binds it around him, pulling tight,
tutting quickly until she is satisfied her work is sufficient.

It is not right or proper, of course, for a gentleman to
be attended by a woman in the same way his mother is.
But somehow Andrew Hilton had made it seem an act
of charity and of no consequence because Sarah is not
a proper person. And, in that, he did his son a favour,
however unwittingly, for she brings Fran comfort. Despite
her obvious incompleteness, her inability to form proper
words and so to reveal to others what is contained within
her head, Sarah seems to understand at least some of what
is going on around her and sometimes has something to
say – by gesture or the look on her face – to those who
care to pay attention. At least, Fran believes so, though he
cannot explain how he knows it.

But that is not what comforts him. Indeed, astonishes
him. For Sarah – who is one of the very few to know his
secret – does not judge him. When Fran looks into her
eyes, he sees only acceptance. In truth, he couldn't care

less if she really doesn't know the meaning of what she sees and hears. So long as she is indifferent to it, he will treasure her.

Though all that humming, those strange animal noises – they are exceedingly annoying.

He finally begins his journey towards Warcop a little after the sun reaches its highest point in the heavens, leaving Dolfyn to stand sorrowfully at their gate. Giles Helbeck, his father's squire, rides with him, squat and dark and noiseful. As with so much else, Fran has not made up his mind what to do with Giles. Much of this particular indecision arises from the fact that he finds the squire a rather haughty fellow, never backward in bestowing his opinion on those he considers his inferiors or even, when he forgets himself, on those who would naturally expect him to keep his mouth shut. It's true that Giles has always shown him proper reverence, serving him as diligently as he did his master. But Fran has been much irritated by the way the squire speaks to Sarah and the other servants, sees how he pushes his horse well beyond what is good for the beast.

But Giles is scarcely his most pressing concern. As they ride south out of Hilton, the unbounded prospect that suddenly rises up before them still makes Fran feel a little dizzy. To their left, hump-backed Roman Fell guards their flank while, far ahead of them in the distance, the angular tip of Wild Boar Fell slices through the sky. Fauvel, Fran's palfrey, is pleased to be out, shaking his sleek chestnut head, his hoof-falls on the rough moorland track blithe and brisk. Fran feels them as a drumbeat heralding the moment when he and Will can sit or walk together. Finally, he will be able to speak with someone who is not only bound to absolute secrecy by virtue of his office as priest, but whom he loves and admires for his good sense, the wisdom so willingly imparted. Who makes him feel alive with one playful glance, hard-won but all the more glorious for it.

And yet his father's voice mocks him from inside his head, for how can he tell Will the truth without his whole world collapsing?

Throwing that thought into the distant fells, Fran urges Fauvel to hurry, counting off each clump of trees, each stream and house on this well-worn route. A wren scolds them, flitting from one gorse bush to another, no doubt luring them away from her second brood of young. A vigorous wind throws itself at them from the south, but it hits them with a caressing warmth, the sun soaring above them. Fran prays quickly for the words that will help to unlock his predicament to Will. He is glad to be away from Hilton.

If only Giles would cease his onslaught of questions. Which does the young master prefer, the sword, the mace or the axe? What does he know of King Edward? Has he ever met Sir Robert Clifford? Is it possible Clifford isn't truly dead? What does he think it's like to ride into battle?

How on God's earth would I know? Fran wonders for a moment if Giles is taunting him for not going with the king's army, but nothing is written on the youth's face apart from a rosy eagerness. Fran sighs to himself. 'Hold your tongue, for pity's sake.'

But Giles is rarely discomfited. 'What's that, sir?' The squire stands up in his stirrups, looking to their left. They are now above Warcop, moving rapidly downhill, the great valley of the River Eden stretching entirely from the eastern horizon towards the west, a busy country of many colours, of light and shadow, of corn and pasture and meadows and woods.

'What did I tell—'

'You need to look over there.' Giles points emphatically to the east, above the trees. A great plume of grey smoke streams towards the heavens.

Fran frowns. 'I don't know what it is any more than you do.' He spurs on his horse, and they are soon within Warcop's boundaries. Hastening towards the priest's house, which lies beside Crook's Beck, a clamour draws them instead to the small patch of grass where stands a maypole set atop four well-worn steps. A press of men is gathered round the sheriff, Will's brother, Sir Henry Warcop, who stands resolutely on the second step trying to answer questions. Some turn to look at the newcomers and Fran raises his hand in greeting. They nod, turn back quickly towards Sir Henry.

'Fran! I didn't expect you to come.'

Fran's gaze leaps down, all thought turned fugitive, to find Will standing beneath him, heavy black hair falling into his eyes beneath his cap, the white of his woollen habit drawing the eye like a great light. But where is the smile of greeting, the complicit glance that feels like an embrace? 'God keep you, Father, I didn't. I came to see *you*. My father is dead.' He speaks quickly, forced into talking about what is necessary but not so weighty on his mind.

'Oh.' Will places a hand on Fauvel's flank near Fran's leg. 'I see. I will ... Look, the Scots are coming. They have already burned Brough.'

'Damn!' So that explains the smoke. Fran's eyes leap towards the road east, though houses impede his gaze.

Will looks that way too. 'We were brought word an hour ago. Please God it is not too late.' He nods towards his brother, the sheriff. 'They seem to be heading west, to go back over the border north of Carlisle. They have countless beasts with them, and it is best we do not try to stop them. Harclay and some of the men from Carlisle tried up on Stainmore ...' His face twitches. 'But we should do what we can to get our people out of the way.'

Giles has been unnaturally quiet, twisting and gawping all around. Now he draws in a sharp breath, no doubt as the prelude to some insistent pronouncement or other.

Fran turns quickly to him. 'Go back to Hilton and tell Harry Sowerby to move our beasts up into Swindale. Then ask my lady mother to gather all the women and lock themselves in somewhere. I don't want you to delay for any reason.'

Giles frowns, opens his mouth.

Fran gives him his fiercest look. 'Go!'

The squire shrugs, turning his horse with a clatter.

Will strokes Fauvel, speaks quietly, as if to the beast. 'Jamie Dickinson's boys are not yet come back from

Scotland. Nor Adam Fothergill.' He looks up, touches Fran's boot lightly. 'I should ready myself.' And then he smiles, suddenly boyish again. 'I would not want you getting too far ahead of me.'

Fran is thrown back more than ten years, to piles of books and parchment and Will – then a novice in the monastery at Shap – teaching him Latin and Greek, some mathematics and a little theology, the sun slicing through the window. How he had loved the time they spent together and how hard he had worked to justify and honour Will's patience with him. He marvelled at all the things his teacher knew, the mysteries he became privy to under Will's firm direction. He smiles.

But already Will's face has grown heavy again. He raises a hand in farewell and benediction.

Sitting entirely still on Fauvel's back, Fran is not afraid. But only because he cannot yet imagine all this, the familiar and the ordinary, washed away in a tide of hacking, burning, yelling savages. Getting down with a sudden leap, he ties Fauvel to a fencepost and edges forward to stand at the back of the crowd. But almost immediately men begin to run, no doubt on some signal from the sheriff.

'Where's Andrew?' Sir Henry bustles up, tugging impatiently at his glove with only two complete fingers on his left hand, a constant reminder of another battle in Scotland, but one that was lost a long time ago. He has none of the priest's vivacity, nor his fine proportions, bringing to Fran's mind a great boulder stuffed into robes that are much too small, his features pinched and creased where Father Warcop's are elegant and smooth. Nearly a score more in years and a different mother. But Sir Henry is a man who gets things done.

Fran whips off his hat, bows low. 'God speed, my lord. My father is dead. Yesterday.'

Sir Henry blinks. ''Tis not possible. I saw him yesterday myself. We talked about the battle. He was in an almighty ill humour about it.'

'Well, he's dead now, for certain. I came to see about his burial. But' – Fran gestures vaguely – 'it'll have to wait.'

'That it will. I doubt . . .'

He's going to tell me to go home, that this is no place for a . . .

'. . . he ever thought you'd be fighting his battles for him quite so soon.' Sir Henry clasps a great hand to Fran's shoulder. 'I sent my squire off with Jamie Dickinson, so you can come with me.'

'You do me much honour, sir.' Fran had hoped to wait for Will. This day has not turned out anything like the way he'd imagined.

Chapter 3

It is a warning for their own people that Sir Henry intends them to deliver, sending them in twos or threes up and down the byways that criss-cross the valley and the lower slopes of the Pennines, the great line of hills that lie like slumbering giants to the north of the valley of the River Eden. There is nothing to be done about the standing grain, but if even some cattle and sheep can be saved, it will be worth the effort. The hope is that those devils have enough booty already and will be eager to return home. What they must not do, Sir Henry tells Fran with a grimace, is attract their attention. 'No one can say I wish ill on our neighbours, but if it's us or them . . .'

Fran nods. They are riding not so very far from Hilton, heading towards Appleby. 'Could we not lead the Scots away from here?' He thinks his voice is a little too shrill, but vigorous enough, and marvels that he should already seek to make himself heard.

But Sir Henry shakes his head. 'That would be beyond foolish. They know what they're about, that's for certain, and there's nothing we can do to try to change their minds.' He sniffs, looks down on Fran. 'Why didn't you and your father go with Sir Robert to Scotland?'

There was something to be said, Fran decides, for not drawing attention to yourself. He shrugs, scans the horizon again. 'He thought we should stay here and protect our own.' In truth, Andrew Hilton had told his son he would break his sword and slit his horse's throat if he even thought about going. By then, Fran no longer knew what sort of man he wanted him to be.

Sir Henry sniffs again. 'He was a strange man, your father. You know that, don't you?'

More than most. 'I should have chosen better, I suppose.'

'Don't be clever. You could have gone.'

Fran closes his eyes. 'He wouldn't let me.' It sounds wretched, a coward's excuse.

Sir Henry snorts. 'You should be glad, and that's the truth of it.' He gives Fran a long look. 'This isn't a game, you know.'

They ride in silence for a while. Fran does not think it a game. In truth, he hasn't thought all that much about the war these past years, though it's always been there, worrying at them all like a tick bite, growing angry and painful every now and then.

Something stirs in his mind, a drift of purple spread beneath a host of ancient oaks, the delicate smell of bluebells as pleasing as laughter. And his mother smiling, arm draped over the shoulders of an older woman. Her mother, his grandmother. He cannot have been more than two years old, trying to find his own feet. In Scotland, before the war began. He remembers his grandmother's smell, dry and warm, cabbages and roses. She liked to tickle him, he remembers that too, rub her nose on his belly. Does she still live? Why has he not thought on her these long years? Where has he been all this time?

They ride quickly along the edge of a great field, the barley dancing and rustling in the breeze. A chorus of barking dogs heralds their approach to a jumble of houses smoking gently. High up on a little hill, the square church of Great Ormside stands on impotent watch. The manor house at its foot is solemn and quiet, for John Derwentwater has been near to death this past twelvemonth.

Stopping abruptly, Sir Henry eases himself out of the saddle and raps on the first door, kicking at a mangy dog baring its teeth at him. But already women with very young children and a few men of the more decrepit kind emerge from round corners, from behind doors, some lingering, others gathering close.

'The Scots are at Brough. They're coming this way.' Sir Henry directs his gaze at an old man with oily locks and pale, cloudy eyes.

But it is a fine-boned woman with a child on her hip who answers, moving her child deftly to her other hip as it begins to whimper. 'What do you want us to do?' It is nearly a shout.

Fran studies her, the darkness circling her eyes, the way her body swings and shifts so as to accommodate her child, the glittering force of a gaze that speaks of a life only just holding together.

Sir Henry's mouth tightens. 'Get out of the way. Until they've passed. Go now. Take your beasts, if you can, but go quickly.'

The woman gives them a look that falls like water through fingers, cleanly, quietly, without artifice. It seems to Fran she is telling them she is hopeless because she understands perfectly all that is wrong with the world.

They ride up to the church, which commands a good view over the River Eden and the ancient road on the ridge beyond. For a moment, all is peaceful. But at last, with a jolt in Fran's spine, he sees a dark shivering fill the valley floor from the right, an unstoppable flow of men and beasts.

Sir Henry's face burns to the dark, distressing colour of an engorged flea even as he raises his chin. They nudge their horses deeper into the shadow of the church.

Fran feels a great anger, against the Scots certainly, but it is their own impotence that hurts him most. 'Is there nothing to be done?' He thinks on the woman with the child. She has good reason to think them negligent, surely? And something else leaps into his mind, the recollection that Sir Henry's own hall was violated a year or so ago by a group of armed men, Englishmen all, who took some of his goods, his widowed daughter Isabel and a boy who was his ward. To be the king's own officer on the king's own business and unable to protect your own, that must have hurt to the quick.

The sheriff stares straight ahead, eyes unblinking. 'There's some of them up there on the road too.' He points across to the ridge on the other side of the river. 'They must've gone off somewhere else to be behind those driving the cattle.' His other hand beats urgently on his thigh.

'Where do we go now?'

'That's what I'm trying to decide. Flakebridge was the plan. But that means crossing the Great Road.'

Fran feels something hard lodge in his belly. 'Couldn't we—'

But instantly Sir Henry turns to him. 'No. I've already told you. Others have tried and failed. The Scots on the road can easily ride off it to make mischief, if they think it worth their while. We can either get out of the way and let them do their worst. Or pay them off, but I'm not minded to give them any more unless we must.'

'What about trying to get them to go a different way?'

Sir Henry shifts in his saddle, nose twitching. 'What do you mean?'

What do *I mean?* 'If we could make them think something untoward is happening further on, something they would be foolish to ignore ...'

'Such as?'

Fran's mind gallops through various possibilities, all equally reckless. But he becomes more and more certain they could – nay, should – do something no one would expect them to do. 'What if we made a great smoke somewhere over there.' He waves vaguely towards the west. 'Make the ones behind think the ones in front have been attacked.'

'They don't need any help to destroy us!' Sir Henry looks down on Fran, solid face turned molten with alarm.

'It's to *stop* them destroying us, don't you see? Once they're past, they won't come back.' Fran knows there's nothing certain about this plan, can see the madness in it, but the simple logic too. 'They might not come back.'

'No, I don't see.' Sir Henry looks at Fran as if he is a strange object he has found beneath his boot. Then his mouth twists. 'How old are you?'

'Twenty.' Fran feels a sharp heat, wondering what lies behind the question.

'You're small for your age, aren't you?'

The heat fills Fran with intensity, pulling him out of shape. 'That's no reason to think less of me.' The words slip out like pennies from a hole in a pouch. He wants to kick Fauvel in frustration that Sir Henry will not give his plan proper consideration, wonders why the sheriff thinks he has time for foolish observations when there's still work to do.

Sir Henry's eyebrows reach for the heavens, but already he is pulling on his horse's reins. 'What in God's name are you talking about? I've scarcely spoken two words with you till today. If you want the truth, I thought there was something wrong with you, Andrew kept you at such a distance even when you were there among us. Now I see you're just as bone-headed as he was.'

Fran contemplates the sheriff's words as they descend the hill, moving towards a loop of the Eden where it turns towards the south. He finds it grimly amusing that he and his father should be thought equally stubborn. They reach a clump of oaks beside the riverbank.

'Stay here.' Sir Henry does not wait for a reply, plunging into the water before heading steadily up the other side.

Fran grinds his teeth but knows better than to disobey. He worries that Sir Henry will come to harm. There is a kindness to him, for all his blunt words. Fran can see the sheriff is trying to do his best as everything shifts wildly around him.

Wiggling his shoulders to ease the pain in his chest, he hums a little tune to himself, a band of sparrows chattering noisily in the branches above his head. At last, Sir Henry reappears on the crest of the hill. Relieved, Fran advances out of the trees. But he has not even reached the river when there is a shout. With his heart in his throat, he turns his head towards it.

For a moment Fran sees only a shifting cloud, dark and menacing, but he soon understands that a small party of horsemen and beasts is travelling at speed towards him along the north bank of the river. Tugging at his sword, he realises too that they will soon come between him and Sir Henry. He glances round for an escape even as his father's voice hammers in his head. *Fight, goddamn it! If he hits you, hit him harder. Don't you dare give up.* But Fran has never been allowed to fight in anger before.

He pours all his attention on the two Scots who have broken away from the other three, riding fast. Young and swarthy, their broad grins tell Fran they are looking forward to seizing an Englishman for ransom. If they do not decide to kill him for sport first.

He knows the sheriff is too far away to help him for at least another few minutes. Grasping Fauvel's reins tightly in his left hand, he urges his horse into a gallop with a sharp kick to both flanks, his passage on to their side of

the river greeted with excited hollas from his pursuers.
Fran feels the air rush at him so impetuously, it threatens
to make away with every last breath in his body. Earth and
sky, gorse and grass, the things that are up and those that
are down, all are thrown together so violently, it is as if God
Himself has decided His creation needs to be shaken up.

But inside, a voice guides him, reaching out from a
place beyond thought. They are two; he is one. To gain
advantage, he must go uphill, then turn and use the hill to
give him more speed. Whatever weapons the Scots carry,
he knows without thinking what he should do to repel
them and to make his own blows count.

His sword – given to him by his father with gloomy
reverence on his fourteenth birthday – sits comfortably in
his hand. A little over two feet long, it is light but very
strong, tapering away to a point he is sure will never bend
or break. And there is no denying that Giles is adept at
polishing it, the diamond incision along the length of the
shaft as clear and clean as the day the sword was forged.
But it's not just a thing of beauty. Fran has been learning
how to use it since he was six years old, is as comfortable
wielding it as he is sitting on Fauvel's back.

Looking down upon the Scots, he feels a tremendous
power flowing through him. There is only one thought
burning within him: to maim or kill, to do whatever he can
to send them to Hell. A great cry surges from his lips, the
whole world shrinking to this hill, this river, this moment.
Within a trice he reaches the flat ground. The two riders
coming towards him are less than ten horse-lengths away,
spears lowered. Fran shakes his head violently to loosen the

sweat dripping into his eyes, down his nose. He feels there is something strange about them, something he should know.

One of them is left-handed.

He only has time to twist the reins even more tightly in his grip before pulling them hard to the left, his whole body tilting over to that side even as his right leg presses deep into Fauvel's flank. Instead of heading straight between the two Scots within reach of both their weapons, Fran comes round the outside of the left-handed one. Slicing his sword briskly through the air as he passes, he has nothing to fear from the spear held in the rider's other hand. A scream rends the air.

Fran feels a trembling take hold of his limbs. Gritting his teeth, he forces Fauvel round to face the Scots before they charge again. They turn quickly, ruddy faces pulled taut, spreading out to make it harder for him to pull off a trick like that again. He has no idea which one he struck.

Once more he digs his heels into Fauvel's flanks, charging forward at full cry, a great yelling and bellowing from men and beasts assailing him from behind. And only now does he realise Sir Henry is galloping towards the two Scots at full tilt. Fran's heart leaps and a marvellous vigour grabs hold of him. Perhaps they see it in his face, for his assailants glance round. One veers off into the river, the other moving in the other direction, out of reach of Fran's sword. Both are intent only on getting back to their fellows.

Fran slows down, he and Fauvel both panting hard. For a moment, he watches the man he struck pass him by on the river side. In truth, he is scarcely a man. His spear has fallen somewhere, a hand now clutching the top of his arm, blood seeping through his fingers, his entire face puckered and twisted. Fran feels his pain, imagines how this day has changed the boy's life forever, presuming he survives. Aghast, he throws away these treacherous thoughts, willing himself to believe that one less Scotsman can only be a blessing for England.

But they are scarcely out of the woods yet. Sir Henry gallops up, jerking his head. Without a word, they both ride back up the hill he's just come down. Only when they've reached the top does the sheriff pause, looking closely at Fran. 'You're not hurt?'

Fran shakes his head. For a brief moment, he bends towards the sheriff, leaning awkwardly on the solid expanse of his chest.

Sir Henry grants him that moment, but no more. Laying his hand on Fran's shoulder, he shakes him. 'What were you thinking, coming out of the trees like that?'

Fran's eyes bulge. 'I thought you meant for me to come to you.'

'Did I signal?'

'No. But . . .'

'You could have been killed.'

Fran drops his head, blinks away tears.

'At least you proved you could use that sword of yours.' Sir Henry shakes him again, but gently this time. 'Come, we should not tarry here.'

Fran bites his lip, urging Fauvel forward, but a smile takes hold when he finally winnows out the praise hidden within the rebuke. And then he frowns, greatly troubled by the way his horse is sweating and trembling. Not that there's anything to be done about it. Once more they stop, looking around to make sure they're not riding into another ambush. Fran feels a stinging in his nostrils. 'What's that smell?'

'Fire.' Sir Henry jerks his head to the west, towards the town of Appleby. 'But at least that means most of the Scots are gone past us now. Let's go.' He moves quickly now towards the north, down towards a great wood a mile or so distant. Sir Robert Clifford's park of Flakebridge, though he won't be hunting there anymore.

Advancing along the edge of a cut field, the remains of the corn lying like the massacred dead, they catch sight of a single timber hut crouching low to the ground. No smoke froths from the chimney. No dog prowls nearby. Only an axe set deep into an old log stands guard.

Sir Henry slows his horse to a trot. 'That's the woodman's house. It's just his wife and child there now. He died, the woodsman. At the battle. I came out to tell her myself a few days ago.' He pauses, looking somewhere else, somewhere unpleasant. 'I wouldn't speak of this abroad, but she was quite overthrown, wailing and lamenting as if the world had just ended. God willing, she's in a better humour now.' He glances towards Fran so that he too might acknowledge the unseemly foolishness in such a display of grief, even if it is only to be expected of a woman.

Fran does not feel inclined to oblige him. 'Shall I try the door?'

'Go and look for her round the back, in the woods. There's a stream there. She could be washing clothes.'

They jump off their horses, tie them up, do it quietly,

as if there's something here that does need to be shown reverence. Fran opens the gate into the park, branches swaying and creaking in the wind. The ground becomes soft and unsteady beneath his feet, herbs and grasses profuse, stars and tendrils laced tightly together, ravelling the earth. The stream rushes by a short distance away but nothing disturbs its banks, no linen spread out to dry across the bushes. He cannot imagine a place like this being turned upside down by Scottish riders and is glad of it. But he turns quickly all the same, eager to be away from the wood's primitive dankness.

Turning the corner of the little hut, he sees Sir Henry standing by his horse, a stiff, defeated look on his face. And Fran is suddenly uneasy, looking around, listening hard for the sounds of hooves, passing his glance through a square hole cut into the wall of the hut. Something rises up to meet his gaze. A face, perhaps, but so lacking in warmth, in the supple invigoration of blood and air beneath the skin, that he has little cause to believe it a living being. And yet he feels as much as sees the eyes of polished grey, like pebbles that have sat too long at the bottom of a river. He thinks she has not seen him, for the face hangs there, like a painting framed by the opening.

But he is mistaken. Slowly, as if making a play of it, she brings a hand – a hand that would be plain and ordinary with work and weather scored into it were it not for the blood that drips so unquietly – and shows him the knife she clutches. Just as slowly, she extends her first finger from the second bloody hand, brings it to her lips. Carefully she turns, runs a hand through lank, dirty hair as unbound as any nymph's. And throws herself away from the window towards the door.

Fran does not think. In three strides, he is round the corner of the hut, groping for his own knife in his belt. He reaches her long before she is anywhere near Sir Henry, throws himself at her. He is aware of the ache of her bones beneath him, the penetrating weight of her knife somewhere in the tangle of their hands. But it is her scream he feels most, beyond his flesh, dragging him into the very depths of Hell. She is certainly not in a better humour. She is in the grip of a most powerful madness, the kind of grief that banishes all hope.

With every ounce of his strength, he drags her to sitting, his own arms embracing her like the staves of a barrel. But he is not careful enough and with one vicious slice, she jerks the knife up and across her throat. The blood feasts on his skin, his hair, his eyes. Whimpering, he lets go, clambering hurriedly away from her. She slips to the ground, as if desirous of gentle sleep. Fran looks across at Sir Henry, who stands, mouth open, a few steps from his horse.

Sir Henry rouses himself, striding forward with a hand outstretched to haul Fran to his feet. They stand very close together, looking down at the dead woman. Fran sees she is not much older than he is, sturdy in figure and features, thin-lipped and square-faced. He imagines her marching about, getting things done, her speech direct, everything about her straightforward. But in truth the only thing he knows about her is that her feelings ran through her as forcefully as a contagion.

'Go and wash in the stream.' Sir Henry speaks gently.

Fran is brought back to the blood tightening on his skin and cannot wait to be rid of it. He runs so fast his heart rides high in his chest. Kneeling on the bank, he sinks his head deep into the water so that it caresses his hair, his face, his neck. He wishes he could take everything off and leap in, let the sharp cold cleanse him. But he does not dare. Throwing his head up and out again, he thrusts in his hands and arms, rubbing violently, the water running redder and redder till at last all is clear again. But still he sees those eyes looking at him through the hole in the wall, neither alive nor dead, and a great shivering falls upon him. It's not just the river's cold embrace. He has seen something much more potent than anything he has ever known. He even wonders if whatever possessed the woodsman's wife was stronger than God.

But that is too weighty a thought for now.

He walks back, water dripping down his neck. Sir Henry has been diligent – a boy no more than three years in age lies stiff and lifeless on the ground near his mother, mostly covered by a sack. Fran is glad. He has no desire to see any more blood. He had not thought of the child when he first saw the bloody knife, but he must have known what it signified because he is not surprised. Only heartsore that a mother should be so warped in feeling as to kill the fruit of her own loins.

Sir Henry stares out into nothing beside his horse, which swishes its tail vigorously against the flies. He turns, smiles vaguely.

Fran feels the cold spreading within him, cannot stop the shivering. The sheriff stretches out a hand as rough and knotted as a piece of wood to place it on his forehead. 'You should be in front of your own hearth.'

Mounting Fauvel, Fran wonders how such a glorious day should host such terrible goings-on even as he fixes his mind on Hilton and how it might have fared. He hopes with all his heart that his manor has proved too far out of the way, thinks it must be so because he cannot imagine otherwise. Riding in silence, they reach a track that will take Fran back home.

Sir Henry tugs a strand of hair out of his mouth. 'I'm praying you haven't caught a chill.' It is gruffly said.

'I'll be fine.'

'You're strong, right enough. Will always says so. For all you're so small.'

'I'm glad to hear it.' Fran would rather no one mentioned his stature, but he would very much like Sir Henry to say more about him being strong or brave.

A boy runs up the road towards them. Aidan, son of one of Warcop's blacksmiths. He stops, flaps his arms.

Sir Henry leans heavily on the pommel of his saddle. 'Which is it? Good news or bad?'

The flapping stops, but Aidan keeps his hands in the air, fists clenched. 'Good news, sir. Mostly.'

'Go on then.'

''Tis the Dickinsons. Wat and Rob. They're back. From the great battle. Thin as broom handles, they are, but hearty enough. Glad to be home, and that's the truth of it.'

'And Adam?'

The boy shakes his head slowly. 'Not Adam. No.'

'Well, I'm sure he won't be long.'

'He's not coming back, sir.'

Sir Henry plucks at his beard. 'Did the Dickinsons say so?'

'That they did.'

'They saw him die with their very own eyes?'

Aidan nods vigorously, kicks a stone, poised for flight. 'I mun get back, sir.' He runs off, leaping from one side of the road to the other, long-legged, uncontained.

They sit on their horses for a moment longer, each contemplating the meaning of Adam Fothergill's death.

'Did you know him? Adam.' Sir Henry stares after the boy leaping down the road back to Warcop.

'Yes. But only a little.'

'I'll say this for him, he didn't have much luck.' Sir Henry presses his lips tight together, eyes still held by the far distance. At last, he turns to Fran, dropping a heavy hand on to his shoulder. 'You did well today.'

A few moments ago it would have been welcome, this hearty praise. But Fran feels only the weight of the sheriff's hand, into which all the dolorous words and deeds of today, of this year, of these miserable times, seem to have been poured. He does not think he can bear it. But he will. Just like everyone else.

Fran has no need to look carefully at Fauvel to know he is utterly exhausted. The horse's breathing is quiet but quick, his gait slow. They have not gone so very far today, but the riding has been hard. He gets down, so Fauvel need not bear his weight, and they plod up the hill back towards Hilton, the river running heedlessly alongside. The track is endless, its slope entirely unreasonable, however unremarkable on any other day. Fran worries that he cannot make sense of his thoughts, which tumble over each other in vague leaps and bounds. But then he thinks he shouldn't disturb them, for they are disturbing enough. He has not the strength to put them in order, is the truth of it.

And then he sees he is approaching the ancient rowan that hangs its head over the lane that leads into Hilton. His shoulders begin to relax as he stops for a moment to fill his nostrils with evening air, the lingering distillation of today's many scents hanging heavily. The next moment, a creature rises up with a great cry from the foot of the rowan, causing him to gasp, fumble for his dagger. But it is only Luke Elliot, the shepherd's boy, running towards him at full tilt, Dolfyn by his side.

'You is home, young master. God be praised!' Luke comes to a stop, mud flying everywhere. 'Your lady mother is bidding me look out for you and tell her when you is coming.' With that, he turns and flies away again, presumably to fulfil the second part of his task.

Dolfyn thrusts his nose into Fran's hand as they follow slowly after, past houses falling quickly into slumber. Fran is aware only of the things he must do so he might at last sit down, take off his boots, eat something, sleep. But even before he has reached the front door, hands are all around, taking Fauvel's bridle, handing him a glass of warm wine, guiding him up the steps and, finally, to a seat by the fire. Everything swirls around him, as if he is the only real thing in the room. He quite likes it that way.

His gaze floats towards the lady astride a playful horse on the tapestry opposite. She looks straight at him, half-smiling, and he is sure she knows a secret, although he has never noticed it before. He studies her more closely, the intensity of her green eyes, the firmness of the lines carving out her face. She seems neither young nor old, but infinitely wise, as if there is nothing in this world she hasn't seen before. He is sure she would understand, no matter what he told her. As the wine's warmth reaches his belly, he wonders if once she had a name, if she lived and breathed somewhere. And as he watches and wonders, the lady begins to unwrap him with her keen eyes, first his clothes, then his bindings, and on to his flesh so that there is no him or her, just muscle and sinew and a hot tide of blood, until there is only a beating heart. It is the greatest freedom Fran has ever known, there, just for a moment.

But he cannot hold it. Turning his head, he sees that the hall has settled into a state of sleepy activity. His mother sits near him, calmly working at her embroidery. He wonders if the Scots really did come today, the riding out to tell the people, the felo-de-se with her murdered child. He shifts slightly, pulls the blanket that someone has wrapped around him even tighter, feels a surprising contentment that he should have been so vigorous and useful and not found wanting.

His mother looks up and throws him a quick smile, pinning her needle into the cloth. 'We were worried.' It is brisk, practical, as if the temporary loss of him was of no greater moment than if he'd been a key or a shoe. It occurs to him that this is the way she always negotiates the limitations of her situation, seeking what is possible, not what is desirable. If he had not come back, if the Scots had killed him, she would have mourned, of course. But she would have found a way through. He sees it but does not understand it. If he had been the one waiting, contemplating such a loss, he would have wanted to roar and punch something.

But such thoughts, ones that scratch away at the differences between them, are not what he desires now, not when they suggest his nature is more akin to the woman with the bloody hands. She surely did not sit quietly either, waiting for her husband to return from Scotland. Or, if she did, her unquiet silence soon festered and turned foul once the enormity of her loss was confirmed, spilling over into madness. Is that the choice, an easy heart living at arm's length from its true desires, or a passionate one cast adrift in a world it can scarcely influence, let alone change? He shifts and sighs within the blanket, thoroughly miserable now, desiring to squeeze a little pleasure out of this gloomy day. 'Will someone fetch Luke. Tell him to bring his whistle.'

There is a pause, a murmuring. At last, a door bangs. Fran takes a sip of wine, dips his bread into the bowl of broth, glances at his mother. 'So, you—' he begins.

'Did you?' Christian asks, hands clasped tight around her embroidery.

'Go on. I just wanted to know if you saw anything of

the Scots?' He expects her to say she did not. Dipping his bread again, he feels the hunger burning in him at last.

But she nods slightly. 'A few hours ago. They came up the road from Warcop as if they owned it. About five of them. Willow was watching out, so we knew in plenty time.'

'But you had done as I asked? I sent Giles to tell you.' He sees the squire start, eyes leaping across their conversation. But it is his mother who captures his attention, her head dipping slightly, and he thinks she smiles. 'Do not laugh at me!'

She looks him straight in the eye. 'I do not. And, yes, we did your bidding, never fear. We would have been foolish not to.'

He chides himself for thinking himself slighted. 'Did they take anything?'

This time she shakes her head. 'They never reached here. It was probably the lateness of the hour. We waited a while, and I sent Willow out again to see. But they'd gone.'

He nods, the unease receding.

'And you?' She leans forward, elbows on knees, fingers kneading into the line of her jaw.

'Yes. Sir Henry and I put a few of them to flight near the river down at Great Ormside.' He feels a surge of pride in putting it like that, ignoring his own foolishness but not wishing to push himself forward as the only player in the story.

'You fought them?'

'Yes.' He smiles, searching for signs of esteem.

She nods. 'Your father would be proud.'

He considers that. Doubts it. And wonders too why she will not give him something of herself.

'Then we went to Flakebridge.'

'Did you see the woodsman's wife?'

He says nothing, for he can either lie or walk a perilous line.

'She lost her husband, poor woman. In the battle.'

He wonders how she knows this when he didn't. 'Who told you?'

She picks up her embroidery again, settling into her tale. 'Edie was visiting one of her friends in Warcop yesterday and it was the talk of the kitchen. She said the woodsman wasn't much given to passing the time of day with anyone even before he married. But he was quite besotted with his wife – I can't remember either of their names – even though she was such a plain little thing, and he hardly left his house unless to work. And, it must be said, no one ever heard a word of complaint—'

'Be quiet, for pity's sake.' He can scarcely breathe. Rushing up off the floor, Sarah leans over the back of his chair and strokes his hair, cooing gently. He knows she means only to bring comfort, but he wishes he might think over this day in peace.

The door bangs again and Luke, the shepherd's boy, strides in, his whistle held carefully in front of him. He walks right up to Fran, bows, his gaze solemn. 'What is you wanting me to play, master?'

Fran cannot help but smile at the gravity his request has inspired, but he realises that what he really wants is to be lying on a hillside beneath a generous summer breeze listening to the dancing notes of Luke's whistle silencing the larks and meadow pipits. If he just shuts his eyes, perhaps he will be able to imagine himself there. 'Just play,' he says at last. 'You choose.'

Luke nods as if giving the matter heavy thought. He goes to perch on the floor near the fire, shutting his eyes and letting the music flow through his fingers and out into ravenous ears. Not everyone is entranced, of course – Giles, for one – but such indifferent souls are wise enough to keep their chattering discreet. Fran feels himself grow heavy, rising on his chair into air pressing so thickly against him he can scarcely see anything. He senses the oblivion hovering nearby and turns towards it.

On the way up to bed later that night, his mother tells him that when she was giving orders about the sheep with Harry Sowerby, near to the place where their neighbour, Robert Bacon, has his barn, one of his servants spat at her and said he supposed they would escape any damage. She understood him to mean because she is of Scottish blood.

Fran spins around, puts a hand on her arm. 'He will answer for that.'

She nods, a great sigh agitating through her. Drifting away along the passage, her hands are wrapped tight around her ribs, shoulders hunched.

Chapter 4

Fran is shown into a small room just off Thomas Bacon's hall by a maidservant with all due courtesy and no warmth whatsoever. Thomas Bacon is inordinately proud of his parlour, another of which cannot be found, so he says, for thirty miles in any direction. But this pride pales into indifference next to the store his wife sets by the very thought of having such a pinnacle of privacy in which she can entertain those few she considers her betters and impress upon everyone else the unbreachable distance between them and the Bacons. In truth, Fran thinks it a small, hard-edged room where even the cushions discourage lingering.

That husband and wife are difficult to deal with is not in doubt, for many a merchant or gentleman at least as far west as Penrith has found himself on the uncomfortable end of a bargain, whether of a sale of silk or a purchase of wedders. But this pride and arrogance was not something Andrew Hilton had ever remarked upon about his neighbours, just as he never noticed the hurt his devotion to his sister inflicted on those he did, in his own way, care about deeply.

He disliked the Bacons, of course, not least because they occupied the manor house at Hilton Beacon, even though both families held the land equally. But any difficulties in his dealings with them – and there were many – he charged through as if intent merely on scattering a field full of impertinent jackdaws. Indeed, Andrew Hilton was their equal in churlishness, just as unwilling to put on a pleasant countenance and seek an agreement that might bring honour and profit to both parties. As a result, Fran learned early how to bargain fierce and hard.

But what Fran is entirely unprepared for is the fact that the Bacons have already spent an entire evening discussing the opportunities offered by Andrew Hilton's demise. Investigating these possibilities has become necessary, indeed imperative, now that various loans taken out by Thomas Bacon as far away as York require repayment. Thus it is that Fran has been permitted to wait in the parlour instead of freezing in the hall, though his impatience grows with each and every passing moment.

He idly turns the pages of a small, bejewelled copy of the *lais* of Marie de France carefully placed on an oak side table beneath the window, looking up with relief when the door to the parlour finally opens. But it is not Thomas who steps briskly through it, but his wife. Egidia Crackenthorpe stops, waiting for him to turn and see her, framed beautifully within the simple solidity of the wooden door. She is a small woman with pale yellow hair, slight as a feather (if that feather were constructed entirely of steel), and still, for all her thirty-four years, possessed of a beauty that does not enhance the world but disdains it.

Fran whips his hat from his head, heart sinking as he bows.

She moves forward gracefully, sinks into a chair and adjusts her skirts, her maidservant scuttling into a corner and busying herself with some darning. Waiting just a few moments longer than is either necessary or courteous, Egidia finally waves a hand at the only other chair. Fran sits, wishing he still had the advantage of standing above her, and that it were Thomas he must deal with.

She presses her hands together, lowering her eyes for a moment. 'We hope your father did not suffer.'

Fran is unsure if this is a question, but he answers it anyway. 'It was . . . not a bad death.'

Her lips purse slightly. 'God be praised.'

'Indeed.' He wonders why he feels she holds him responsible in some way, will certainly not tell her there was no time for the last rites, though she surely knows that already, given that rumours travel from his house to hers quicker than lightning. He reminds himself that he visits to seek redress for a wrong done to his own family, not the other way round.

'And, of course, if you need any advice, any guidance, you need only ask. You are still so young.'

He sighs inwardly, wishes again that Thomas Bacon would hurry up.

'But not so very young.' Her owl's eyes are on him now, unblinking, searching.

But for what? Fran cannot imagine what purpose this

conversation might serve, though he's sure there is one. Everyone knows Egidia Crackenthorpe never wastes even a belch or a fart except in her own interests.

The door creaks open and a girl stumbles in, coming to linger near her mother's chair. Emma Bacon is as downcast and ephemeral as Egidia is bold and unwavering. At thirteen years old, she should be blossoming, but instead holds herself ready for flight, her limbs seemingly unconnected to the rest of her body and threatening to topple her over. The only thing of beauty she has inherited from her mother is her hair, which ripples and shines over her shoulders before sweeping down her back. She tugs a strand of it quickly into her mouth, gnawing at it as if to save her life.

But already her mother darts out a hand, tearing at the strand of hair before grasping her daughter firmly round the waist and drawing her hard against the arm of her chair. The girl squawks in fright, perching there like some caged creature desperate to curl up somewhere far away.

Fran wonders if he can find some excuse to leave. He imagines collusion between husband and wife to waylay him, thinks they must have somehow uncovered the slight to his mother and seek now to divert him from his purpose. He clears his throat, puts his hands on his knees. 'Well—'

'You will be thinking, of course, about your marriage. A fine young man like you shouldn't wait too long, not with things so uncertain. How little time there is these days to linger on what is pleasant.' Egidia pulls down her mouth, sheathing her eyes. 'And we must stick together, I think.

Would you not agree?' Now she turns the full force of her gaze upon him, leaving no room for doubt.

He blinks, wondering what on God's earth she's talking about. And then it's as if the air is sucked out of this small, stifling room. He knows exactly what she means and is appalled. Even if he were a ... But he is not. And cannot. He is trapped, bound to give offence, whatever reason he might proffer. And only a fool would not have thought of this before. Emma has no brothers or sisters as yet. It would make perfect sense to unite their families and the lands they hold, for they have some fine hill country between them, enough to clear a good £20 a year so long as the Scots do not prove too burdensome.

And, with this great revelation, Fran feels an unholy anger seize hold of him, setting fire again to the memory of his father, who has left him to deal with this terrible mess by himself. He believes with absolute certainty that this cannot have been the first time the marriage has been mooted, that Andrew Hilton will have been accosted bluntly by Thomas Bacon and in countless sideways comments, suggestions, assertions, musings by his wife. Fran even wonders if his father did not put much effort into discouraging this ungodly union, imagining somewhere in his troubled mind that what he had willed into being had somehow become godly flesh. That he had a son in truth and not just stubborn fiction.

Egidia Crackenthorpe is looking at him, a great heat scorching her cheeks. He must think of something to say, and quickly. At the very least, the girl does not deserve the disgust that is meant not for her but for himself. He draws a deep breath, fixes his gaze on a small painting on the dark blue wall above Egidia's head. The Christ-child sits on His mother's knee, a finger pointing upwards as if demanding everyone to hush and listen to His words of wisdom. Fran implores Him for advice even as he wonders if this plump, assured baby already knew what lay before Him, the sacrifice He was sent to Earth to make. He decides it would be a terrible burden to carry for all those years as a mortal being. But fathers can be cruel.

He stands, forcing himself to look at Egidia while trying not to stumble over his words. 'You're right. We should stick together. But my father is not yet buried, and I have much to attend to.' He lets the reproof lie heavily between them, sending a smile to Emma so she might know he means no pain or insult to her, at least.

Egidia inclines her head, the narrow press of her lips betraying displeasure. But only for a moment. 'You will think on it, then? When the time is right? A marriage with Emma would bring honour to us all.' It is a singular concession, for she is much given to exalting her own and Thomas's families by denigrating everyone else's.

'I will think on it, yes.' He can scarcely say anything else, though he feels he will choke on such a pretence.

'Perhaps next spring would be—'

'Do not run too fast, madam. I said I would think on it.'

Egidia rises too, chin held high. 'Surely you are eager to prove the gossips wrong, Francis?' Though she has not raised her voice, her words hit him with all the force of a well-aimed staff.

But he has spent a lifetime weighing words, suspecting friends, neighbours, acquaintances, almost everyone, of divining his secret. He has learned to hold his breath, wrestle his unruly heart back into a normal rhythm, swiftly search the words and their speaker for signs of discovery. And every time he finds he has invented a meaning that was never there. This time, however, he has no idea what Egidia is implying, though he does reassure himself that she would surely never offer him her daughter's hand if she thinks him no more a man than Emma. So he raises his chin too. 'I did not think you would listen to rumours, madam.'

She holds his gaze. 'Sometimes one has no choice.'

He pauses, eager to know, afraid to ask. 'Pray tell me what is said.'

Egidia turns to her daughter. 'Leave us.' She waits until the girl's heavy footsteps disappear before sitting back down and looking steadfastly at the hands folded in her lap. 'All I will say is that it is entirely natural that men should find wisdom and even solace with other men.'

Fran's cheeks burn. Though he cannot deny the lustful thoughts and feelings that sometimes run riot through him, he does not – cannot – think of himself as a carnal being. It is shameful to imagine that others do.

She turns her head, spears him with a look. 'I'm sure it was nothing more than a youthful passion.'

He frowns. 'What was?'

She turns away again, lips pursed. 'You do not need me to say it.'

'Whatever you've heard, it's false!' He is vehement now,

outraged that he should be denied what others take for granted but accused of it all the same. And with whom? He has been courteous to all the girls of his acquaintance, but it is clearly ridiculous to suggest he has ever desired anything more.

'If you say so.'

He is in no doubt she means the opposite. 'I do.'

She picks hard at a nail. 'As I said, a man's business is his to direct as he chooses. But only if he is careful ... if he does what is expected of him, so far as everyone else is concerned.'

'In what way do I fail to do what is expected of me?' He has spent every waking moment doing exactly that.

She throws down her hands. 'If you do not understand my meaning, you're a bigger fool than I thought, Francis Hilton.'

'Then it's a wonder you think me a worthy husband for your daughter.' Thrusting his hat back on his head, he gives her a careless bow and strides to the door.

'It is a good offer,' she shouts after him. 'But we will not beg. Come back when you've seen sense.'

Plunging down the steps and out into the blustery day, Fran feels the wind finger his hat. He stands for a moment, gulping air. But now Thomas Bacon arrives at his front door, stoking Fran's fury, for if the man had seen fit to do so even five minutes before, he would not have had to endure such an ordeal. He is tempted to berate his neighbour for his wife's intemperance. But he has not forgotten why he's here. Moving back up a step, he folds his arms, tries to make more of himself.

Thomas comes to stand beside him, a red-faced man with a fulsome brown beard but only a few long strands of greying hair clinging limply to his shiny head. 'You've no need to leave. I was just speaking with my shepherd. We'll have some ale, shall we, and you can tell me how you fared yesterday. By God, you were much honoured, to ride with the sheriff.' He strokes his beard as if in wonderment at such a thing.

'I'm expecting someone.' That's an outright lie. Fran reminds himself to be civil. Thomas is not Egidia, and anyway, he must live beside them both. But he does not wish to speak of the woodsman's wife and her child; he still has no words for such a hellish, incomprehensible thing. No doubt the Bacons will hear the sorry tale soon enough and be annoyed he did not offer them it first. And he thinks sourly that Egidia, for all her protestations, loves to be the one to tell others the newest tidings, especially if the news is bad or even slanderous.

'There's nothing much to tell. We were close to the Scots, but . . .' He imagines Thomas will most want to hear about that terrible, glorious encounter on the riverbank, but his neighbour is nodding quickly, apparently eager for him to finish. Fran does him the favour. 'What about you?'

Thomas shakes his head slowly, as if lost for words himself. 'It was a terrible thing. Down at Sandford, we were. They came upon us that quickly, I thought my time had come.'

'You fought them?' Fran is somewhat impressed even as he deeply regrets not mentioning his own fight.

'Chased them all the way to Little Ormside.'

'The ones with the cows or the soldiers?'

Thomas rubs his nose vigorously. 'It was hard to tell.'

'Really?'

'They were taking a piss, see. Down by the ford.'

'So, they weren't with their fellows?'

'That's right.'

'How many of them were there?'

Thomas waggles his head from side to side, as if counting in his head. 'Three or four?'

Fran is entirely sure Thomas really means one or two but knows he must not laugh. 'I see. So, what were they like, close up? I've heard they have really sharp teeth.'

He nods vigorously. 'And small. About your size, I'd say. Dark, too. Like devils.' He sniffs. 'You have Scottish kin, don't you?'

'My mother's family. But I have not seen them since before the war.' He knows now is the time to speak. 'That's what I came to see you about.'

Thomas grunts. 'Your mother's family?'

'No, my mother.'

'A most . . . estimable lady.'

'Indeed. But one of your men doesn't seem to think so.'

'Oh?' Thomas doesn't ask which one. Or what this rogue thought or said or did.

'It was yesterday. Near to your barn. I had given them orders to take the beasts up into the fells, so she was there with Harry Sowerby. I suppose your servants were doing the same. One of them spat at her, for being a Scot. She didn't recognise him.'

'That'll be Dod Liddell. He's new come from near Carlisle. They've suffered even worse up there.'

'I don't doubt it. But that has nothing whatsoever to do with my mother.'

'I'll speak with him. If he's forgotten his place, he'll be punished.'

'You don't believe me?'

Thomas lowers his eyes. 'That's not what I meant.' He studies the stone beneath his feet for a moment. 'Tell your lady mother I'm sorry for it.' Thomas smooths down a strand of hair that hasn't moved. 'Did my wife mention—'

'Yes.' Fran pulls his hat down firmly over his ears. 'Yes, she did. And I have promised to think on it.' He bows with heavy politeness and marches quickly away, up the road towards their house, the great fells gathered high above him. When he reaches the line of blackthorn that marks the border between his land and the Bacons, he stops, looks round carefully. The sky is a dappled grey, with rain weighing heavily over Roman Fell, but not yet on Hilton.

Running heedlessly down the blackthorn hedge towards the river, he slides onto the bank and falls to his knees. Below him the clear water sings its merry tune, indifferent to hearts full of joy or misery. A bee speeds past him, intent on finding harebells or bog star. Clutching a rock, he feels a great convulsion in his belly. And, at last, he weeps until his head aches and his face runs with tears. He doesn't know why he weeps. Only that he will not be able to go home until he does.

Chapter 5

Autumn comes gracefully, eschewing wind and rain for a gentle blushing and withering that lasts well past All Souls. The harvest has, despite everything, been plentiful, so most rents are paid promptly at Michaelmas, with few excuses offered and almost none accepted. Since he is newly become master at Hilton, Fran knows he will be tried and tested for weakness and is determined to show none. He is, however, content to let Harry Sowerby come to him quietly with requests for help.

Winter is less agreeable. Though, as always, the shortening of the days brings an easing of the cares and duties that accompany the growing seasons, there is something unsettling about the smothering snow that falls throughout December. Even when skies clear, the air is so cold it could choke the breath out of a man. Great icicles form beneath the roofs of houses, causing all sensible people to scuttle about, eyes torn between the threat above and the difficult ground underfoot. By Noel a rock must be thrust down the well to break the ice before a bucket can be sent after it. Even the hardiest of women is not inclined to tarry there in idle talk.

Fran has scarcely seen Will these past months. The priest's mother, who lives near Alnwick in Northumberland, is dangerously ill and so he spends much time there. Besides, Fran does not wish to burden his friend, for he knows there is a great affection between mother and son. Yet it irks him he is left with no one to guide him when there is so much he would like to try to understand. And now that so many months have passed since his father's death, he cannot imagine saying the things that need to be said to unburden himself, even to Will. But then ... who is he fooling? Fran knows perfectly well he could never tell Will he is in truth woman, not man.

As the days struggle through the weeks, Fran busies himself in reading out loud to whomever wishes to listen, one foot pulled up on to his chair by the fire, a hand resting on his knee or caressing the top of Dolfyn's head. Harry Sowerby's son is a particularly rapt listener, sitting close to the leg of the chair, occasionally peeping over the back so he can mouth the words on the page that contain so much wonderment.

Willow Sowerby's baptismal name is Simon but not even his own mother calls him that. A youth of great suppleness, he is also blessed with hair that hangs over his shoulders in straight golden rods. He has long refused to have it cut more than an inch at any one time, in the belief – and who knows for certain whether he is wrong – that this was how the Arthurian knights wore theirs. Quite a few girls from Brough to Penrith dream of stirring their hands through his locks, coiling them round their wrists like the fur trims to their gloves.

It is, in part at least, the youth's eagerness to hear about King Arthur's knights in general, and Sir Galahad in particular, that explains why Fran's copy of *The Quest* – purchased from Paris by his father nearly three decades ago – is so well worn that the green leather cover has become a soft yellowy blue, its metal corner pieces chipped or missing. If he's not careful, Fran fears the book will fall apart altogether, and he vows to purchase another copy in the spring.

Giles Helbeck sits at the table behind him. The squire is fond of stories about King Arthur and his knights too, but he has no liking whatsoever for Willow Sowerby. When Willow claps, shouting words of encouragement as Galahad unwittingly bests his father Sir Lancelot, Giles covers his ears with both hands and groans loudly.

Fran shuts the book as gently as he can for fear it will finally crumble. 'If you two can't sit in peace . . .'

Both leap to their feet, protesting, drowning each other out. Edie, the cook's daughter, leaning against the door like a rosy-cheeked statue, wipes down her hands with a sigh before wandering off back towards the kitchen.

Fran gets to his feet, stretching out the muscles in his back. Willow slinks away, shoulders hunched, head hung low.

Giles bustles up. 'You shouldn't waste your breath on a coxcomb like him, sir.'

'God's bones! It's not for you to say what I waste

my breath on!' It irks him that the squire pretends to know what Fran wants or thinks, so he must always be contradicted, creating needless arguments between them. Fran prefers not to think of himself as an open book. Indeed, he likes to imagine his thoughts are kept safely hidden. On days like these, he regrets that allowing Giles to stay on at Hilton is probably better than trying to find a new squire.

He has made up his mind, even if he hasn't confessed this to his mother. As they say, 'a known evil is best'. If it had been the other way round, if – and this is of course scarcely worthy of belief – he had been in nature a boy but raised as a girl, there would be every reason to let nature take its course. So, though the disquiet remains, the frantic yearnings in deepest night from those parts of himself that might as well be dead, he is determined not to listen.

But now he sees a familiar look of disquiet tug at Giles's face, eyes suddenly fluid and threatening to overflow. Fran cannot understand the extremes in his squire's nature. But he supposes he'll have to live with them. He pats Giles on the arm. 'Forgive me, I am most tired. What say you bring me some ale? And an apple tart, if cook has one to spare.'

Giles sniffs, nods gravely before turning quickly on his heel. A few moments later he can be heard shouting for Edie to come right away or she'll earn herself a slap.

Fran sighs and walks over to the window, his heart sinking to see heavy feathers of snow once more vanquishing the sky and everything beyond the wall around his house. And yet it is beautiful, this great blossoming of white overwhelming everything, extinguishing the traces of men and other living creatures.

He feels a shivering of skirts beside him, a hand on his back. Without thinking, he stiffens and the hand retreats.

'I do not wish you harm, Fran.' His mother speaks hesitantly, as if full of regret.

Biting his lip, he turns his head towards her. 'I didn't know it was you.'

She closes her eyes, but not quickly enough to hide a glint of tears.

Heart stinging, he looks at her closely for the first time since the day his father died. He sees that she ages quicker than her years, lines digging deep, skin sallow and sagging. 'Does something ail you?' Now it is his turn to put a hand on her.

Christian shakes her head firmly, blinking away the tears. 'I was going to ask you the same thing.'

'I am perfectly well. I lack only a considerate squire.' That was supposed to make her laugh, or at least draw forth a smile.

But she folds her arms tightly around herself, shoulders drawn towards her ears, a habit she has learned these past months. 'He is a man to be reckoned with.'

Fran frowns. 'Giles?'

'Of course not. His father.'

He does not dispute it but wonders what brings her to say so. 'I didn't know you'd spoken with him.'

'At your father's burial.'

He nods, none the wiser, chilled by the distance between them, the hunted look on her face. 'Tell me what he said.' He speaks quickly, roughly, fearing some huge wave is about to overwhelm them without any notion where it's coming from.

Her throat contracts, swells out again. 'He was courteous for the most part. When others were within hearing. But he looked for me when he wished to leave and took my elbow to bring me out of the hall. I thought he wished to ... I imagined he had something important to tell me privily. He's been a widower himself these five years ...' She kneads an elbow. 'But it wasn't that. He said I had nothing to keep me here and it would be better if I went back to my own people. I think he believed he was speaking kindly, to save me from others.'

'Why didn't you tell me?'

She turns then, eyes urgent. 'I only want to explain ... There were others. Most were unpleasant but not really threatening. No more than the kind of thing young girls say to each other when they fall out of friendship.'

'I still wish you'd told me.'

'There's nothing you can do.'

'You don't know that.' He wishes he'd been able to protect her. But it angers him more that she seems to think he can't.

'Perhaps. But that's the least of it.' She puts out a hand, pulls it back.

He feels like a rabbit caught in the path of a fox, unable to move.

Christian glances round the room to reassure herself no one else can hear before offering her face to the window's steady gaze. 'Do you remember when I went with Hawise to market in Appleby just after Michaelmas?'

'Of course. You have refused to go ever since. I thought it was the weather.'

She snorts. 'Aye. The weather. You probably didn't notice, but when I returned, I told Hawise to warm a bath for me. And burn the clothes I was wearing.'

'I remember the first, for certain. I thought you'd caught a chill. I had no notion of the second.' He licks dry lips.

Her chin has set to steel. 'I was just coming back from taking a piss behind a hedge, so I was on my own. Two men were coming up the lane. I knew them and they knew me. I was ready to smile a greeting, but the one pushed at the other with his elbow. Their faces ... They were giving me such black looks, I was suddenly afraid. But I had nowhere to go.'

She pauses. Fran feels the agony in her heart beating in his, for all that she speaks calmly, quietly.

Turning to face him, she pulls at his hand, clutching it with both of hers. 'I will not tell you what they made me do. Or who they were. I understand perfectly well they have good reason to hate the Scots. But I never thought ... After all this time, I have long ceased to consider myself one of them.'

He cannot look at her, giving back only dull words. 'We all have reason to hate those who come to destroy us. But that's no reason to behave like savages.'

'I fear it is too late.'

He is suddenly alive with fury. 'Then tell me who they were. I will speak with Sir Henry. He will see justice is done.'

She pulls away, shakes her head. 'I never want to speak those words, so I cannot accuse them.'

'Then I will have justice another way. But you must tell me!' It is a cry born as much out of frustration with her as anger at her unknown assailants.

'Lower your voice, I beg you!' She moves closer, words urgent. 'Do nothing on my account. You should think only of what is best for everyone at Hilton.'

'You don't have to tell me that. But I cannot allow this . . . this outrage to be . . . to pretend it never happened. For you to live here dishonoured, whether anyone else knows it or not.'

Placing a hand on his chest, she breathes deeply. 'I'm going back, Fran.'

He blinks, struggling with her meaning. But, in truth, he knows. 'No.'

'I must. My mother is old now and she needs me. You do not.'

I do. I do. I do. Fran feels it as another betrayal, choosing to abandon him, just as she's done all his life. And yet he had thought – hoped – he would have the time now to mend what has long been broken between them, though he has done nothing these long months to breach her watchful restraint. Or his own.

She is speaking. 'This war cannot go on forever. Perhaps there will soon be a truce. You could come and see me.'

He nods, doubting it very much. 'When will you go?'

'With the first signs of spring. Before the roads are too busy with people.'

'Does Hawise know?'

Christian nods. 'She will come with me. If it pleases you.'

'You don't give me much choice, do you?' He opens and closes his fists. 'I will ride with you. To the border. And you must remember me to my grandmother.'

But she twists her face. 'You need not come. I know the right ways to keep us safe. Women travelling alone are not so suspicious.' She pats his chest, removes her hand.

They both know that women travelling alone are also more vulnerable.

But already he feels lighter at the thought of one less responsibility even as guilt plucks at his heart, pushing at him the feeling that this too is his fault. Yet still – despite how little he knows her, the lack of a bond between them – he cannot imagine waking up to her not being here. 'You are sure you must go?'

She nods, happier now she has told him, turns back to her women.

Fran stands by the window drenched in nothingness. He wonders how long it will take for him to forget the outline of her face. That he should feel even more alone than usual is not, he realises, because she is a friend to him. It is the loss of the hope that she might be.

The three girls are standing by the wall, Edie picking away at the moss as she listens and nods, the fingers of her other hand gently stroking the smooth fair hair behind her ear. Her hair flows past her face, delicate strands of red and gold dancing in the wind. She stretches out a hand, milk pale, unblemished, to curl a lock around soft fingers. Awaiting news from her lover – whose face is utterly familiar but strangely vague – she drifts through the day, disdaining food, sipping wine, trying to read. She feels her love as a sickness, its stifling embrace filling her mind completely. But she is loath to throw it off.

And, anyway, turning over the meaning in her lover's every word or glance before embellishing them in a hundred faithful digressions provides ample entertainment for her friends. Fran revels in imagining the hours spent in earnest conversation, arms, legs, heads pressed so tightly together it is scarcely possible to tell where one girl begins and another ends. Closing her eyes, she conjures up the warm earth living in their skin, the blossom in their hair. Last, but not least, she savours the tingling feeling of hands in her own tresses, binding, stroking, undoing.

Fran throws open his eyes, pushing aside such idle imaginings, recovers his bearing. The murmuring below pierces his heart, and he must pull back from the window, a fire in his cheeks. He has been accustomed for as long as he can remember to watch others closely, noting every agitation causing lips to part, cheeks to redden, eyes to dim or brighten. These attempts to understand the ways in which feelings are imprinted on everyone else are, so far as he knows, successfully unremarked. But now he feels exposed, fear charging in to dispel what had once brought him some understanding of what it must feel like to belong. Though he has no idea what sin he might be guilty of, shame engulfs him all the same.

Did Edie look up? Or did he just imagine a moment when she did because the thought was already in his mind? He moves closer to the window, ready to push himself away if he is indeed discovered.

The other two girls have their backs to Fran, but it takes no more than a glance to realise the one on the left – half Edie's size, reed-thin but formidable in disposition – is Luke the shepherd boy's sister, Agatha, who also works in the kitchens. The girl on the right is one of Edie's many friends from Warcop. Fran struggles to remember her name but does know she is servant to Jamie Dickinson. A pretty thing, she is blessed with a froth of light brown hair that bounces down her back.

Though he cannot see her face, it's clear she is the one doing the talking, slight shoulders rising and falling, hands beseeching the air, reaching out to Edie, who nods slowly. Occasionally the girl turns towards Agatha for a reassuring smile.

But it is Edie who is the fount of all wisdom and at last she pushes herself away from the wall, heedful, no doubt, of the rain that will return as surely as her next breath. Reaching out with both arms, she enfolds her friend in a brief embrace that completely swallows her up. The three then link arms, dipping their heads to pass beneath the low-hanging sweep of a cherry tree swollen with snow-white flowers. They laugh as they bow in harmony and are gone, leaving Fran to fall back from the window as if they had slammed a door shut in his face.

He aches with the desire to share confidences with others who are at ease with all he is and is not. But no one at Hilton – apart from Sarah, of course – knows his secret. And there never can be, now his mother and Hawise have gone.

Around the fourth Sunday in Lent, Christian Kirkbride began to study the skies, sniffing the air for signs that winter, which had slunk away quietly, might return in a fury. Fran understood these signs, but they had agreed she should not tell him her intentions, that she would slip away quietly so no one might plan any mischief.

She and Hawise could no longer be found on Good Friday, that dismal day when our Lord suffered for the sins of mankind. Now, half a moon later, Fran wanders through the house trying to feel her absence. He might have ended up in the kitchens, seeking freshly baked bread to smear with the new butter Edie churned yesterday. But he would surely encounter the girls he's just been watching.

If he feels a great heaviness upon him that wearies him to his very bones, it's not for lack of things to do, despite the mercilessness of the weather which already disquiets the crop farmers down in the valley. For one thing, it presses upon him that Will sent a most precious copy of *The Seven Sages of Rome* over ten days ago. The priest had borrowed it from the bishop of Carlisle and would, so he wrote, have to send it back within the next few weeks.

Though this transitory gift was in part an apology for Will's many absences, Fran felt a spasm of distress on reading the rest of the missive enclosed with the book. *I am sure*, it said in the priest's brisk, imperious tones, *you would rather I had sent you* Le Roman de la Rose, *for I know young men find it pleasing. But I think you will find this more*

useful, not least in educating you in the wiles and sinfulness of
women. You are too trusting by nature and must learn to be
on your guard now your father is not here to guide you. The
reproof is softened by a drawing of the two of them, a
crude depiction of their heads and shoulders added to the
margin of the letter. They are both smiling, though Will is
the more commanding figure, his arms entirely encircling
a much smaller Fran.

Fran still winces at the condemnation of his true nature,
however unwitting. It does not help that Will's words also
remind him of the unpleasant consequences of his decision
to leave things as they are. It's common knowledge that
Francis Hilton is ripe for marriage, and he has received all
manner of invitations from across the county to hunt or
spar or dine. After the first painful experience at Thomas
Bacon's manor house, he vowed to venture forth only if
no unmarried daughters or sisters lurk in the household.
Never again will he endure an interminable banquet in a
draughty hall as guest of a boastful father or brother eager
to describe the virtues of a pale-faced girl.

But he knows he is acquiring a reputation for being
cold to women. He has, of course, declined Emma Bacon's
hand. The recollection of that moment still makes him
shudder, for Thomas Bacon had blinked, thrown his hat
on the ground and jumped on it before turning sharply on
his heel. For several months, they scarcely exchanged more
than a grunted 'God speed', though more recently Thomas
has succumbed to his urge to chatter.

But Egidia Crackenthorpe will never forget. If she sees
him, even at a distance, she stops to stare, arms crossed,

eyes hooded. He tries not to let this deter him from going
where he pleases, but there's no doubt it preys on his mind.

So, Fran has no desire to begin Will's book today,
though he promises himself he will do so before the
Sabbath. He considers asking Giles to play chess, but the
squire has a habit of sighing during his own interminable
turn and yawning during his opponent's. Willow Sowerby
is a better player, but Fran is in no mood to listen to his
chatter. He stares out of the great window in the hall, hands
behind his back, Dolfyn sprawled at his feet, eyes fixed on
the grey-swollen sky cascading down Murton Pike. He
imagines the rain flooding through him, breathing in its
soft distillation of earth and heavens, and tells himself to
be done with these low spirits, for they serve no purpose
except to distract him from the business of living.

Harry Sowerby's dog barks. A mournful-looking creature, he roams the courtyard all day, every day, in search
of something to announce to the rest of the world. Fran
knows better than to pay any heed, though something
causes a prickling on the back of his neck. Dolfyn feels
it too, lifting his head with a brisk flick of his ears. Is it
voices they can hear? A little too loud, too strident. And
now most certainly there are footsteps coming this way.
Fran turns, just as Harry Sowerby himself throws open the
door, snatching the hat from his head.

'God keep you, sir, and forgive me for disturbing you.'
The tautness in Harry's face forewarns Fran of what is still
to be said.

'Never mind that.' Fran curls his hands into fists,
prepares himself. He thinks for a moment of his mother.

Sarah shuffles through the door, a low, breathless moaning escaping her lips.

Harry does not glance at her. ''Tis the shepherd's lad. He's fallen into a ravine round the back of Roman Fell. The mud's that slippery. I know you're fond of him.'

'Is he . . .?' Fran is not sure which way he wants to ask that question.

'He was well enough to shout for help, but he's been down there a while and the rivers are still rising. 'Twas Sim Taylor himself who came.' The shepherd is rarely seen around the house.

Fran feels a powerful urge to move. 'Gather all the men you can. And ropes. We'll need ropes.'

Harry nods. ''Tis already done. I just wondered . . .'

'I'll come too.' Fran says it quickly, before anyone can tell him it's foolish. 'Sarah, find Giles for me.'

She lifts her skirts, pushes past the bailiff, her moaning keeping pace with her steps.

Chapter 6

A crowd has already gathered beyond the upper gate, men and dogs restless with the damp and worry. A dozen faces turn Fran's way and he wonders if he provides any reassurance at all, as his father had done. Ahead, hovering at the point where the ground dips away towards the confluence of Hilton and Swindale Becks, stands Sim Taylor, the shepherd. Holding himself taut and a little hunched, eyes flighty, it is as if his strength subsides the longer he is away from the hills. His dogs are just as uneasy, tails slung low, teeth bared at the slightest provocation.

Fran has no wish to stand around thinking of the right words to say. Setting his own face to the hills, he strides forward, Dolfyn at his heels, the crowd shifting and reforming behind him like an evening congregation of starlings. The shepherd contemplates his approach, cap kneaded between great-knuckled fingers. His dogs sit back, eyeing their master whilst keeping most of their attention on Dolfyn, who does not even throw them a glance.

Fran has not the height to clap Sim on the shoulder, so settles for a quick pat of restless hands. 'Lead us.' He says it softly, but leaving no room for equivocation. So close to such ill-used flesh, the harshness of wind and weather written into brow and cheek, the clotted disfigurement of raw-red skin on bone, he wonders how old Sim is. He certainly has no recollection of a time when he did not work at Hilton, infrequently observed, but undoubtedly relied upon.

The shepherd takes flight immediately and becomes another creature altogether, casting off any decay as if it were a cloak. Fran has difficulty keeping up, unaccustomed in recent years to making swift progress on foot across ground that is rarely as firm or flat as it seems. But they are soon far ahead of the others, keeping to the south side of Swindale Beck as it creeps through Swindale Edge towards Swindale Crag. The grass is vibrant green and plentiful lower down, and both cattle and sheep are already supping well there. But here all is rock and treachery.

They do not speak, for Fran has no breath and the shepherd no inclination. And always the rain, filling the threads of Fran's cloak till it is sodden wet and heavy. At last he must stop, to free himself even for a moment of the tedium of climbing and slipping and feeling his heart complain in his chest. 'Is it much further?' He knows he sounds like a querulous child.

'Just a little, young master.' The shepherd speaks to him like an infant, and Fran knows he must bend his head once more to keep a close watch on his feet, Dolfyn dancing in front of him and no help at all.

At last Sim stops, looking down eagerly, a hand reaching to fondle one of his dogs. Fran rushes up, follows his gaze, wipes the drops of water from his face, looks again. 'Is that him there?' He points. It is no more than a smudge of colour below a gap in the rocks, the rushing of water assaulting their ears.

The shepherd nods. 'He fell down the other side, I'm thinking. It's o'er steep there.' He draws in a great breath. 'Luke, boy, can you hear me?' His cry is hoarse, but loud enough to send three rooks watching them from a thorn bush into the air with outraged croaks. He shouts again, in case the croaking concealed the response. But there is nothing.

Willow Sowerby arrives with a rope. He and Sim look at one another, then at Fran.

'You must do as you think best,' he assures them.

Sim Taylor nods. Quickly tying the rope around his waist, he hands the other end to Willow, who braces himself against the far side of a great boulder. Without a word, the shepherd begins his backwards descent, face set, feet spread apart, hands bouncing and tumbling on to anything that might keep him steady. He is nimble, of course, and soon reaches the line of rock that falls away towards the beck. And there he stops. Turning, he shakes his head, throws up an arm to encourage Willow to pull in the rope as he climbs steadily back up the steep slope. 'No use,' he says, finally out of breath. 'I be too big to get through.'

Willow immediately steps forward, but the shepherd puts a hand on his chest. He turns to Fran. The other

men have arrived now, sides heaving, hands on knees.
Harry Sowerby pushes his way through. 'What's going
on, sir?' He throws a quick glance out towards Willow, but
immediately brings all his attention back to Fran.

'It seems I'm the only one small enough to get through
the rocks.'

'No, sir. That is beyond foolishness.'

'I'm not going to argue with you. There isn't time.' Fran
throws off his cloak, looks around for Giles, who creeps
towards him, eyes fixed on the drop. Fumbling for the
cloak, the squire retreats quickly to clutch a boulder.

'You know how to do it, sir?' The shepherd is uneasy
now, hands restless once more.

Fran doesn't wish to think long over what he's about to
do. It's better just to do it. 'I saw what you did.' Everyone
is staring at him. Harry Sowerby opens his mouth. Fran
looks at Willow. 'Ready?' For once Willow does no more
than nod. Dolfyn whines once and lies down with his head
on his paws.

Fran stretches a foot out over the edge. Immediately
he feels it slide, brings his other one beside it, but ends up
on his knees, hands scraping on rocks and stones, the rope
digging into his waist. The company above him catches its
breath.

'You mun lean back, young master. Don't let yer legs
be getting too far away frae you.' Sim Taylor is wandering
back and forth like a bullock ready to charge.

Fran is not convinced, but there must be some sense in
it. Getting to his feet, he wipes his hands on his breeches,
takes one breath, two, and leans back. Slowly, he moves

one foot a little way, then the other. It is better, he can feel it, more in balance. Keeping his gaze steady on the grass and herbs, he soon hears shouts from above, calling to him to stop.

He removes the rope, which will not stretch much further, turns to contemplate the narrow gap. It will not be easy to get through, but he thinks he'll manage. It will be a different matter going the other way, though, and for the first time he wonders how he's going to get Luke Elliot back up with him. The boy is slight, that's true. But if there's no life in him, even if he's not actually dead, he will prove a great weight.

He throws such thoughts away. Turning sideways, he forces himself through the gap in the rock and is suddenly released. For a moment he thinks he must fall, but though he trembles, arms flailing, he keeps his balance and finds himself looking down at the untidy bundle that is Luke Elliot. A few feet away lies a ewe, one of last year's lambs. It is most certainly dead, legs sticking straight up in the air, head twisted. In a less anxious time, it might provoke mirth, but Fran curses it for leading the shepherd boy astray.

The beck is indeed rising and already Luke's right arm hangs in the water. His head has fallen on top of it, leaning awkwardly over his shoulder, but his nose and mouth are still free to breathe air. Fran plunges into the beck, feels its mighty chill and the force of its passing, but it is shallow enough here, with several big rocks to keep him steady. He prays all the same, a feverish repetition to guide him safely to Luke's side. Kneeling above him, his heart stumbles

over a beat. The boy's eyes are open, yet he does not seem
to see. Fran reaches out a hand, and the eyes fasten on to
him, a frown half-forming.

Fran breathes again, a great smile bursting out of him.
'It's me. Francis Hilton. Don't try to speak.'

Still the frown, a cloud of unknowing across the eyes.

Fran sees the water rush closer. At the very least, he
must get Luke on to higher ground. He cannot see much
blood, but the rain has probably washed most of it away.
He hopes it will not hurt too much when he lifts him. It
certainly won't be easy, for he cannot get beneath Luke
to get the boy up. Breathing in and out, long and deep,
he glances back up to where he came from, to where he
must go back. But the others are obscured beyond the
wall of rock. There is fear upon Fran now, and not just for
Luke. He cannot imagine being anywhere but here, in this
dripping, painful place. And that is not a thought to bring
comfort.

Filling his lungs to the very bottom, he gets behind
Luke and quickly hoists him so that he sits up. The cry is
horrible, and Fran tries not to imagine the consternation
above. At least it proves the boy lives. He does not stop,
getting on to one knee and throwing Luke over his
shoulder. In the same movement, he rises onto both feet
with a mighty grunt. His muscles protest so fiercely that
he is sure they will refuse him, heart beating fit to leap out
of his throat. But by a miracle he stays upright.

Luke shrieks again, short and terrible and abruptly
ended.

Fran has no breath to answer him. And what would he

say anyway? It's time they were moving, away from this godforsaken place more suited to fish than men. Staggering forward, he feels his legs begin to tremble, wonders why it is so much harder to go up than down. Placing each foot carefully, he inches forward, eyes fixed on the rock wall. He knows it's not the end of their journey but cannot think beyond it. At least Luke has not cried out again. Is that because he no longer lives? If so, the dead weigh as much as the living. Thoughts flit like bats through his mind, scarcely alighting. He is sure he cannot go on and yet he does.

If he had the strength, he could stretch out his hand and touch the rock wall. And now he feels the ache of tears, for it is too much, the thought of getting Luke through it. He stands swaying, everything turned to water. And yet, there is his hand in front of him. No, not his hand. It seems to come from the wall itself, knotted and gnarled. And it is talking to him, but he cannot latch on to what it's saying.

It speaks again. 'Let me take the lad, sir.' Insistent, anxious.

'I cannot.' He says it sadly, but it is the truth.

'One more step and I can reach him.'

He's heard it before, this talking hand, he's sure of it.

'Master!'

He blinks, sees Sim Taylor's face stretched taut at the top of the gap, and falls towards him. The hand holds him up, a second coming through to take hold of Luke, before suddenly the weight is gone from him. He gasps, wonders where he is for a moment before it finally strikes him that

he has done what he set out to do. Sim will take the boy
up and he need only tie himself to the rope he came down
on, snatching lightly at the ground as if the hand of God is
pushing him upwards.

Harry Sowerby reaches down to bring him up over the
edge. 'God be praised.' The bailiff says it over and over
and they are all slapping Fran on the back, chattering like
magpies. Dolfyn forces his way through, jumps up. Fran is
astonished at the warmth he feels in his heart, despite the
worry over Luke.

And now they all turn, falling silent as the shepherd
nears the top with his burden. Once more, hands reach
out and Luke is laid on the ground. Fran is sure he's dead,
so still does he lie, so pale. And yet, as they all hold their
breath, his eyelids flutter, a moan escaping from lips edged
with blue.

Gently, Sim Taylor lifts him up again, cradling him in
his arms.

Fran puts out a hand to move the wet hair out of
Luke's eyes. 'Take him to the house. He'll be warm there.
And send for his mother. I'll ride down myself for the
physician.'

Harry Sowerby frowns. 'Should you not leave it till
tomorrow, sir? It'll be dark soon. You must certainly get
yourself dry first, or you'll catch your death.'

Fran thinks the bailiff is too eager to take his mother's
place, but he pats Harry's arm, still invigorated. It's true
what he says, though. He feels the cold creeping towards

him and is eager to be gone. And it is probably sensible to wait until tomorrow unless Luke is in imminent danger. And then he wonders where his cloak is. 'Where's Giles?'

The squire emerges from behind a boulder looking shamefaced for once. Taking a few steps, he stops some distance away, head hanging. 'I felt queasy, sir. I didn't think I should get in the way.' He looks up quickly, then down again. 'Forgive me.'

Fran nods, having no desire to chastise anyone, even Giles. 'Give me my cloak, then go home.'

The squire does not need a second bidding, scuttling fast when the ground looks solid, walking like an old crone where it threatens to overturn him even a little.

Fran pulls his cloak tight around him, but it is so wet that it provides little comfort. He can think now only of a bright fire, warm wine. At least the rain has stopped, the wind dropping. His muscles ache and he is glad they are on their way home, but he feels a peace in his heart that keeps a smile on his face. Willow chatters endlessly to begin with, but soon even he falls into his own thoughts. A shaft of light strikes Murton Pike as the clouds lift, and Fran feels blessed.

Dolfyn stops first, ears flat on his head, a low growl forming in his throat. It takes a moment for them to make any sense of what catches their eye down below, on the other side of Swindale Beck. That it stands upright like a man is certain, but in every other way it has more of the beast about it, with matted hair and horrible, scaly skin. They catch only a glimpse before it gives a stunted cry and lopes quickly back up the hill away from them. But that was enough for a great fear to grip them, for Willow to move closer to his father, all of them reaching for their daggers.

They stand for a moment, eyeing each other.

'That was no mortal creature.' Harry Sowerby says what they're all thinking.

Fran nods. He has so many questions, but knows they will likely remain unanswered, for the moment at least. Hurrying now, they are eager to reach Hilton, to be away from this wild, ungodly place.

'Where do you think it lives?' Willow is already more bemused than afraid.

Fran shrugs. 'You know as well as I do there are a million places a creature could hide up there.'

Harry Sowerby shakes his head.

'What?'

'It's certainly a good place if you don't want to be found.'

'Indeed.' Fran would rather they both kept quiet so he can consider the strange apparition and what it might mean.

'But what does it want?' Willow skips a little.

'Hold your tongue, for pity's sake.' His father cuffs him round the ear, but gently.

Willow sighs, dances away.

Hilton looms above them now, the houses falling into shadow as the sun makes a brief appearance, dropping beneath the cloud before plunging finally behind Murton Pike. Fran has already changed his mind about not going to Warcop even as he laments to himself that he cannot spend the rest of the evening beside his own fire. Running up the steps, he shouts for clean clothes, for Fauvel to be saddled and for something to eat and drink. And then he descends to the kitchen, where the gloom is cast out by the great heat of the fires, smells of baking and roasting seeping from the very walls.

Tom Strickland, the cook, whips off his red hat, wiping his hands quickly on his apron. A giant of a man, his bare forearms are scored with the scars left by ancient burns and blisters, his fingers equally well carved by his wayward knife. He is not a careless man, but he likes to work fast and suffers for his impatience. Mercurial too, he can be carried off by riotous laughter one minute before falling into terrible low spirits the next. In such moments, Edie comes quickly to her father's side to lead him to sit sobbing out of the way. She is careful to remove all sharp objects from his reach, for he has been known to threaten himself when such a mood takes him.

But today he is all smiles, leading Fran to where Luke lies on a pile of straw covered in a thick woollen blanket, his sister Agatha by his side. The boy's eyes are open and bright, if a little glassy. He tries to rise up at Fran's approach.

'Don't be foolish.' Fran cries out as Luke moans and twists his face in pain. 'I only came to see if you are comfortable. I'll ask the physician to come from Warcop. He'll mend you soon enough.' Fran knows that might not be true even as he prays it is. He pats Luke's hand and rises, intent now on changing his clothes.

He passes Giles, who is enthralling Sarah and some of

the other servants lingering in the hall with the stirring story of Luke's dramatic rescue, in which the squire's own part seems to have undergone considerable embellishment. 'Come with me.'

Giles frowns. 'But—'

Fran slips without warning beneath a molten tide of anger. Walking right up to his squire, he stabs his finger through the air in front of Giles's nose. He speaks quietly, but there is no doubt he means every word. 'If you say "but" to me one more time, you will leave here and never come back. And if you choose not to come with me this very minute, you might as well pack your bags now.'

Giles's mouth opens, the blood entirely fled from his face. 'I did not ... Pray forgive me ... I will ...' And he is gone, leaving Fran both ashamed and more than a little awed by the power of his wrath.

Chapter 7

They are on Hag Lane within the hour. Fran can see that Giles has been crying, eyes smeared and red-rimmed, a hopeless look on his face. And he refuses to say more than a sullen 'yes, sir' or 'no, sir'. Fran cannot say he regrets saying what he did, but fervently wishes he did not have to suffer the consequences.

There is an endless darkness to the night, speared now and then by silvery threads of moonlight. Fran contemplates this day of great oppositions: the triumph of Luke's rescue against the dread possibilities of his injuries and the terrible creature out in the hills. But there is no danger of them becoming lost in the night's deep folds, for Fauvel could bring Fran safely down to Warcop in his sleep.

All the same, it is a relief to catch a glimpse of Warcop's squat church glowering in the shadows at their right hand, slivers of moonlight glancing off its walls through the surrounding trees. Every sound – the chink of a bridle, a surreptitious sniff from Giles, the thud of a stone kicked by one of their horses – rings out a thousand times louder than it does in the daytime. Fran wonders now if Will might chide him for coming at such an hour. He bites his lip.

He's not sure if he bids Fauvel to stop or if the horse senses something first. Giles feels it too, for he comes closer to Fran than he has the entire journey. It takes only one more breath to realise that something foul lies close by, its putrid stench cutting through the night air like a brutish fist. Fran jumps down, pulling his cloak tight across his nose and mouth. Advancing towards the church gate, a sudden movement beneath his right foot makes him gasp. But it is surely only a rat or some other creature disturbed in its nocturnal activities. Steadying his breathing, he steps out again across another strip of darkness until he reaches the safety of the patch of moonlight in front of the gate.

But now his breath is knocked from him entirely. He stands blinking, struggling to understand what lies before him. What devilment can possibly conjure up three copies of his own face, wan and wide-eyed, right there in front of him? And set within the ghastly portals of a horse's head, the flesh sunken and bloated.

He lowers his gaze, shakes his head, forces himself to look up again.

'What is it?' Giles sounds like a shrill child.

Fran sees himself frown three times, three hands sweeping across brows studded with beads of cold sweat, just as if he were looking in a ... He stretches out a quivering finger towards one of his counterfeit faces, closes his eyes tight. And then he gasps again, for he does indeed touch the cool hardness of a mirror. 'It is a charm of some kind.' He tries to sound surer than he feels. 'Left by the Warcop folk, I suppose. Don't ask me why.' But he has some idea.

He could easily imagine the strange creature they saw up on the hill was responsible. But, judging by the smell, the amulet has been here a few days and such profanity on the threshold of a holy place would have been quickly taken down and buried far away if it had been put there by such a malignant being. All the same, he cannot help thinking the people here surely profane their church themselves, for Will has taught him that scripture is most clear on the subject of magic. Fran frowns, wondering why the priest has permitted such a thing.

But he will find out soon enough. Riding on into the silent village, nothing moves apart from a dog slinking round a corner and under a fence. Glancing about with an icy stone in his guts, Fran imagines something watching him from the distant fells. He tells himself it is impossible, that the creature has surely travelled far beyond where they saw it, making for who knows where. But he cannot shake off the feeling that something evil lurks nearby.

He brings Fauvel to a halt before a resolute stone house overlooking Crook's beck. Giles gets down, looking from left to right and back again, though he can scarcely see more than a stone's throw in front of his eyes. At last he scuttles towards the house. Jigging up and down on his toes, he raps as loudly as he can on the wooden door. The sound strikes Fran as excessive, utterly startling, and he cannot help but glance round too. After an age, they hear the slow rasping of a bolt, and the door opens a little. Giles runs headlong back to his horse.

Leaping down with a sigh, Fran advances towards the door, which remains mostly shut. He coughs, to clear away something tight in his throat. 'Is Father William at home?' Fran knows from a recent message that the priest is indeed in Warcop, but he is no longer sure of anything except how much he wishes to rest easy in Will's company.

There is a long silence before, finally, a querulous inquiry is thrust round the door. 'Is that you, Master Francis?'

'Yes, Michael. I am come on urgent business, so pray let me in.'

The door is pushed a little further open and a pale face emerges like a sullen moon out of the darkness. 'Forgive me, sir. Be coming in quickly. We was not thinking anyone would be abroad tonight.' Michael is pitifully old, a wild tangle of yellow-white hair sprouting from head and chin, eyebrows bristling. 'You knows where the stables is.' He retreats at a quick shuffle.

Fran nods to Giles, who nearly opens his mouth, but thinks better of it, disappearing at a trot with both horses.

Pulling open the door, Fran soon catches up with Michael, but they are already submerged in utter darkness. 'For pity's sake!' – he is losing all patience with this strange behaviour – 'We need a candle.'

A clatter leaps out of the darkness beyond. At last, a light flickers above, descending quickly towards them and hollowing out the smooth contours of Will's face. He stares at them for so long that Fran imagines he has lost his wits. But at last he gives an abrupt cry, stretching out a hand. 'Come in, come in. I never thought for a moment . . .' Turning, the priest runs back up the stairs, Fran following close behind the dancing flame.

As soon as the two of them are gathered in the low-ceilinged room Will uses for his studies, he slams the door shut, turning to embrace Fran most frantically. 'I have been meaning to write all week, but what could I say?' He loosens his grip, holding Fran at arm's length. 'So, the contagion has spread to Hilton. We are truly cursed.'

'I . . .' So many words, pouring out like boiling water. Fran has never seen him so discomfited. 'I don't know what you're talking about.'

Will drops his hands, narrowing eyes and mouth. 'But surely, at this hour . . .'

'I have things to tell you, most urgent things. And obviously you have things to tell me.' He has come for solace, but this is disturbing. And then he remembers that his pouch contains *The Seven Sages of Rome*. Handing it over, he is relieved that at least all this horror will disguise the fact he has not read it. He tried the first page but couldn't stomach an entire treatise on the wickedness of women.

And indeed Will scarcely glances at it, throwing it on to his desk before thrusting himself into an ornate wooden chair stuffed with cushions, the only place it is easy to sit. Everywhere else in this small room has been appropriated by parchment indifferently folded, books thrown down with no consideration for their proper care, clothes heaped on chairs and in corners. The priest could not be said to be a tidy man, however well kept he is in his person.

Fran shoves a pile of books onto the floor and settles himself on a stool. In the warmth of the room, he is quite overcome, yawning long and hard. 'Forgive me.' He shakes his head vigorously to loosen the lethargy. 'It's been a long day.'

Will frowns. 'Do you want something to eat?'

'No. But a little wine would be good.' Will often needs to be prompted into providing even a little sustenance.

They say very little as they wait for Michael, and Fran feels he has come to a familiar place that is not itself. But at last the ancient servant trembles his way into the room and furnishes them with goblets and a long draught of a pleasant red wine. He tells them Giles is already asleep on a mattress at the foot of Will's bed, if it pleases them. It does, they nod and he leaves.

'So . . .' They both say it at once.

And then Will smiles, though there is a melancholy to it. 'I am not myself, I fear.'

Fran says nothing, afraid the same thought is already written on his face.

'Anyway, you obviously thought I could help with something?'

Fran takes another swallow of wine, feels a little less unmoored. 'Two things, really. The first concerns the physician.'

'Ah. I do believe Master Halkirk has gone to Carlisle to visit his sister. Is someone sick? Is it your mother?'

Fran reminds himself to tell Will his mother has gone for good. 'One of our shepherd boys fell down Swindale Crag. We've spent most of the day getting him out. He's in much pain, but I can't tell if anything's broken.' He knows Will has some medicinal skill himself.

The priest nods, unstiffening. 'I will come back with you in the morning. He should be looked at as soon as possible.' Will leans forward, placing a hand on top of Fran's head. 'I hope you did not do anything foolish.'

Perhaps it is a benediction, though Fran isn't sure what for. It doesn't matter. He closes his eyes for a moment, letting the warmth of Will's touch trickle through him, eager to tell of his adventure. 'I went down for Luke on a rope.'

The hand seems to grow heavier. 'Someone else could have.'

Fran doesn't wish to dwell on his lack of stature, but he wants Will to be proud of him. 'No, they couldn't. I had to squeeze through a gap in the rock.'

Will withdraws his hand, narrowing his eyes. 'You are sure it was just an accident?

'Of course.' Fran sighs to himself, imagining words of approval that, so far, have not been forthcoming. 'He went after a sheep and the two of them fell. The sheep was dead there beside him. I saw it with my own eyes.'

'But you didn't see them fall, did you, so you don't know what caused them to do so.'

Fran feels an exasperation. 'I haven't spoken with Luke, if that's what you mean. But everyone knows he cossets those sheep as if they were lapdogs.' He suddenly grasps at why Will is being so obtuse. 'Is this to do with the creature up on the fells?'

Even in the indifferent flame of the single candle,

Will's face is suddenly become greyer than a corpse's. 'You have seen it?'

Fran nods, eyes locked on Will's. 'Is that what the . . . amulet, or whatever, is at the church?'

'Yes.' Will looks away.

'I thought the Church frowned on such things.'

The priest throws his head round. 'Do you not think I have considered that?'

Fran reaches out a hand, stops short of Will's sleeve. 'I would not dream of reproaching you. I just want to understand.'

Will turns his gaze away, towards the fire. 'There is such a fear abroad, I thought it might . . .' He stares into nothing before finally looking back at Fran. 'Tell me exactly what you saw.'

'We were coming back down Swindale Beck. I think Dolfyn growled, so we looked over to the other bank. It was walking towards us and then it just turned and ran away. I don't think it had seen us until that moment.' These are the things he remembers with some certainty.

Will leans forward, fingers plucking at lips. 'What did it look like?'

Fran considers for a few moments. 'It was terribly thin, I remember. Like a birch sapling. And covered in hair. When I first saw it, I thought it was very old. But when it ran off, I would say it moved surely, if a little stiffly.'

'And was it . . . would you say it was some kind of a man? Or more of a beast?'

Fran thinks carefully. 'It's hard to say. It moved like a man.'

Will nods. 'I know what you mean. Others here have seen it, though I have not myself. They said something similar.'

Fran shifts on his stool. 'What do *you* think it is?'

Will presses his fingertips together. 'I know you would like a firm answer. But it is a most difficult question. I would not like to say anything that might cause more distress. When I have more information . . .' He waves a hand airily.

Fran thinks that Will is now restored to his usual self and wonders with some surprise if he prefers the one that is a little less superior. 'But what has it done? I mean, it must be of ill character, looking the way it does. But perhaps it deserves our pity.'

Will stares at him. 'It most certainly does not. That devil killed animals, left their corpses at people's doors, entrails arranged like . . . like . . .' He waves his right hand about, clutching for the right words.

'I'm sorry. I didn't know. But why on God's earth should it do such a thing?'

Will is so disturbed that he motions to Fran to pass his goblet, refills it and his own, sits back. 'Exactly. And why here?' He leans forward urgently. 'Do you think you recognised it?'

'Recognised it?' Fran squints up at Will. 'But I told you I didn't . . .'

'I do not mean what kind of creature it was. I mean, do you think it bore a resemblance to someone you know?'

Fran blinks, turns away so as to compose his thoughts. He remembers thinking he'd never seen anything like it.

And yet, was there a moment, when it turned away? 'I don't think so.'

Will falls back, holds on tight to the arms of his chair. 'Rob Dickinson thought he did. But then he said it was not possible. He would not tell me who. He said it was not worth his life.'

Fran almost laughs. 'Rob Dickinson was frightened?'

Will rolls his eyes. 'I know. There truly is a first time for everything.'

They sit in silence for several long moments. Fran feels giddy, a great tiredness weighing upon him now. But he wishes to be certain of what is known. 'So, you think the creature on the moors intends some kind of evil towards Warcop?'

Will traces a pattern on the arm of his chair. 'Not Warcop as a whole. It has come here three times in the night over the last week and each time it has left these devilish gifts at the same doors.'

'I suppose it was on its way here again tonight.'

Will nods slowly. 'You saved us from that, thank the Lord.'

'Do you think it will try again?'

Will sighs.

'So, who got these gifts?'

'The Dickinsons. All of them. Jamie, Wat, Rob.'

'Then we must catch it.' Fran forces the words out as a great yawn pushes at his mouth. 'And I must go to bed.'

They stand up. Fran breathes in Will's smell, the comforting suggestion of lavender on his habit and the soft earthiness of his skin. Yet the thought comes upon

him that he has provided as much solace to the priest as he
has received in return.

Will examines Luke thoroughly the next day, ordering the
boy to be brought up from the kitchens and placed on a
blanket on the table in the hall. Fran paces up and down,
trying to keep his eyes fixed on the lady in the tapestry, but
falling away from her reassuring gaze time and again to
follow the priest's progress.

At last Will stops, puts his things away and – placing
a hand on Luke's head – intones a prayer as those in the
room venture closer. Finally he looks up, eyes searching for
Fran's as he pulls down his sleeves. 'There is considerable
bruising. But I do not think anything is broken. The cut
on his head worries me a little, but I have cleaned it.' He
hands over a small pouch. 'You should have your servant
girl put these herbs in a little wine twice a day.' Will does
not approve of Sarah, either her person or her position,
and will not call her maid, for he considers Fran having
one most improper. 'If you have reason to worry, I could
come and purge him in a few days.'

Fran sits down heavily in his chair. 'You have earned all
our thanks.'

'Indeed.' Will comes to sit beside him as the cook picks
Luke up and carries him away. 'And the good Lord too, of
course.'

'Of course.' Fran thinks that that remains to be seen.
He lets Will take a few sips of wine, a mouthful or two of
bread and cheese. 'So, what should we do now?'

'I've just told you.'

'I meant about' – Fran bends his face close to Will's – 'the creature.'

'Ah, yes. Of course.' Will puffs out his cheeks. 'Henry will be back soon. From Carlisle. Sir Andrew Harclay sent for him to make plans about the Scots. He will know what to do.'

Fran frowns. 'Couldn't we—'

But Will cuts him off, shaking his head. 'We do not know what we are dealing with.'

'Then let us at least ask questions. Find out all we can.'

'I do not see what that will achieve. But I could go to Carlisle myself. Look in the abbey library, speak with the bishop. So long as you promise not to do anything foolish.'

Fran rolls his eyes into his sleeve. 'I'm not a child, Father.'

'And if I were you, I would keep all your men and beasts as close to Hilton as possible.'

'Of course.' He feels Will's eyes upon him for a long moment, wonders what he's thinking.

The priest rises, putting a hand on Fran's shoulder. 'Forgive me. I forget sometimes that you are a grown man. Do as you think best.'

Fran leaps up, warmed by such an unexpected concession. 'I would not wish to disappoint you.'

Leaning down, Will kisses Fran on the forehead and weaves his way gracefully out of the room.

Fran feels the weight of the kiss lingering warmly on his skin until the very moment many hours later that he descends into a deep and silent sleep.

For the next few weeks, the creature does not return to Warcop, filling them all with the hope it has been startled out of its evil doings, whether by an encounter with mortal beings or for some other reason. Fran no longer dwells on that brief moment when he laid eyes upon something both terrifying yet strangely sad. But not long after Whit Sunday, the visitations resume.

And on that day the creature dared to come out in full daylight, waiting for the herd boys high up on Musgrave Scar, lifting its arms slowly from its sides and letting its head drop. It stood entirely still like that as they looked up in terror. But then it lifted its head and began to run down the hill, arms flapping, the herds fleeing ahead of it, abandoning their flocks. Now none of them will go out beyond Warcop's bounds no matter how much their masters beat them. This mischief will cost them all dear, one way or another.

Upon his return from Carlisle, Sir Henry is not best pleased with the news of a vile creature haunting the moors and creeping to within a stone's throw of his own door. The sheriff's first thought is to scowl at his brother, on whom it fell to tell him, before gruffly asserting that he has enough to do to prepare for the coming of an enemy that he, at least, took far more seriously. But he can see the fear digging deep into his own people and those in the surrounding countryside. So he orders the men of Warcop to gather on the green, all ages and armed with bows, old swords, sticks or anything else that can be fashioned into a weapon. They move off up into the hills, but always walking within clear sight of one another, stern-faced and tight-lipped.

They discover almost nothing, though more than one swore something was watching them, glimpsed on the brow of a hill but gone before they could even cry out. They do find the remains of several fires in dips and hollows sheltered by trees, which does little to reassure them, for this creature ranges so far and so widely that it surely cannot be human.

From then on doors are kept securely locked even during the long hours of daylight. Needless to say, no one witnesses the leaving of dead birds or animals outside someone's door or even on the church's altar, but every inhabitant of Warcop dreads the coming of morning, for the creature is spreading its net far beyond the Dickinsons now. Will tells Fran that Martha, the maidservant who comes to his house in the mornings, found a dead crow cut into four pieces and spread over the ground outside. She came running to him weeping and wailing in the middle of his devotions, much to his annoyance, for such an important duty should not be interrupted. He bid her carry off the remains to the midden but did confess to Fran that he found it hard to return to his prayers.

Fran, sitting opposite Will with their knees nearly touching in the window seats in his solar, feels a certain distance from all this horror, given that Hilton remains unscathed. He nods in sympathy, of course, but cannot help feeling it is only to be expected if no one is prepared to do anything about the creature. And anyway Will is causing him much anxiety for a completely different reason.

He listens with a great agitation rising in his breast as the priest once more laments his mother's departure as an act of folly and even – though Will does not use the word – cowardice. Fran turns this judgement over and over, searching for the wisdom in it. It's true, of course, that he can't tell the whole story. He'd been glad, to begin with, that his mother had not provided the details of the outrages she claimed upon her person. But, for a moment, Will's words prompt him to wonder if perhaps she had embroidered the meaning of those insults. Or if he himself had misunderstood the import of what she had not said.

But, in his heart, he knows that isn't true. So, for once, he thinks Will is in error, that the priest is blind to the hatred taking root across the border counties. The good Lord knows they have every reason to detest the Scots. But this is something different, an insidious, vengeful poison that seeks only to hurt and destroy close to home. His mother is innocent. But she is tainted and so has fallen under suspicion or blame, however unwittingly, by those she lived among. And he cannot help but wonder if anyone would have dared to treat her so badly if his father were still alive.

But it seems impossible to make Will understand this, not least because he seems convinced that women are naturally foolish, their decisions thrust upon them by their feelings, not reason. So now Fran must suffer yet another sermon on the need for fortitude in the face of adversity, that God sends such trials as a test that one must endure. He has had enough. 'How fares *your* lady mother?'

Will stops, mouth open. And then a great smile floods his face, bringing colour and light to his cheeks and eyes. 'Very well, God be praised. She is weak, of course, after such a long sickness. But I do believe she will recover almost entirely.' This woman is the exception to his low opinion of the female sex.

Fran smiles too. 'I am glad to hear it. Does that mean you'll be able to go to Carlisle?'

Will rubs his chin. 'What for?'

'I was just wondering what is to be done about the creature.'

They both look out of the window, though there is nothing more to be seen than the usual view of Murton Pike, dressed now in the vivid greens of late spring.

Will leans back, hands clasped tight in his lap. 'In truth, I have felt unable to find a way to begin such enquiries. We know nothing about it, other than that it has a great resentment against us, though for what reason I honestly cannot say. I have not divined anything that joins together those of us who have received its "gifts" beyond the fact we live in and around Warcop. Nor do we know what sort of being it is. You yourself were unsure if it were man or beast.'

Such an admission of inadequacy is so rare in Fran's experience that he cannot think it has ever happened before. But there is no denying the happiness he feels, sitting here in his own house discussing such weighty matters as if Will thinks his opinion worthy of consideration, as if they are equals. But weighty matters require action, for they should not be made to feel afraid on their very doorsteps and banished from wandering any distance from them.

Fran leans towards Will, taps him on the knee. 'I want to see it again.'

'Why on God's earth would you want to do that?'

'Because I don't want it to rule us.'

Will sighs even as he nods slowly. 'And I suppose I must come with you.'

It is a most unusual day, for the sky is the colour of cornflowers, strands of white cloud combed across a firmament that grows almost limitless as they climb. A day such as this should bring joy to the heart, but now he is setting off into the hills, Fran feels he is walking into a trap. It helps, of course, that Will walks beside him, Giles close at their heels. They are vigilant, casting their heads from side to side, twitching at any sudden noise. Only Willow defies their fear, leaping hither and thither till Fran tells him sternly to stay close. The track, once frequented every day by the herds coming up from Warcop, is entirely empty.

Up close to the giant curving mounds rising sternly out of the grassy plateau, the valley below is so faint, so trifling, Fran finds it impossible now to imagine being there and not here. And he thinks it beautiful, the naked heather still glistening with the residue of a pre-dawn shower, tiny, delicate spheres clinging to each stubby branch. Streams force their way through the rough ground, their babbling no doubt reassuring in other, more innocent times.

He wants to get higher, to the very top, for surely the nearer he is to the heavens, the more he'll understand. And it is understanding Fran seeks, for he is weary of labouring under the constant unease that comes with not knowing what kind of threat the creature poses, what it is, and what it wants. But there is something else too. Ever since that unearthly being came into their lives, he has been gifted the same energy and purpose he felt when he took part in rescuing Luke. He would never say such a thing out loud but vanquishing the creature has become his quest.

They pass beneath one of the great mounds, its long edge seemingly protected by ruined ramparts. He reaches down into one of the streams to drink its freezing waters, throwing a handful over his face. 'We should go up there.'

'Why should we do that, sir?' Giles's nose is red and overflowing, his face ashen.

'It will afford us a better view and we will know how the land lies.'

The squire gathers his arms around himself, shoulders hunched.

'Is that wise?' Will squints up at Roman Fell as if it were about to throw rocks at him.

'Stay here, if you like. I won't be long. Just keep an eye out, will you? For anything . . . you know.'

'No.' The priest lays a hand on Fran's arm. 'If you go, we all go.'

Willow nods vigorously. Giles looks away.

They leave the path, stumbling through the heather, hearts beginning to pound. Fran turns now and then, still astonished that the valley should diminish so. Though he and Will roamed long and far into the fells in their youth, they never ventured up on to the high tops and never thought to do so. He turns back again, eyes fixed now on the beginning of a line of boulders, thrown across the slope as if an engineer had devised it so. It will not take them long to reach—

A pipit springs away, startled out of its hiding place in the turf. But that is not what brings them to a sudden stop. It is the smell. Without saying a word, they throw themselves to the ground, even Willow. Fran stays entirely still for several moments, waiting for the hammer blows in his heart to stop. He listens as hard as he can, quietening his breath. But there is only a gentle ruffling through the grass.

Raising his head at last, he expects to see something ungodly rushing towards him. But all is peaceful. He bows his head, mumbling a prayer. And then they all get to their feet, turning their gaze left towards the stink.

It is a sheep's head, or at least it was, one eyeball sinking back into the skull, the other already lost. Bits of wool lie all around, some of it sticking to the ends of its horns. And the flies are legion. The head sits on a boulder, held up by countless stones and pebbles, so that it stares balefully out across the valley. There is nothing particularly malevolent about a dead sheep, for they are often to be found out on moors or in streams, struck down by some malady or their own foolishness. But this is entirely different.

And then Willow gives a little cry, pointing to the right. A second head sits on another boulder some distance away. And, now that he looks properly, Fran can see that still more sit beyond on either side into the distance. To kill these animals and place them so deliberately is surely meant as a warning. Or a sign of possession.

A violent chill strikes him, then a great heat as the remains of the bread and cheese with which he broke his fast rushes out of his mouth. He knows his stomach is strong – the vile horse's head at the church gate sickened him, but not beyond endurance – but this … He supposes this is the proof he did not truly imagine existed. That something evil lives here beyond the laws of God. He thought he'd seen something deeply unhappy in the creature, fooled himself into finding a momentary connection with it. And now he has been proved utterly wrong.

When the vomiting passes, he looks up, sees Giles sobbing on his knees, Will crossing himself and Willow tugging at his hair. But it is not the smell that so distresses them. Scarcely a stone's throw away, the creature stands entirely motionless, arms stretched out and head fallen to one side, for all the world as if it were Christ on the cross. That it should blaspheme so monstrously is bad enough. But what is truly shocking, what takes Fran's breath away entirely as they flee down the hill, is that they all recognise him. Or they would, if they hadn't known that the gaunt, butchered man who had stood before them is dead.

Part Two

Chapter 8

'You're telling me Adam Fothergill's come back from the dead?' Sir Henry looks at them with disbelief hammered hard into his great face. 'And what in God's name am I supposed to do about it?'

His brother the priest tries to explain. 'I am not fully acquainted with the scripture on the subject of revenants. Nor am I entirely sure how Adam died.' The Dickinson brothers, Wat and Rob, have refused to say anything about what happened, shaking their heads in horror whenever they're asked. 'But I imagine it was not a good death.' Will pauses, tongue testing the side of his mouth. 'I mean, I doubt he was prepared to meet his Maker. Perhaps he still possesses an excess of spirit that animates him even now?'

Sir Henry puffs out his lips. 'When did Adam die?'

Will frowns. 'That is what perturbs me. It was some time after the battle in Scotland. Early August, perhaps?'

Fran nods, remembering when they heard the news, the day of the encounter with the Scots and the woodcutter's wife.

Will's frown deepens. 'Which means he's been dead for nine, ten months.'

'So?' The sheriff rises, stalks over to the window.

'Obviously his physical remains are still in the ground wherever he was buried. Or, I suppose, on the ground wherever he fell. It is only his spirit that visits us here.'

'I'm not sure I can tell the difference.' Sir Henry stares out of the window.

Will raises his eyebrows, waits, goes on. 'It is my understanding that a revenant can leave the grave only while there is flesh on his bones. I am no expert. But I would have thought that was more than enough time for his body to decay entirely.'

Sir Henry turns, walks back and forth in front of the window with his hands behind his back. 'But presumably he was buried far away from here. He can't be travelling back and forth every day, surely?'

Will opens his mouth, closes it again. Fran shrugs his shoulders.

'Then we'd better speak to Wat and Rob, hadn't we?' Having decided to act, the sheriff immediately strides out of the room, his dog Whitefoot leaping up after him.

Warcop manor lies immediately to the south of the church, but Sir Henry does not waste time going by the road. Marching through his garden, he makes for a little gate that will take him across the fields towards Crook's beck. The sun is moving behind them now and Fran wonders how long he should stay before heading home. But he is glad they are going to talk to Wat and Rob Dickinson, for they are the only living beings in the whole world who know what happened to Adam Fothergill.

Fran has never met a revenant before, though his mother spoke of them, and they all heard tell of one a few years ago somewhere near Sedbergh. He would be entirely glad never to meet another, for he is troubled by the boundless changes wrought on Adam by his death. Though Fran did not know him well in life, he remembers a quiet man between thirty and forty with smooth skin and features regular enough to make him pleasant to look at, especially on the rare occasions he revealed a smile that seemed to come straight from his heart. And he was always neat in his person, hair and beard kept within proper bounds and his clothes free of tears and holes.

But that's not what Fran saw today. Today Adam Fothergill is become monstrous outside as well as in: the skin on his face and arms horribly marred by dappled patches of bloody red that seem to pull him out of shape; his hair – once a rich reddish-brown, but now turned entirely white – left to grow wild; his clothes turned to rags. And he is no more than skin and bone, the gaunt remains of a man that look as if they would blow away. It's no wonder Fran hadn't recognised him in that first glimpse by the side of Swindale beck. But for all Adam's lack of substance, his spirit has clearly grown so powerful and wicked that he seems a giant.

And that makes Fran think that whatever the Dickinson brothers can tell them about how Adam Fothergill died, they will get more help from the library in Carlisle and the monks who tend it. Getting rid of revenants is no easy matter and they don't want to make matters worse by doing the wrong thing. He murmurs a quick prayer, asking God to speak with Will, that they might be in agreement.

They reach the main part of the village soon enough, crossing Crook's beck on a narrow plank. The houses leading up to the green are, like Will's, neat in stone and thatch, though a closer look reveals some stonework lacking care, wooden doors and shutters in a state of some distress. But such decay is to be found all over the county and beyond, the coin that might be spent on repair given to the Scots.

Sir Henry turns up the street but only takes a few steps before stopping to shout down a narrow gap between two houses. A few moments later, Jamie Dickinson emerges. Striding over until he almost stands on Sir Henry's boots, Jamie slowly removes his cap before crossing brawny arms that strain against the sleeves of his tunic. Squat and broad as a bullock, it's easy to imagine the fights of his youth from a nose that bends and swells quite unnaturally, ears thickened and deformed (though Fran has often wondered what is written of them on the faces of his adversaries). Jamie is at least forty, the lines and fadings of age written deep into his hair and face, which has the appearance of old leather. But his strength seems entirely undiminished.

His beady eye holds Sir Henry firmly in its gaze. 'What is you wanting, sir? I mun finish off the bringing down o' our sheep afore nightfall.'

Sir Henry nods. 'Are your boys with you?'

'O' course.' He glowers. 'What business is you having wi' them?'

The sheriff claps a hand heavily on Jamie Dickinson's

shoulder. 'Your labours are done for the day. We have weighty matters to discuss.'

They decide, after some to-ing and fro-ing, to go up to the place where Jamie's sons are busy with the sheep. After a sharp climb out of the village, they find themselves among a riotous cacophony of bleating and shouting.

'This will not do.' Sir Henry thrusts a finger at Jamie Dickinson.

'Whit?'

But the sheriff is already marching away, having spied Wat and Rob. Pointing vehemently, he manages to lead them all to a place of quiet, with a fallen oak they can sit on, presuming they would not rather stand with their arms folded, as the Dickinsons do.

Sir Henry plunges straight into the matter at hand. 'We have news of the revenant.'

'Begging your pardon, sir, but whit revenant?' Rob Dickinson is the younger of the brothers and his father's favourite, which doesn't stop Jamie from cuffing him whenever he thinks it necessary.

'The creature up in the fells. Francis here saw it this morning.'

Jamie spits on the ground. 'You're saying the young gentleman is seeing a man whit is deid, sir?' His words are polite enough, but the ridicule hangs heavy.

'Yes.' Fran says it firmly, looking straight ahead of him. Jamie Dickinson makes him uneasy, with his insubstantial allegiance to the hierarchies God has decreed should bring order to human affairs. He is the kind of man who seems to have hauled himself straight out of the ground and can still taste the soil's tang in his mouth. For such a man, what are kings and nobles but meddlers and thieves?

Rob Dickinson clearly cherishes the same beliefs, but in looks is cut from entirely different cloth. Indeed, Fran finds it differently troublesome that, without even noticing, his gaze is drawn to the younger of the two Dickinsons so that he must keep telling himself to turn his head back towards Jamie and Sir Henry, past Will, who seems to be scowling, though only the Lord knows why.

In truth, if Fran could stare at Rob Dickinson without being seen, he would like to do so – for the strong curve of bone stretching delicately from ear to chin, for the pale warmth of Rob's skin that looks as if it is lit from within, for the smile irresistibly commanding. It cannot be denied that God makes such beautiful beings as a sign of His great favour. Fran feels the blood within him … 'Not just any dead man.' Sir Henry stretches out his legs. 'Adam Fothergill.'

The sheriff might as well have struck the two younger Dickinsons with a hammer, they are become so insensible. Fran has never seen such a transformation, faces taking on the pallor of the dead, limbs soft and unreliable. Rob cries out, 'So it's true,' as Wat sinks to the ground. Fran feels a great anguish rising in his breast on their behalf, even if he does not entirely understand why they are so undone. He remembers that Rob Dickinson thought he recognised the monster, but no wonder he believed himself gravely mistaken.

But Jamie Dickinson will not endure such a spectacle, pulling Wat to his feet and giving Rob a shove in the back.

'Staun up like men, the pair o' you.'

Fran watches them closely. He has forgotten about going home, for this is entirely fascinating. Impatient now to hear the proper story of Adam's death, he hopes Sir Henry won't mind if he asks a question or two of his own.

But it seems he must wait. Rob Dickinson, still deathly pale, turns to his father, whispers in his ear, long supple fingers held taut against his breastbone. And, at last, his parent shows some compassion. Scratching the side of his thigh, Jamie Dickinson directs his gaze a little beyond the sheriff's left ear. 'Beg pardon, sir. My lads is happy tae speak free-like come morning. But' – his face twists with the difficulty of such an admission – 'they crave some time tae recover frae this news.'

Sir Henry stares hard at Jamie before firmly shaking his head. 'Go home, if you must, but come to my hall before the sun is over there.' He throws an arm a little further towards the western horizon. 'Don't you dare make me send someone to find you.' With an emphatic nod of the head, he turns and strides back towards Warcop.

Fran falls into step next to Will. 'That was extraordinary.' The priest raises his eyebrows. 'You didn't think so?'

But Will has turned away, eyes fixed on the path ahead. 'I do not think anything. We have not learned anything as yet.' He sniffs. 'I doubt we will learn anything, anyway.'

'Why do you say that?'

Will turns his head at last, a contemptuous curl to his upper lip. '*You* might think Rob Dickinson has half an intelligent thought in his head, but I do not.'

Fran is stabbed by melancholy anger, a hand reaching

out to catch the priest's sleeve. 'They were there, Will!' It is almost a shout.

Will says nothing, marches on.

Fran drops his hand, walking faster. 'Are you displeased with me?' He cannot imagine what he has said or done to merit reproach, but he feels bereft all the same.

Will's jaw is locked in stubborn restraint. But at last he speaks, eyes darting towards Fran but never settling. 'I am just surprised you give such credence to a boorish creature like Rob.' He takes off his hat, wipes his brow. 'I have told you before that you are too trusting.'

Fran has indeed heard this before and has been prepared to believe it. Now he wonders if what it really means is him giving credence to anyone other than Will. But he is eager to escape this sudden storm. 'They know what happened, is all I meant. You'll be able to go to Carlisle and find out what we need to know to overcome this creature.'

Will's face softens. 'Forgive me. I thought . . .' He looks down at his feet.

'What? What did you think?'

Will glances round, but Giles and Willow are nowhere to be seen. He speaks quickly, head close. 'You do not seem to need my help.' Fran opens his mouth, but Will hurries on. 'You have changed since your father died. It is to be expected, I suppose. But I was not prepared.'

'I don't understand.' In his perplexity, Fran thought too little had changed.

Will walks quickly away. 'You are master now.' The words are thrown behind him like hailstones.

Fran stands utterly still, eyes blinking. And then he smiles, warmth returning. Did Will really think that wouldn't happen? Running at full tilt to catch up, he feels suddenly taller. 'We must work together. Neither one of us master.'

Will gives him a quick look. 'Of course.' And then his chin goes up, the smile demanded of the sides of his mouth doing little to leaven the steel in his eyes. 'But please forgive me if I forget. You are a brave man, everyone knows. But so small! And you have no more hair on your face than you did when you were at school.' His smile widens further, as if this were a marvellous jest. 'Just be patient with me.'

Fran forces the muscles in his face to prop up his own smile. 'Patience is not one of my virtues. You know that.'

Will puts on a great pretence of sorrow and despair. 'Ah yes. If only I could have cured you of it before you grew too old for me to chastise.' He waits for Fran to reply, then slaps him on the back. 'What? No witty words in revenge?'

But Fran's smile has withered away entirely. 'You're too clever.' He struggles to keep his voice steady. He cannot bear the thought that the familiarity which has sustained them for so long might not be enough to protect him now. He curses the rapture he felt in imagining he was Will's equal, for it was no more than pride tempting him to forget his monstrous deceit. How could he believe he would ever be whole, ever be worthy . . . He looks up.

Will stands before him, hands ravelling and unravelling, shoulders hunched. For a moment he looks Fran straight in the eye and Fran thinks he's going to say something more, something that will bring them both comfort. But the priest is already turning away. They walk on in silence.

When he finally reaches the stone steps leading up into Sir Henry's hall, Will is already at the top, despite Fran's efforts not to let him get ahead. As the priest reaches out a hand to open the door, Fran looks down at the ground, heartsick, feet dragging. But when he reaches the last step, he looks up again to find Will waiting, hands pressed together at his lips. They look at each other for a long moment.

Will takes in a long breath. 'We should not quarrel.'

'I do not wish to.'

'Then say you forgive me.'

Fran hesitates, because this is Will, who is worthy of an honest friendship. And he alone knows that what lies so heavily between them is an untruth. 'There is nothing to forgive.'

Something shifts in Will's face, a trembling that transforms swiftly into a venerable smile. He puts an arm round Fran's shoulders as they enter the hall. And now, at last, Fran can turn his mind to the Dickinsons. Once Wat and Rob have spoken and been questioned – illuminating the revenant's origins, its composition and disposition – he believes that what has tormented them these past weeks will be understood. And once it is understood, Fran is also sure, it can be destroyed.

The Dickinsons arrive at the very moment Sir Henry's gaze turns to interrogate the door so furiously he is surely only seconds away from striding over to kick it. Jamie Dickinson enters at a trot. Rob follows close behind, his pace equally commanding. Only the wildness of his gaze, which flits from window to hanging, from face to face, suggests he is at all uneasy in his mind.

A few moments later Wat Dickinson drags himself in as if under the command of some invisible chain held in Jamie's hand. Rob's elder by one year and three months, Wat is the very double of his father, a great bullock's head sitting on a short, bullish neck set atop a sprawling trunk of solid flesh. If he were in the habit of smiling, perhaps his face might be considered handsome, for there is an evenness to his features that is not unpleasing. But the slackness that draws down his mouth lends him an air of eternal perplexity that is certainly not opposed by the slowness of his speech. He rarely ventures an opinion when his father or brother is nearby, seeking refuge in any task requiring strength and endurance.

But if Wat considers that Nature saved her best handiwork for Rob, at least Jamie Dickinson's impartial use of his fists as his preferred means of communication gives his elder son no reason to imagine he is less favoured. Indeed, what is most striking about the Dickinsons is the way they seem to think and act as one, jealous not of each other but of any neighbour or acquaintance whom they imagine is intent on disadvantaging them. And yet they are so deep-rooted in the Eden valley, and so scrupulous in their dealings, that most of those same neighbours and acquaintances willingly take their side in any quarrel.

Fran searches through his mind for what he knows

about the Dickinsons. Their paths have not crossed often, for though Jamie and his sons live and work in Warcop, they also rent land in a number of other villages, but especially at Flitholme a mile or so to the south-east, where – so it is said – their ancestors long guarded their interests just as jealously and where a cousin, Richard Salkeld, still lives.

Adam Fothergill came from Flitholme too, Fran thinks. And Rob Dickinson's wife, who is snaggle-toothed and far too tall, for all that she has molten gold-flecked eyes, pretty lips and two acres of arable land. Fran cannot recall a single thing about Wat Dickinson's wife, except that it is said they are happy together, which must mean she is as dull-witted as he is.

Jamie Dickinson has no wife. Evidently he once did, though Fran cannot remember her. But he thinks it strange that Jamie should not have married again, since he never misses an opportunity to spin more coin or grow more acres. And something stirs in Fran's mind: a story going around some years ago about a woman Jamie wished to marry, but she would have none of it. People had laughed behind his back then, and Jamie thought himself furious enough to kill with his bare hands, so he joined the old king's army in Scotland in order – so it was said – to put his wrath to good use.

Gesturing at the newcomers to sit, Sir Henry pulls his own chair nearer the fire, scattering the numerous dogs and cats gathered there. The Dickinsons cluster together in the middle of a bench pulled away from the wall, feet placed square-wise on the floor, hands flat on thighs. They look impregnable, and Fran is reassured. Now he thinks on it, he was greatly troubled when he saw them so disturbed. That men who wore their strength so openly should seem to break at the very idea of Adam Fothergill's return from the grave was almost as frightening as the revenant's actual ghastly presence.

Fran is content to remain standing near the window where he can watch everyone without drawing attention to himself. He only hopes he will not be too distracted by the throbbing in his guts, the tenderness in his belly. He knew, of course, that his courses would soon be upon him, but now is most inconvenient. There's no blood as yet, just the constant, gnawing pain.

Sir Henry sets out what he wants to hear, a thorough recitation of the hours or days – it matters not, so long as they establish what happened in full – before, during and after Adam Fothergill's death. Jamie and Rob Dickinson nod. Wat stares at a black cat sprawled so close to the fire it's in danger from the sparks and cinders.

Sir Henry sits back, fingers pressed together across his belly, eyes hawked. Rob Dickinson stirs himself, leaning arms on his thighs, clasping his hands, taking a deep breath. But before he can utter a word, Sir Henry barks at Wat. 'Well, what are you waiting for?'

Wat throws up his head, eyes blinking. 'I . . . Whit is it you're wanting exactly, sir?'

'God's bones. I just told you.'

'Aye. You did that.'

Rob Dickinson unbends himself with the grace of a waterfall. 'Mappen I can—'

Sir Henry turns on him. 'Hold your tongue. You can have your say when he's done.'

Fran wonders how long it will take to prise any information at all out of Wat Dickinson and decides he must sit, for fear the pain in his belly will overwhelm him. Slipping quietly down the wall, he clasps his hands round his knees, wishing he were in front of his own fire.

But Wat surprises them all. Clutching his cap tightly in both hands, he stands up, nods at Sir Henry and begins to speak quietly but firmly to the wall behind the sheriff's head. 'We was chosen, Rob and me, to go wi' the king's army. We had to leave afore the lambing was done, I remember. It were a bad year.'

Fran groans into his knees. Sir Henry leans forward. 'Did you march to Scotland with Adam Fothergill?'

Wat pauses for a moment, his eyes wide and unblinking, jumping down to hold tight to the sheriff. 'No, sir. We is not. There be a hatred between us these many years. I thought you was knowing. I saw him, sure enough, when we was on the road, but we was not going anywhere near him.'

And in an instant Fran remembers. It was Adam Fothergill who married the woman Jamie Dickinson wanted for himself. A hatred indeed. He throws himself up from the floor, grabbing a stool and bringing it near to Will, who pats him on the shoulder. Already a whole host of questions flit across his mind. But he will wait.

Sir Henry sits back. 'Tell us about the battle, and what happened afterwards. That's what we need to understand.'

Fran leans back on to Will's chair, an arm wedged against the priest's leg. He feels better.

Wat returns his gaze to the wall, licks his lips. 'The battle.' He stops, mouth half open. 'It were a terrible thing.'

Rob Dickinson slaps the bench. 'It weren't meant to be!' All eyes turn on him. 'We thought, after all these years – I mean, when was the last time we took on the Scots? It should've been a great thing. Mebbe we'd get some gold or weapons off dead Scots. A knight, or summat. Or capture one, and get the ransom, see. Aye, it were going to be a grand adventure.' He spits out the words, a curl in his rosy lip.

Sir Henry's mouth twists, as if half wants to say one thing and half something else. He nods. 'That's enough now, Rob.'

Everyone turns back to Wat. He stands utterly still. But then his shoulders rise. 'It were no adventure. It were hell. We was at the back. It were the knights what charged first. I think so, anyway. We didn't really know what was happening, but the lads in front passed back news now and again. We is hearing them in the distance. Horses and weapons making a terrible noise. We'd move forward a little. That were a fearful thing. But marvellous too. We had no idea what was supposed to be happening.'

Rob springs to his feet, glorious in his fury. 'We was meant to win, that's what was supposed to happen. We're English, see. And they're Scots. It were a marvel, just tae be looking round and seeing so many Englishmen in one place. But then everyone is starting tae shove. And then we is running. It shames me tae think on it, even now.' He sits back down fiercely, before the sheriff has time to say anything.

'So you ran too.' Sir Henry speaks quietly, as if this was something that should not be spoken abroad.

Wat nods. 'We is following everyone else to start wi'. I'm not remembering much 'bout it.'

'We wasn't staying together long, that's for certain, or those devils would have caught us.' Rob speaks to the floor. 'Then it were just me and Wat. We was sleeping in woods and thickets in the daytime, moving on when it were getting dark.'

Wat nods again. 'Mony's the time we wasn't moving at all, if the night were too black. And we was sore afraid to search near houses for food in case someone is catching us. I mun confess, I wasn't thinking we'd ever win home.'

Fran tries to imagine the sorrow of it, being so far from Hilton among those who would harm him on sight. And he thinks on the Scots he fought over towards Appleby. They had no fear of riding among their enemies. He feels a potent stab of anger, a desire to move Heaven and Earth to keep England safe from these monsters, for there is no doubt the king cannot or will not lift a finger to help them.

And yet he wonders now if the revenant is not only something malevolent in itself, but a manifestation of the evil that now stalks this land. But then he sighs, for where will such thinking lead if not to a prison of the mind, casting them into the darkness of knowing God is punishing them? He knows they should examine their consciences, that there will be a good reason for the misery inflicted upon them. But he has not the stomach for it now. He looks up, having not meant to sigh out loud. Everyone is staring at him.

'Did you have something to say?' Sir Henry glares down at him.

'No.' Fran turns his gaze on Wat, taking great care to make sure it doesn't linger on Rob. 'Actually, yes. How did you come upon Adam Fothergill?' Wat's eyes widen, while Rob grins behind his hand, so Fran knows this has already been spoken of. To make matters worse, he blushes. 'Beg pardon, tell me again.'

Wat looks away, speaking quickly this time. ''Twere coming towards nightfall after many moons skulking and running. We was creeping down this track high on the moors. No food. Nothing at all. He rose like a devil out of a ditch and is giving us some ale. So, we bid him stay wi' us. 'Twere natural we should be going together.'

'Was it?' Fran ponders that for a brief moment. 'I thought the hatred between you was' – he struggles for the right word, one that will not offend, but still do justice to a feud so notorious that few would dare mention Adam's name to any of the Dickinsons – 'enduring,' he says at last, unsatisfied.

Wat glances at his father, but Jamie refuses to meet his eye. Rob is silent too, so Wat takes a deep breath. 'Aye, that's true enough. We isn't liking Adam Fothergill before then. But three is better than two, we is thinking.'

Fran supposes that fleeing such a battle could've changed their thinking, given them good reason to bury their quarrel so they might all come safely home. He nods, settling back to listen again. But Wat stands with his thoughts buried in the wall.

Rob wades into the silence. 'Tae tell you the truth, young sir, I was thinking he'd be handy wi' his knife. So, I were glad he were wi' us.' He looks round them all, chin up, and Fran feels a warmth rise to his cheeks to have been spoken to directly.

Sir Henry nods, shifts in his seat. 'Tell us how he died. Either of you.'

Leaning forward again, Rob spits out his words as if he's glad to be rid of them. 'We was near tae Elsdon, back o'er the border. We thought we might find food and rest there.'

'Where's Elsdon?' Fran interrupts. They all look at Sir Henry.

But Will answers. 'It is up in Northumberland. A country of high moors indeed. The village is pretty enough in summer, but bleak in winter. I have visited the church. A resting place of St Cuthbert.' He says this as if no other explanation is necessary.

Rob's eyes skim the room. When no one says anything else, he recites a story that must have lain heavily on him all these months. 'We looked in the houses in the village, but the doors was locked, no one there. It were getting dark and the rain coming. We had seen there was a castle. Ruined, it is. Walls all fallen down. We thought we might rest there. We was fearful hungry, but had no spirit left tae go looking for anything.' Like his brother, Rob's gaze clings to the wall, as if he would fall down insensible in removing it.

'But we wasn't the only ones thinking that. When we

was getting closer, we was seeing a fire burning. An' we was taking oot our knives, a cause of all the thieves and vagabonds in these parts. There's being quite a few inside. Some men, none too young. And women, one wi' a bairn. I remember the smell like it is still being on my lips. Venison. Well cooked a'ready.'

'How many?' Fran is trying to put himself in this dreary castle, to feel the hunger and the fear.

Rob shrugs.

'A handful? More than ten? Twenty?'

Rob shrugs again.

'Wat?'

He shrugs too, not looking.

Fran frowns but does not press them. He can see these memories are disturbing.

Rob scratches his cheek. 'So, Adam, he's going mad wi' hunger. He goes up tae the fire and the woman tending it. She had the bairn tied on her back. Asked her for some food, bold as anything.'

Fran leans forward again. 'But not you?'

'No.' Something throbs in Rob's neck, the skin on his face so full of blood it looks as if it might burst. 'I mean, aye, we is looking for some of the meat. But we isn't doing the asking.'

'Indeed?' Fran cannot imagine either of them sitting back, not going after what they wanted.

'We is not ourselves.' Rob cries it out from his very soul. 'You is needing tae understand that.'

Sir Henry gives Fran a piercing look. 'Finish your story, Rob.'

There is a pause, but only for a moment. 'The woman was saying no tae Adam. Was laughing in his face. An' he was going for her like a mad man.' He looks around them all, a tremble on his lip. 'So he kilt her. And the bairn.'

Sir Henry rises half off his chair. 'Adam killed a woman and child?'

Rob talks to the floor, as if the rest of the hall is too tender for such words. 'Aye, Adam, right enough. We is allus saying he were a queer one wi' a wild temper on him if he is being thwarted.'

'Aye,' says Jamie Dickinson, moved to words at last.

Sir Henry scratches his neck, blows out his cheeks, still disbelieving. 'Adam did that?' He shakes his head.

Fran hastily removes the woman and child from his mind. 'But how did he die?'

Rob turns his gaze on him, more sure of himself now, as if telling the story is exorcising the revenant. 'I is coming to that, young master.' He gallops to the end now. ''Twere a great confusion. They was setting on him like animals. We was wanting tae help him, but they was coming for us too. I kilt one o' the men and we was running out of the castle and the fire was growing, spreading o'er the whole place. We spent the night under a tree.' He hunches his shoulders.

Fran frowns. 'But these were old men, women with children.'

'They was animals. The women just as wild as the men.' Rob looks Fran straight in the eye. 'What is it you're thinking we should hae been doing differently?'

Fran raises his hands, for he does not know. 'And you saw Adam die?'

Rob and Wat nod their heads vigorously.

'Who killed him?'

Wat looks at the floor.

''Tis hard to say.' Rob strokes his chin. 'But we saw the knife going in, and him falling and not moving again. I reckon he would be burnt anyway, like the rest o' them.'

'So they were all killed?' Fran has no doubt about the confusion, for he feels it himself.

Rob looks at Wat, who shrugs. 'We isn't knowing that for certain,' he says at last.

'But you knew about the fire, that it was truly fierce?'

Rob grunts. ''Twould be hard not to. We was seeing it frae miles away.'

'That's enough.' Sir Henry gets up, strides to the window. 'I know little about revenants, but Adam Fothergill's death sounds devilish enough to explain his ungodly presence here.'

'Does it?' Fran ponders what he's just heard. 'Why would he want to avenge himself on Rob and Wat and the people of Warcop? They did nothing to bring about his death.'

Rob leaps to his feet, eyes burning. 'That devil is cursing us.' He brings both hands to his head, rubs vigorously. 'Just afore they was pulling him to the ground. For bringing him to Elsdon. He was raving that he were fine on his own. That we wanted him dead, to have our revenge for what happened all them years ago.' He looks around them all. 'But I is thinking he wasn't in his right mind.'

Sir Henry turns sharply from the window. 'You brought that devil here and said nothing. Did you not think you were putting everyone in danger?'

All three Dickinsons move closer together, muscles taut. Rob looks Sir Henry straight in the eye. 'We isn't knowing, is we, till the young gentleman is saying that creature is Adam.' He puts his cap on his head, though no one has dismissed him. 'But you is not needing tae worry. Wat and me, we is thinking we is wanting tae be going away. Up tae the border to be safe.'

'To a garrison?' Sir Henry comes away from the window.

They nod vigorously.

'How long have you been planning this?'

They study their feet. But Rob looks up, jaw tight. 'Sir Thomas at Helbeck is saying they is needing men up there. We is wanting tae fight the Scots. Do it properly this time.'

Sir Henry twists his face. 'I would know where you are.'

Rob gives the sheriff a pleading look. 'We isn't planning on saying onything tae onybody.'

Sir Henry shakes his head. 'I could find out anyway, so you might as well tell me .'

'Aye, sir.' Rob Dickinson looks discomfited once more, shoulders hunched. 'Sir Robert Tilliol's new castle at Scaleby. He is asking for men to go.' He speaks quietly, looks away. 'You'll no be speaking of this abroad?'

'Of course not. Nor will the others.'

With a sigh and a grimace, all three Dickinsons nod their obeisance to the sheriff and are gone.

Fran lingers outside, as he always does when he must sleep anywhere other than his own bed. That way, everyone else will be ready for sleep and he need only discard his tunic and breeches as quickly as possible and not be left standing in front of them all in his shirt and braies. He has been taught to make sure this happens but rarely, just as he avoids bathing in rivers or pissing in public. He knows it's another reason for some to whisper he must be hiding some physical defect, which he supposes he is. But it's better than worrying about prying eyes or a misstep of his own.

And yet he knows he's in more danger every time he sleeps in the same bed as Will, because they've known each other so long and it's easy to forget his deceit in the depths of their long friendship. Shivering beneath rain-swept skies, he hastens back inside, running up the stairs and removing his outer garments in one swift motion. Giles has long since given up waiting to help him when Sarah is not at hand.

He and Will whisper long after darkness has fallen, the curtains drawn around Will's bed against the chill of the night, Giles and Willow tossing and turning on mattresses on the floor. Fran is agitated, and not just because of the distracting ache in his belly. 'I don't know what to make of it.' Leaning on his elbows, he looks down and across at Will through the thickening darkness.

Will lies on his back, arms under his head. He stays silent for a few moments, staring up at the black

nothingness where the ceiling should be. 'I will ride
with my brother to Carlisle when he goes to see Harclay
tomorrow.'

Fran nods. 'That will bring us some answers. But I wish
the Dickinsons were not going so far away.'

Will stretches out his arms, yawns. 'God willing, the
revenant will leave us in peace if they are not here.'

Fran grunts, unsure, throws himself onto his side. 'Do
you remember what happened between them, the wife
that Adam got, and Jamie Dickinson thought was his?'

Will turns to face him, the warmth of his skin, his
breath, flooding the air. Fran wants to reach out, to feel the
thick softness of his curly hair, or have Will put a hand on
him in comfort . . . He closes his eyes.

'I do not know the rights and wrongs of it.' Will's
fingers lie only a hair's breadth from Fran's hand.

'Can I ask your opinion of Adam Fothergill when he
lived?'

'Which question would you like me to answer first?'

Fran is not dismayed, for he can feel the imprint of a
smile nestling in Will's words. 'This second one. Then go
back to telling your story.'

'Hmmmph.' Will reaches into the darkness to give him
a playful slap. 'In truth I found him sober, hard-working
and honest.' This is the highest praise the priest can bestow
on one of his flock below the rank of gentleman. 'Though
I believe that he was the strangest child anyone ever laid
eyes upon.'

'How so?'

'My brother says he was a thin, wild-eyed thing in

those days and used to run about up on the fells as if he were a Will with the Wisp. His father was a shepherd up at Helbeck, though they lived in Flitholme. No one liked Jack Fothergill. He had a wicked temper on him, and drink only made him worse.'

'But I thought Adam was of good stock.'

'Indeed. His grandfather was bailiff to old Sir Thomas Helbeck. But no one would trust Jack with a dog, never mind a year's revenue. Still, they say his son adored him. It was painful to watch the boy slinking after his father. He would know he was only going to get a beating, but it did not stop him.'

'And his mother? Did he find comfort there?'

'Dear God, no. She was a strange woman. And she never forgave Adam for being the one to live when her beloved first-born was carried off by a fever at sixteen. I believe she went back to her own people up in the moors near Kirkby Stephen when Jack died, and no doubt thought herself the better for it.'

Fran is once more entirely enthralled. 'How old was Adam then?'

Will taps a finger on the coverlet. 'He is some ten years older than me. I mean, he was. Eleven or twelve, I would reckon.'

'So what happened to him?'

'He disappeared.'

Fran gasps. 'Really?'

'No, not really, you goose.' Will lightly slaps Fran's arm again. 'A cousin in Appleby took him in. But few saw him for three, four years. Then one day, Adam came to my brother's steward and asked to be one of our herds. It caused quite a stir, for no one recognised him to begin with. Let us just say there had been a great transformation.'

Fran leans up on his elbow. 'There must have been. He was a sturdy fellow, as I recall. And taller than most. Even you. Certainly not a slip of a lad.' Fran is careful not to mention he also thought Adam Fothergill handsome. Not as handsome as Rob Dickinson, perhaps, but most pleasing with his dark red curls and strong nose. Whatever lay behind Will's anger earlier, Fran does not want to earn more of it.

Will yawns. 'Adam turned many a girl quite giddy when he came to Warcop. But I do not believe he even noticed. And Henry was pleased with him. You probably do not remember, but he made Adam reeve by the time he turned twenty.' He sighs. 'That is when the trouble began.'

'With the Dickinsons?'

'Yes. Though I have only recently remembered that there was bad blood between Jack Fothergill and Jamie Dickinson long before then. It was over the death of one of Jamie's cows.' Will's hand comes down, sweeps across Fran's arm for a moment. 'As I say, I do not know who was in the right over the quarrel between Jamie and Adam. Jamie swore he had made an arrangement with Roger Mauchell for his daughter. He had a great desire for the land over at Crackenthorpe that she would bring in dowry. But Roger denied it, said he would never hand over his Joan to such a lout, that everyone knew Jamie's first wife died from the blows he gave her.'

'Was that true?'

'Who knows? But it is not hard to believe, is it?'

'Was that why Adam left Warcop?'

'I do not know. He did not have any land round here, thanks to Jack drinking it away. But perhaps it would not have been wise to stay. All I can tell you for certain is that my brother was sorry to lose him when he went to Crackenthorpe. He had tender feelings for Adam. That is why Henry found it so hard to believe he could have done such a thing at Elsdon.'

'I do not mean to forgive it one jot, but who knows what a battle like that, having to flee like that, can do to a man.'

'It should not turn him into a savage.' Will speaks sharply, leaving no room for doubt.

But Fran wonders why Will is so sure, when he has never looked death in the eye as it came hurtling towards him lodged deep within another man's face. And wondered if that same madness showed on his own face. But that is something else he could never say to his friend. 'Was it worth it, Adam's marriage?'

Will draws in a long breath. 'For a while. I only heard of him occasionally, when I had reason to go to Appleby. But, yes, it seemed they were blessed. Until God saw fit to take Joan in childbirth and the boy a few weeks later. The rector at Kirkby Thore told me that Adam found it hard to accept God's will. That he was grown bitter. But the only time I saw him – some two years past, at the horse fair – he was pleased to see me. Told me to give Henry his best greetings.' He yawns again, rearranges himself below the covers.

Fran knows Will is ready for sleep. He listens to his breathing slow, become a regular reassurance. And he thinks about Adam Fothergill, torn in two when he was alive, one part of him determined to overcome fate, the other entirely constrained by it. Fran shivers at the thought of what Adam is now become but cannot help feeling sorry – a sentiment as sincere as it is futile – for the man he once was.

Chapter 9

Will was right, it seems. As the days steal wantonly from dark night in the weeks leading up to Midsummer, the revenant and his ghastly deeds are seen no more. Soon, the herds are content to take their flocks into the hills. Neighbours flit between each other's houses even after dark, as they were wont to do before Adam Fothergill came to terrify them.

At last, the whole horrible affair wanes in the mind, becomes something to discuss in the open air, to mock or deride even by those who had once quivered behind barred doors and windows. Now the people of the north wait to hear word of a terror they have become accustomed to, for Robert Bruce is known to be gathering his men close to the eastern border. It is whispered he will try to take Berwick, the only piece of Scotland still held by the English king. Or will ride towards Yorkshire to harry the country there. Either would please the people of Westmorland.

Fran's mother writes, her words set down in the hand of a priest. She must have had it written soon after arriving in

Scotland but found it difficult – unsurprisingly – to find a messenger willing to cross the border. She finally managed to entrust the tiny scrap of parchment to a Franciscan monk from Dumfries visiting a cousin at Lanercost Abbey. One of the brothers there brought it to Hilton on his way to copy a text in the library at Fountains.

Fran reads it with a haunted feeling in his heart. He is glad to know she is safe and well, Hawise too. But it grieves him to hear his grandmother died last winter. Having so recently thought of her again, imagined her kindness as a living thing, he feels it as twice the blow. He wonders what she thought of their great deceit, tries to believe she argued against it, growing ever more generous and reasonable in his mind. And even his mother – who, to begin with, had slipped into the strange half-life of those who are absent but largely unremarked – is now become an ache in his heart.

At the same time, he feels the revenant's removal to the realm of macabre recollection most keenly and not necessarily as a source of pleasure. He will not tell anyone this, but he had been most distracted by the hunt for Adam Fothergill, both his actual malevolent person and in pursuit of an understanding of his lamentable transformation. Now Fran finds the return to his customary life – attending to any difficulties with the washing of the sheep before they are clipped and marked, their wool readied for sale, the fattening of his cattle – hanging heavily on him again.

He is also much preoccupied by rumours of sheep falling down dead further south, struck with a sudden plague as if by the hand of God, cattle labouring under a fever, blisters appearing in their mouths and near their hooves. Down in the valley, too, the hay has lain so long under water it seems most unlikely it can be mown or gathered, while the corn, including Fran's own meagre crop, will doubtless fare no better. Prices have risen so much that even the king has noticed and decreed what they should be while this scarcity lasts.

Fran does what he can to protect his beasts. He tells Harry Sowerby they should not buy any new stock this year, in case they bring disease, praying Thomas Bacon is just as prudent. But the last time Fran tried to speak with him, Egidia had run down the steps as they were standing at Thomas's gate, ordering him away with bitter tears as if he were a plague.

But none of this is what causes his heart to freeze or catch fire. For though the weather is unreasonably cold, the rain smothering the hills and filling up ground and river alike, it is still the season for love. Everywhere he looks, Fran sees glances exchanged, trysts arranged, kisses stolen. He does, in truth, mistake many entirely innocent greetings for tokens of outrageous affection, mishears merry conversations between those who wish only to give and receive a smile. But often enough he is made miserable even by those much younger than himself eagerly following the urges that come so furiously upon them in the summer months.

It is easier, of course, to take a girl by the hand and run with her to a secluded spot when they are out anyway attending to the beasts. But Fran can watch the gilded words drip enticingly from mouth to ear even in his own hall, for it seems that Willow – who remains in Fran's mind a child of little sense, however good-natured – has become smitten with Edie. And, more surprisingly, she with him.

Fran watches Harry Sowerby closely, but the bailiff gives no sign he has noticed the unfortunate bewitching of his son. Fran finds this bewildering, for he himself seems to trip over them almost every day lingering behind doors, out in the herb garden, down by Hilton Beck or any other part of the manor. They make a great show of meeting as if by chance, or they invent unlikely reasons for being together. Willow will pick a bunch of flowering thyme and proffer it to Edie as if it were a gillyflower – supposedly so she can teach him its use in cookery – encouraging her to smell it, leaning his head towards hers . . .

Fran realises he has followed them, hiding behind a blackthorn hedge. He loathes himself for doing it but can scarcely pull himself away. He has known these two for all of their lives and yet he scarcely recognises them, so animated do they seem, so unlike the innocents he is used to. It is Edie who intrigues Fran most. He watches her eyes turn so fluid and bright they seem about to trickle off her face, while her lips, their rosy hue deepening to blood red, eagerly part whenever she sees Willow. The pair of them giggle at the slightest provocation, even – so it seems to Fran – on none at all. It's as if a madness has fallen upon them, but one that clearly spreads a great swell of happiness to overcome the trials and tribulations of these unholy times.

With a sigh he steals back inside and throws himself

on the settle. Finding his book behind a cushion, he turns the page, thrusts it back down again, swings his legs on to the floor and brings his head into his hands. For a moment he manages to fix his mind on nothing, to hold back the tide of misery. But he can feel the tears gathering, does not know whether to indulge them.

The inside door opens and Sarah hurries in, head first, feet scurrying to keep up. She wears a new dress, the one Fran gave her last Christmas but which she has saved for Midsummer, that strange and magical time when the light – such as it is this year – is triumphant. There is nothing special about the dress, though Fran did think the dark red colour would look pretty on Sarah's pale skin, her dark hair – streaked with grey now at the temples – curling over her shoulders to rest on the ample shelf of her breasts.

He peers at her round the settle's high back, knowing she does not yet see him. Sticking her nose in the air, she raises her arms a little, moving her weight from one side to the other, almost as if she would dance. And she sings to herself, a gentle, happy tune, but with a powerful touch of longing to it. Fran wonders if Sarah too is thinking of a lover, has somehow become ensnared in the season's mysterious promises of abundance and satisfaction. But that is a ridiculous notion. And yet some might see her as an ideal wife, infinitely caring and entirely unwilling or unable to express her own opinion. He watches her smooth her hands down the length of her bodice, pick up her skirts most delicately and step around the floor, kissing the tips of her fingers and wafting them around the room.

Only then does Fran think he trespasses on her tender heart and ill-formed mind. He knows there are many and not so far from this very house who would ill-use her if they could, who would point to her lack of intellect and the rudeness of her features as evidence of God's own displeasure with her. He can only hope he really would box their ears if they dared to do or say anything in his hearing. And then he remembers with a stab of desolate fury that even Will has pronounced that Sarah surely finds little favour with God to have been given so little intelligence and even less beauty.

Slipping back behind the shelter of the settle, he rests his head on the pillow and pretends to sleep. He soon hears her come to stand in front of him, opening his eyes a crack so he can watch her regard him with her best bird's gaze, turning her head from side to side and cooing gently.

Opening his eyes fully, he smiles at her. She claps her hands, dress shivering and shaking with the joy so easily inspired in her. And Fran knows what he must ask her to help him do.

Sarah stamps along the passageway to Fran's mother's chest, which lies in a corner of Christian's old room, its contents mostly garments she had grown too plump to wear but had been loath to part with. Fran goes to his own chamber, uncertain now. He had told himself it was merely a game, something to divert him on an afternoon when he did not know where to put himself. But now he thinks it is a most serious thing. He does not know how it will end and this frightens him.

Sarah seems to know it is serious too, nodding gravely when Fran told her what he wanted to do. She had run off immediately before coming back again to look him up and down, standing with her head cocked to one side, finger tapping chin. It made him feel naked already. But, at last, she nodded again.

He sits stiffly on the chair, heart beating wildly. When Sarah returns, she frowns, drops the things she carries on to the floor and begins to pick and tug at his clothing. Knowing he could easily have taken off his tunic, shirt and breeches himself, he stands up, feeling wrong and helpless.

Fran closes his eyes as she undoes the bindings round his chest. He takes off his braies, leaving on only his favourite sage green hose tied on with a red silk garter. But when Sarah starts on the knots holding the pouch, he pats her away. Pressing her mouth together, she looks him in the eye, shrugs and goes to put the clothes on the back of his chair. He moves away from her, pads round the room while she watches, never taking her eyes from him. Then he turns. 'Take it off.'

She smiles then, comes to bend her head to the knots.

Staring at the wall, he wills her to be quick. At last he feels the cloth slither across his skin, hears the thud on the floor.

But already Sarah is stamping away. She turns at the door, lifts up one finger, and is gone.

Pulling his shirt back on, he stands with his back to the

fire, eyeing the rest of the clothes he took off, wondering if there is a madness in him.

Soon enough, the door is hipped open violently and Sarah enters carrying a great copper pot steaming with hot water. She looks very pleased with herself.

He smiles, throwing off his shirt. And then he is seized with a terrible fear, running full tilt to the door, bolting it.

Cooing gently, Sarah sets down her pot, clean rag in hand. He stands, scarcely breathing, feeling only the caress of the warm water. He can smell the scent of lavender on his body, the stink of confinement vanquished at last. She is so gentle he can easily imagine she isn't there, that he is becoming beautiful.

Fran keeps her eyes closed. The gentle rubbing stops. She opens her eyes. Sarah stands before her with a chemise, an old one, certainly, but the linen clean and soft. Fran lifts her arms, bends her head, feels the cloth billow, then settle.

Next, Sarah holds up two kirtles, one in a lighter green than the hose, the other a dark purple, for she knows Fran likes some colours but not others. Fran chooses the purple, feels Sarah tug it down, the swell of her body clinging to the linen. And now there are only the three cotehardies hanging on the back of the chair. Fran remembers Christian wearing them long ago, sees herself now as her mother was then for lack of any other imagining.

She plunges her fingers into the dark rose-coloured one which alone is made of silk. Handing it to Sarah, eyes gleaming, she lowers her head once more.

And once more Sarah guides it down and Fran feels her heart in her mouth wondering if her arms will fit, for the narrow sleeves are not meant to conceal the swell of muscles. But with considerable pulling, easing, scolding and clucking, Sarah finally tugs them free. Now she must only do up the buttons at the sides, groaning at the girth of her fingers stumbling over each fastening.

At last, Sarah releases her. Fran smiles, lifting her skirts and letting them drop so they fall neatly. She stands up straight, feeling excitement and unease in equal measure. 'What do you think?'

Stepping back, Sarah looks at her wide-eyed.

'What?'

Wrapping one arm across her belly, Sarah brings the other hand up to her chin. Then she steps around her, still pondering, and Fran is filled with the urge to scream, to rip these ridiculous garments off.

But again Sarah turns, running head down this time towards her own chest in the corner of the room. Fran shivers, wondering. But she does believe Sarah will have thought of something else to make things better.

Sarah rises, running back. Opening her hands with a triumphant smile, she shows Fran the cloth neatly folded there. Fran reaches out to take it, unsure what it is, but Sarah snatches it away.

Pushing her into the chair, Sarah places the wimple carefully on Fran's forehead, folding and pinning the layers of cloth around her head, letting them flow on to her shoulders. And Fran wonders how she could have forgotten that her hair of all things marks her out as man, not woman. Sarah's fingers still stumble, but she is sure in what she is doing, even though, as an unmarried woman, she need not wear one herself. If Fran were not tied to every movement of her hands, the strange warmth and weight cossetting her head, she might have wondered whose wimple she wears, why Sarah held it with such reverence, where she learned to arrange the headdress of a wife. But Fran is wrapped in other thoughts entirely.

Once more Sarah stands before her, surveying her handiwork. But this time she blushes, casting her eyes down and away, stealing looks from time to time.

Fran does not like this any better. 'What is it?' Standing up abruptly, she begins to walk, nearly stumbling over the length of her skirts. Sarah rushes to catch her but draws back, miming the taking of small steps. Fran nearly laughs, for Sarah never takes small steps.

She tries again, stops, starts. But slowly she acquires a kind of poise, a little grace, walking as if in a dream that will soon fade away, leaving only a tender residue of regret. She burns to see what she looks like, stands opposite the window. But only a quiver of colour is thrown back, a faint apparition in a shape she doesn't recognise.

Sarah has thought of that too. Reaching into her gown, she pulls out a hand mirror – a plain thing, polished pewter set within a wooden frame – moving so she stands in front of Fran, but some distance away. Fran spins slowly on her heel to face her, eyes lowered. The moment hangs heavy. But there is no point in having come so far and not going any further.

Fran lifts her eyes. There is no shock. Just incredulity. Before her stands a young woman, swarthy enough to be a peasant but otherwise miraculously convincing. For a moment she cannot move, speak or think. And then she decides she's conjured up a charm and woven herself into it.

With a low cry, he tugs at the veil, trying to find the pins, to rid himself of this absurd possibility. For that is what he has proved this afternoon. That it is possible. And he finds now he does not wish to know it.

Robert Bruce and his hounds of Hell do indeed despoil the eastern counties, reaching – so the carriers of news insist – as far south as the town of Hartlepool belonging to the bishop of Durham. The people of the western march wait to see if the Scots will go home along the Great Road with their booty, as they did last year, but soon dare to hope they will be spared. It does not help that their own king has forbidden them to make truces so they might avoid the worst.

But the Scottish usurper's ambitions have grown ever more monstrous since his great victory, and so, in the middle of July 1315, his army begins to arrive outside the walls of Carlisle. Sir Andrew Harclay, the sheriff of Cumberland and keeper of Carlisle, has been energetic in his preparations, burning so many buildings outside the city walls in the preceding weeks that some began to complain the medicine was worse than the disease. But they did marvel when great towers were built upon the

walls to look down upon the siege engines Bruce was said
to be bringing with him.

Sir Henry rushes off to help with the preparations to
defend the city, sending his brother, who has spent the
last few weeks in the library there, to Newcastle to buy
him a new hauberk and gauntlets. Fran had written some
weeks before to tell Will that the revenant seemed to have
gone back to whichever hellish hole he had come from,
but Will wrote back to say he would finish his studies,
for who was to say whether Adam Fothergill had gone
for good.

Fran had hoped Will would return immediately, but
that was before his experiment with his mother's clothes.
Now he is relieved, for he has become uneasy in company,
preferring to read quietly in the solar when he is not
practising his sword with Giles and Willow or listening to
Harry Sowerby's quiet judgement on the number of their
cattle infected with the murrain and the diminutive size of
their sheep, which – God be praised – are still spared.

Sometimes Giles or Willow slips into the solar to ask
him to read, eyes downcast, hats abused in unquiet hands.
He does not always say no. But he is glad when he can
close the book and send them away.

The only thing that gives him joy is Luke Elliot's
recovery. When Will reassured them there were no bones
broken, Fran thought the shepherd boy would soon be
back on his feet. But a few days later, a fever descended.
Luke lay utterly still, so close to nothing, in a corner of the
kitchen, yet his absence was felt the length and breadth
of the manor. Indeed, it was his long illness that unloosed

love's arrow on Willow and Edie, for Edie's knowledge of herbs and Willow's willingness to help her prepare them was enough to transform their concern for Luke into a deep fascination with each other.

But now Luke is returned to the fells, his gaunt, sprightly figure often seen traversing the slopes, or trudging back to Hilton, a lamb with one ailment or other cradled in his arms. It is as if there had been no tumble and fall, no confrontation with death. And no revenant. Just the terrible afflictions men visit on one another.

It disturbs Fran to know the Scots are but a day's ride away, as if Hilton sits unperturbed in the very eye of a storm. He has resisted Giles's determination to have him give his opinion on which is the best Scottish knight, dogs though they certainly are. Giles thinks Sir James Douglas is no more than a brigand who would slit a man's throat as soon as look at him. But Sir Thomas Randolph – who is, after all, the usurper's nephew – is surely a most chivalrous man, even if he is clearly in error in his loyalty to that murderer, Robert Bruce.

Fran finds the question an interesting one, even if he is loath to answer it. The Scottish boys he fought last year were not even men-at-arms, never mind knights, even if they did ride tiny, stalwart horses. In truth, they were no different to the young men herding and harvesting the length and breadth of Westmorland: boastful, swaggering creatures who still have one eye on the comfort of their mother's laps. Giles has tried as many tricks as he can to press the story out of him. This might easily be another one. So he bids the squire go and fetch Luke from the

kitchen so the boy might play his whistle in the hall and
bring them all a little cheer.

It is the time for bats and owls to overtake the evening
skies, and Fran finds a little peace at the quietening of
the day. Sarah sits in her customary spot on the bench by
the window, mending a pair of hose. Edie slips in beside
her, winding wool, but her gaze shifts often to Willow,
playing chess with his father. When their eyes meet,
both redden, smile as if they know something no one
else does.

Fran tries not to watch them, wonders if even they
whisper about him, expecting there to be talk of his
marriage. He wills Luke never to stop, to hold him here
in this moment when all is at peace. But eventually Edie
jumps up to light the candles and Luke puts down his
whistle. 'I mun be going now, sir. Mither don' like me out
after dark wi' the creature about.'

Fran smiles gently. 'But it's gone, Luke.'

Luke shakes his head earnestly. 'Oh no, sir, it hasn't.
But it's not coming down here, is all. I is telling Mither
that, but she isn't caring.'

Fran leans forward in his chair. 'You've seen it? Him?'

Luke nods again. 'Aye, sir. It be living up at King's Pot.'
He crosses himself. 'I is seeing it frae far away when some
of our sheep is getting lost, but it were him for certain.'
They all nod. King's Pot is well beyond their pasturelands.

'Can you take me there?' The words fall out of Fran's
mouth even before the thought is fully formed.

'Why would you want to do that, sir?' Giles looks up
at him from his stool, horror pulling his face out of shape.

Because it will give me something to distract me from questions that have no answers. 'We cannot allow it to live up there. What if it does decide to start its nocturnal wanderings again and we had the chance to deal with it long before?'

Giles comes then from a different direction. 'Shouldn't we ask Father Warcop? Didn't you say he's been studying what scholars have written about such creatures?'

Fran scowls. It does not please him when Giles is right. 'Yes. But he's not here, is he?' Will is still in Newcastle dealing with Sir Henry's regular demands for equipage and other supplies.

The whole company draws nearer, Edie and Willow standing close together behind Harry Sowerby, who has come to occupy the bench nearest Fran. Only Sarah sits entirely unaware of the weightiness of what's being said, eyes screwed up as she struggles to see her sewing in the dwindling light.

Fran gets up. 'I'm going to bed. I will think on it.'

But Willow steps forward eagerly, his face full of fire. 'We must act, sir. There can be no doubt on the matter.' His father gives him a little kick from his place on the bench. 'Surely.'

Edie frowns, opens her mouth, closes it again.

'What is it, Edie?' Fran knows she is held in high regard by her friends. He has also never heard her speak in company. Both these things make him curious.

Giles snorts.

'Hold your tongue.' Fran glares down at Giles, who glares back, face reddening.

Edie looks at them both, tying her hands together. 'I'm just thinking ...' She stops, lowers her head. 'I is sure it don't matter.'

'Let me decide that.'

She studies the floor. 'I been knowing Adam Fothergill since I were a girl. My aunt was being maid to Joan Mauchell, see.' She looks up, acknowledges the question on a number of faces. 'His wife, that is. He were a good man then. I is knowing that for certain. But he were not a man to forgive easily, and if he is deciding summat, he isn't stopping till he'd done it. If he be that creature and still up there, then there'll be summat he still needs to do. That's what I'm thinking.'

Fran sits back, eyes gleaming. All this time, Edie knew far more than Will what kind of a man Adam Fothergill was. Speaking of Will, he knows perfectly well the priest would tell him not to be foolish. But he is sure in his own heart there comes a time when the thinking and talking and reading must end. He springs to his feet. 'Edie, will you come with us? Would your father allow it?'

Edie brings a hand to her mouth so that Fran is not sure if she's appalled or delighted. Willow certainly manages to look both pleased and unhappy at the same time, a light leaping into his eyes even as he frowns and chews on a strand of hair.

Giles, on the other hand, is utterly horrified, leaping up from his stool. 'I will not come. I will not be led by *her*.' He spits out the word. 'And I will most certainly tell my father about this.'

'Tell your father what, exactly?' Fran is still a tiny inch

taller than Giles, but he realises it won't be long till the squire overtakes him. 'Surely even you can see that if Edie is known to the revenant, that might help us find out what it wants?'

'It's not right.' Giles can scarcely get the words out.

Fran wants to box Giles's ears. But he does not wish to annoy his father, Sir Thomas Helbeck. Putting an arm round Giles's shoulders, he draws him away from the others. 'I know this is ... extraordinary. And you might feel insulted.'

Giles nods, but the violent redness flooding his face begins to recede.

'So, if you wish to stay here, I would have no objection whatsoever.'

Giles hangs his head, mumbles as if to himself. 'I should be with you, sir. I would feel dishonoured if I stayed here.'

Fran swallows a sigh. 'Yes. Of course. I'm glad. I might have need of your sword arm. To protect Edie.'

Giles's eyes widen. 'Really? I hadn't thought of that.' He stands straighter.

Fran pats his shoulder. 'Good.' Giles trots away, and Fran turns back to Edie. 'It could be dangerous. You know that, don't you?'

She nods, shrugs. 'If you're thinking I could be useful, I is wanting to go.' She glances at Willow, who has moved close.

Harry Sowerby stands up, wincing as he does so. 'I should come too, sir.'

Fran shakes his head. 'I need you to stay here. Adam Fothergill's not the only thing we have to worry about.'

Harry nods, takes a deep breath. He puts a hand on Willow's shoulder, pushing him towards the door.

Edie watches them go before bobbing her head at Fran and hurrying off back towards the kitchens.

Only then does Sarah look up.

Fran feels a great agitation at the thought of their impending journey, a resumption of his quest. For he is still certain that, if only he can uncover enough about Adam Fothergill, he will be able to find the means to send the revenant back to the grave.

Fran must work hard to persuade Tom Strickland to let Edie go, for the cook cannot understand how his daughter could be of any use up on the wild fells that all honest folk avoid if possible. Edie, for her part, obeys her father's commands with the least grace imaginable. In the end, Fran promises Tom a set of new clothes for them both, wincing at the cost but more determined than ever to find Adam Fothergill.

They set off on a tempestuous morning in late July, each lost in thoughts that flit from the revenant to the Scots still intent on stealing Carlisle to the rain that never seems to cease for more than a few hours at a time. It is a long hard walk, the sodden earth waiting to catch them unawares, setting them to slip and slide as if all were girt with ice. But that does give Willow cause to keep step with Edie, though she is the one holding fast to his elbow as he rolls and slithers around like a duck on a frozen pond. Only Luke is undaunted, though even he is careful whenever he approaches a fearful drop.

They must cross numerous becks, clinging fast to one another as the waters tumble incontinently all around. Their cloaks grow heavier and heavier, Edie's hair clinging to her face in long, ragged strips. But at last they come up on to the higher ground, the mournful sound of curlew keeping them company. A great mist hangs all around, obscuring where they've come from and where they're going, the wind rushing at them as if to send them away. Fran feels an unease fall upon him now, in this strange, unearthly place so utterly removed from the land of the living. He even wonders if Adam Fothergill is being held here as some sort of punishment.

He wonders, too, how long they still have to walk, unable to imagine this will ever end. But at last Luke turns, comes back to them. He waves a hand to where the ground seems to fall away before rising up again towards the misty heights of Mickle Fell. 'He be down there, in the hollow.' With that, he crouches on his haunches, bringing out a piece of sheep's cheese to nibble most delicately.

Fran looks at Edie, who looks at Willow. Giles is content to crouch near Luke, not meeting anyone's gaze.

Fran thinks for a moment, surveying this vast country of subdued colour. 'If I go by myself and he sees me, I might frighten him away.' He looks at Edie again and this time she looks back at him, nods. He turns to Giles and Willow. 'Come after us in a little while. But be vigilant. I might need you if he proves violent. But if he's gentle, you must stay away.'

Willow shakes his head. 'Begging your pardon, sir . . .'

Edie goes back to him, places a hand on his heart. 'It's best there be not so many of us.'

Willow catches hold of her arm. 'You shouldn't be the one to talk to him.'

'You is knowing why.'

He opens his mouth, but already Edie is walking away.

'The cook's whelp,' Giles taunts Willow. 'You're aiming high.'

The sound of scuffling hangs in the air. Fran fights the urge to look back, mostly for fear the greyness has already swallowed them up and he will feel lost, even with Edie at his side. But when the ground begins to fall away from them, he can hold nothing else in his mind but where his feet should go. A wall of rocks above King's Pot is visible now, a desolate place but no doubt a safe one.

Edie puts a hand gently on his arm, knocking him out of a reverie where a few of his well-chosen words lead Adam Fothergill back to righteousness. 'You mun stay here, sir. I'll cry out for you if I be needing to.'

He wonders why he thought this was a good idea, to bring the girl here and let her go down there alone. But even as this burden of guilt grips him, he knows she's just as brave as he is and a lot less given to thoughts that circle round and round like buzzards.

All the same, he prays now that Luke is wrong, or at least that the revenant has grown tired of this cursed life and is truly gone away. He watches her clamber down between two rocks, push her hair once more out of her eyes, and disappear. Holding his breath, he wonders how long he should wait, worrying that the wind will run away with Edie's cries into the far wildness.

Every second that he hears and sees nothing assails him with bruising force. And yet Edie scrambles back up through the gap less than a minute later, a hand clutching tight at her cloak. He rushes towards her, searching hard for signs of violence.

She quickly stops, breath unruly. 'He is flying away afore I could be saying anything.'

'Damn him!' Fran feels a fool for coming all this way for nothing. 'Did he see it was you?'

She nods. He bites his lip.

But they need not debate what to do next. A cry rends the air, prolonged, sinister. Throwing their heads towards it, they draw closer to each other.

Adam Fothergill stands atop a rocky knoll a short distance away, his hair, shirt and tunic – what's left of them – fluttering furiously in the wind. He stretches out his arms, as if to gather them to him. But they are rooted to the ground now, all speech fled. For one horrible moment, Fran thinks Adam will fly at them, smite them with the dagger thrust into his belt. He thinks too, with grim irritation, that, for all his training, no one thought to teach him how to fight off a revenant.

Adam holds fast to his perch, swaying there for several long moments. But Fran has not come all this way to turn on his heels. Forcing enough courage into his legs to get them to move, he steps forward.

Instantly, Adam thrusts out a hand, a deep growl rising out of his throat. 'What do you want?'

Fran feels Edie by his side, swallows his fear, for in truth they do not come to harm him. 'To speak with you.'

Adam lowers his arms. 'Why?'

Fran looks at the ground, his boots soaking in a puddle of water. But he must raise his head to force his words across the distance between them. 'May I come closer?'

Adam seems to grow taller. 'Stay where you are.' It is a shriek, but commanding nonetheless.

Fran sighs to himself. It is perturbing to converse with the dead, but especially like this. He shouts again. 'We wish to know how long you intend to stay here. We were frightened by what you did, the things you left down in Warcop.'

'I meant you to be.'

Fran fingers the pommel of his sword. They stare at each other for a long moment as he wonders what to say, what not to say, for fear Adam might yet decide to fly upon them. But there's not much he can do to make the story any less appalling, and it's not as if Adam doesn't know it already. 'I heard what happened at Elsdon.'

'Hah!' It is a shocking sound. The revenant stretches out his hands, as if he wishes to throttle something. Or someone. 'And who was telling you?'

'The Dickinsons. Rob and Wat.'

There is a pause, as if a reckoning is being made. 'And was it a truly terrible tale?'

Fran thinks he jests and is outraged. 'It was so terrible even their father was kind to them for enduring it.' The words slip out and he regrets them, though he's not sure why. Stumbling on, he hacks his way towards what he hopes will be the truth. 'They said you were hungry. And the people there wouldn't give you any food. So you killed—'

Immediately, as if Fran has released a dragon, Adam becomes an unholy spire of clamour and movement. Edie gasps. But already Fran is drawing his sword, pushing her urgently out of the way. He leaps forward.

But Adam is gone, just like that, in the merest blink of an eye.

Fran throws his gaze all around, anxious now they might be attacked from behind. But all that is left is the wild fells screaming in the wind. He breathes again, sees Edie rushing back the way they came. All he can do is follow her.

Willow emerges from the mist, running hard towards them, stopping with his mouth open once he sees they are both entirely whole. 'You shouldn't have gone.' He says this to Edie, anger frosting his words.

'Leave her be.' Fran is suddenly angry.

Giles puffs up behind. 'I didn't think you'd be coming back, sir.'

Fran nods, wondering if his squire is disappointed. 'We shouldn't stand round here talking.' He finds himself utterly bewildered.

They walk as quickly as they can. Luke is still sitting where they left him, though he rises as they approach. 'We mun be leaving a creature like that alone, sir.' It is solemnly said.

Fran bites his tongue.

Edie hurries to his side. 'What be happening there, my

lord? He is being such a wild thing. Not hisself at all. Is it being your words is making him fly away like that?'

He doesn't know if she reproaches him. Thinks she might, which angers him. 'It speaks of his guilt, Edie, that he should not wish to say one word about Elsdon when I was most gentle with him.'

'It be distressing 'im, you talking 'bout yon place.' This time her words are certainly laden with reproof.

He stops. 'Do you know what he did there?'

She steps away from him, shakes her head.

'He killed a woman and her child. They wouldn't give him any food, but even so.' He looks at each of them, unbowed in the face of their horror.

Luke bites a nail. 'I'd best not be telling Mither that.'

'No! I's not believing it.' Edie leans towards Willow, pulling her cloak tight around her.

Fran shrugs. 'Really? Can you be sure the man you knew wouldn't have done it, if he were desperate enough?'

She says nothing.

'What do we do now, sir?' Willow slashes an arm through the air as if he has his sword in his hand.

Giles snorts. 'Go home and lock the doors.'

For the moment, Fran thinks that's as good a plan as any, though he certainly won't say so.

Chapter 10

Will paces the room, rubbing his face and pushing a hand through his hair so that it sits like a crown around his tonsure. Everyone watches him, even if they pretend to be doing something else. 'It is not what I expected,' he says at last.

'You've already said that.' Fran pats the chair next to his. 'But I don't understand why. You must tell us more about your studies of revenants, so we might compare the ones in the books with Adam.'

'I know, I know.' Will throws himself into the chair. 'But it is not so simple. In truth, the books are not agreed on the subject, so I was unable to come to a firm conclusion as to their nature. To give but one example, it is claimed by some – Bishop Thietmar, for one – that the undead are a most potent proof of the Resurrection. But I cannot believe that. Their murderous behaviour is entirely opposed to Christ's gentleness. And why should their barbarous activities be rewarded with such a precious gift, paid for by the ultimate sacrifice?' He is clearly most disturbed by what he's read, scarcely able to sit or stand still.

It should be more satisfying, Fran thinks, to see Will so discomfited. But he needs the priest to collect his thoughts, so he might advise them. Though nothing has been seen of Adam Fothergill since their encounter with him, knowing he is still out there unsettles them. Once more they feel under siege, prisoners in their own homes and unable to attend to even the most mundane of tasks without trembling thoughts. 'But are revenants always badly behaved? I mean, *necessarily* so?'

Will turns a frown on him. 'Why do you always take Adam's part?'

'I do not!' Fran is bewildered. 'I only wish to have some notion of what he might do next. He frightened me, is the truth of it.' The image of that haunting figure flits often through his dreams. He had been much dismayed up on the fells, with Adam, with himself, even Edie. But since then, in his waking hours, he has turned a less fevered mind back on what happened. It's not as if the revenant actually harmed them, though he surely meant to cause them to imagine he might. Fran scratches the side of his neck. 'We all know what he's capable of. But up there he did no more than yell and look malevolent. Is that fair, Edie?'

Edie sits quietly on the floor at Sarah's feet, arms wrapped around long legs. She is content now among company that once she would never have kept, occasionally offering a thought that Giles and even Willow try hard to contradict, but which only makes them sound like fools.

More than once, Fran has gone looking for her in the kitchen or outside in the herb garden, speaking out loud the thoughts that have plagued him all day. By the time he's spoken, and she's asked him questions so as to be sure in her own mind what he means, and offered something in return, he is much surer in what he thinks.

Now Edie rubs one hand along the back of the other, staring hard at her feet peeking out of the bottom of the dress. Giles sniggers, and Fran throws him a warning look that he refuses to catch.

But Will is impatient. 'I hear what you say, but he is playing you for a fool! That ungodly creature has killed God's creatures and defiled them, deliberately putting them out for innocent people to find.'

'But that's the . . .'

Fran stops as Edie unwinds herself and moves a little towards them. Lowering her gaze to the floor, she addresses the priest. 'I is happy to answer, sir. I am thinking the same as my lord Francis. When I is first going tae speak wi' him, he is frightening me wi' the way he's flying about away frae me, and later too, when this place is being spoke of. He's like some kind o' demon, like you all is saying. But I is thinking after that it is being like some kind o' show.'

'Exactly so.' Fran leans forward. 'And though he wasn't overly friendly, it was only when I spoke of Elsdon that he became monstrous. But even then . . . I expected him to attack us, but he didn't. He just disappeared. It is most strange.'

Edie steps forward even further. 'I would say, sirs, that he is still—'

'Be quiet, Edie.' Will's face is fallen into peevish folds. 'We have no need of your foolish opinions.'

Fran feels the blow and stiffens. He knows he cannot rebuke Will, their priest, in front of everyone. But he sees Edie flinch, the colour withdrawing from her face, and feels the injustice most keenly. Of course, Giles sniggers. If the squire were nearer, Fran would kick him, just to feel a brief deliverance. But that will not help Edie, who is looking at him now, eyes shimmering. Inclining his head towards the door leading to the kitchen, he proffers her a slight smile. She scuttles away, head down.

Will settles back in his chair, quite indifferent to the humiliation he's just inflicted.

But Fran is too dismayed to swallow his words, out of respect or affection. He leans over, keeps his voice low. 'If I wish to hear Edie's opinion, I do not see why you should oppose it.'

The priest blinks. But then he smiles, shaking his head. 'Ah, Fran, you still have much to learn. You really should not encourage her. If she learns to speak up now, she will only find herself disappointed when she marries. No husband wants a wife who thinks she knows better than he does.' He rolls his eyes. 'Can you imagine what kind of a household that would be!'

Fran withdraws in dismay, a host of unruly thoughts rushing to his lips. For the first time in his life, he mislikes Will, thinks him cruel. Such a thought makes him miserable, but not as miserable as imagining Edie's dismay, the injustice of her dismissal, the stupidity in not letting her speak when she knows far more about Adam

Fothergill than any of them. What purpose can God have, to put sense and wisdom in a girl's head even as he counsels men to silence her?

But then he realises Will is still speaking about revenants, fingers pointing and stabbing, black locks falling gracefully into his eyes.

'... the night creature Grendel, who is vanquished by Beowulf. Grendel is cursed, of course, because of the punishment the Almighty inflicted on his ancestor, Cain.'

Fran struggles to give proper attention to the words, sees himself as if from a distance sitting in his own hall like an unwelcome stranger. He coughs. 'And he was an undead creature?'

'Indeed. A grim spirit banished from the company of men and unable to feel the joy of their companionship.' Will smiles at Fran, who does not smile back.

Willow is rapt, for he loves this story almost as much as those of King Arthur and his knights. He claps his hands. 'That's just like our creature, isn't it?'

Giles glares at him. 'How would you know?'

'Yes. Just like him.' Fran grasps at Willow's eagerness as cover. 'But the question is, what do we do to get rid of him?' He will not meet Will's gaze, though he feels it charging him down.

'I was just coming to that.' There is no warmth in Will's voice now, only judgement. 'Brother William of Newburgh's *History* was most instructing, providing a number of powerful remedies. I have taken care to commit them all to memory. One was to take turns as watchmen, though we would have difficulty knowing where to stand guard. On more than one occasion he mentions that the corpse should be dug up from where it rested and burned. We should bear that in mind.' He pauses, studying the toe of his boot for inspiration. 'Ah, yes. Attacking it with a battle-axe also worked, as did putting an absolution written by a bishop in the tomb with the corpse.'

Fran sighs, reminding himself they have work to do. 'But we don't really know where he's buried, do we?'

Giles and Willow compete to look the most solemn, shaking their heads vigorously.

'Yes.' Will kneads his forehead. 'That is a problem.'

Fran leans forward, elbows on knees, carried away once more by the devilish enigma that is the revenant. 'Though presumably he's not very far from where he fell at Elsdon. Perhaps the people there know something.'

Will brings a thumb to his bottom lip, stroking it gently. 'What about the Dickinsons?'

Fran looks away, shakes his head. 'They seem to have left almost as soon as the killing began. We could ask Jamie if they said anything, but I doubt it.'

Will gets up, begins to pace around the room. 'How did he seem to you? I mean, the state of the body. Did it look as if it were decaying?'

Fran considers the question, knowing it is important. He remembers Will saying that revenants can only roam among the world of men while there is flesh on their bones. 'I would say so. It's not just that he's so much thinner than he was in life, though that's certainly true. There's something awful about his skin.'

Will stops. 'In what way?'

Fran considers this, keeping his gaze on his hands. 'It's as if it's been eaten up from the outside. All down one side of his face and one of his hands. I couldn't see much more, of course. I'm sure Edie would say the same.' He could not resist that.

'And was he—'

The door bangs and everyone starts, turning towards the sound. Fran rises, awaiting whoever has arrived so peremptorily. Will moves towards him and they stand, shoulder to shoulder, arms folded.

Sarah stomps in, hands a-flutter. This time, whatever it is, she has understood and is dismayed. She sees Fran and pours forth a loud lament, wordless but potent.

Behind her, Aidan, the blacksmith's son – the same one as came to tell Sir Henry of the return of Wat and Rob from Scotland – nearly trips over the back of her skirts. With an ungentle arm, he pushes her out of the way, bowing to Fran and Will, but locking his eyes on the priest. Fran is about to rebuke him for his rough treatment of Sarah, but the look on his face stops him.

Aidan's face is bright red, his breath arriving in short eruptions, as if there's not enough of it. They know he has run here and quickly. It is impossible to avoid the conclusion that something terrible has happened.

Will steps forward, lays a hand on Aidan's shoulder. 'Gather yourself before you speak.'

Aidan nods, a hopeless look in his eyes.

They wait, silent and afraid, and at last the gasping and panting is subdued. 'Jamie Dickinson's dead, sirs.' Aidan bows his head.

'How?' Will looks incredulous as if he will not believe it. 'He was in rude health but yesterday. Was it a sudden sickness?'

'No, sir. It be murder.'

'Adam?' Fran whispers it, knows it, but cannot comprehend it.

Aidan nods, a fierce look on his face.

Will snatches up his cloak.

'Shall I come too?' Fran does not really mean it as a question.

'If you think it might make you see what that devil is really about, then yes.' That is not a question either.

Jamie Dickinson hangs on the church gate, arms outstretched. Blood is everywhere, seeping from the many wounds on his body, pooling on the ground beneath, splashed on to the gate itself.

They sit on their horses looking at this fearful, incredible sight with no words between them. Aidan slips down and runs off. No one comes out to speak with them. Giles and Willow, at the back, look round most carefully. They all cross themselves.

Fran gets down too, throwing Fauvel's reins to Giles. The thought does not come upon him to let someone else deal with this. He is not sure why, but he feels a certain responsibility, the seeds of a belief he might have poked a hornet's nest when he went to see the revenant.

No one else moves. The smell is powerful, apt to overwhelm, as Fran knows well from his monthly courses.

In truth it's not the blood that discomfits him, in spite of its profusion. What truly sickens him is Jamie's face, eyes bulging, mouth locked open. Fran tries not to dwell on it, for that face can only tell him what all sensible people would know already: that Jamie Dickinson was terrified when he died.

And yet, Fran thinks, it would be better not to assume anything. Jamie was tied to the gate by his arms and legs, his feet still on the ground. All three Dickinsons are forceful, well-built men, the father no less than his sons, despite his age. But surely the revenant possesses unimaginable powers to make light work of any living being, however strong? Fran is perplexed, for the way Jamie Dickinson has been left – awkwardly propped against the gate – suggests Adam Fothergill had not the strength to pin Jamie up off the ground. He turns to look at Will, who has covered his nose with his cloak. 'I would cut him down.'

Will nods. 'Do you wish for me to help you?' He must shout it if he desires to keep his cloak up.

'Let me help, sir.' Willow leaps from his horse.

'Where's Giles?'

Willow jerks his head back behind him. 'He's not feeling very well.'

Fran grunts. 'Come then.'

Willow walks towards the gate as if it were a holy relic, eyes never moving from Jamie Dickinson's inert body. 'I never thought to see such a thing.'

'You don't need to whisper, Willow. He can't hear you.'

'Who can't, sir?'

'Jamie Dickinson. I would have thought that was obvious.'

'I wasn't thinking of him.'

'Ah.' Fran fights the urge to look round too, telling himself the revenant is long gone. 'I don't think *he* can hear you either. If you cut the cords, I'll hold the body and we can lay him down over there.' He points to a patch of grass a few feet away, beneath the church wall.

He braces himself for the mortal remains of Jamie Dickinson to press heavily upon him and indeed he is nearly knocked over when the last cord is cut. Grunting a little, he manages to remain upright but is heartily glad when Willow comes to help.

'He's so stiff. Why is he so stiff?' Willow looks outraged.

'I don't know.' They lay Jamie down carefully. Fran gets on to his knees.

'Close his eyes,' Will calls from a muffled distance.

'Yes.' Fran is glad to disguise the horror imprinted there. He closes his own eyes, the better to imagine what the revenant must have done. But then he decides to count the wounds. Seventeen in total, but none to the heart or the vital organs. He sits back on his heels, deep in thought. Jamie surely bled to death, and the revenant must have meant him to do so. He cannot imagine what possessed the creature that had once been Adam Fothergill to even think of such a thing.

'What are you doing?' Will sounds more fearful than annoyed.

'Wait a minute, please.' Shuffling on his knees towards Jamie's head, Fran waves at Willow to come down beside him. 'I'm going to bring him up to sit. You must take him from me. There's something I want to look at.'

Willow nods eagerly, putting himself across Jamie's legs and taking the weight of him with clenched teeth. Fran wonders, not for the first time, how he can see anything with all that hair.

As soon as the corpse is bent over, Fran knows he was right to imagine that the revenant had surprised Jamie Dickinson. What he sees on the back of the head is a great gash very different to the stab wounds. These edges are not sharp and smooth but jagged, the hair folded into it where it's not come away altogether. And the rock, or whatever else was used to inflict it, was brought down on Jamie's head so forcefully, Fran is dismayed to see pieces of bone in the gaping hole. Now, at last, he feels a great revulsion in his stomach, turns away and spits out bile. He turns to Willow, but Jamie Dickinson is already lying flat on the ground, the back of his head safely hidden in the grass.

Fran stands up on shaking legs, walking carefully back to Will. 'I think I know what happened.'

'Just by looking?' Will tentatively removes his cloak.

'It's written all over him.' He sees Giles slumped over on his saddle but decides to say nothing.

Will looks disbelieving, but he too says nothing.

Fran composes his thoughts. 'The first question I asked myself was how the revenant got Jamie Dickinson up there.'

'But the accounts say he might well have prodigious strength—'

'Will you wait until I've finished, please?' Fran tries not to glare at the priest in front of Giles and Willow, forcing a smile.

Will narrows his lips, nods.

'That's why I looked at the back of the head. It's clear Jamie was hit from behind, very hard, with a rock or something similar. The wound is not at all like the others.'

Giles sits up, fixes bloodshot eyes on Fran.

Fran raises his eyebrows at his squire but quickly turns his gaze back on Will. 'I think the revenant brought Jamie here and tied him to the gate. That would have been hard enough even if Jamie were insensible, as he must have been. After that, it would have been no trouble to inflict the knife wounds. But what I also noticed is that those wounds wouldn't have killed him outright.'

'Really, sir? I would have thought that most unlikely.' Giles is feeling well enough to copy Will's disbelieving tone.

This time Fran does glare. 'You can go and look if you like.' That is cruel, but he thinks it justified.

Giles turns even whiter. 'I just meant—'

'Well, don't. But perhaps you can answer this question. Where would you stab a man if you wanted to kill him?' He hears himself sound just like Will all those years ago, trying to coax him into looking at the facts of a particular matter and drawing conclusions.

Willow opens his mouth, but Giles spits out the answer first. 'The heart.'

'Yes. Anywhere else?'

'The other organs?'

'Indeed. You might not die immediately, but it would be certain. Poor Jamie over there has no wounds in such places. Which means?'

Giles stares at him, shakes his head.

Fran turns to Willow, but he too looks blank.

'It means that—'

'Wait, sir!' Giles has been twisting his face quite dreadfully. 'He cannot have wanted him to die in a short time.' He lowers his voice. 'He wanted him to suffer.'

Fran nods. 'That's what I think too. It was the bleeding that killed him and who knows how long it took. The thing that confuses me . . .' He tries to knot the strands of his imaginings together. 'I would have thought a revenant was more than a match for Jamie Dickinson.'

Will shifts in his saddle. 'What do you mean?'

'I mean, hitting someone hard on the back of the head so they become insensible suggests he wasn't.'

Will frowns. 'Wasn't what?'

'More than a match. Strong enough to overpower Jamie face to face.'

Will frowns again. 'I am not sure what you are suggesting.'

Fran shrugs. He's not sure himself. He reminds himself that the Dickinsons saw Adam die. And Adam himself is playing the part of a revenant to perfection. There can be no doubt on the matter. 'What do you want us to do with the body?'

Will breathes out long and slow. 'We should move it inside the churchyard. I am loath to put him in the church itself, but he should be taken away from the road. The people here will be frightened enough.'

'We need to speak with Aidan again. How did he know for certain it was the revenant, for one thing? And before you say it, I'm not looking to excuse that creature. But Aidan must have seen something, and I want to know what it was.'

Will nods. 'I should send word to Henry. I doubt there's much he can do about this at the moment. But he should know.'

They leave their horses at the church, walking close together along the road and down towards the wattle houses growing along the riverbank. The blacksmith does not live quite there, but a little nearer to the village green, his house timber-framed and immodestly plastered, as if intent on showing the world he does not belong among the peasants who are his neighbours.

The shadows have grown long now, creeping towards night. Will raps on the door, its wooden frame no barrier to his preacher's voice. 'Aidan. It is me, Father Warcop. I would speak with you most urgently.'

There is a loud rustling, voices low and strained, a lowing and bleating coming from the animals brought inside many hours ago, thanks to this new and terrible danger outside. The door creaks open and Aidan's father, the blacksmith Edgar Simpson, puts his head round it. 'Come inside quickly, Father.' He speaks in a whisper, a low rumble emerging from the depths of his powerful body.

Fran tells Giles and Willow to stay outside, which causes Giles's eyes to leap up into his hair, his hands to twitch at his sides. But he will say nothing in front of

Willow. Ducking their heads, Fran and Will enter the dark, smoky room, stifling coughs behind their hands. The smell hits them like a blow, so ripe and powerful it could hold up the entire structure on its own. Nose outraged and eyes stinging, Fran can scarcely see the people gathered there, but slowly he becomes used to the heavy, pungent gloom. He wonders how they manage not to trip over each other every time they turn around.

Besides Aidan and his father, he recognises the blacksmith's wife, Ava, a small scrap of a woman whose nose drips constantly. Then there's the other son still at home, the one whose name Fran can't remember, who now takes advantage of the confusion to dip a finger into the pot in the middle of the room. Finally, he notices Ava's mother, a pile of bones and rags lying in the corner waiting to die.

After more shuffling and scraping, Ava presses her way through with a stool for the priest. She gives a brief squawk when she sees Fran too, but he waves a hand, shakes his head, and she retreats into the far shadows. Grasping Aidan in one hand, Edgar forces his son through all impediments so that he lands, swaying and unsettled, at Will's right hand. Aidan bobs his head up and down to the priest before finally coming to rest, as hunched and unhappy as a heron. 'I don' know nowt.'

Will waggles a finger at his captive. 'You know more than you think you do.' He surveys the company, though he can scarcely see any of them. 'You all do.'

Ava, sniffing loudly, appears at Aidan's elbow with two cups of something dark and smouldering. Will seizes one, passing the other up to Fran, who supposes the priest is used to dealing with unwanted gifts from his flock. He smells it tentatively and is pleasantly surprised that the newly brewed ale's earthy pungency comes from the sage used to give it flavour.

A few seconds later, Ava returns with a scraping of bread and cheese, which Will once more takes with a curt nod. Fran is unsure how to receive his tiny portion, struggling to slip the cup into his pocket to free both hands. He is become impatient now, but his stomach tells him he is hungry and, anyway, since this gift cannot easily be spared, it would be churlish indeed to refuse it. For the next few minutes everyone watches them eat and drink until at last he swallows the last morsel and smiles. Ava claps her hands as her husband growls at her to get back out of the way.

Aidan, meanwhile, stands as if the earth is trying to drag him down into it, while Will dusts the crumbs from his habit and places his hands to his lips in his customary position of readiness.

Fran is unsure how this will proceed. He fervently wishes he could ask the questions himself, but knows Will is unlikely to give up this privilege. He tells himself to pay close attention, so he will remember what else needs to be found out.

But Will is skilful in his questioning. He is also adept at putting Aidan at ease, gazing attentively at the boy as if his words were most precious and important. 'I suppose that you were the one chosen to find me because you are the most fleet of foot?'

Aidan nods vigorously. ''Tis true, sir. Most certainly.'

'And did someone have to find you for this task, or were you already at hand?'

Aidan turns his head right round, searching for his father.

Will leans forward, touches him lightly on the arm. 'There is no right answer, Aidan. It is just what you remember.'

Aidan nods, swallows. 'I were at the forge, bringing in more charcoal fir the fire. It were the time o' day when folks is a-finishing o' their work and ready tae stand chattering wi' their neighbours. I wis lookin' tae go fishin' wi' some o' the ither lads, I is minding o' tha.'

Edgar Simpson gathers himself as if to say something, but, at a glance from Will, looks away.

'I is not knowing who is seeing the creature first. I is hearing summat coming, like a storm o' words, ivveryone cursing an' crying. I isn't knowing whit tae dae. Faither is awa' wi' Si Harrison, tae see if he's really wanting a new plowshare. So I peeked outside. An' I is seeing it, staundin' in the road wi' its arms pointing and poking at ivveryone, aw bloody on its hands. An' they is running away a little an' gathering outside the forge tae listen tae whit it's saying.'

Fran is astonished. But then, he ponders, Aidan has eyes and ears the same as everyone else and why should he not be able to use them even if no one ever asks him what it is he sees and hears?

Will can scarcely stop nodding. 'This is most useful, Aidan. Can you remember what it was the creature said?'

Aidan nods slowly, gathering the words together. 'I is not unnerstanding ivverything. It were saying summat 'bout reteri ... retri ...'

'Retribution?' Fran cannot help himself.

'Aye, jus' so. Whit is it meaning, this reteribooshun?'

'Vengeance.' Will says it simply and they all fall silent for a moment. 'Who did he want to take vengeance on? Jamie Dickinson?'

'It is sayin' aw' o' them, Jamie an' Wat an' Rob. He is saying their sins is being found out and must be punished, an' it is the one tae dae it.'

Fran bends down so he can talk directly to Will. 'Do you think that means Adam wishes to be avenged because they've been speaking about what he did at Elsdon?'

'It is no sin, surely, to bring to light such terrible deeds.'

'Not for us, but it's possible the undead see things differently. Or maybe Adam is angry with Wat and Rob because they didn't stay to help him fight off the others that were there – and if they had, he might not have died.' *Or maybe Adam didn't do what the Dickinsons said he did.* Fran wants to take that thought away into the quiet, so he might search it for possibility. But that will have to wait.

Will scratches the side of his cheek. 'I do not know, is the honest truth. But I see the logic in what you say.'

They smile at each other, forgetting for a moment this day's terrible doings. But not for long.

Aidan is agitated, rising up and down on his toes. 'Whit kind o' a creature is it, sirs? I's thinking it mus' be the Devil hisself.'

'Not the Devil, no.' Will speaks carefully. 'But

something hellish, that is certain.' The room falls utterly quiet, and yet the unspoken words, the desperate thoughts, disturb them all.

Edgar Simpson speaks at last. 'An' whit is we doing tae deserve this creature? We is having enough tae worry 'bout, what wi' the Scots and a' the things like to ruin honest men.' He doesn't say God sent the rains and the winds and the diseases, but Fran doesn't doubt that's what he means.

Again, Will speaks carefully. 'We must not despair. If God is angry with us or if He is testing us, we must find a way to appease Him. Together. But do not forget that the revenant only wishes to take revenge on the Dickinsons.'

'It is saying it'll curse us all if we is trying tae stop it!' This bursts out of Aidan like a summer storm.

Will's mouth works silently, but no words of comfort pour forth.

Fran looks round everyone, feels an ache in his heart for the fear now sown here again. He knows about fear. The way it shifts shape so that black becomes white, friends are quickly suspected of enmity, and strangers must be come to do the Devil's work. They do not need the revenant to teach them that. 'If I can perhaps explain a little of what we've found so far. You know, of course, that Jamie Dickinson was brutally murdered.'

There is a great nodding, a wail quickly stifled.

'And you know that the creature is the undead remains of Adam Fothergill?'

Clearly not everyone knew that, for there is horrified chatter that he puts up a hand to quell.

'We know that Adam did a most terrible thing over in

Northumberland, near the border, and that he was killed shortly after. We also know that Wat and Rob Dickinson were both there. What is unclear to me now is why *Jamie* Dickinson should have suffered the way he did, for he had nothing to do with what happened at Elsdon. Did any of you see him this afternoon?'

It is the other boy who speaks, the one whose name Fran suddenly remembers is Ralph. Rubbing the evidence of his thievery from round his mouth, he rises like a spectre from his place by the fire. 'I is seeing him. Going up Hayber Lane, he was. Wi' a right sour look on his face.' He pauses, twisting his face. 'God be resting his soul, o' course.'

'Did you exchange words with him?' Fran squeezes his bottom lip between thumb and first finger, praying for a helpful answer.

'That's the thing. He's not even looking at me usually except tae gi' me a clap roun' me ear for getting in his way. But today he's asking me if I'd seen anything – I is coming down frae fishing in the gill, see.'

This earns him a clap anyway from his father, who clearly does not know this and certainly does not approve.

Fran waits until the 'ow-ing' and other reproaches have ceased. 'Did he say anything else?'

Ralph straightens himself. 'Summat 'bout a message and Simon Harrison better no be making mischief. They is having themselves a feud, those two, 'bout a bit o' meadow o'er at Flitholme.'

Fran thinks on this. 'Can you remember what part of the day this was?'

Ralph shrugs, eyes fluttering. ''Twere afore the creature

came, that's for certain. After that, I is going tae see if I can be spying on Maggie Murton. She be Jamie Dickinson's servant, so I's knowing he—' All becomes confusion as Aidan throws himself on his brother, the ensuing struggle only ended by their father picking both of them up by the ear. It's only by a miracle – or so it seems to Fran – that neither he nor Will is caught up in the fight.

Will stands up, a perplexed look on his face. 'I thank you both, though I am disappointed too that you should behave so churlishly.'

Aidan and Ralph try hard to look contrite, but grins lurk impatiently at the corners of their mouths.

Nodding at the company, Fran follows Will outside, nearly stumbling over Giles, who sits so close to the wall he seems to have attached himself to it. Willow stands nearby, kicking at stones. It is nearly dark. 'Go and get the horses and bring them to Father Warcop's stable.' Fran turns away so as not to endure any pouting or moping, from Giles at least. He is become cold and unsteady, at odds with everything and everyone around him, the shock of today finally grasping hold of him, shaking him free of all good feelings. The thought comes upon him that Jamie Dickinson might come back to haunt them, so unprepared must he have been for such a death. And what will they do then, if they are doubly cursed?

That night he is so tired he can scarcely speak. Will asks him every other minute if he is well, sighing often in Fran's direction or giving him a searching look. But when they go to bed, Fran lies awake through the quiet of the deep night, thinking over this curious day, their quarrel over Edie, the horror of Jamie's murder, but the invigoration he felt in dealing with it. And now, as all lies quiet, he only wishes he could bury himself in Will's arms, to feel repose at last.

When Fran returns home the next day, he sends Willow up on to Hilton Fell to find out from Sim Taylor, the shepherd, when he is thinking of bringing down the sheep from the summer pastures. It is a question Fran does want answered, so as to be properly acquainted with how his own affairs stand this year. But he has another reason for wanting Willow out of the way.

Waiting and watching in the hall, he sees Edie stride outside, no doubt heading towards the herb garden. He has not forgotten what happened when they were discussing the revenant, has begun to doubt in his own mind the wisdom of encouraging her to leave the hall, fearing she thought it for his own benefit rather than what he believed she would want.

He walks slowly down the stairs and outside, wanders through the flourishing roses, the orchard trees adorned here and there with plums and cherries, their leaves mottled and wilting. He can see Edie now, armed with her hoe in the kitchen garden, removing the weeds from among the beetroots and onions with grim determination. She is so strong, so vigorous, that Fran feels even more unhappy about her exclusion from their discussions. He knows he should feel protective of her. But nothing about Edie brings forth such a desire, not in him at least.

Instead, he is the one feeling reassured when she is there, even when she says nothing.

All the same, he doesn't wish to startle her, coming upon her so unexpectedly. Moving closer, he hears her singing some country ditty, slipping carelessly from one note to another whether or not the two sit well together. And yet there she is, in perfect harmony with herself.

'Good morrow, sir.' She bobs her head at him before leaning on her hoe, toes wriggling in the earth and a wary look on her face. 'I is not meaning tae disturb you.' Lowering her head, she picks up the hoe and her skirts.

'I'm the one disturbing you.' He was not expecting this to be difficult, had meant only to bring her some comfort that would comfort him too. 'Please don't go.'

She hangs there, hoe in hand, eyes roaming over the plants and trees as if they are her friends and might come to her rescue.

'I wish ...' He does not like her like this, uncertain, ready for flight. 'I wish we could have heard what you thought, about Adam.'

'It's being my mistake, sir, to have spoken so.'

'But I asked you to.'

She looks at him now, dark clefts between her brows betraying her annoyance. 'I'm thinking you shouldn't have, sir.' She throws a sleek coil of hair over her left shoulder.

Fran bites his lip, angry with himself and her and Will. It irks him almost to tears that she should no longer converse easily with him. He wants her to bend her head to his, to smile and whisper in his ear, a hand on his arm. In truth, he wants to be her friend, to enter the magical circle he has watched her form with other girls, an impossibility without bounds. He wishes he could make her, but of course, in that at least, she has all the power. And so, he forces himself to nod, to admit his foolishness. 'I am sorry to have distressed you.' And he is, for all it is a mumbled apology.

Edie looks away, a raw, roughened hand clasped to her swan throat.

He cannot bear this. 'Edie, I need your help. I promise not to bring shame on you in front of the others. But you know Adam better than anyone else here and that's worth ten of me. Maybe even ten of Father Warcop.'

She giggles then, the back of her hand trying to smother it.

He was being serious but is delighted with her better mood. He smiles. 'Why is that mirthful?'

She laughs openly now. 'I is just thinking o' ten o' you, sir, and ten o' Father Warcop all running about and how you is both getting so much more done than you do already.'

'Oh.' He considers her words and finds the warmth in them and perhaps the jest.

'I been thinking o' Adam and the terrible thing he is doing tae Jamie Dickinson. I is quite turned upside down wi' it. And' – she gives him a quick, sly look – 'I is wishing wi' all my heart I can be speaking wi' him.'

He is astonished. 'But, Edie, he most certainly didn't want to speak with *us*. And don't forget, he just murdered a man who played no part in his death.'

She has no difficulty holding his gaze now. 'I is knowing

that, sir. But I is just wanting tae try. And I is thinking he's not wanting tae harm me.'

He scratches the side of his face. 'You can't know that.'

But she nods her head so vigorously her blonde tresses bounce off her shoulders.

He wonders how he has got himself into the situation where Edie, now entirely unbowed, is begging him to take her to the revenant. But he does not wish her to think him ungrateful, that he does not want her opinion. 'The truth is, we don't know what to do about him. I mean, we think we should let Sir Henry decide, now there's been a murder. But perhaps if—' He stops, Adam's infernal, disfigured face rising up before him, mocking them both for ever thinking him gentle, not one of the damned. If it crossed his mind that Jamie Dickinson was killed by a man, not a living corpse, there is more than enough evidence to contradict such a notion.

She nods, seemingly satisfied. 'If you is being so kind as to tell me what you all is saying, sir, and you is not thinking it too bold, I is most happy to listen. Not wi' the others, o' course.'

He has what he wants, or something of it, at least. If only he didn't want more.

Jamie Dickinson is buried quickly two days later, almost before the pale light of dawn has had time to gather round them. His sons do not attend, though Will sent word to Scaleby telling them the terrible news. It is shocking, of course, that Wat and Rob do not come to put their father in the ground, but no one complains of it. The few attending the burial are too busy looking over their shoulders as Jamie is lowered into the ground, Will committing his soul into the Lord's care as swiftly as he can without sounding as if he gallops. There is no wake, no drink taken after. Jamie Dickinson's mortal remains slip away out of sight as if he were a leper.

Sir Henry sends a breathless message to his brother, underlining the haste with which he wrote it and the important business on which he's engaged. Though the Scottish curs left Carlisle in early August, on word of the approach of the earl of Arundel's army, they cannot be trusted not to appear somewhere else. So he rides with Sir Andrew Harclay to protect the border as best they can. *Besides*, he tells Will in obvious perplexity, *the murderer is not a living man, and so does not come under my jurisdiction. This revenant is more your concern than mine and I would urge you to deal with it as quickly as possible, for the sake of our people.*

'That is easy for him to say.' Will sits in Fran's hall, chewing carefully on an apple, for he has a sore tooth.

Fran nods, sits back, gives his thoughts time to breathe. He is in a quandary, for he knows he shouldn't tell Will about Edie's desire to speak again with the revenant. He is almost certain the priest will vigorously seek to dissuade them, and fighting Will is the last thing he wants. He could suggest that, with Wat and Rob out of the way, there is nothing left for Adam to attack. But he's said such things before, only to be ambushed by a new outrage. 'What did you say should be done to get rid of revenants?'

Will looks up, mid-chew. He throws the remains of the apple into the fire, watches it spit and smoulder. 'The problem is, you need to know where it's buried.'

'Should we go to Elsdon, then?'

Will sighs. 'I knew you would say that.' He searches for Fran's gaze and holds it tightly. 'I do not wish you to think me a coward. But it would be foolish to travel so close to the border with the Scots still riding out.'

Fran nods. He does not wish to go to the place where so much horror is gathered together. But just now he is enthralled by Edie's desire to find out why a man of honour and some gentleness is intent on slaughtering, if not innocents, then at least standers-by. And if she says she feels no danger from Adam Fothergill, then he believes her. Though he has not asked her if she thinks he too would not be harmed.

He knows Adam has left King's Pot, because he asked Luke about him after Jamie Dickinson's murder. But now he wonders if the boy has seen the revenant or signs of his prowlings since then. He feels the sting of impatience nipping at him and decides to seek out Luke again, wishing with all his heart he could confide in Will. But he can't. And it's not as if he is a stranger to hiding things from his friend.

Chapter 11

Fran would like to keep Edie to himself. It's not just that he finds her company less irksome than Giles' or Willow's, who must joust with each other in giving an answer or vouching an opinion. He also likes to study her without worrying what anyone else thinks, in the hope he might learn more about being a woman than just the way she carries herself. He can see she is wise, not least because she thinks carefully before she speaks. And she is kind, as well as brave and easily impatient, though she hides it well. He feels at ease again when they speak together, though he's not so foolish as to imagine they really are friends. It's not just that he is master and she servant – many a lady finds solace in the confidences shared with a maid. It is, as always, the firm prohibition placed on him by the line beyond which he cannot be himself.

But Fran cannot ignore the rest of his household. He knows Giles resents the fact that Willow accompanies them almost everywhere these days, but Fran deems it prudent they should be three swords instead of two. He has, of course, explained to Willow that they must protect Edie if they go to find the revenant, but was surprised when the youth protested that women are less in need of it than they like to pretend.

Yet, now he's thought on it, Fran realises Willow speaks partly out of frustration. His passion for Edie has been restricted to infrequent caresses of short duration ever since Harry Sowerby finally realised what was going on between them and shook his son till his teeth rattled. Harry has a paternal fondness for Edie, having known her since she was a baby, and is most concerned that Willow will dishonour her. 'Clearly,' he told his son in a fury that was all the more notable for being so rare, 'you cannot marry her, and I won't have you fuck her either.'

Fran was not party to these harsh words, of course. But he sensed all was not well, that the love he had watched blossom, far from thriving on obstacles, was becoming a restless, inconvenient thing, at least for Willow. All the same, he is still somewhat jealous of their intimacy and fearful of what might happen to Edie. Once or twice he has come close to broaching the subject with her. But he cannot find the words.

She has not mentioned going into the fells in search of the revenant since she first suggested it to Fran. But he knows she will expect him to keep his word now that Sir Henry has refused to pursue Adam. As August edges miserably towards September, he sends word to Luke to come to the hall.

But he is diverted by the lack of Giles. One minute he's

serving at table, the next he's gone. Fran sends Willow to find him, remembering the squire had been much given to holding his belly and moaning throughout the day. Willow returns at last, flinging himself on to the bench with perfect carelessness. 'He's downstairs in the cellar, sir. Says he's sick and wants to be by himself to sleep.'

'What kind of sick?'

Willow shrugs. 'In his guts, he says.'

Edie rises from the floor. 'Should I be preparing him some herbs, sir?'

Fran contemplates that thought and the certainty in his own mind that Giles is playing with him. 'No. I'll go and see what's wrong.'

He walks slowly downstairs, forcing himself to confront his feelings for his squire. In truth, he feels a powerful loathing every time Giles walks into a room. He should have sent him back home when his father died. It would have been remarked upon, of course, would certainly have provoked some unpleasantness. But it would have been done and mostly forgotten by now.

As he eases the door open, the room is in perfect darkness, a strange unbodied moaning filling the void. Fran throws open the door so a little more light ventures in. The moaning stills but only for a moment.

'Stop it.' Fran stands over the mound that is Giles.

And the moaning does stop. 'I'm sorry, sir.' The voice is small and bleating. 'But I don't think I can get up, for fear of falling down again.'

'I see.' Fran folds his arms, anger seizing him by the throat. 'You expect me to believe that, do you?'

The silence fills with a thousand wordless voices, re-proachful, humiliated, deeply uncertain until Giles finally wraps every shade of outrage and injustice into a pathetic appeal. 'You think I lie?'

But Fran feels only revulsion, his anger cooled now to an icy determination. 'Of course I do. You've done nothing but prove your cowardice every time the revenant is mentioned. I almost expected a trick like this.'

Giles sits up, his hair plastered at odd angles across his head. 'Why would you say such a thing?' His face is crimson, eyes bright. 'Have I not served you as well as anyone? If I have done wrong, then you must show me my error, not store up my faults to cast them at me later.' He looks away, voice falling apart in earnest this time. 'And if you do not think me sufficient, you must write to my father.'

'Hold your tongue. In case you haven't noticed, there's a murderous beast out in those hills and I need you to behave like a man, not a child. Get up and stop this babbling.' Fran turns on his heel, pushing the door hard behind him, not caring if it bangs.

But within a few steps, his anger turns on him, remorse flooding in. Giles is right. He has paid almost no attention to the instruction his squire has every right to expect beyond practising with weapons. It matters not he has been so overwhelmed by his own thoughts and feelings, the dilemma that haunts his every waking moment. Shame sitting heavily on his shoulders, he stops, hand reaching for the wall. Throat dry, he turns. Creeping back, he pushes open the cellar door as gently as he can. The mound quivers and quakes to the tune of a quiet lamentation.

Fran stands at a loss. He can deal with Giles when he is vigorous in his own defence, insolent even. That is to be expected. But not this.

Something takes him by the hand, leads him to the mound, gently pushing him down so he sits on the floor beside it. Stretching out a hand, he lays it on top of the blanket. 'I am truly sorry, Giles.' He hopes very much the crying will stop.

But it only grows the more violent, as if the world is ending and all goodness has already vanished. There is nothing to be done but to sit and wait.

A hand appears, followed by a head, though Giles is still turned away. 'Everyone hates me.' The words hiccock out, thickly intent on discouraging any objection, defiant once more.

Fran can scarcely deny the loathing that was in his heart only minutes ago.

But Giles does not need encouragement or approval, deceiving words of kindness. 'I killed my mother.'

'No, Giles, you didn't. You were only a child.'

The head bangs against the floor. 'I did. I hid behind the hangings and saw her die, and there was so much blood, and it was because I was there and I shouldn't have been. He said so. Every night he told me he wished it were me and not her.'

'Your father?' The banging continues. 'Please stop.' He lays a hand briefly on Giles's head. 'I cannot bear it.'

Giles lies quietly then, his head on his arm. 'I *want* everyone to hate me. I mean, I thought I did. That way, they won't be disappointed if I kill someone else.'

Fran sees the strange logic in that, will not seek to overturn it. 'What changed?'

'I want you to care for me, as you do Willow and Edie and Luke. It's not fair. They're just servants. God's blood, one of them's a girl!'

Fran looks up at the wall, bites his lip to stop from laughing or crying. 'Just because they're ...' He swerves away. 'I can still think well of them.'

Giles sits up, turns his swollen, tear-streaked face on Fran. 'I like them too. Even Willow, though he's an annoying arse.' His head seems to become too heavy for his neck, falls down on to his chest. 'I don't mean to.'

'It brings no dishonour to speak pleasantly with those who happen to have been born in a lower station. It is God who decides these things, so it's no more their fault than it was yours that your mother died giving birth.' He speaks very firmly.

Giles stiffens. 'And you won't even let me serve you in the morning and at night, like I should.'

'But you know that's just because my father bid Sarah attend to me. I can scarcely tell her not to after all these years, can I?'

He hiccocks. 'It's just as well she's not a proper woman.'

Fran tightens his lips, but keeps his voice low, gentle. 'I'm not sure I know for certain what a proper woman is. God has made her, and that's enough.' And now it occurs to him how hard it must have been for someone like Giles, who has a strong notion of what is 'proper' and likes to be surrounded by it. Putting a hand on his hair, Fran strokes it gently, as he remembers his mother and grandmother doing when he was very small. Time passes slowly and he wishes he might return to the warmth of the hall, to the urgent matter of Adam Fothergill.

'You were right, though, sir. I *am* a coward.' Giles delivers this too as an undeniable fact.

'Are you a coward? Or are you afraid?'

Giles sniffs. 'What's the difference?'

'It's easy enough to do something hard or dangerous if you don't fear it. And there are some things you *should* fear.' He remembers the fight with the Scots, the unfathomable despair of the woodsman's wife.

Giles begins to rock backwards and forwards. 'I cannot stand the thought of it.'

'What?'

'That thing. The creature.' He can scarcely breathe. 'It's the priest who should go after a devil like that.'

'I don't agree. I will admit he has confused me and made me sore afraid. But I still want to know what he is and what he wants. He's part of our world, whether we like it or not.'

Giles shakes his head. 'I don't understand.'

'And that's what makes you afraid. When I went with Edie to meet him, I was terrified. But I'm not sure why exactly, apart from his strangeness and all the things I don't know about him.' Fran swallows another sigh. 'I suppose you think you have no choice but to come with us? For your honour, I mean?' He feels his legs grow numb from sitting in such a strange way.

Giles gathers himself together, scrambles to his feet. 'If I don't go, will you make Willow your squire?'

'I've never thought of it.' He wants to say more. That he would rather Giles didn't come up on to the fells if he's going to cause them aggravation. That, yes, he has thought of writing to his father. He jumps up. Giles is already an inch taller since earlier in the summer, so that they stand eye to eye. 'I would have you by my side.'

Giles nods, a great smile on his face. 'That is as it should be.'

'But you must let Edie and Willow and Luke play their part too. I have decided this, and you must accept it.'

Giles's mouth tightens, but he nods again. He puts a hand out, lets it feel its way towards Fran's arm. 'I will not be afraid, sir.'

Fran breathes out heavily. 'Yes, you will. We all will.' He puts on a smile, pretends to cuff Giles around the ear. 'Come on, we have work to do.'

Luke is appalled at the idea of looking for the revenant again, standing in front of them all and flapping his hands in consternation. ''Tis an ungodly thing, sir. We hae no business wi' it.'

Everyone turns their gaze on Fran. Giles looks hopeful. Willow vigorously shakes his head. Edie, as always, gives nothing away.

Fran pushes his hands along the arms of his chair. 'I know I ask much of you, Luke. But I wouldn't put you or any of us in danger.'

'Begging your pardon, sir, but you is not knowing what is the danger.'

'Is it still up there?'

Luke nods, eyes flitting round the room. 'I is knowing how to keep out o' its way.'

'But surely it would be better if we got rid of it, one way or another, so you need not worry?' He glances at Edie, but she has turned her gaze on the window. 'Luke, we cannot go up there without you.'

The boy flings himself to the floor, hands cupping his chin. 'It be moving all about. And I is only seeing it two, three times these past weeks.'

'But do you know where he sleeps?'

Luke shakes his head. 'Only afterwards. Sometimes I is seeing he is bin lying somewhere.'

Fran nods, discouraged.

Willow leans forward, hands alive. 'It doesn't matter how long it takes, we must hunt it down and be rid of it.'

'He be a man, Willow. Not an "it".' Edie speaks quietly, but she holds herself tight, as if trying to contain herself.

'And what would you know about that?' He rolls his eyes, not even looking at her. 'Of course it isn't, is it, sir?'

Fran blows out his cheeks. 'I don't know. He *was* a man, obviously. And now he's dead.' He frowns. 'But it doesn't matter what he is or isn't. I don't know how we're going to find him.'

Giles stretches out his legs, his face not showing his feelings for once. 'I don't know how it can stand to be up there and never a nice warm bath.'

'Mmm.' Fran doesn't know if he jests or is trying to turn the revenant into something he can understand. He is grateful for either. His mind trips through other things

Adam Fothergill might want or need after this time in the hills. But he quickly bumps up against his ignorance. Do they eat? Shit? Surely not. Do they feel the cold? Perhaps a blanket and some new clothes might tempt him. Otherwise, he is at a loss.

Leaping up, he strides as if with confidence towards the fire, hands behind his back. They all look at him expectantly. He puts on a reassuring smile. 'I doubt the revenant will let us find him unless he wants us to.' There is a babble of agreement, much nodding. 'So, as Giles suggests, we must make the revenant have confidence in us, give him something useful to improve his existence up in the fells. Something to keep him warm, for example. And then we might arrange to speak with him.'

Giles manages to look astonished, proud and dis-believing that he did, in fact, suggest such a thing.

Willow thrusts an arm into the air, waving it about. 'There's no need for all of us to go.' This time he gives Edie a stern look. 'I'm happy to take the things myself, if it pleases you, sir. So long as Luke will guide me.'

Luke raises his eyebrows, but since his head is bowed, none sees it.

Fran watches Giles struggle with the part of him that hates Willow besting him and the part that abhors the fells and its monstrous inhabitant. But if he himself does not go, there will be no honour lost by his squire, even if Willow earns the right to boast. 'Very well. Edie, do you know if Adam can read?'

'Aye, sir. 'Twas his wife what is teaching him.'

He nods. Adam must not receive these gifts and give

nothing in return. He must let them come to him again and answer questions fully this time.

With sheep and cattle dying in their droves all along the border and the harvest likely to be a stunted, sodden one, Fran baulks at spending any coin. So he bids the women of his household and any willing wives or daughters of his husbandmen to mend blankets that might make Adam Fothergill more comfortable. He does not tell them who they're for, of course, mentioning only the destitute of the parish. Fran then writes a number of short letters beseeching the revenant to desist from more violence and to speak with them at Arnside Rake – a place not quite so far as King's Pot – so they might know his mind. All these Willow and Luke take to the various places Luke thinks Adam most likely to use for moments of safe repose.

They wait for a full week to pass until the day named by Fran in his letters when they will all venture forth once more, to meet with the revenant around the time the sun reaches its highest point. Arnside Rake lies near a shelter of stones and stunted bushes that Luke is certain Adam likes to frequent. In the meantime, as the rain carries them ever deeper into despair, Fran thinks they must be nearing the end of days and Judgement will soon be upon them. He has no doubt he will be judged harshly, waking often in the night drenched in sweat, clouding his mind throughout the day.

───── ∞ ─────

Fran and Giles slip out of the manor gate. For once, the day is set fair, and Fran feels a pleasing agitation at going up into the fells under a benign sky. Turning left, they spy Edie, Willow and Luke already standing above the dip that will take them down alongside Hilton Beck. He smiles, waves.

They walk on, sleeves pulled up, tunics loosened. Giles and Willow wonder aloud when the king will next scrape together an army to march against the heathen Scots, casting covert glances at Fran, who does not take the bait. He hasn't given any thought to fighting and, anyway, now is not the time. Edie ties back her hair with a kerchief, singing one of her ditties. Giles suddenly looks wistful. 'My mother's maid used to sing that one,' he says at last. Edie smiles at him and he smiles back.

But soon enough they begin to climb, and talking costs too much. They toil in silence across hillsides misted in purple. But however delicate the heather looks from a distance, its tough wiry fronds nip at legs, hold tight to boots and cloaks. Only Luke scuttles about with ease. It's only as they near the Rake that he falls back, his gaze drawn hither and thither, sniffing the air as if it were wine. At last, he points in the direction they should travel and squats down among the purple so that only the bright green of his hat betrays him.

The four of them choose their way carefully over to the narrow sanctuary offered by the tangle of juniper and ash. Willow and Edie hang back for a moment, talking in low, angry voices. Giles fixes his eyes on the trees. Fran moves close by his side, matching him step for step. If the squire sees him, he gives no sign.

Before they reach the trees, Fran stops, lays a hand on

Giles's arm. He turns to Edie and Willow, who hurry to reach them, the one hastening apart from the other.

Edie comes to stand before Fran. 'Is you wanting me to go and find him?' She does not speak with quite such assurance as last time.

Fran shakes his head vigorously. 'No. We go together.' He glances at Giles, who swallows hard. 'We have nothing to fear if we stay vigilant.' Giles stares even more keenly ahead.

Fran walks on, heart beating so fervently he fears all can hear it. He wonders now – as he always does when it's too late to change course – at the wisdom of coming. His fear closes in, hunting him down. It's not so much the revenant he dreads, but the thought that it will be his fault if anything happens to the others. That will be his memorial, foolhardiness become everything about him.

And if he is killed, they will say it was because he was no man.

He almost stumbles, feels Giles's hand reach out to steady him. The others press close. He looks around, trees swaying and creaking in the breeze. The sward grows thick here, smothering the ground. It is a good place to hide. 'Adam!' His cry is quickly overwhelmed, carried deep into the trees by the wind.

'I's thinking he's not here.' Edie whispers it.

Fran nods, turns to Willow. 'You brought a blanket and letter to this place?'

Willow nods, restless now, dipping under branches, poking into the longest grass. 'It's not here.'

'The blanket?'

'And the letter.'

Giles unglues himself from Fran's side, catching hold of a branch with both hands and hanging from it. 'So, what do we do now?'

Good question. 'He might be coming from afar and not be here yet.' Fran says this with no firm belief it's true. They haven't seen or heard a soul.

Edie stoops to pick willowherb. Straightening, she arranges the bunch in her arms, standing like a statue for several long moments, mouth half-open. At last, she frowns. 'Why is Adam Fothergill killing the poor woman and her bairn?'

'I told you.' Fran sits down on a fallen log, pulling out his flask of ale. 'He was sore afflicted with hunger and the woman wouldn't give him any food.'

Edie moves closer, comes to sit on the log, somehow still drawing Willow to hover nearby. 'You is saying that, yes. But I is not understanding.'

'What don't you understand?'

'Hunger is not for making that kind of anger.'

Giles lets go of the branch. 'I get angry when *I'm* hungry. But your father always chases me from the kitchen.' Clutching his belly, he staggers about till Edie giggles.

'You look stupid.' Willow sits down on the log with a thump.

Giles steps forward, but Fran holds out a hand and he turns away, jaw hard.

Edie rushes on. 'I is not meaning the hunger afore dinner, when you is gurgling in your guts. They is walking owt o' Scotland mony days wi'out food, isn't they?'

They all nod.

'That's making 'em weak as a bairn. I is seeing it last year, some o' the Stainmore folk coming tae beg in Brough when they isn't getting any flour. Like tae fall over, they was, not go rushing at folk wi' daggers.'

Fran thinks she is over-fond of Adam and will not believe what seems entirely possible to everyone else. 'He was a strong man. And his need was great. I don't see why he couldn't have lost his mind when the woman refused him.'

But Edie smiles, as if she's just tricked him. 'Then why is the Dickinsons not going for the food too, if they is that desperate? They isn't the kind tae shrink frae using their fists or their knives if there's summat they want. But they is saying they is just running away. That a bunch o' old men chased them.' Her hands chastise the air, leaving no doubt as to her disbelief.

Fran knows his heart has been shyly suggesting for some time that the story Wat and Rob told Sir Henry doesn't ring true, not in its most important details, at least. He has argued back that he can't know what a man might do in such circumstances, which is reasonable enough. But he has not faced up to the fact that the Dickinsons' story does nothing to explain what the revenant is doing in the fells above Warcop and why their father was killed. 'What are you saying, Edie?'

She shrugs, looks away, and Fran understands. She knows he has been remiss when he should have been bold. Just because the story they were given seemed to be the only one they could ever have, he should still have given it proper scrutiny. Of course, it's hard to believe the deformed creature that was once Adam Fothergill is honest. But Fran burns now with the desire to hear from the revenant's own mouth why he came back. And he is certain that, until he does, the evil lying so heavily upon them will grow and grow until they are swallowed up by it.

Fumbling in his pouch, he brings out pen and ink, a well-folded square of parchment. The others come closer, Giles and Willow trying to read what slowly emerges from his quill. Gathering his thoughts, he ponders what he really wishes to say, scratches out what little is already written. At last, the words form clearly. *Adam, I want to know what happened at Elsdon. It cannot be as the Dickinsons said. I will come back here on the day of the next full moon. Francis Hilton.*

Fran regrets his letter by the time they reach Hilton. But he doesn't know what else is to be done. Riding slowly down to Warcop alone with his doubts the next day, he also knows Will is unlikely to give him much comfort, expecting an exasperated interrogation as to why, by all that's holy, he thought it wise to hunt down the revenant again, even as he wishes the priest might release him from his agitation.

But it is Warcop that is in a turmoil, for the news is remarkable, of the kind to bring all and sundry out into the street to debate it. Even Michael is full of it when at last he opens Will's door, almost clapping his ruined hands and asking Fran if he is come to see the treasure.

Fran holds his tongue until he is seated and ale brought with painful attentiveness by the ancient servant. Even here bread is no longer served except with dinner, and then there is only enough to make you feel the need for more. Despite the dullness of the day and the smallness of the window, no candles are lit, so that darkness hangs around the edges of the room. But Will's embrace is warm, lingering, his smile a distillation of joy. 'I have not seen you for so long. I was beginning to think you were avoiding me.' He says it lightly, as if such a thing were clearly impossible, but there is a wariness in his eyes which holds it to be true.

Fran tries not to hang his head, knowing he has kept away for fear the priest would oppose contact with the revenant. He sits on the edge of his stool, unwilling to puncture this pleasant bubble with his confession. But he needs guidance.

Will picks up a quill, twists it in his hand. 'You have heard our news, then?'

Fran has no real desire to find out what is exciting Warcop, but he can see Will thinks it of some importance. 'Michael said something about a treasure. But we have heard nothing.'

Will laughs. 'What a hermit you are!' He puts down the quill. 'Your neighbour is not so ignorant. Thomas has come down three times in two days, though I imagine his wife has been the one trying to sniff out any advantage. She'll have her daughter pledged to Wat Dickinson's son quicker than you can snuff out a candle, even if the boy is only six years old and his father little more than a husbandman with a few fields to his name.'

'Wat Dickinson?'

'Well, Rob has only girls, so—'

'Will, you're speaking in riddles. Start at the beginning.'

'Forgive me. It is all we have been talking about this past week. Some of Jamie Dickinson's men were going to mend his hedges, as Wat and Rob had instructed them to do while they wait for the court to settle their father's affairs. Coming along the lane past his house, one of them noticed a pile of soil like a mole might leave beneath the hedge that goes round Jamie's garden. He probably would not have noticed it, but there was something shiny near the top. So he pushed away the soil and found a small heap of jewels and coins. He brought it straight to me.'

'A treasure, indeed! Does anyone know how it came there?'

Will shakes his head. 'I thought at first it must have been buried long ago and some creature had pushed it to the top. But the coins are from the reign of this king and the late one. If they were Jamie's, I cannot imagine him forgetting he had hidden a single one, never mind a handful. But perhaps it was someone else.'

'Do Wat and Rob know?'

'Yes. I sent word that day.'

'Will they come back?' Fran does not know what to think.

Will looks up, startled. 'They arrived last night under cover of darkness. They are not complete fools. They know what happened to their father.'

'They *are* fools, even for a good reason.' It would have been better for them all if Rob and Wat had stayed away.

And now Fran feels himself becoming entangled in this curious happening when all he wants is to ...

Will frowns. 'I had no choice but to tell them. In my opinion, the treasure is theirs and I do not want to keep it here any longer than I must. Everyone knows I have it.'

Fran nods, reassured. If they are here but for a short time, there can be little danger. He should not imagine that, if something needs to be done, he's the only one can do it. 'Do they stay somewhere safe?'

Will runs a hand through his hair. 'Not in their father's house, that is for certain. I thought it best they should stay at the manor. Henry is still away with Harclay, but I have organised the tenants to take turns looking out for anything untoward.' He throws Fran a rueful smile. 'Five of us will gather today to decide if the treasure is theirs or not. Once that is done, they can come here at nightfall to get it, and leave straight away, God willing.'

'Then I will stay here until they do.'

'Has something happened? I am glad you are here, but you seem ... Do you know any more than we did when Jamie was killed?'

Fran feels suddenly tired. And hungry. 'No.' That is the sad truth of it. 'But we tried to find Adam again.' He gives Will a sidewards glance.

Will shakes his head. 'And you think we are fools!'

'I knew you'd be angry.'

'I am not angry.'

'Then please listen. I need you to listen and tell me what you think.'

Will frowns, bringing his fingers to his lips. He nods.

Fran searches his mind for the right words to mould everything he has thought and learned into something that will fly straight and true. But he feels it's still a confusion. 'The story Rob and Wat told us. I think I believed it largely because it's the only story we have.' He searches his thoughts. 'And because Adam is now so ugly in looks as well as deeds, I couldn't imagine he might speak the truth.'

'No, indeed.'

'But I've been thinking . . .' He knows better than to mention Edie's part in all this. 'We have to understand why he's here, and he's the only one can tell us.' He thumps his fists onto his knees. 'And we must listen to what *he* says happened at Elsdon.'

Will says nothing, his face hidden behind the clasp of his hands. And then he removes them. 'You do not believe the Dickinsons' story?'

Fran sighs. 'It makes some sense in itself. But there's much it doesn't explain.'

Will sits back, hands in his lap, eyes blinking.

Fran knows there's nothing more to be said or done in this moment. It's enough that he's made Will stop and think, his words clearly requiring a weighty answer. Yet he still feels ill at ease, as if he's waiting for a blow to fall but can't see where it will come from. He wonders too if there will ever be an end to all this bloodshed and want and worry, for this is not a country for the weak of mind or body. And, yes, that is something to make them all feel shame, for did Jesus not say the meek will inherit the earth? And in that moment he's fiercely glad his father made him change his nature, a thought that burns him with the heresy of it.

Will goes to his gathering to decide on the fate of the treasure, returning satisfied that it does indeed belong to the Dickinsons. Fran doesn't wish to speak of the revenant or anything else unpleasant for the time being, so he suggests they play chess, something they have not done together for so long, neither of them can remember when. Will has inherited a set of bone chess pieces, well-worn but still intricately carved, said to have come from the baggage train of an ancient Scottish king who made the mistake of crossing the border and was vanquished by stalwart Englishmen in the days when stalwart Englishmen knew how to defend themselves.

They are so wrapped in the game that both are alarmed when the knock on the door finally comes. It's not yet dark, but the night is gathering the sky to it, a great beam of golden light falling through the window from beneath a rampart of dark cloud. The Dickinsons are in a hurry, grown anxious so far from the walls of Scaleby castle. Rob stretches out his hand for the pouch into which the treasure has been poured. He and Wat peer inside, bouncing off one another's heads in their eagerness. 'How much is it worth, d'you think, Father Warcop?' Rob pulls the cords together, holding the pouch tight within graceful fingers.

Will shrugs. 'The coins amount to some £23. As for the jewels, I could not say.'

Rob and Wat both nod. They make the room seem small, a cage they are eager to escape.

'Francis and I will accompany you as far as the Great Road. You will be safe then, since you are on horseback, and Adam . . . is not.' Will tugs at his cloak on the back of a chair.

They all nod vigorously, as if the more they agree, the greater the reassurance.

Fran takes a deep breath. 'We should go south across the bridge and then to Sandford before riding up to the Great Road. It would be less expected.'

''Tis further.' Wat's formidable hands beat insistently at his side.

Rob casts a smile at Fran. 'But better.'

Fran feels the unexpected warmth of Rob's gaze as if it were the proffering of a rose, but it is a fleeting, inadequate gift now. They follow Will's flickering candle down the stairs, slipping through the quiet kitchen and out of the back door. The stables are just across a narrow lane. Speaking boldly among themselves to keep up their spirits, they gather in the passageway between the stalls. Fran holds up the candle so Will might put on his saddle, for there's no time to wait for a groom. Then he turns to Wat, whose horse is ready. Wat tugs at the reins to lead him out.

Out of the darkness a demon flies. Wat screams, a terrified howl of pain. The candle falls and is extinguished. Fauvel jerks his head, and Fran must hold tight, but he cannot see what's happening. All he can hear is a great grunting and gasping. He lets go of the reins and pulls out his knife. 'Will!' His cry is shrill and frightened, but not for himself. The noise dies away to quick gasps of breath. Staggering out of the door, he's greeted by a feeble moon resting on the rooftop. He stands ready, arms outstretched, a furious sob tearing at his throat.

A ghastly shape appears in the doorway, knife in hand. Instantly Fran throws himself at him.

The revenant twists out of the way, seizing his wrist so he cannot use his own knife. 'Leave me be!' Adam can manage only a gasp, a plaintive command. The smell is overwhelming, as if a great sickness has risen up in human form to pollute the earth. But in the next instant Fran is thrown backwards. By the time he has scrambled to his feet, the revenant has been swallowed up by the darkness.

Bending over, he vomits a thin string of phlegm, quivering from top to bottom. Legs shaking, he staggers back into the house, shouting for Michael. At last, the servant finds him with his candlelight. 'What the devil, young master . . .'

'Give it to me.' Fran seizes the candlestick, throws himself out of the house and into the stables.

The first thing he sees is Wat lying on the ground, a great wound across his throat. He is most certainly dead. Frantic, Fran raises the candle, spies Rob face down. Beyond him, Will sits with his back against the end of one of the stalls, clutching his left side. Fran springs towards him. 'Do not mind me.' Will smiles wanly. 'See to him.' He nods at Rob. 'Though I think it is too late for him too.'

Fran puts the candlestick down, kneels so he can wrestle Rob onto his back. He feels the damp on his hands, smells the blood. Bending his head to Rob's chest, he is astonished by the distant rhythm still beating there, lets out a fierce cry. Throwing off his cloak, he begins to tear at his shirt.

A hand falls lightly on his. He looks down. Rob stares up at him, eyes shining with tears. The hand falls away. Fran is helpless, staring once more at Death, knowing it is futile to argue. He no longer thinks Rob sees him. Putting his head down again to his chest, he prays for a beat, however faint. But there is nothing. Fran takes Rob's head in his lap, rocks back and forth and lets the tears pour out of him for no good reason other than it is all that is left for him to do.

But at last he removes himself, crawls over to Will and wraps himself close around him. 'You are not hurt, then?'

'I do not know. I have been holding my side tight these past minutes, but I have not been able to look.'

'God's teeth, Will. You should have said.' Fran retrieves the candle. Together they gently pull away his tunic and shirt, reveal the taut, pale skin gathered round a sinuous river of red. It seeps blood but does not run very deep. 'We should not stay here.' He helps Will onto his feet, bids him hold tight to the stall while he ties Fauvel up again. Moving slowly past the two dead men, Will crosses himself, but Fran would rather not let go of the warm solidity of Will's body within his grip.

Depositing Will on a stool in the kitchen and the candle on the table, Fran attends to the fire so it is soon ablaze again. He brings the water bucket to the table, and Michael comes to the door, hovers there. 'Fetch wine,' Fran commands. 'But do not get in my way.'

He changes his mind. 'Michael, fetch me a clean shirt. I'll get the wine. Make sure it's clean, mind.' Michael shuffles off, wringing his hands. Fran finds a flagon of wine, pours them both a large measure. 'Drink that.'

Will leans back against the table but does as he's told. 'I was trying to stop him.'

'Adam?'

'Yes. I mean, I do not think he intended to strike me.'

'Well, he definitely meant to strike Wat and Rob.'

'Yes.' They sit in silence for a moment.

Fran laps up the wine, is eager for more. 'He had me in his grip. Outside. But he didn't strike me either. Told me to leave him be.'

'Sweet Jesu! We have both been saved tonight.'

'Saved? I think it's more he has no quarrel with us.'

They fall silent again, pondering a miracle that isn't, turning over the knowledge that the revenant will only kill by design.

Will looks up at Fran and smiles just a little.

Fran tries to smile back. 'You need to take your shirt off.'

Will struggles, unable to pull the linen up over his head. Fran stands over him, tugs it free, eyes drawn now to the bloody confusion stretched across the pale tautness of Will's stomach.

Michael returns, waving a clean white shirt. 'Will the master be well soon, sir?'

'I'm sure of it.' Fran tears off a ragged strip. 'Go to bed now.' He glances at Will, who nods. There's no need for anyone else to watch. Dipping the cloth in the cold water, Fran gives Will a rueful glance, for they both know this will hurt. Will closes his eyes. He moans a little, gritting his teeth as Fran gently cleans the blood away, red rivers meandering down to gather in the soft web of hairs at the top of Will's breeches. Fran moves the cloth down, over the gentle swell of Will's belly.

Will reaches out a hand. 'Let me do that.' He looks away.

Fran busies himself ripping up more strips of cloth.

At last, the wound emerges as an angry gash from just beneath the ribs to an inch or so below the navel.

'Do you have any herbs?' Fran strides over to shelves full of bottles and pots.

'There is some fresh mint in that one, near your right hand. Second top shelf. Fifth from the left.' Will is brisk, in command.

Fran gently sticks mint leaves along the gash, the blood on the lip of the wound holding them in place. Then he winds cloth strips round Will's body, trying hard to think clearly as his hands pass lightly across warm flesh. When he's finished, they sit close together, drinking their wine and wondering.

'Where should I put them?' Fran feels light-headed, but there's no one else to attend to the dead brothers.

Will shifts uncomfortably on his stool, winces. 'Leave them where they are, but cover them. I might ask John Burdon at Musgrave if he will attend to the funerals.'

Fran twirls the wine in his goblet round and round. 'Will, do you think we were played?'

'Played?'

'When I think on what happened, it all feels so inevitable, as if Adam was somehow making us do what he wanted.'

'But how could he have known those two had come back?'

Fran shakes his head. 'I don't know.' He gets to his feet. 'You should go to bed now. I will sleep on the floor, in case I touch you in sleep.'

'Hark at you!' Will tries to smother his smile. 'I will have to get better soon, or you will become far too accustomed to your mastery.'

Fran smiles. 'You never know. You might decide you like it.' Their eyes meet, trying to speak of fear and loss and something else even as their words skip away from such weighty matters.

Will puts both hands on the table to push himself up. He looks down on Fran. 'I am most grateful for all you have done tonight.'

'You would do the same for me.'

Will yawns. 'And I would be even more grateful if you could help me to my chamber.' He reaches out to clutch Fran's arm. 'But before we go, I have one last laurel to put in your crown.'

'Indeed! My head is swelling as it is.'

'I can see that.' Will's smile is grim. 'No, I was just thinking we have very little choice now. You must go and speak with the revenant. This must stop.'

Fran nods, adjusting his arm so it is wrapped around Will's good side. 'The only question is whether he will speak with me.'

'I will pray for it. I think, from all we have said already, that you are safe enough. But you must promise me you will take a proper retinue with you.'

'I promise.' Fran wonders if his little band of followers in any way constitutes a proper retinue. But he has no other and, in truth, does not wish for one.

Chapter 12

Adam Fothergill sits shrouded within one of Fran's blankets, coughing as if his lungs are determined to escape his chest. He seems entirely fragile, more of a wisp than anything else. Fran watches him carefully. In truth, he's disappointed this infernal creature should look so decrepit close up. But he knows what Adam is capable of.

He's grateful, though, that the revenant's face is largely hidden, either by the blanket or the bird's nest of his hair. Raw red and ridged, the skin on his face is a potent reminder of his demonic half-life, for Death will ultimately prevail. The only question is how long it will take.

Fran glances over at Giles and Willow standing in the trees, out of sight unless Adam turns his head some distance. Giles grips the pommel of his sword tightly, but Fran told them they must draw their weapons only if they're sure violence is threatened.

Edie, sitting just behind Fran, is entirely compassed by Adam's gaze. She keeps her own eyes absorbed on the ground, busying herself with pulling up various herbs and flowers, examining them closely. Fran is unsure whether she plays a part or is able – unlike the rest of them – to detach herself from the reason for their being back at Arnside Rake. It matters not. He must turn his whole attention on this conversation, for he cannot imagine he will wish to repeat it.

Adam twitches, rubbing his nose most gently, as if his face is a trial to him.

Edie looks up. 'Is you needing summat for that, sir?'

He stares at her, blinks. Fran is unsure whether he's angry or just astonished. 'That is a hard question to answer, young Edie. Perhaps we might come back to it?'

She nods, lowers her head again.

Adam sighs deeply, turns his red-rimmed eyes, sunk deep within great puffs of skin, on Fran. 'You keep bad company, Master Francis.'

'If you mean the Dickinsons, it was not by choice.'

Adam grunts.

'But I meant what I said. About Elsdon.'

'What if I don't believe you? What if I think you said that just to get me to come here?' There's menace in the soft words.

Fran doesn't let his gaze leave Adam's. 'If I'm come here to listen, what does it matter?'

'That won't do.' Adam shifts in his seat, and Willow's hand moves to his sword.

'Very well. I don't believe what the Dickinsons said happened at Elsdon can be the whole truth.'

'And why is that?' Adam doesn't move a muscle but

somehow those four words seem to hang above an abyss.

In that moment, Fran thinks this must be what Hell is. The struggle to do good even as evil goes unpunished all around you. He can scarcely keep his gaze on Adam's, for fear his bewilderment will overwhelm him. But he knows he must speak. 'If what Rob and Wat said is true, you can have no reason to kill them, let alone their father. So what they said cannot be true.' He blinks, amazed to have come to this conclusion, so firm and clear. But then a cloud comes over his mind, blackening his thoughts. 'Unless . . . I know so little about revenants. Perhaps, when you die, you do not think as you might have done when you were . . .'

Adam laughs almost merrily, until the coughing overtakes him again. He wipes his mouth. 'There is that, I suppose.'

Fran is becoming most agitated by all this prevarication, the way the revenant turns every question aside as if it were swordplay. 'For pity's sake, Adam. I want to know what happened! Either tell me or I shall depart.'

A potent silence falls on them all. Edie stops plucking at her herbs. Willow steps out of the trees, thinks better of it, stays where he is.

'I see.' Adam pulls his blanket tighter. 'In that case, I'd better tell you. I would hate to think you came all this way for nothing.'

You need not mock me. Fran grips his hands tight together.

Adam lets out a long, shuddering breath. 'Tell me what those devils said, exactly?'

Fran looks up, sees that all traces of incivility are flown away. He casts about for an answer. 'I would rather . . . If I don't tell you then I will know which parts match together and which parts don't.'

'And the parts that don't? What will you do with them?' Adam leans towards Fran, eager now to guide their talk onward.

'As I said, I couldn't find the sense in your actions if what was supposed to have happened was true. I can only hope you have a better story.'

Adam smiles, but now there is no mirth. 'I have a much better one, never fear. Though you still might not like it. I am none too fond of it myself.' And to Fran's astonishment, great sobs rock Adam like waves crashing ashore. Edie rises, crouches beside him, shushing him as if he were a baby. Willow steps forward.

'Keep them away.' The words are not harshly said. Adam dabs at his face. Edie jerks her head at Willow, directing him back to Giles as she settles herself next to the revenant. Willow scowls, looks at Fran, who nods.

Adam struggles to free a hand from his blanket, but finally he picks up a strand of her hair, wraps it round a finger just as scarred and abhorrent as his face. 'I'm glad to see you again, Edie. You always were a lovely girl. My Joanie was fond of you too, do you remember?'

Edie nods. 'I is wishing you is both not dead, sir.'

'There are worse things, believe me.'

Fran thinks he's going mad, he's so far adrift from his native shores. But he doesn't think it will help if he chides Adam again.

Adam looks up, beyond Fran's face, into the heavens above the dark swaying of the trees. He speaks now as if in a trance, as if something or someone speaks through him. Yet it is Adam's voice, strong and clear. 'I was with some Yorkshire folk after the battle, but they left me at the border to go a different route. That was fine with me. I wasn't so far from home. Maybe I was more foolish than I should've been. I don't know. It's easy to think of that afterwards, and I've had plenty time for thinking.' He brings both hands to his forehead, kneads it as if he's in pain.

'I met the Dickinsons the day we came to Elsdon, somewhere up on the moor. If I'd seen them before they saw me, I might have saved us all a lot of trouble by keeping myself hidden. But Wat spotted me. He seemed glad I was still alive. I'd often wondered if he was less of a toad than his father and brother.' He lowers his eyes until they meet Fran's. 'But I was wrong.' He flicks his eyes away again.

'Rob didn't say much. I'm sure he wasn't happy about me being there. He took on his father's quarrel like it was his own. But he wasn't himself then, sitting and staring at nothing. I gave them some of my ale and they were happy enough. They only had water and were sore afraid of catching something. We moved on together. None of us knew about Elsdon castle, that it wasn't lived in anymore. But we saw it soon enough, the timbers fallen down and the fire in the courtyard. We weren't foolish, though. We'd seen broken men moving round the moor, so we knew we shouldn't march straight in. But it was just old men. And the woman.' He closes his eyes.

Fran feels himself grow tight over the entirety of his body. He walks across a high moor, sees the jagged outline of a castle in the far distance, a great shadow of walls, the fire within a beacon in the gathering darkness. It should have been a sanctuary.

Adam keeps his eyes closed, voice little more than a murmur in the trees, hard to hear but Fran is nothing but ears. 'They were roasting a deer. The devil knows where they got it from. Probably found it, for they had nothing to hunt it with.' He shakes his head. 'We were pulled in by the smell. It got into our guts and turned them over, so we were all a-tremble. I remember thinking they had more than enough, that they wouldn't mind sharing it.'

'Did they?'

'They were scared when we first came in, flocking together, the woman at the back. But I put down my knife and told them we meant no harm. I thought the others would do the same, but they must've just put them away. It's something else I've thought about all these weeks. Why did I put my knife down and forget where I'd put it? But it's done now. Only fools think anything'll change if they keep chewing over the past.'

Fran knows he's entering another country now. But he must let the story unfold slowly, so he can remember it and lay it against the other. 'How many of them were there?'

Adam still has his eyes shut. 'Two old men. The woman and the baby.'

'Is that all? I thought there was a multitude.'

''Twas enough to be dying.' It is a rebuke.

'Yes. Of course.'

'If you would stay quiet, Master Francis, I will be the quicker telling it.' Now Adam does look at him, gaze molten.

Fran nods, in thrall to the story.

'They passed us some meat and we ate with our hands as if we were beasts. I don't need to tell you how good it was. The old men said they were father and father-in-law to the woman. Between the Scots and bad harvests, they'd nothing left to pay their rent, so they'd gone up on to the moors. Her husband had been with our army and wasn't home yet. I think we gave her hope he might yet come back.' He stops, hand over his mouth, wondering.

Fran can scarcely breathe, but there's nothing to be said. Edie is crying without shame, but what does it matter?

'I fell asleep. Maybe those devils did too. When I woke, Rob was sitting next to the woman. She was trying to feed her baby, but he had his hand on her bare shoulder, whispering in her ear. She tried to shrug him away. The old men gathered round them, begging him to leave her alone. He just laughed. But then he saw me watching. He got up then, went back to sit next to Wat. But he wasn't done – he was waiting till we all lay down. I couldn't sleep. Just lay there, looking at the stars and wishing I was home. I watched him get up. I thought he was going for a piss. He disappeared anyway, away from the light of the fire. But when he came back, he went over to the woman. I could see her begin to struggle. I sat up. That's when I remembered I didn't have my knife. I looked around for it, but that was foolish, it being dark except near the fire.' Once more he falls into silence.

He bows his head. 'It all happened so fast. The baby woke up, started crying. Rob seized him with both hands and shook him hard, let him fall to the ground. And he was pushing the woman down and she was fighting him, and I was running over. He let her be then, but she started screaming because her baby was dead, snatched it up and held the corpse out to him and he turned and came at her, just one thrust of his knife and she was gone, and he was turning to the rest of us, a snarl on his face. I told him to put the knife down and Wat was there, by his side, the old men stumbling awake and crying at him for what he'd done, and Rob killed one and Wat the other. That only left me.'

He stops, out of breath, coughs, on and on. Licks dry lips. 'Wat put his hand on Rob's arm, said something. But Rob shook his head. I was the only one could tell the story. I knew they knew that. It was Wat came for me, and I ran from him, and he thrust at me with his knife, caught me on the arm, but it was like the blow filled me with a great demon and I ran hither and thither so fast he couldn't get near me. So he threw a rock at my head from behind, and I don't remember anything until later.' Once more the tears run down his face, and Edie clings to him, so they are become a great waterfall, the two of them.

'So you didn't die from the blow to the head?'

Adam sniffs, snorts. 'No. Do you wish I had?'

'Only time will tell.'

'You don't believe me?' Adam looks too exhausted to fight anyone now.

Fran looks away. 'It's a much better story.' A terrible story.

'It's not finished yet.' Adam strokes Edie's hair. 'When I woke up, I was lying in the middle of the courtyard, next to the fire. The others, the dead, were lying on top of me, so I could hardly see or breathe. I wanted to scream, but I knew better than to let them know I wasn't dead too.' His words begin to drag, as if reluctant now to go on any further. 'The child lay next to me, his little hand resting on my cheek, curled up as if he slept. I hoped his mother was nearby. I couldn't bear to think she wasn't.'

He pulls out a long stammering breath. 'But those devils were still busy, pulling bits of timber on to the fire so that I could feel this terrible heat coming closer and closer. I knew I'd have to take my chances with them or I'd be burned up. And then I heard Wat yell at Rob to get going before the whole place went up in flames, so I started to roll away and a piece of timber fell down on me like a flaming arrow. I don't remember it hitting me. I just remember the burning.'

His eyes are shut again, the words coming with such reverence. 'The pain was a living thing, everywhere at the same time. My clothes, my hair, everything was fire. *I* was fire. It would have consumed me, but there was a bucket of water they'd drawn up from the well and I came up against it and it fell over me so I hissed and spat, but the flames were destroyed. The pain was still in me, but I knew I shouldn't stay because of the fire.'

He opens his eyes. 'I couldn't understand how I was still alive, but I've come to believe the Lord saved me to exact His vengeance.' He looks up, straight at Fran. 'And my own.'

Fran says nothing. It's too hard a thing to judge.

'And He told me to crawl outside, into the cool grass, and took me into His arms and watched over me while I slept. And then the day was upon me, and I could see the skin all mangled on my arms and knew it was the same on my face, all of this side.' He draws a hand down the length of him.

'I will confess it, I was not worthy of the Lord's protection, for I didn't want to live. But He is wise and told me I needed to attend to the dead. And that was when it came upon me so I've not been able to think of anything else, looking at that charred flesh, no better than the venison we'd eaten: I vowed then I wouldn't rest until those devils were dead, and I swear the Lord gave me strength in my anger so I could dig deep into the earth and put those poor innocents to rest together in the shade of a sycamore tree. I slept again, I don't know how long, and then I walked down out of the moors the long miles to Hexham where the monks tended to me. Though I think they thought they'd soon have a corpse on their hands.'

Fran feels something shift in his mind, an understanding buried there finally released. 'You're not dead.' It's not a question. 'Of course you're not.'

Edie raises her head, stares at Adam with bewilderment and joy. Giles and Willow come close, crouching beside Fran, wan-faced, restless.

Adam gently dabs at his face with the blanket, wiping away the tears. 'No. I'm not dead. Not yet.'

'But you—'

'It pleased me for you all to think I was a revenant. I wanted to put the fear of God into those devils. I thought I could make them confess, because I was come back to haunt them, and they would be punished by their own confessions.'

Fran springs to his feet, pacing around, trying to wrestle all this horror into something he can live with. He thinks back through everything that has happened these past months so he might weave it into a different pattern. And then he stops, suddenly dismayed. 'You didn't know they were telling another story, did you, the one that blamed you, until I came to King's Pot that first time?'

Adam nods as Edie gasps.

Fran kicks the ground, groans. 'Did I say something about Jamie Dickinson too?'

'That you did. But you need not take the burden on your shoulders. I would have found out they had slandered me beyond belief and that he stood by them, encouraged them, the knave.'

'But how have you survived up here? You need food. It's not possible.'

'I've lived only to do what I have done. And there is food enough up here.'

'Even so.'

'I have money. A treasure I buried before I left for Scotland. I never imagined I'd use it for such things, but I will not take the blame for that.'

Fran sits down, buries his head in his hands. 'I cannot compass all this. It is evil beyond belief.'

Edie goes to bury her face in Willow's chest and, for

once, he holds her close. Giles edges closer to Fran. Feeling the squire's body beside him, Fran wishes it were Will.

Adam begins to cough again, as if he cannot hold it back any longer. He is truly become a shadow of a man, no longer either revenant or living being, a walking corpse. But he has an urgent question. 'Do you believe me?'

Fran draws his hands down his face. 'I want to. But there is no one left to gainsay it. And you have had a long time to stitch your story together.'

'There are those who would tell my story. But we must go far from here.'

'Where?'

'To Elsdon. And you will see with your own eyes.'

Fran nods slowly. 'Till then you must stay at Hilton. It would do you good to have a proper bed and better food. Just for a few days till we're ready to go north.'

But Adam is entirely unmoved by the idea. 'This is my home now. I'm not fit for anywhere else.'

'But you have suffered so much and wholly innocent.' Fran feels the injury most keenly, a part of him still flitting through the corrupted shell of Elsdon castle.

'I'm not innocent now, am I?'

Fran hides. The water was too hot to begin with, but now it's so pleasant, it feels as if she's melting into it. If she sits with her arms curled around her knees, the sides of the wooden tub become her battlements, and even Sarah – bustling about, noisy and oblivious as always – can scarcely see her.

She rests her mind for a moment on her mother, wonders whether they would have been friends if Christian Kirkbride had been allowed to keep her daughter. Christian has written again, this time with nothing in particular to tell. The weather is no better in Scotland. She has suffered from a rheum these past weeks that disturbs her sleep and will not leave her. She wishes Fran was with her, to give advice, for she doesn't know if she should marry again. There's no one in particular. But now she's settled with a portion of her father's land, it's something she's begun to think about. She craves a reply to her letters, to hear something of life at Hilton, of what Fran has been doing.

There was something plaintive in her words, a suggestion woven through them that she misses what she's left behind, misses Fran. This was shocking. Her mother always seemed so little concerned with the stirring up of feelings, preferring to push them away so all might proceed calmly on the surface. Fran found herself wishing they might start over, begin to know each other without pretense. But that's all she ever wants. She wrote back this time, though there was so much not to be said.

She wishes she could stay here forever, warm and out of sight. She wishes she'd never heard the story Adam Fothergill told them, never thought to leave her own hearth, to lead them all in a dance of death. The water cleanses, but does not remove the stain of such wickedness. Only unknowing can do that.

Does she believe Adam? And, if she does, is that belief to be trusted? Not so long ago, she had faith in Rob and Wat's simple story that portrayed the revenant as a monster. She had looked Adam in the face, that first time up on Roman Fell, and found him monstrous, is the truth of it.

But she knows that looks deceive.

Moving her hands, she lets the water dance through her fingers. What foolishness it is to believe you can control anything. Yet that is what men believe; what Fran believes when he thinks it will satisfy him to chase after the truth. But what use is the truth when it reveals a world so full of folly, any act of compassion or decency is no more than a piss in the wind?

Cupping the water in both hands, she splashes it over her face, her hair, feels it drip wantonly onto her breasts. They seem so unnatural, those exuberant accumulations of flesh, that every time she bathes or on the few occasions she bids Sarah dress her in women's garb, she cannot help but squeeze and prod, anxious to own her own flesh. And still she is astonished. But this time she is only dismayed, afflicted by a vision of the woman at Elsdon feeding her child.

The water is cooling now, the wind's chill breath whipping through the window frame, settling on her skin to disquiet her. She knows it is an indulgence, all this searching for answers. It matters not which clothes she wears.

Fran hastens down to Warcop two days later. He would like to have gone sooner, but there's much to do with the approach of Michaelmas, when rents will be paid and the last of their beasts brought down. Harry Sowerby has been wringing his hands for weeks already, worrying about how benevolent they can afford to be when Fran's tenants come – as they surely will in such a dismal year – asking for deductions on their rents because of the disease among their beasts and the poor grass. Fran looks at the rough figures Harry brings to him and sighs.

He's glad to escape the sitting and the worrying. Giles rides eagerly alongside, but Fran's mind is wholly fixed on Will now. He wants to see for himself there are no ill effects from the knife wound, but he's also most impatient to know how the priest will judge Adam Fothergill's revelations.

As they begin the descent towards Warcop, Fran's mind leaps from one thought to another, without alighting for long on any particular one. Mercifully, Giles is mostly content to leave him to his thoughts – in that, he is much improved. But, from time to time, the squire bursts into solemn reflections on their adventures: 'I would never have believed it if I hadn't heard it with my own ears;' 'I did wonder about those Dickinson brothers, if they were telling the truth.' Or excited questions laced with fear: 'Do you suppose there'll be vagabonds at Elsdon now?' 'What do you think the bodies will look like after all this time?'

These are not thoughts that had occurred to Fran, but only because his mind is already too crowded. He tries to answer as best he can, unwilling as yet to tell Giles he won't be coming with them.

He finds Will in need of visitors who will neither gawp (though Giles is still capable of that) nor make demands the priest is unable to carry out. Egidia Crackenthorpe, for one, finally decided she could not entrust their business entirely to her husband, endeavouring to discover to whom the treasure now belonged if the deceased Dickinsons were guilty – as was rumoured up and down the Eden valley – of a most terrible, if as yet unspecified, crime.

'Mistress Crackenthorpe ...' Will tried to keep the astonishment out of his voice. 'We do not even know where the treasure is, never mind—'

'Then that is something else to be remedied as soon as possible.' She said it in such a way that the priest was left in no doubt she had a long list of things in which he was remiss. He wanted to tell her to hold her tongue as it was none of her damn business, but had not the stomach for the consequences in his weakened state.

Fran tells himself not to allow Giles to tax Will with too much idle chatter, though he's inclined to allow his squire a little crowing. And then, though there's scarcely any bitterness or reproaches between them, he hopes to think of a reason to send Giles away. Fran tells himself this is merely so he can talk freely with Will about all the things that have been troubling him.

He fights the urge to push Michael out of the way so he might reach Will's study without delay. But when they enter the chamber and Will turns to look up at him from his couch with a look of joy on his face, Fran finds himself in such disorder he can scarcely speak. He tells himself it matters not what he feels, for he is well used to suffocating all desire as soon as it threatens to become more than an urgent flame quickly spent. But he blushes, all the same.

Will reaches up to embrace him, smiling as if a long dearth of happiness has finally come to an end. 'The hero is returned.'

Fran settles himself on the stool. 'Heroes. I didn't go alone. I promised you.' He means to speak lightly, but worries he sounds fretful. He tries to imagine they're what they've always been, old friends, fraternal in love and affection.

But Will is in no way discomfited, turning merrily to Giles. 'Forgive me! There has been much talk, of course, but it is all so confused in the telling that I have grown weary of not knowing the truth. And now here you are to ease my mind.'

The truth. There it is again, so full of promise, so unequal to the task. Fran beckons to Giles to come and sit on the floor beside them. 'You tell it.'

Giles gives him a radiant look before becoming very solemn. He begins hesitantly but is soon using both hands to summon up the horror and the turmoil so that Fran is once more at Elsdon and this time Will is there too.

Will asks questions, stopping the flow of words when he's unsure. Sometimes Fran answers, but mostly he does not. At last, Giles falls into silence. They all do.

Will lies back on his couch. He shakes his head. 'I never imagined I would hear of such things.' He turns back to Giles. 'That was well told. If you go to the kitchen, tell Martha to give you something to eat and drink. You will need it, I imagine.'

Giles is so pleased with himself he has no inkling he's being got rid of.

The door closes. Fran stands up, moves towards the

window, pretends to look out. 'How is your wound?'

'Tolerable.'

Fran cannot stop himself from turning back. 'No infection?'

Will shakes his head. 'You need not worry. I will recover perfectly. It will just take time.'

Fran nods.

'So Adam is no revenant, and you believe what he says?'

Fran sighs, is drawn to sit back down, to rest his head against the couch. 'He has promised to take me to Elsdon so I might see for myself.' He rubs the smooth skin beneath his chin. 'He says there's something there he can show me that will prove the matter of his innocence beyond all doubt.'

'What on God's earth might that be?' Will lays a hand for a moment on Fran's hair.

Fran closes his eyes, feels the flame flicker, grow stronger. He blows it out, lifting his head out of Will's reach. 'I don't know. He wouldn't tell me.'

Will shifts uncomfortably, tries to sit up. His hand lies close to Fran's arm, but he doesn't move it any further. 'That is most suspicious.'

'Perhaps.' Fran breathes deeply. 'I did try most earnestly to persuade him to tell me, but he said it was too monstrous to speak of until he absolutely must.'

They sit in silence for several moments. 'I can only put my trust in him.' Fran stares gloomily at the fire. 'Anyway, it's in his interest to find something, or else he has nothing to convince a judge and jury that he had good reason to do what he did.'

Will thrusts both hands through his hair. 'Perhaps it's . . .' He struggles again to sit up.

Fran looks around for a cushion, leaps across to the chair by the fire to retrieve one. Holding Will by the shoulder, he gently pushes him forward so he can slide the cushion behind him. For a moment, everything is as it was, when they were young and their world was small, easily contained.

Will's eyes are bright. 'Did you not say that Adam carried the bodies out of the courtyard and buried them under a tree?'

'Yes. A sycamore.' Fran is not sure where this is heading.

But now Will shakes his head, shrinking back into the cushion. 'Forgive me, I am being foolish.'

'What were you going to say?'

Will twists his face. 'So you can laugh at me?'

'No! You know I am here for your help.'

'I was going to say that, if the Dickinsons were right, Adam would have been dead when he buried them . . .' Will shakes his head. 'I am tying myself in knots. I thought a revenant would not be able to dig a grave, but look what he did to Jamie Dickinson. And he was not dead anyway. Though it makes little sense to kill them the way he did and then feel enough charity to bury them.'

'I suppose he could have wanted to make amends when he woke up from the fire and saw what he'd done.' Fran sighs. Up on the fells he believed Adam without a shadow of a doubt. He still believes him. He just has to convince everyone else.

'When will you go?'

Fran looks away. 'Tomorrow. If it must be done, we should do it quickly.'

'And how many of you will go?'

'Just the two of us.'

'No!'

'I'm sorry, Will, but I've no coin to spare to take even Giles. We'll be careful, I promise you.'

Will stretches out a hand, lays it gently on his shoulder. 'It is not your fault what you uncovered was so ...' He sighs.

Fran resists the urge to lay his cheek on that hand. He forces his mind back on to Adam Fothergill. He prays with all his heart that whatever Adam intends to find is still there and that it will be enough in the eyes of the law to save him from the hangman.

Will turns his head away, laying an arm along the back of the couch. 'You are sure it is worth going all that way?'

'I hope so.' Fran knows he must see this journey through to its end.

Will nods slowly.

'And when we return, I'll hand Adam over to Sir Henry. If you could speak with him, ask him to show mercy. If that's possible ...?'

'Will you tell Adam that?'

'I don't know. He might suspect anyway.' Fran still has a terrible feeling nothing good will come out of their journey. Or is it just that, when they return, their adventures will be over and there will be nothing between him and the rest of his life?

———— ⊗≋⊗ ————

They arrive at Hexham as the light bleeds away, the priory's great towers rising out of the shadows to greet them. They're exhausted, but the monks who cared for Adam all those months ago are overjoyed to see him, welcoming Fran too with open arms. Adam has been transformed now into a gaunt gentleman in as good a set of clothes as Fran could find in his father's chest. But only once the priory's great door is pushed shut behind them does Adam remove the hood he has kept low over his face to hide its hideousness.

Brother Ralph hovers, debating with Brothers William and Edwin as to whether Adam should be taken immediately to the infirmary. But the cellarer, Brother Philip, shoos them away, bidding the visitors follow him. The monk hurries off, habit swaying, candle held high, leading them through the cloisters and into the dining room. The abbey has suffered much from the depredations of the heathen Scots, so that some of the outer buildings stand in a confusion of burnt timbers. The dining room itself is thankfully complete, though the smell of burning lingers even now, causing Adam to tremble when he first entered the priory.

They need no second bidding to dip their bread in a broth of duck with beans as a host of monks tiptoe quietly in and wait for them to finish. Once they have put down their spoons, Brother Philip brings over a little more wine. He sits down opposite Adam, the others flocking to join them. Even Brother Robert, the prior, hobbles in, scattering his monks until he has been found a comfortable place to sit near the fire, for he is not young in years and has seen much to make his hair turn a downy white.

Fran thinks that Will would have found much solace here, wonders if the priest thinks of them, of him. He feels the long day's ride settling into his bones, less insistent now that he's sitting here in the warmth, listening to the monks ply Adam with questions. But he's surprised that Adam offers them nothing but the truth in return. Fran watches the monks grow troubled, crossing themselves, staring hard at the scratches on the table, bringing hands to mouths or foreheads. He himself feels the appalling strangeness of the story once more and is filled with a dread that is the more wounding for being slow to fall upon him. Tomorrow, all he has heard and imagined will be made real. He takes a sip of wine, savouring its dense sweetness.

The prior, whose head had fallen on to his chest so that Fran is certain he sleeps, suddenly turns eyes like dark coals on Adam, beckoning him over. Adam hesitates, though not out of anxiety or shame, for his gaze is steady, thoughtful. At last he rises, walking like an old man afflicted with numerous aches and pains. He kneels before the prior.

Brother Robert looks him full in the face, but Adam is not perturbed. The prior sits back. 'Do you wish for forgiveness?'

Adam shakes his head. 'I would need to repent of what I did, and I do not. I know what I have done is unforgiveable. But I also believe God knows my heart and, though He must judge me harshly, He will understand.'

Brother Robert smiles, giving a childish look to his decrepit face. 'That is a good answer. You are an honest man, Adam.'

Adam nods.

'We shall add you to our prayers.'

'I thank you. I have already made arrangements for you to receive a small sum each year when I die.'

The prior raises his hand as if in benediction, thinks the better of it.

Fran has not considered the state of Adam's immortal soul before, but now he wonders if Adam weighed up the consequences of his actions before he came back for vengeance. Fran has the feeling it would have made no difference. But now? Perhaps he will spend the rest of his life atoning for the deaths of the three Dickinsons and God might well have reason to judge him less harshly. It's a comforting thought and Fran clings to it, for he's growing fond of Adam.

At last, Brothers Ralph, William and Edwin swoop down, bidding Adam come with them so they might put more unguent on his injuries from the fire. Adam smiles, protests it's too late now, but they bustle him out of the room with unyielding tenderness. Fran feels himself grow drowsy, leaning one elbow on the table. A young monk comes to his side, guides him to the visitors' dormitory. Sleep comes to him as soon as his head reaches the pillow, his dreams passing unremarked through the long night and the rising of the monks for the divine offices. He wakes, head filled with the velvet lethargy of a good sleep, fleetingly uncertain where he is or what it is he's about to do.

———◁∞∞▷———

Adam is grown quiet as they ride towards Elsdon. Sometimes Fran thinks he weeps, but it's impossible to be sure what passes beneath the hood. He would rather they spoke together, to pass the time and keep him from his own dark thoughts. He wonders out loud how Adam knew with such certainty that Rob and Wat would come back to Warcop to claim the treasure. But Adam doesn't want to speak about the ones he calls devils, gives him a look that says only a fool would imagine them doing anything else. All he will say is, he took the treasure back when he killed them.

Fran is unsure if that is just. 'I suppose it was your treasure to begin with.' Adam says nothing and he takes that as affirmation. 'But if you won't tell me about that, at least help me understand how you fooled Jamie Dickinson into meeting you alone. That's what you did, isn't it?'

Adam takes in a long shuddering breath. 'I suppose you cannot work that out by yourself, and I wouldn't want to perplex you for all eternity. You're right. I needed to get him out of the way of everyone else and to a place where I could surprise him. I didn't think I could best him in a straight fight, not a great ape like Jamie Dickinson.'

'I heard it was something to do with his feud with Simon Harrison.'

'Aye, another feud. It's a wonder anyone spoke to that man, never mind did business with him. But they did. There's more fools in England these days than sparrows.' He falls deep into thought once more and Fran waits impatiently. But at last Adam coughs fit to bring up his lungs, continues his story. 'I spent most of my time hiding around Warcop, to see what I could find out and use. That's how I learned about Jamie and Simon Harrison. I'd hoped there'd be a woman to lure him up on to the fells, but that was one vice he didn't have. So Simon it had to be.'

'But he surely wouldn't go alone to meet a man sworn to be his enemy?'

'You'd think so, wouldn't you? But not Jamie. And especially not if he thought that enemy had weakened. Simon was hoping to inherit some land from his wife's cousin over at Cockermouth. But he'd need to ride over there to pursue it in court. I spent an age thinking how that might work for me. You've got to keep these things simple, see.'

Fran considers protesting he has no need of such deceitful practices, but keeps his mouth shut.

'So I thought if I pretended to be Simon and let Jamie know the court case over at Cockermouth was likely to be at the same time as the one here, and I – Simon, that is – wanted to come to some arrangement, that would do it. Maybe. I wasn't sure. But, if not, I'd think of something else. It was only a tiny portion of a meadow they were arguing over, the one almost as bad as the other.'

'But how did you get him to believe you were Simon?'

'Oh, I couldn't have managed that. But I didn't have to. All I needed was a fool eager for coin to carry a message, and there's plenty of those around. I had to watch Simon for days, till I saw him go out on his horse, wife behind.

Then I hid near his gate with my hood up till I spied one of the herds Jamie sometimes uses, told him I had a bad rheum so he shouldn't get too close. This one wasn't quite as much of a dolt as the others, so I knew the message would get to Jamie without too much loss.'

'But what did you say to get him to come up on to the fells? There was no good reason for that.'

'And I'd say it wasn't a good reason, but good enough. I said Simon felt the shame of his capitulation and only wanted to discuss it where no one could overhear them. I wouldn't have been surprised if Jamie didn't come, but in truth, I thought his greed would get the better of him. And it did.' He says it grimly, but with a certain satisfaction. 'I had a horse I'd taken from the sheriff's stables to bring him down, in case you were wondering.'

'I was. You knew Jamie well.'

Adam gives Fran a sharp look.

'I mean you are good at judging men.'

Adam looks away. 'If I was that good, I wouldn't have gone to Elsdon with those devils in the first place, now would I?'

Fran knows this moment will soon pass, that he might not get the chance to ask this again. 'But if I might say so, I'm not sure Jamie Dickinson deserved to die.'

'Because he didn't draw his dagger at Elsdon?'

Fran nods.

'He didn't need to. He killed the truth so there could be no justice. Not for the people his sons butchered. And not for me. He treated our lives as if they were no more than thistledown on the wind. And he made you all believe I was capable of ...' Adam punches his thigh. 'That's why Jamie Dickinson deserved to die a thousand times.' Once more he falls back into silence.

Fran ponders those stern words, wonders if Adam has always been so attached to the truth. Like a beacon on a hill, it lights his way, with no room for error or ambiguity. It is what Fran finds so comforting, so admirable. But he himself has not found the truth to be so good a friend.

The road they follow is better than Fran had imagined, firm beneath their horse's feet for all it passes up and down mile upon mile of moorland. The monks at Hexham said this road was built by the Romans, whose great empire stretched across the known world. Fran tries to imagine that ancient army marching through the north of England, wonders if they are fated to suffer invasion until the end of time. Rain threatens from the west, great black clouds covering the sky. A buzzard passes overhead, its cry full of sorrow. Fran thinks it ominous. He says so to Adam.

Adam sighs. And then he turns stiffly, pushing back his hood a little. 'There's nothing for you to worry about, Francis.'

'I know.' They pass on in silence for a few moments. 'You're certain we'll reach Elsdon before nightfall?'

'I'm not certain. I was on foot last time, and I can't remember much of it anyway. But I think so. You can ask at the next house, if you want.'

Fran shakes his head. And it strikes him with a surge of credulous hope that perhaps Adam might better throw himself on the mercy of Sir Roger Clifford's court if he vowed to become a monk. It would surely be more pleasing to God than seeking pardon by serving in the king's army. 'They seem to love you.'

'Who?'

'The monks in the priory.'

'Perhaps. But I think they love the work they did on me more.'

'Oh, I don't know.'

Adam laughs gently, before being overtaken by coughing. At last it subsides. 'Do you think I should join them?'

Fran shrugs, a little discomfited at being so easy to read. 'It's not for me to say.'

Adam raises his head to the distant horizon. 'I have thought of it. But if God knew my heart when I killed those devils, He'd know I was serving Him for the wrong reasons. For me, not Him.'

'Would it matter? You might grow into such a life.'

'I don't think so. I have an unruly spirit. These months in the fells, when I had no one to answer to but myself, have only fed it.' He shakes his head, as if dismissing the idea for all time, and sets himself to examining the horizon attentively again. 'I remember that wood over there. I don't think we're too far from Elsdon now.'

Fran swallows, tells himself he has nothing to fear from the long dead, though a part of him does think that, even if Adam was no revenant, those poor souls have every reason to come back and haunt the place where they died so horribly.

They ride on in silence. Fran is impatient now but dare not risk pushing Fauvel any faster. They seem to have come to a great high wilderness, many of the houses up here burnt to a few timbers by the Scots, their inhabitants long gone to the surrounding villages and towns where they might find work, if they're lucky, or beg if not.

Adam turns to him. 'That's Elsdon over there.' He gestures to a gathering of houses around a squat, handsome church. 'There's no one there.' And indeed there is a forsaken feel to this place too, as if a great breath has been sucked in and not yet blown out. There are not so many hours of daylight left, certainly, but instead of neighbours talking idly as they shake off the day's toil, the streets have nothing to say. They ride past houses in a state of mean repair, the only signs of life the restless warbling of birds.

Fran has no desire to linger, encouraging Fauvel into a trot. They come round the side of the church, where Adam stops, ties his horse to a tree. Fran does the same, not sure yet where they're going.

Without a word, Adam takes off his hood and together they walk further up the road before turning right. Immediately they're confronted by a great mound, as if some giant lies buried beneath the sward. Fran hastens up it, scattering a host of rabbits scurrying about the holes won out of the soil. Reaching the top, he looks down to see Adam struggle for breath, no longer the man who strode across the fells so easily that he seemed to be in two places at once.

Fran turns away, surveys a scene he has imagined many times. The top of the mound is not so very broad, the tower that once stood there reduced now to a low wall surrounded by a tumble of stone. They soon stand in the courtyard with its well, but Fran can be forgiven for not realising. All he can see is burnt wood everywhere, piled up and scattered about, a layer of black, muddy ash spread incontinently across the cobblestones. And always the faint, bitter whiff of fire. He feels the bile rise within him, wipes his mouth and settles his mind on the one thing of beauty in this godforsaken place, the remains of a delicate piece of stonework that was once perhaps the bottom part of a window.

Adam stands before the fire that nearly consumed him, head bowed. Fran lingers a short distance away, unwilling to intrude on what he imagines to be a tumult of feelings that belong only to Adam. He shuts his eyes, prays quickly they will find what they're looking for, whatever it is.

Looking up, he sees a gap in the wall and a dark gathering of trees beyond. But he does not wish to go there alone. Searching the sky for an inkling of the hour, he is also eager not to stay here beyond sunset for fear of what might roam freely when Christian folk are abed.

Adam lays a hand gently on his arm. 'Come now.'

Fran stumbles over a rock hidden in the grass, steadies himself, sees Adam fall to his knees ahead of him. He feels suddenly alone, as if only the dead or the near-dead have dominion here. Gritting his teeth, he dips beneath an ominous weight of sycamore branches and kneels beside Adam. 'They are here?' He whispers for no good reason, just as asking the question is entirely unnecessary. The soil has clearly been disturbed, mounded up a little and the grass on top as meagre as anything else trying to grow this year.

Adam nods. 'Do you want to see them?' He does not look at Fran. 'To be sure.'

Fran's hand shoots onto Adam's sleeve. 'No. There's no need.'

Adam shuts his eyes, crosses himself.

'They're all here together. That's what matters.' Fran prays they rest in peace. He stands up.

But Adam kneels still, muttering to himself. At last he looks up at Fran, face wet, ill-defined. 'You believe me, then?'

Fran feels his dismay swell up, sticking in his throat. Now comes the hard part. 'Yes. But it's not me you need to worry about.'

Adam pushes himself slowly to his feet. 'You mean the sheriff?'

'Yes.'

'I'm not worried about him.'

'You said there was something here that would prove your story.'

Adam blinks. 'All in good time.'

Fran feels his impatience rising. 'I would like to find somewhere better than this to rest tonight.'

Adam walks away, into the courtyard, hand busy in his pocket.

Fran follows, hoping all will now be revealed.

But Adam only holds out his hand. 'You have been a most constant companion, even when you didn't mean to be. I want you to have this.' In his palm he holds a pretty little ring, a garnet nestling at its heart.

'You have no need to give me such a thing.' Fran is

astonished, a great warmth spreading from the tops of his ears to his cheeks.

But Adam takes his hand, folds Fran's fingers over the ring. 'Take it. It would please me very much.'

'I thank you with all my heart.' Fran puts it carefully in his own pocket. He will look at it properly when they're away from this place.

But already Adam has moved to the other side of the courtyard. He stands with his back to Fran. 'And you must promise me you'll go back to Hexham. The monks have something else for you. It's most important you do this.'

'But surely you'll be—'

Adam turns round. 'Take out your sword.'

'My sword?'

'Take it out.'

Fran's hand twitches, and he looks around in terror, but all is utterly still. 'What for?'

'You must kill me now.'

There's so little sense to Adam's words that Fran almost laughs.

But Adam isn't laughing. 'I cannot bear to live any longer now I've done what I set out to do. But it's a mortal sin to take my own life, so you must do it.' He says it calmly, as if this is entirely logical, wholly reasonable.

'No! I will not.'

'Would you rather I was hanged or died in prison because of those scoundrels?'

'That won't happen.' He is not so sure, of course. 'I will think of something to prove your innocence for everyone else.'

'Perhaps.' Adam stands there, forlorn, a great weariness pulling at his limbs. He speaks quietly, but with a great longing, this life long since spent. 'But do you think I can sit quietly by my own fire for the rest of my days looking like this? Do you think people will forget what I did? Who I became? Do you think *I* will?'

Fran struggles to breathe. Darkness has fallen and the sun not even set.

'I'm dying anyway. The fire did it. But it will not be a good death. Just a slow one.' Adam has his own sword in his hand, though Fran doesn't remember seeing him draw it. 'Take it out!' Now he is become vehement.

But Fran cannot move, will not believe this strange, vital, honourable man has asked such a thing of him. He folds his arms, shakes his head, eyes fixed on Adam's. For a moment the Earth stops turning, the sun stays its course, nothing breathes.

And then everything begins to move at once. Lifting his sword high above his head in both hands, Adam runs towards him as if possessed, screaming like a demon. Fran only has time to duck out of the way, Adam's fists glancing off his shoulder with the blade only inches from his face. He runs to the other side of the courtyard, pulling at his sword, cursing slippery fingers.

Adam circles the remains of the fire, but he coughs now, stopping to try to draw breath.

'Enough, I beg you!' Fran keeps his sword down at his side, the other hand held out in supplication. 'We should go back to Hexham to see if the monks can do anything more.'

But Adam merely rouses himself, runs at him again. Their swords ring out before Fran manages to slip away. He is younger and stronger, but a reluctant fighter, while Adam is full of impossible conviction. He comes at Fran again, sword above his head. Fran steps back, trying to avoid a scattering of rocks. But he is nearly at the remains of the back wall, great ropes of ivy reaching for him. He puts his left hand against the wall, intent on turning Adam's sword aside, sweeping his own blade across his body where he expects the other to come.

But Adam never brings his sword down, running on with a scream that suddenly pierces the very heavens. His sword falls, he clutches at Fran, the blood leaping from his neck, seeping through his tunic. And Fran is screaming too, his mind full of the woodsman's wife, drowning in the blood. And he goes on screaming, clutching at Adam, long after Adam's spirit finally escapes his exhausted body.

Part Three

Chapter 13

Fran has locked herself in her chamber. She lies in bed for most of the day in a state of complete undress, her nakedness a failure, not a comfort. Sometimes she sits by the fire, arms clasped tight around her legs, chin on knees, looking for signs in the flames. She will not allow anyone to come to her, even Sarah, sipping water from a jug when she can no longer bear her thirst. Though she is undoubtedly here in Hilton, in truth her mind cannot leave the desolation of Elsdon, feels Adam still pressing heavy upon her, his blood binding them together.

Edie creeps to the door, whispers in a low voice. 'I is bringing something for you, tae mak you feel better. We is wanting tae see you, sir. We is wanting you not tae be sad.'

But Fran scarcely hears, his thoughts consumed by Adam, his perfidy, his desperation, the way he seemed to control everything, the way his fortunes were knocked entirely off course, the look on his face when he died, the look on his face when they talked on the fells, his gentleness, his unflinching determination. The inventory is endless.

Fran hates him. But only because she wishes Adam had been able to live. Without him, she can see no resolution for herself, the two worlds she hovers between set to collide, to shatter, to tear her apart just as Adam could live neither as beast nor man.

For he cannot help but think that what Adam asked of him was just, that he had no choice in seeking his own death at the end of Fran's sword.

Giles knocks this time, speaking so gently that Fran cannot help but try to pick out the words. 'I don't know what ails you, sir. But I don't think you should keep your troubles to yourself.'

Fran wants to cry out, throw open the door. He wants to throw his arms round someone, anyone, even Giles, and cry her heart out. And because she cannot, she stays here alone, nursing her black mood, nurturing it through a constant dwelling in it. And already she's grown sure of one thing. She cannot, will not, live as a man among men. Their world is full of evil, throwing them all under a curse. Above all, she wants someone to care for her, to look after her, take away all this pain and strife.

They come together, Giles and Edie and Willow. They tell him he must eat something, that Tom Strickland has made a venison pie and they cannot eat it all.

She wonders who they're talking to.

Harry Sowerby coughs just once behind the door, prays forgiveness for disturbing him, but there are petitioners come to ask about their rents and other pressing matters.

Fran feels sorry for them, but as if they importune someone else, a distant calamity. Sarah comes often, rattling the door as if she would pull it off its hinges. Fran turns her head away, lets Sarah's howls flow through him, feels them as her own.

And then, perhaps on the fourth or fifth day after Fran's return, a voice reaches out to him. It is as familiar as his own, though she only dimly recognises it, cannot understand what it's doing here, so near and yet not at hand. Will speaks gently, though there is a quiver in his voice that escapes from time to time. He regrets not being able to come sooner, but he had to administer the last rites to Simon Blackstock over at Sandford. The old man lingered longer than anyone expected, so that a visit of a few hours became a vigil two nights long. Will talks as if there is nothing amiss in his being sat on one side of a locked door. And yet sometimes he can speak no more, the silence filling the space between them, morose and empty.

And then he begins again, using every argument he can think of to try to turn aside the evil that seems to have Fran in its grip. He speaks of God's will, that it is impossible for mere mortals to understand it, of the infinite ways in which His mercy can and will be shown to those whose hearts are true. He reminds Fran why our Lord was sent to die on a cross. The silences grow longer until he too submits to the desire to press hard at the door, as if it has miraculously sprung open. He cries out then, finally escaping his priestly patience. 'You can have until the morrow. Then I swear I will fetch the blacksmith to prise you out.'

Stamping away, he comes back almost immediately, leans his head on the door with a dull thud. 'Forgive me. It seems I do not have the words for you.' His voice is thick with resentment and despair.

Fran lies in bed facing the wall, the blanket pulled right over him. She doesn't want the voice to stop. If the voice keeps talking, he will be safe, for when people are talking, there's no blood. That comes later. But it always comes. She wants the voice to come nearer, pulls the blanket around her, stumbles to the door. The voice is there, just behind it.

'For pity's sake, Fran. You torment me beyond all reason.' Will sinks down on to the floor.

Fran puts his hands on the door. She listens but can hear only muffled weeping. 'Is that you, Will?'

'Jesu!' Will springs to his feet, leans his head once more on the door.

'How did I come here?' Fran's mind twists to try to find the answer.

'Can you not remember?'

'I don't want to.' Fran closes his eyes, feels Adam beside him.

'Will you open the door?'

Fran tries to remember why she locked it, wants to curl up in bed again. But he should not, if Will has come to visit. 'Let me get dressed. I will come to the solar.'

'You promise?'

'Yes.'

Fran waits until he hears Will move off along the passageway. But still she doesn't move, wrapped in the blanket in the middle of the room. At last, he goes to his chest, drops the blanket, pulls out clean braies, a shirt and breeches. But even dressed he still feels uncertain, exposed, so he wraps the blanket round him again. He considers the stink on him, of sweat and horse, and suddenly remembers approaching Hexham for the second time, the pain of being there without Adam.

He shakes his head, pushing Adam away. She feels the cold of the metal bolt chilling her fingers, walks unsteadily out of the door, catching a glimpse of a tousled autumn day shaking with leaves. Swaying on his feet, he must steady himself, leaning a hand on the wooden panelling, feeling its roughness. She looks down at the place where she once scratched her name and earned herself a thrashing. He thinks he walks on air, or perhaps angels carry him, it's impossible to tell. All she knows is that the world is not as it was. Or at least he has changed her opinion of it.

The door to the solar opens and Will stands in the half light, his white habit spattered with mud. He gives a little cry to see Fran walking towards him, puts a hand over his heart as he turns back into the room. It's cool inside, no fire lit, nothing to bid them welcome. Fran sees the book she was reading before she left for Elsdon lying on the window seat, as if there is no reason why she shouldn't pick it up and read on. But all that came before is now turned to dust.

Will can scarcely stand still for even a moment, walking this way and that, a hand pushing at his hair, tugging at his mouth. But he stops suddenly. 'You must eat. Edie must bring you something.' He launches himself at the door, as if suddenly eager to escape.

'I don't want to.' Fran goes to the window seat, sits

there hunched in her blanket, watching.

Will turns back, stands in the middle of the floor, slipping his hands inside his sleeves. 'You will fade away to nothing if you do not. And there is little enough of you as it is.' Neither of them smiles. He goes to sit in the seat opposite Fran, hugging himself tight. 'Will you tell me what happened?'

Fran breathes out, a noisome fluttering.

'Then pray tell me where Adam is.'

'He lies at Elsdon.' Fran gently traces a finger over her lips, as if astonished such words should leave them. 'With the others.'

'He is dead?'

Fran nods, still wondering that she sits here, so near to Will, in her own house, seemingly alive. 'I killed him.' She hears himself say it, knows it's true. But those words have no real meaning.

Will gasps, all the same.

Fran gnaws at the back of a finger, the blanket falling from her shoulders. She doesn't pull it back up, lets it rest at her waist. 'He meant me to.' She looks straight at Will, biting the knuckle of her thumb now.

Will leans forward, seizes Fran's hands. 'Tell me.'

Fran shivers, rocks endlessly to try to ease the pain.

'Please.'

'Everything happened the way he said. Everything was as he meant it to be.'

Will frowns. 'I don't understand. You mean, what happened at Elsdon was as *Adam* said, not the Dickinsons? As you thought? Did he give you the proof?'

Fran blinks, suddenly sees Will there opposite her as flesh and blood talking about earthly things of the kind you think you can tie neatly together, make clear in the mind. She nods, but already she's slipping away again, back into the dark. They sit together, saying nothing, for what is there to say?

But, out of the darkness, Adam appears to Fran, urging him to tell the story, to give voice to its ending, the sacrifice that had to be made because there was no other way. 'When we went to Hexham the first time, he told the monks privily what he was going to do. I have been remembering the things we said as we rode towards Elsdon: he was already speaking as if he were a dead man. But I did not know it then.'

Will lowers their hands, holds them tight in his lap, keeps his eyes fixed on Fran's face.

'They didn't want him to do it, the monks. They told me afterwards they begged him to hold his life more dear, to God and to himself. And not to burden me.' She lowers her head, tears trembling, falling.

Will gets to his knees, tries to make Fran look at him.

Fran bites her lip, the world clouded with tears. 'He told them he would think on it, but that was the only thing he said or did that wasn't honest. And he made them take a paper, to give to me if I came back alone, that explained . . . that said he would force me to defend myself, and he would . . . he would run on to my blade and it was entirely his wish that he should die, that he could not live any longer now he had avenged the people of Elsdon but hoped one day he would be forgiven, in this world and the next.' Fran pulls her hands from Will's, slips off the seat. Stumbling away, she wraps herself in the folds of a hanging, lets the tears overwhelm her, sobbing until she has no breath left.

Will follows him, puts out a hand, draws it back inside his sleeve. He waits, puts out his hand again, reaches for Fran's shoulder. 'Then you have nothing to reproach yourself with.'

'How can that be true?'

'It *must* be true. You said Adam was honest. Then take him at his word.'

'But that's it exactly!' She turns to look at him, fire in her eyes. 'There *is* no truth here!' She knows that wasn't what he was talking about, but it's all that matters to her now. Adam has ruined the pretence. For what use is imagining himself at ease, loved even, by those he cares for too when it's all a lie?

Will puts both hands on Fran's shoulders, tugging him towards him, lifting his face so their lips collide, teeth collide, breath extinguished.

She spins out of time, all feeling absorbed by the places where they touch, their mouths, their hands on each other's faces, speaking so furiously though they are beyond speech.

But already Will is hauling himself away with a cry, stumbling to the door, face in his hands.

Sinking to the floor, Fran lifts a hand to the tapestry to trace a finger down a filigree of leaves and flowers. She thinks it's more real than she is.

After Will leaves, she walks downstairs, her mind still trapped in the solar and at Elsdon, both at the same time. But suddenly Sarah is before her, clapping madly, a great hollaing calling the rest of the household. They enter the hall, Dolfyn rising from his doleful watch by the door, bounding towards Fran, threading himself between her legs. Giles comes running into the hall, bows deeply to disguise the breadth of his smile. 'That is good, sir. To see you. To have you among us.' He nods most sagely, follows Fran to the table, sits down, stands up, retreats to the wall where he leans with his arms crossed, eyes flitting around the room.

Edie has dashed up the stairs, stands at the door, Jack the kitchen boy peeking round her skirts. 'I is bringing you food, sir. Don't be going anywhere.' They both dash away again.

Harry and Willow Sowerby come rushing in together. Willow keeps running, coming to a halt at Fran's side, putting a hand on his shoulder as if to be sure he is flesh and blood. 'God keep you, sir. We were at our wit's end what to do about you.'

Fran pats his hand, nods, more tears threatening.

'Willow, come out of the way.' Harry Sowerby sits at the far end of the table, a hand placed flat in front of him, his face fallen into sorrowful lines.

Edie returns, placing a thin potage in front of him. 'My father is being most sorry not tae have summat better for you, sir. 'Tis the price o' goods now. He isn't knowing you'd be feeling better today.' She too retreats to sit on the floor nearby, keeping a strict eye upon him.

Fran turns her attention to the potage, her belly gurgling despite the lack of anything much beyond warm water and the suggestion of a few worts in the bowl in front of her. She feels all eyes upon her, is both warmed and discomfited by it, for it is him they love. Could they ever love her?

She knows they want to hear what happened, have a right to know, considering they have been so often by her side these past months. And always Will calls to her through the leaf-strewn miles between here and Warcop, though what they might say to one another is so huge, so monstrous, it leaves her utterly despondent to dwell on it for even a moment.

She pushes the bowl away after a few sips, a nausea rising harshly up into her nostrils. 'Pray thank your father, Edie. I am still somewhat unwell.'

Edie nods, removes the bowl, goes back to sit with it beside her.

Willow looks over at Edie, a curl in his lip. 'Don't you have work to do?'

She reddens, looks at her feet.

'Leave her be, Willow.' Fran is annoyed with him for trying to break even one of the bonds that hold them all together. He gets up from the bench, strides over to his usual chair, Dolfyn close enough to trip him up. Sarah follows, leans on the back of the chair singing softly. Luke scuttles through the door, head down, slipping on to the floor near Edie as if he's been blown in. Fran smiles at him and Luke finally looks up, smiles back.

'I suppose I must tell you what happened.' He glances round the expectant faces.

They all nod, settling themselves so as to be comfortable.

He tells it as if it were written in a book, each word exact and true and almost certainly not what happened, at least in its entirety. It is only just bearable. Sometimes they ask questions, and that pains him. But he shuts himself away as much as she can.

She tries to shake off the questions buzzing round her mind. *What can Will be thinking? Will they ever speak again? How can they not?*

She finishes her story, the exhaustion pressing hard. Her head aches so badly the room begins to shift and drop. 'I must . . .' She stands up, swaying.

Edie rushes to her side, an arm across her shoulders. Sarah leans over the chair, tries to push her away.

Instantly Fran takes hold of Edie's hand, trying to pull herself free as gently as she can. 'Perhaps I stood up too quickly.' She watches Edie carefully, sees a question flit briefly across her face. But then the girl just smiles, goes to pick up the bowl before disappearing back towards the kitchen. Fran doesn't know if she's been discovered, if that would be a relief, cursing herself for being a fool and a coward.

Sarah is distressed, bringing clean bindings, looking all over for the pouch. Fran wonders if she's in possession of a particular knowledge or is merely upset that something they have always done is now abandoned.

But Fran is still certain she is done with her life as a man. She will not pretend. She will not hide. She has courage, she knows she has. It's just that the consequences of becoming her true self are bewilderingly difficult to imagine.

And still Will does not come or send a message. The thought of him brings her such torment, and yet she can scarcely think of anything else. She remembers the moment he kissed her. Did he embrace her as man or woman? But if he had guessed her secret, why did he say nothing? She must tell him, imagines his relief, to have so much explained. And, with a sudden icy twinge, she conceives of the great gulf that would surely spring up between them. Then it occurs to her that she, like his mother, would be incomparable in his good opinion. Alas, it quickly falls upon her that such a notion is nothing but foolishness. He is a priest. They could not be friends. She must learn not to think about him. She goes on and on thinking about him.

On the third day, Fran wakes once more in great agitation. She sits again with Harry Sowerby, and they decide on what can be done for her tenants, which is little enough. A summons has arrived from their new young lord, Sir Roger Clifford, demanding that Francis Hilton come to serve on the jury at Sir Roger's next court, to be held at Appleby on the third Monday of October. She thinks this has gone on long enough.

She waits until they have eaten an early supper, the potage made more palatable by the addition of a rabbit snared down by Hilton Beck. Fran pleads tiredness, turns aside Willow's requests she should read to them. Sarah bustles out after her, sewing in hand.

But when they reach Fran's chamber, she bolts it, telling Sarah to retrieve her mother's clothes from the bottom of the chest. Sarah can see this is not a game, her fleshy face held taut, mouth turned down to give her a dull, sullen look. She holds out the linen chemise for Fran to dive into, a girdle and hose, followed by a pale green woollen dress, for, though the daylight will linger for a while yet, already there is a chill slipping through the walls. Fran draws her hands down the front of her gown, still enamoured with the way it clings to her shape.

Sarah sniffs when she's finished.

'What is it?' Fran has been busy with thoughts that leap from despair to a strange, agitated bliss, is not used to Sarah being anything other than content.

But Sarah merely draws a hand down Fran's cheek, shaking her head as she does so. And Fran comes to understand Sarah is frightened for her, for the unknown that beckons.

Fran smiles, opens her arms and is swept into Sarah's great softness. 'Don't worry. It's for the best. It was wrong, what I was before. You do know that, don't you?' She is gabbling, a goose waiting to be plucked. 'And I only go out for a ride, to see what it feels like.'

Sarah releases her, turning away to fold up the clothes discarded on the floor.

Fran runs to her again, kisses her on the cheek. She finds her boots, her cloak, unbolts the door. Listening carefully, she slips downstairs, still looking out for anyone to surprise her. In the stables Fauvel nuzzles her hand, whinnies when the saddle is put on. And, at last, they fly, Fran's dress riding up almost to her knees, cloak billowing behind her.

For some time, her heart beats hard to the rhythm of Fauvel's hooves on the soft ground and she has little room in her mind for clear thought. But, with Warcop in sight, she tells herself again she is in love with a monk and should not expect anything in return. She must desire only that he know the truth.

She knows she lies. It's not what she wants. Not at all.

Her heart beats faster again as they pick their way through the bog that lies near Cringle Beck. She has decided her fate, but does not yet know if it will taste sweet or . . . It doesn't matter.

Of course it matters. That's why her heart is running so fast she fears it will burst. It's like a sickness, this not knowing. This loving and not loving. She wonders what Will is doing and thinking now. Does he feel this anguish, this fever that burns and chills and cannot be cured? She tells herself she only wishes to know if she is loved. She even tells herself that, since marrying Will is clearly impossible, she can endure it if he turns his contempt for women upon her. Soon enough, she will be married to some suitable local gentleman and the shape of her life up till now will be swept away, Will along with the rest.

A light rain begins to fall. She feels it caressing her face, licks her lips. The beck splashes and gurgles and she feels a great thirst. If she is drawing out the moment when she will arrive in Warcop, so be it. Leaping down, she leaves Fauvel to wander a little, for he never goes far. And then it occurs to her that a gentlewoman would never ride out by herself, and what reason would she give?

Someone is walking down past Bell Nook on this side of Deep Gill. Fran thinks he'll surely keep going down on to Hayber Lane. She hastens to the beck, already discomfited by the length of her skirts, the need to hold them to get anywhere easily. Crouching down, she drinks her fill, the cold water restoring her spirits. She looks around for Fauvel, spies him a little upstream, tugging at a juniper bush. It enters her mind that she could just ride home. No one would know her cowardice.

And then she sees him. He must have turned west instead of south, heading towards the path they've just come down, his white habit shuddering and leaping with each determined step. If he turns his head, he'll see her. She can shout.

But she cannot move or speak. In a moment, once he's crossed the beck, he will gain the path. And he must surely turn up it, for if he were going back to Warcop he would not come this way.

Does he go to Hilton?

A great excitement seizes her and she starts forward, a cry in her throat. Will turns his head, stops, squeezing hands into fists, tossing hair from eyes. He stays where he is, watching her run up the other bank towards him.

She stops, quite out of breath, apprehensive now, for he makes no move at all to come nearer. 'Will?'

'Lady, I do not know you.'

She gasps, entirely discomfited. And then she picks up her skirts, wades through the water until she stands before him, a dripping, disconsolate changeling.

He looks at her, mouth half open, reaches out to steady himself on a stunted alder leaning out of the bank.

She thrusts her hands behind her back, fearful she will lay them upon him. 'I'm sure how I appear now will distress you. And that you may not . . . forgive me for the deception, which in truth began with my father.'

He groans, as if in great pain, backs away as if he might run.

'I only want you to know me as I truly am. I've wanted it since my father died.' It is torture not to step closer to him.

He moves behind the tree. 'Is this some kind of devilment?'

'No! I swear. A deception, certainly. But it's what I've always been.'

He circles the tree, looking at her through its branches. 'It's not possible.'

'You know it explains much.'

'But . . . why on God's earth should you do such a thing?' He is angry, face heavy, stiff.

'It's a long story. From before I was born.' All she wants now is for him to understand it was not her doing. Not to begin with, at least. She bites her lip, fighting a rising, choking fear.

'Your father did this?' He looks at her with such astonishment that she begins to wonder if he'll ever believe what stares him straight in the face.

'Yes.'

He sits down abruptly beneath the alder.

She sits too, but some distance away. She thinks he is like some injured creature too frightened and upset to do anything other than sit and shake. She tells herself she cannot expect anything more, tries to imagine his shock.

He wrestles with his hands. 'I was coming to see you.'

She nods.

'To say sorry. I have spent these past days walking and walking to try to . . . And now . . .' He puts his head in his hands, sobbing.

She moves towards him, puts a hand on his back, but he shrugs her away. 'Leave me be, for pity's sake.'

She feels her heart shatter into a thousand sharp pieces that fly away on the wind but not before piercing her flesh all over. She stands up. 'I was coming to see *you*. To tell you. It's a torment to me too.' She walks away, wondering that she has the strength. She imagines him fighting his way through the alder to reach her, to demand why she leaves him, to take her in his arms.

But she reaches the other side of the beck quite alone, throwing herself at the far bank, stumbling over her dress, wet and angry. She will not look back, stamping over to Fauvel. Furious tears sting as her heavy skirts restrain her so that she must hoist herself up into the saddle as if she were a crone. She hopes he doesn't see how diminished she is, even as she longs to know if he watches. The path home has never felt so long and tedious.

Chapter 14

She does not sleep and does not care. The heavier the feeling inside her head, the more it agrees with her mood. Nursing her anger and despair through dawn's bewitching of the night, she rises from her seat by the fire, holds up her gown. Sarah lingers nearby, not looking at her.

Fran knows she's undone, her secret become a weapon in Will's hands. For that, she does not blame him. She still feels she had no choice but to admit her deception. And yet these wild feelings – of love, of fury, of all that brings her every fibre to boiling point – have weakened Adam Fothergill's hold upon her. But it's too late now. She knows she's delaying the inevitable, putting on her usual clothes but doing nothing to hide her shape. She considers speaking with Giles, who should certainly be told and soon. But she wouldn't wish for the others to find out and not be the one to tell them. She knows what must be done. Once she's dressed in tunic and hose, she tells Sarah to fetch Giles.

He arrives in haste. 'Do you have something for me to do, sir? I must confess I find it wearisome now our adventures are over.'

She raises an eyebrow, unable to forget his former reluctance to go out against the revenant. 'Those kinds of adventures are over for good – for me, at least.' She hears herself say it, cannot yet believe it. 'But I wish to speak with you and everyone else, if you would tell them to gather in the hall after supper.'

His face falls. 'Have I displeased you, sir?'

Fran reaches out, touches his hand. 'No, not at all. It's just . . . it's important, that's all. For everyone.'

He smiles, turning away eagerly. 'Of course.'

He will enjoy the little lording to be got out of delivering her message, she thinks, turning again to Sarah. Now she must begin her transformation.

Sarah works quickly. The day drags on, the weight in Fran's mind now disabling. She tries to imagine standing before them all but cannot find her breath. Pushing herself up, she walks about her chamber, clutching her skirts, the walls, her chair. Sitting down heavily on the bed, she catches Sarah's sorrowful glance, shuts her eyes. But then Will rises up before her, reproachful, dangerous.

They walk downstairs, every step imprinted on Fran's mind. Stumbling ahead, Sarah opens the door to the hall with a stifled sob. Fran steps forward.

She has never imagined being so looked at, eyes unwilling to believe, mouths agape. Eyes sweeping across the room, she tries to smile, but her throat is a dry riverbed choked with weeds. Everyone stops talking. Someone drops something with a clatter. Fran fixes her eyes on the lady on the horse, who watches her too from the hanging. At least she is gentle with her.

Fran wonders if she should sit or stand, remembers the moment she had sunk into her father's chair just after he died. What a long time ago that seems. Does he watch her now? She pushes him out of her mind, though the old anger has faded. It's a long walk across the room, but at last she reaches the other side, her chair. She stands in front of it, faces them all.

Harry Sowerby wipes his face with a kerchief, looking up at her and down again to stare at the floor. Luke has moved closer to his sister Agatha, who sits next to Edie and Jack the kitchen boy, Tom Strickland standing behind and clutching his red cook's hat. Giles whispers to Willow, the two of them standing with their arms crossed near the window. Sim Taylor and the rest of the herds lurk at the far door.

She wonders if she feels worse than when she faced Adam Fothergill, tells herself this is no time to feel sorry for what is done. She has made her choice and now she must begin her life anew. 'Forgive me for my appearance among you now.' She hears herself falter, searches for a friendly face but finds only horror, disbelief. Even Edie looks as if she suddenly finds herself in the presence of a monster. Fran draws her gaze back to the lady on the horse and her inscrutable smile. 'It was my father's decision to raise me as a boy and I was not ... I did not know how to behave otherwise when he died. I knew it was an offence against God and against you all, and for that I'm sorry. I know too that I cannot tell you with any certainty what will happen now.' She feels the room shift, a tightening of faces already taut.

She stares for a moment at the floor, breathes deeply, looks up again. 'Most of you have known me all my life or yours. I am still Francis Hilton. You, of all people, know who I am.' She sits down.

No one speaks or moves. Then Sim Taylor, looking as if he would hit something, turns away. The other herds follow. Luke stands up, watches them go. But before he runs out after them, he skips up to Fran, leans over and kisses her hand.

Tom Strickland thrusts his hat back on his head. 'I is not sure what's going on, sir. You'll be telling me, Edie, won't you?' He ambles off back down to the kitchen.

Harry Sowerby gets up slowly, painfully. 'I would speak with you privily when you're ready ... mistress.'

'Yes. We have much to speak about.' She smiles and he nods. Willow runs to his side, speaking in a low voice as they leave.

Giles lingers still by the window, not looking at anyone, brows furrowed, mouth pulled down. Edie has risen, pulling Jack with her.

Agatha stands too, staring at Fran all the while. 'Is it the Devil what is changing you, mistress?'

'Now you is being foolish again, Aggie.' Edie puts a hand on her shoulder, pushes her towards the kitchen stairs. 'There's being no change. Our lady's always been a girl.' Agatha's eyes grow bigger, staring over her shoulder as she walks away.

'Edie?' Fran springs after them.

Edie turns, mouth firm, gesturing to the others to go ahead of her.

'Did you know?'

Edie shakes her head. 'I isn't thinking anyone could be doing such a thing.'

'But you wondered?'

Edie twists her mouth. 'I is thinking you is being somewhat strange in your person this last while since you is coming back from Elsdon, begging your pardon. I is thinking now 'tis better this way.' She looks Fran straight in the face, throwing down a challenge. 'Is you thinking it better, mistress?'

'I don't know. I still feel strange in my person, as you put it.'

Edie nods slowly. 'I is supposing 'tis most likely you will.' She frowns, walks away.

Fran turns to Giles, but he's gone. She sighs. She has nothing to steady her now except herself.

Giles is nowhere to be found the next day. They know he's taken his horse, so there's no point looking for him nearby. But on the day after that, he rides back up the path, tired and hungry. Fran sees him from her chamber, where she sits trying to learn how to sew, glad to throw the cloth with its wayward stitches onto her seat. She meets him as he comes up the front steps, hunched and miserable once more.

'Come.' She leads him into the hall, bids Sarah bring something, anything, then sits opposite him at the table.

He will not look at her. At last Sarah returns, carrying a bowl of something hot, a piece of yesterday's bread.

He eyes it resentfully.

'Go on.' She tries not to sigh. 'You'll feel better.'

'No, I won't.' But he picks up the bread, thrusts it in the potage.

'Where did you go?'

He glances up then, thin-lipped. 'To my father's.'

Her heart skips a beat. 'What did you tell him?'

He shakes his head. 'I didn't go in.'

She raises her eyebrows.

'I didn't want to go back.'

'I see.'

'*I* don't. I don't see anything at all.' He stabs at his potage with the bread. 'How could you? I feel such a fool.'

'I don't see why. My father trained me well. No one else knew apart from my mother and Hawise and Sarah.'

He keeps chewing, seizes the ale that Sarah now brings, swallowing noisily. And then he brings his hands flat on the table. 'You said you don't know what will happen.'

'No.'

'I'll stay here till you do.' He throws this at her as if she should be grateful.

Fran wonders if he's trying to reassure himself. She nods, gives him a shy smile. 'Perhaps we might still practise our sword?'

He looks at her as if she's suddenly grown three heads.

She gets up, wondering what to do with herself. She won't go back to her sewing. Perhaps she might go out for a ride? Giles could accompany her if she must not go alone.

It's a pity Sarah has never learned, though it's impossible to imagine her leaving the confines of the manor.

She decides to speak with Harry Sowerby, had thought he would try to find her yesterday. She has told herself not to be so impatient. She has known her true state for as long as she can remember, but her confession must have taken an axe to everyone else's certainties. Still, it saddens her to have disappointed Harry, for he does not often judge and is kind even when moved to do so. Sending Giles to find him, she paces up and down the hall, not noticing how often she listens for the sound of horse's hooves, someone knocking at the door.

Harry comes, cap in hand, eyes resisting her person. He bows. 'My lady.'

Fran imagines he has thought about this moment already. She smiles, goes to her chair, gestures towards the bench next to her, something they have done a thousand times. But not like this.

He seems to gather himself tightly together, sitting cautiously, making sure they will not touch. He waits.

Fran breathes deeply. 'I ... I'm sorry. That you didn't know. My father ...'

Harry says nothing, staring at the table in front of him.

Fran turns her gaze quickly round the room, seeking courage. 'It doesn't matter. The question is, what will happen now?' It is her turn to wait, looking straight at him.

At last he looks up, scratches his chin, throwing small glances at her, recoiling away again. 'We must write to Sir Roger.'

She nods. 'And what will that mean? For me?' Again

her gaze sweeps the room, as if it is full of people, her household, her tenants. 'For everyone?'

He puffs out his lips, places both hands on the table. 'I'm trying to imagine.' He says it grimly.

She's not sure if his gravity is directed at her or her situation. 'He will have my marriage, I suppose.'

Now he looks her full in the face. 'We must pray for a good husband.'

A new master. Fran wants to put a hand on his arm, thinks better of it, tries to keep her mind off Will. 'Yes.' It is an entirely strange thought, her marriage. Before, that most ordinary of states was forbidden, a source of shame and grief he tried not think about. But now she must wrap herself in its possibilities, embrace it as an occupation, perhaps even a vocation. The thought catches her like a blow to the ribs, knocking out her breath. She gasps, throws back her head.

Harry Sowerby leaps to his feet, shouting for Sarah.

But she thrusts herself up from her chair too. 'Stop it, Harry. I'm quite fine. It's just … perplexing, for me *and* you.'

He draws a knuckle across his mouth, looking her over carefully. 'I'm thinking it'll get harder before it gets easier.'

She doesn't doubt he's right. 'But we can continue as before, with what needs to be done.' She doesn't say it as a question, though she knows she should.

He thinks about that, twisting the cap in his hands. And then he pulls out a sheaf of papers from his bag and they both sit down.

It steadies her, to sit with Harry like that. But when he's gone and she lingers by the window watching the winds of autumn stir up the leaves, bending the trees, she feels unmoored. Edie and Agatha come and go, sweeping the floor, tending to the fire, scrubbing the table, busy at their usual tasks. If they glance at Fran, she doesn't notice, but when she watches them, she is speared by their indifference. And yet she doesn't speak, does nothing to bridge this monstrous chasm opened up between them. She knows it's not for them to reconcile her confusion of feelings, but she had imagined that Edie would help her, provide both solace and guidance. The truth is, she has no idea what to do with herself.

With peevish clumsiness, Fran wraps herself in her cloak, staggers out of the room, utterly enraged with her skirts, with Edie, with the world. And especially with Will. She considers putting on her hose but cannot bear to divert her charge for the door.

Rushing down the steps, she throws herself on to the mercy of the wind. To be handled roughly is what she deserves. Seizing her skirts in both hands, she runs out of the gate, kicking at the leaves, driving the pain in her heart into a vital, impetuous beat as she flies towards the fells. She imagines never coming back, wandering the high tops, a cloud-driven wraith forever.

But she is mortal and her breath finally deserts her. Standing high above the known world, she knows all she can do is turn back, go home. But not yet. She breathes in each drop of the heady brew concocted from the air, the earth, the stink and toil of the people spread across this difficult, beautiful land. She is nothing, a fleck of dust, her life a brief dance through time, and this comforts her. Her new life is only just begun. She must take one step, then another, not run at it. Of course, it's hard. She will falter. It's inevitable. She is a child again.

A shadow falls across her left side, bringing with it a discomfiting sensation of tumbling from a great height. She knows before she turns her head that he has come to stand beside her, but imagines he is a conjuring brought there by her own unruly desire. She looks carefully. If all were not topsy-turvy, she would think him flesh and blood. She opens her mouth to speak.

'Let me look at you.' It is a command, wistful, angry.

Her gaze drops to the ground, ill at ease. 'I don't like you to.'

'But I must get used to it.'

She reaches for his gaze then.

Seizing both her hands, Will holds her away from him to behold her properly. 'It becomes you.'

'Oh!' She does not know what to say, looks away again. Then she turns back to him, moves closer. 'I am not used to it yet either.'

He still holds both hands tight. 'Does anyone else know?'

She nods. 'I have told them.'

Will frowns. 'And before?'

'Only Sarah. She's always known.'

He grunts, moves away, walks round her. 'I still cannot . . . It is a hard thing to understand.'

'I know.' She tries to follow him with her eyes,

wondering what it is he sees, is looking for.

Will stands before her again, so close she can smell the sour smell of potage on his breath. 'But what brought your father to do such a thing?'

'He meant only to protect me.' She tells him the story her mother told her.

'He was most mistaken.'

She nods. But part of her is disappointed Will should think only that. 'I didn't make such a sorry man, did I?' She remembers sitting in Will's kitchen after Adam had killed Wat and Rob, when he cleansed Will's wound, bound it, when Will needed him, trusted him. And once more it hits her, as if she contemplates her own death, that they will never share such moments again.

But he laughs, reaching out a hand to cup her chin gently so as to bring her gaze back to his. 'I must confess, I do thank God. I know I should be ashamed of my feelings, but I thought my sin was so much the greater.'

She sighs, even as she nods, for already they have reached the end of the road and he must go one way and she another, to whatever God has in store for them. 'I understand.' She moves away, out of his grasp. 'I would like to come to confession soon, though perhaps I should … perhaps you wouldn't wish …'

He nods, stepping towards her as if he's tied to her side. 'I will ask John Burdon to come to Warcop. Our friendship is well known, so he will understand the reason.'

'I have sent word to Sir Roger Clifford and his lawyers. They must decide about my portion and whatever else I might take into my marriage.' She cannot stop herself telling him everything, as usual.

A hand tugs at his hair. 'Your marriage? But nothing is arranged yet, surely?'

And suddenly she sees his hand reach out, feels him draw a finger gently along the great bone below her neck. Now she exists only there, in that burning part of her. 'I must marry, you know that.' She hears the roughness in her voice, swallows.

One of his hands reaches round the back of her neck, the other lifting her chin.

She knows what happens next. 'No!' She stumbles away, knowing only that she cannot live another life full of lies, even for Will. She has not done all this to be a priest's whore.

But he reaches after her, pulling her back towards him. 'Tell me you don't want me.' He is no longer gentle.

But she shakes her head. 'And what then? If I tell you I want you, that I love you. If I tell you I've always loved you. What difference does it make?'

He raises his hand, as if to strike her, but the wildness ebbs out of him as quickly as it came upon him. 'I do not know. It is all so sudden. But perhaps there is a way. I have been thinking of nothing else these past days.'

She looks at him, does not trust herself to say anything.

Fists clenched, he paces to and fro. 'I thought I loved God enough to withstand anything, even you. I mean, who you were before. But I do not know about this. It is become the only thing in my mind.' He throws her a baleful glance. 'I must speak with someone. Henry, perhaps. And my abbot, of course.'

'Will, what are you saying?' She stands there, suddenly superfluous. She doesn't like it.

He seizes her hands. 'Oh, but is it not a joyful thing, my love, if we can be wed?'

'Wed?' It is not possible. She knows it's not possible. She had never contemplated it as something real. And now he says it as if it might be true, with an ardour that overwhelms her, scattering her thoughts so she doesn't know up from down. Is this happiness, such a wild, heady feeling, beyond reason? She doesn't know why the tears spill down her face. All she knows is that he kisses each one before finding her lips. She has no will left to resist, putting her arms up around his neck, through his hair, breathing him in. All becomes fluid, urgent, the voice in her head finally vanquished.

And yet they must breathe. Gasping, they seize the air and laugh, the day the loveliest they have ever beheld and nothing more beautiful than each other. But it will end, and sooner rather than later.

She pulls away, still holding his hand. 'I still don't understand.'

He smiles. 'It is not for you to worry about. Though even I cannot solve this on my own. You must be patient and I will come as soon as I can.'

'You are leaving now? For your abbey?'

He nods. 'The sooner I go, the sooner I will return.' He casts a long glance over her that pierces her skin, leaves her defenceless.

She is suddenly shy, not sure how to take her leave. 'I will be waiting.' She turns, ready to fly back to Hilton.

'Wait!' He strides towards her, seizing her hand. 'I would see you safely home.'

She laughs. 'Will, I have no distance to go. I'm perfectly safe.'

'It is not fitting.' He smiles, shaking his head as if he can scarcely believe such disobedience, but will indulge it.

She doesn't know what to say, it is so ridiculous, entirely unnecessary. But her heart beats faster at the thought he will be with her for a little longer. Perhaps that is what directs him too. 'Very well, good sir, pray take my arm.'

Will leaps towards her, which makes her laugh again at his happy foolishness. They walk with his arm tight around her waist, which is foolish too as they stagger across the rough ground. She wonders when he will tire of such courtesies but is content to lean against him as they plod back to Hilton, which is become an altogether marvellous place since she left it such a short time ago. They arrive as the first star peeps out from the firmament. Once more they kiss, ever hungry for sweetness and giddiness and the other's magician's touch.

Will pulls away, leans his forehead on hers. 'I would come to your bed this night, but ...'

Fran nods, clasping her arms up and around his neck. She cannot imagine letting him go.

He takes off her cap, strokes her hair, what there is of it. 'I wonder what you will look like when it is long.'

Fran wonders too, imagines it cascading over her shoulders, the feel of it cosseting her head. Will it fall straight, or will it curl? 'Tis another mystery. She giggles, ill at ease with such empty questions.

He groans, pulls her hands away. 'Leave me be, woman, or I will never go.' They both laugh.

'Take Fauvel, if you like.' He'll need to be brought back before Will goes to Shap Abbey.

Will nods. 'I had already thought of that.'

She lingers as the stableboy gets Fauvel ready, wondering when this strange, delirious dream will end. At the last moment, she reaches up so he might pull her to sit in front of him. They ride together through the quiet evening, but only as far as the clump of trees that mark Hilton's south-eastern boundary. He stops and they sit joined together until the darkness hangs heavy above them. She slips off. He turns to give her one last smile, though she can scarcely see it.

She stands looking down the track long after he has disappeared into the night. It is done. And, though nothing is certain yet, she dares to hope.

Chapter 15

She tries to sew, to read a book, which is more agreeable, but always her eye is drawn to the window, her ear to the sound of the wind that might be Fauvel's hooves on the path.

At last, she's sure she's not mistaken. 'Go, Sarah. Bring him here.'

Sarah waddles off in no obvious haste.

Fran tries to sit gracefully at the window seat, gets up, stands near the fire, patting her cap, making sure her dress – her mother's best silk this time – lies neatly from neck to ankles. If there was more coin, she would have one made to fit, for even Christian's youthful attire is several handfuls too big for Fran.

But it's not Will who shoves his way through the door. Sir Henry walks straight in, comes to stand before her, walks this way and that, his gaze never leaving her. Finally, he throws himself into the chair by the fire. 'Who would have thought it?' It is a loud murmur, as if to himself.

'Where's Will?' Fran motions to Sarah to go and fetch some ale.

'Gone to Shap. He visited me this morning.' He leans forward, still looking at her. 'So I came to see for myself, brought Fauvel back.'

She sits down on the end of the bench.

He laughs.

'What?'

'You still sit like a man.'

She blushes, moves her legs together.

He sits back, face serious, old. 'You've certainly put the fox in the hen house.'

'I'm sorry.'

'And led us a merry dance.'

She frowns at him. 'I didn't start this.'

'No. Will told me the story. You were good at deceiving us, though. Women are, aren't they? The Bible says so.'

For a moment, she's so astounded she can only stare at him. *Did Will tell him that?* 'That's not fair.'

'What is, these days?' He shakes his head. 'It's a pity. You were brave. Strong too, for all you're so small.' He sighs.

'I still am.' She says it and doesn't know why she says it, except that it's true.

He snorts.

Sarah clatters through the door, thrusts a beaker of ale at the sheriff.

He takes a deep draught, stands up. 'We'll see what happens when Will gets back. I'll settle something on him if he leaves the Church. Not everyone would, mind, so don't forget it.' He gazes at the fire. 'I promised our father

I'd look after him. Lord knows, he needs it.' He twists his face, before turning his fierce gaze back on Fran. 'And he'll have Hilton through you.'

She nods, the words wounding her now they're spoken out loud. But at least Will's a master of her own choosing.

Sir Henry puts his cap back on, shakes his head again. 'Such a pity.' He strides away before she can say anything else, leaving her unsure whether he meant to flatter her. Though why she thinks it matters now, she doesn't know either.

Once more, Fran feels autumn's melancholy press upon her. Without thinking, she runs to her chest, throws on her old clothes, seizes her cloak. Now that Will isn't here, there's nothing to stop her from listening to the anguish in her breast at what she must give up. Rushing into the stables, she bids the boy put Fauvel's saddle on again. She throws herself up on to his back, rejoicing in how easy it is. Riding through Hilton at a gallop, her anguish is surrendered to the wind. But flying on down the hill towards Warcop, she knows it would not be wise to go any further.

She gets off Fauvel on the way back, eager now to stay out as long as she can. Shadows lengthen across the valley, chimney smoke drifting gently. All is becoming obscure, settling in for the night. A blackbird warbles with earnest joy from the hedgerow and Fran feels a moment of peace. But it doesn't last. Egidia Crackenthorpe walks out of her gate.

Fran prays she won't turn her head. But her prayers are not answered.

Egidia's eyes narrow. And she waits, so Fran has no choice but to greet her. 'Good evening, Mistress Crackenthorpe.'

Egidia lifts her chin. 'It's not good at all, living so near to such a sinner.'

Fran lifts an eyebrow. 'Is that so?' She's tempted to ask what Thomas has done now, but the steely look in Egidia's eye prevents her.

'You think you'll not be discovered under cover of night, but I'm not fooled.'

'Indeed.' Fran is bewildered.

'Do you feel no shame?'

'I might, if I knew what you were talking about.'

With one frugal movement, Egidia steps forward, so they are eye to eye. 'Sodomite,' she hisses. 'And with the priest too. I've had my suspicions for long enough, but I saw you riding wrapped up in him with my very own eyes last night, so don't try to deny it.'

Fran wants to put her hands round that lily-white throat, stop the words, the bile, the malevolent discontent. She folds them carefully. 'You have it wrong, lady. There's no sin.' Walking away quickly, she feels the arrows at her back.

'You're a liar, Francis Hilton.'

I have been, Fran thinks. *But no more.*

Three days later, there is a commotion at the front door, a running up the steps and suddenly Will is in the room. He is dressed most strangely, in tunic and hose, and she gasps to see him. 'You are here!'

He dashes towards her, sees Giles, frowns. 'Pray leave us.'

Giles looks at Fran. She nods.

Will's fingers dance against his thigh until the door closes. And then he turns to Fran, seizing both her hands. 'My lady, you are looking at the man who will become your husband.'

'Truly?'

'Truly.'

She throws herself into his arms, feels such a tide of relief she thinks she might be sick. But it passes. 'What did the abbot say?'

He leads her to her chair, sits down and pulls her on to his knee. 'He was most distressed to begin with. We prayed through the night but, in the morning, I was just as adamant that I wished to leave the order. He consulted with Brother Jerome, who knows most about the law and they agreed that the vows I took as a novice, though they are supposed to be unbreakable, must be kept willingly. And so, in much sorrow, they agreed to let me go.'

She traces a finger across his lips. 'Was it sorrowful for you too?'

He catches her hand, kisses it. 'I do not feel so now. Perhaps, when I have had time to think on it, I might feel differently. But there is so much to attend to before we are wed, and I think more on what I must learn that I might govern our lives properly and the children we will have and what I will teach them.' He grins. 'And we must both grow our hair.'

She already feels it as an annoyance, the constant need to wear a cap so her hair should not contradict the rest of her appearance. But that is such a little thing. 'Your brother came here the other day.'

Will laughs. 'How was he?'

'Confused, I think. But he said he would give you some land.'

Will nods. 'He is a good man.'

'And I must go to speak with Sir Roger's man, about Hilton.'

He taps her on the nose. 'Not you, you silly goose. And that reminds me. I should give you this.' He searches inside his tunic, brings out a ring, a plain gold band with flowers carved into it. He reaches for her hand, puts it on.

She looks at her hand in wonderment. 'But I have nothing to give you!'

'It matters less, for I need not confirm or deny what we mean to do.'

'You think I would?'

'No, of course not. I only meant you must show the world you are betrothed, so you will not be judged.'

She thinks of Egidia Crackenthorpe, sees the wisdom in it. 'But can I not come with you, when you go to see about Hilton?'

'There is no need.'

'But all my household, my tenants—'

'They are not your concern. You must run this house.

But the rest is my responsibility. You see how industrious I will be!'

She twists the ring round and round on her finger. 'Will, I . . .'

He smiles, kisses the side of her face, moves towards her lips.

She feels herself fall into him, vanquished by her desire. But there is also rising within her something forceful she doesn't yet fully understand, the part of her that wants to fight against it.

Fran stands once more in her hall, but this time Will is by her side. He speaks gently, carefully, to those who are gathered, as if they are all his children and must be brought to understand the way things are now, whether they wish it or not. When he is finished, he goes to speak with Harry Sowerby, drawing him into one corner, speaking low, urgently.

Fran stands alone. She watches them all departing to their tasks and is grateful when Giles and Willow approach. Willow describes a scene in the book he's reading, *The Quest of the Holy Grail*. There is a part in it, he says, where one of the knights, Sir Bors, must choose between saving his brother Lionel from captivity or a damsel who is being carried off to certain dishonour by another knight.

Fran nods. 'You know I know it. I have read it to you many times.'

'Do you think he was right to save the maid and not

his brother? I mean, is that always the right thing to do?'

She laughs. 'Are you asking me because you imagine I have a different opinion now?'

They both nod.

For the briefest of moments, Willow puts a hand on her arm. 'It's a serious question, though, don't you think, my lady?'

'But I haven't changed—'

Will is suddenly there beside them, pulling Willow roughly away. 'Do not touch your mistress, or on my life I will thrash you.'

'Will!' Fran tries to hold him, but he throws her off. For one pure white moment, she means to push him back. But, at that same moment, she knows without a shadow of a doubt that, if she did, her new life would be over before it had begun. Trembling with anger and frustration, she forces herself to stand entirely still, arms crossed, hands clasped over her elbows.

'Do you understand?' Will jerks a finger in Willow's face.

'Yes, sir.' Willow slinks away.

Will turns to Fran, puts an arm round her. 'You must not let another man touch you.'

She shakes still, but must speak. 'You had no cause to do that. He meant nothing by it, and you know it. Of course we must all learn to behave differently. But you must give us a little time, I pray you.' She can scarcely breathe for the effort of keeping her voice low, her words calm, when she wants to shout at him for browbeating Willow.

Will sighs, drawing her away to the other side of the room, his fury spent. 'Perhaps I was a little hasty. And believe me, I do understand. It is hard for all of us. But what you and your father did was most scandalous, so you must be entirely circumspect from now on.' He kisses the top of her head. 'Do not worry. I will instruct you.' He smiles radiantly. 'Just like the old days.' The smile fades. 'But if this is going to be troublesome, I could easily find another bailiff.'

Her heart skips a beat. 'No need. I can learn quickly. You know that.'

He smiles. 'Do you forgive me?'

He says it so prettily that Fran cannot help but smile and nod. She thinks Will has much to learn too, that she must give him time.

He holds both her hands at his chest, looking down on her with eyes like arrows. 'You must understand, Fran. I have only just acquired you, and at great cost. If you promise me that you will always give proper consideration to your own honour and to mine, I will be satisfied.'

Fran puts on a smile too and nods. But she wishes she could tell him that she is entirely confused as to what it now is – her honour – for it seems to consist mainly of an absence of things, a not doing rather than a doing, as it was before, when she was he.

But now he holds her hand to his heart, speaks gently, eyes beseeching. 'Take care of this, my love, I beg you. I am afraid of what you have released in me.'

Her own heart falters then. 'Of course I will.' And in that moment it's all she wants.

Leaning down, he whispers in her ear. 'I would be alone with you. It is no sin now we are betrothed.' He leads her up to her chamber, shutting the door firmly in Sarah's face. As soon as he turns, he pulls her to him, the kisses once more lighting her from within so that all she feels is her body's eagerness to move with his. His hand slips to her breasts, covering and kneading, but so gently that she burns beyond all endurance, a low moan escaping parted lips.

His breath shudders on hers as he takes her hand, moving it slowly but surely until it comes to rest between his legs. She knows it will be firm, is not afraid to discover for herself what it is she's never had. But suddenly he clutches at her, a great convulsion rising through him. She looks up to see his eyes like glass and far away, his face frozen as if in agony, and that frightens her.

Slowly he returns. 'Forgive me. I did not mean to ...' He turns away, pushes a hand through his hair. 'You see what power you have.'

She reaches for him. 'Are you hurt?'

'No, no.' He pats her hand. 'Just ... I am not used to ... I should go now.' He takes a deep breath, kisses her on the cheek. 'I will return in the morning.' With a nod, he is gone out of the room, leaving her bereft and wondering.

Will returns to Hilton as often as he can, though he still has responsibilities as priest to fulfil until the abbot at Shap appoints another in his place. But as the days grow ever shorter, he arrives most agitated, pacing the solar so Fran becomes giddy if she tries to watch him. She is already accustomed to sitting so as to let him debate with himself, since her previous interjections were either ignored or turned into possibilities of Will's own invention. But what she understands with some anguish is that it's not so simple as Will had been led to believe at Shap Abbey.

He thrusts his hair backwards over his diminishing tonsure. 'There is even talk of having to send to the head of our order in Avignon, so that he might release me from my vows. That will take months!'

'Come, sit.' She speaks calmly, though she too finds the thought of waiting increasingly intolerable. She feels she inhabits a life that is incapable of being lived. What she yearns for now is to be Will's wife, certainly, with the responsibilities that brings; but to be a mother would, she thinks, give consequence and purpose to the days and years ahead.

At last, he throws himself down beside her with a sigh, one arm wrapped around himself, a hand pulling at his mouth. But he is not finished speaking yet, laying out what he must do, who he must speak with. Resting her head on his shoulder, she strokes the side of his neck, imagining the fells turning golden, the grouse bursting out of the heather, owl and merlin hunting. Fran can feel his own heart beating most powerfully, his legs eager to test themselves against the hills.

She blinks, catching herself. But it's true, she does lament the lack of exercise, her muscles complaining of their neglect.

The next day Will rides back up to Hilton, but has time

only for a brief moment when he clasps Fran to his breast
and tells her he must go to Cockersand near Lancaster,
which lies many miles to the south and west of Warcop.
Abbot William of Shap is intending to visit there anyway
and thinks it would help if they consult Abbot Roger. He
lifts her chin. She expects his kiss. But instead he tells her
gently that she must behave as if the eyes of the world – by
which she knows he means his own – are upon her. Only
then does he bring his lips to hers.

For a day or so, she finds herself endlessly tripping
over herself, unable to settle to any task for more than a
few minutes at a time before she starts gazing into the
far distance without seeing anything at all. She has never
missed anything or anyone like this before. She's not sure
she likes it, this constant desiring. It is a most superlative
form of ennui, that robs her of sensible thought, dragging
her through the hours as if she has no will of her own.

But, after those first few days, it is ennui of a more
general kind that afflicts her. She must look after the
household, of course, making sure there is enough food
and drink for the kitchen, firewood for the great oven
and each room, that the manor is kept clean, the rushes
changed, and all paid for. But she has overseen this since
her mother left anyway.

And still her sewing is excessively bad, and Sarah
laughs at her behind her hand. At least she can resume
her reading, Giles and Willow at her feet and even
Edie sometimes standing by the door, deftly mending
something or other. She knows Giles is uneasy, for he has
no clear role in her household now. Fran means to speak

with Will, who needs a squire of his own. But she fears he will be less likely to agree if the idea comes from her, can only praise Giles in his hearing and hope he will decide for himself and soon.

She spends as much time as she can in the herb garden. Sometimes Edie comes, and Fran asks her to tell her more about each plant, what their various uses might be, for she has only a basic understanding. Edie is patient, making her touch and smell and look. And Fran sees her studying her too, but does not ask what she finds.

So the five days Will is away feel interminable, but they end and he clatters into the stable, running to find her, to gather her in his arms. She feels herself spring back into life, flowering once more, and thinks that is both marvellous and terrible, that she must learn to find happiness in herself.

He brings good news. The abbot at Cockersand is of the same opinion as his own abbot, that a monk's vows must be given and kept freely and so, terrible though it is, they are satisfied that he is committed to leaving. There is no need to send to the continent. Now they need only approach Sir Roger Clifford to settle their affairs and give his blessing to their marriage.

He is pleased, too, to find her sitting quietly in her room, wrestling with her sewing. She is relieved that he finds nothing to spoil his return. And Sarah knows now without being told that she must leave her mistress alone with the new master, the door banging behind her.

Will shakes his head. 'Must that creature always make such a noise?'

Fran bites away the rebuke, puts a hand on his arm. 'She cannot help it. She is not like other people.'

'I know that.' He glowers at the door and she draws her hand gently down the side of his thigh so that he turns to her quickly, the fire already caught. 'I have missed you so much.' He kisses her neck, her cheek, nibbling at her mouth before covering her lips entirely, his tongue moving inside.

She feels the giddiness take hold, the ache deep within that swells until it controls everything. She grips him tight, pulling him close.

But already he is tugging her up, swinging her into his arms. Quickly he crosses the room, places her on the bed and himself immediately beside her. She feels her hands moving on to him, under his shirt, over his belly, moving down . . . But he stops her hand, pins them both above her head, tugs at her gown, fighting the cloth.

Arching her back, she feels the ache grow so that her eyes begin to water, her breath utterly unruly. His hands are on her skin now, for she wears no braies, and then her skirts are above her waist and the air below, fanning her desire even as she blushes that he sees her cunt.

The rest follows suddenly. One moment, he is struggling with his belt, letting go of her hands, the next he is on top of her, intent on breaching her, guiding himself inside and her eyes are flung open with the pain of it, so that she is certain she must be broken.

And then he shudders, crying out, and his weight is entirely upon her, so she can scarcely breathe. She lies there, wondering that such a thing, with so much promised beforehand and so much resting upon it, is over.

He rolls away, pulling up his breeches, and she is glad of it.

Lying entirely still, she feels a rawness inside, but also a wetness. Quietly she slides a hand between her legs and gasps when she sees the blood on her fingers, slick and dark. It's true. She is broken.

But he catches her hand, smiles. 'It's just the first time. Because you were a maid.'

And no longer. She wonders if everyone will know. If it's now written on her. And if God wills there should be a child.

He catches that thought. 'If we are blessed, you should not worry. We will be married before it is born.' Standing up abruptly, he tucks in his shirt. 'I must go to speak with Harry.' Kissing his fingers and throwing them at her, he is gone.

She lies very still, a confusion of thoughts slipping through her. But what is done is done. She stands up, holding her skirts so she can cleanse herself. But she is sure now everyone will know, will see she is changed, for she walks around the void into which he has poured himself. She feels it still.

Sarah throws open the door, comes in singing, albeit without any discernible tune. She wanders to the bed, straightens the covers. And Fran runs to her, throws herself into her arms. Sarah pats her on the back and, when Fran finally releases her, continues her perambulation.

Fran watches her closely for any sign. But there is none and Fran picks up her book, wondering if perhaps she was mistaken, and that the greatest gift a gentlewoman possesses, that she is taught to guard so carefully until she is ready to bestow it, is not something that is given, but something that is taken. The thought occupies her mind for the rest of the day. But when Will is finished with all he must now attend to, he seeks her out, hands eager to rest somewhere on her person, to draw her close. Feeling his need of her, she believes he values her gift above all things and is content.

Fran is not sure how the time passes, but it does. Autumn burns triumphantly before fading away in a dismal tumult of wind and rain. She pours herself into preparing for the onslaught of winter; setting out how much meat and grain she'll need for the storeroom; making lists of places in the manor that need mending; getting Edie to investigate if all the kitchen's pots and pans, the many utensils hanging round the walls, are still usable or if the tinker should be sent for; questioning Harry Sowerby, when she comes upon him alone, on the matter of firewood.

Will grows ever more diligent in attending to all his new tasks and sometimes Fran doesn't see him between dinner and supper. There are still tender moments between them, especially when they lie together, lost in rhythms of pleasure that come so easily. But, more often, when they sit in the hall or the solar in the evening, she cannot find anything to say to him that will not sound as if she is questioning what he does. She was eager, to begin with, to hear about their beasts and the corn and any difficulties with their tenants. But he quickly tired of her interest, complaining that it was none of her business, if she presumed to do more than nod.

And so she cannot think it bodes well when, a few days after Martinmas, she hears his impatient step on the stairs even before she's had time to consider what needs to be done this day. The door to their chamber is wrenched open and Will strides in. He holds a paper in his hand, thrusting it towards Fran. 'What is this?'

'I don't know. If you give it to me, I might be able to tell you.'

'Speak to me with proper courtesy, if you please. I am not one of your lapdogs.'

Since Fran keeps no animals but Dolfyn, she knows he means the members of her little company, whose exploits he no longer wishes to hear spoken about. She dips her head, the better to hide her own annoyance. 'Pray forgive me, my lord.'

He pauses for a moment, then thrusts the paper at her.

Turning away, she knows the seal belongs to her mother's priest and feels a moment of guilt and yearning, that Christian should not know about her daughter, nor her impending marriage, nor Hilton. But she will write again, will try to find the words to speak of the things that were hidden and now are not. It would have been so much easier if her mother were here, to guide her in womanly ways, to forewarn of its many pitfalls and strangenesses.

Fran reads quickly, devouring the words. Christian tells her she was most relieved and overjoyed to receive Fran's letter. Once more, she laments the difficult times to which they are all prey, jests that she is half the woman Fran will remember now there's so little to eat. She doesn't mention marriage again, which makes Fran wonder if she is content as she is. That is a goodly state to be in, Fran thinks. She looks up. 'Tis my mother.'

'Let me see.' Will demands the letter back almost as soon as she has finished reading.

She doesn't wish to let it go, but his hand is gesturing to her. Without even reading it, he tears it up and throws the pieces into the fire.

Fran gasps, runs towards the flames.

He catches her wrist. 'What are you thinking, receiving letters from the enemy?'

'She's my mother. And no enemy. I've told you a hundred times, she didn't choose to return to Scotland. She was forced to go.'

'And I have told you a hundred times, there is always a choice. What she did was utter folly. But it matters not. You must not write to her any more. I will ask Harry Sowerby to make sure of it.'

She gasps again, that her own bailiff should be set to spy on her, but Will is already gone. Sitting back down, she opens her book but sees nothing on the page through the tears of anger and a smothering sadness. And at last she cannot help but wonder to herself how she ever thought this was what she wanted.

Chapter 16

Sir Roger Clifford has gone to his castle at Skipton in Yorkshire and will be there for some time. Will is even more impatient for their marriage, eagerly imagining a child growing in Fran's belly that would be his to shape. Fran listens to him, her heart torn between a longing and a dismay. She counts the days until her courses should come, just like he does. And though she prays that new life has come to dwell inside her, a part of her would not be dismayed if the blood did afflict her.

Once more he rides off on their business, his kisses of farewell still full of passion. Since Skipton is some distance away and Sir Roger no doubt has much to occupy him, Will warns her he might be gone for some time. She lowers her head to his chest, but in truth she is glad for his absence, hopes she will recover a quiet mind if she can think on all that troubles her without worrying about pleasing him. She has still not forgiven him for tearing up her mother's letter, but she can see he had good reason for doing so and perhaps she has been foolish. But then she knows she's not the only one sending and receiving missives from the other side of the border, for the messenger had other letters to deliver, and wars cannot unmake families.

But what brings her most anguish is the knowledge that all that had once bound her to Will, the love that had grown and deepened in honour and a sustaining companionship, was bound to be extinguished once she was her true self. The signs were always there. He loved the youth he had once taught and had even learnt to accept him as an equal in these last fraught months. Fran can see Will loves her still, but she cannot help feeling he mostly loves to possess her. No doubt he is glad, she thinks gloomily, to love her as a woman, to restore the mastery over her that he had long thought was naturally his. She curses Adam now, wishing with all her heart she had waited longer to recover from the shock of his death and her role in it. And yet ...

Damned if she does; damned if he doesn't. She tries to tell herself another husband could have been even more demanding. At least her long acquaintance with Will means she understands him. She must learn how to better anticipate his moods, use cunning to flatter and suggest, never declare or demand.

But, God's teeth, she resents it.

Autumn is nearly over. Thankfully the rains have stopped, even if the wind is restless, intent on bringing down the remaining leaves. Fran is once more free of the worry of doing or saying the wrong thing, sitting with Giles and Willow and talking about anything they like.

But mostly she inhabits the garden in the hope Edie will come. She has made the girl confess to her shock at Fran's transformation, her dislike of the thought of a woman acting the part of a man. 'I is most confused, mistress, because I is thinking the world is so much more of a strange place than I is already thinking. It isn't right at all that women should be being men, now is it?'

'I know, Edie.' But she turns her head away, for now she is not so sure.

But Edie is no fool. 'You is still not liking tae be a woman, mistress?'

'It's harder than I thought.' Fran smiles brightly, feeling brittle. 'But I will become used to it.'

Edie smiles too, but her eyes are still upon Fran's face. 'Forgive me if I is speaking when I shouldn't be, but I is not liking you being sad. I'm thinking now, 'tis a curse what be happening tae you.'

And Fran bites her lip, not trusting herself to say anything. She plucks at the last remnants of sage, brings it to her nose, willing herself not to cry again.

She clutches at the small freedom she has been afforded by Will's absence even as she listens to her body for the slightest change. She doesn't know what it feels like, of course, to carry a child. But she thinks she will know even as she puts on her breeches and tunic, marvelling again at how easy it is to walk around, to bend and turn without thinking about miles of cloth intent on tripping her up.

She goes in search of Harry Sowerby, finding him at a portion of the dyke where stones are fallen down. He looks up, smiles, then starts back.

'Will you say anything, Harry?' She holds her face steady. 'I would not blame you if you did.'

Harry scratches his head, takes a deep breath. 'My lord didn't ask me about that, Francis, so I'm thinking it isn't important.'

She nods, puts a hand on his arm. 'Thank you.'

Next she finds Giles, whose eyes nearly protrude out of his head. 'You shouldn't be doing that, sir . . . my lady.'

'It's just for a few days. One last time. If you wouldn't mind indulging me, I promise not to do it again.'

He purses his lips, nods slowly. 'I miss those days.' It is a whisper, his head turned away.

She says nothing, for fear she will be overwhelmed even as she wonders if they both misremember how good they were. She tells him to tell Willow that they will ride out within the hour.

Willow grins when he sees her. 'Where are we going, sir?'

'Wherever we like.'

They do it every day, each taking a turn in deciding their path. She holds tight to every moment, the smell of the lower fells as the bracken turns to rust, the furious cheeping of the little birds feasting on the seed heads. And then she tells them they must stop. 'My lord might return any day now and I must not disappoint him.'

They nod, not saying that she disappoints them instead.

She bids Sarah wash her clothes, lays them back in the chest with a pang that spears her deep within her heart. She is not sure now it has helped, feels it as an indulgence she could ill afford. Returning to her skirts and her sewing, she is unsatisfied with both and thinks Edie is right. She is cursed.

Will is joyful, though, having found much favour with Sir Roger, who is a young man and most intent on making his mark on the world. He tells Fran of the discussions they had about the state of the north country and the realm, of Sir Roger's many courtesies. And his good mood distracts her, brings some respite from her restlessness. He is gentle with her, laughing when she shows him her wanton stitching, eagerly seeking her pleasure as well as his own when they lie together. He strokes her belly, puts his ear to it as if he might hear their child and she laughs, strokes his hair. He tells her they will soon be man and wife in law, though he believes God has already blessed them.

But the next day she hears a great cry as he comes in the front door and she feels a shiver crawling up and down her spine, her guilt flooding back upon her, though she was sure none would betray her.

Rushing out of the solar, she tries to take his arm, but he throws her off. She follows him into their chamber. He turns to her, a wild look upon his face. 'Give me the key.'

She knows he means to her chest, fumbles with the chain attached to her waist. When she finally releases the key, he snatches it from her hand, throws open the lid. Pulling out everything else, he finally reaches her breeches, tunic, braies. Seizing them in his arms, he throws them all on the fire and her heart stretches so taut she fears it must shatter.

But she will not weep, nor will she beg. She just watches him and wonders who he is. 'Who told you?'

'Someone who would never betray her husband as you have me.'

And she curses her stupidity, knows beyond doubt that Egidia Crackenthorpe must have seen her when they rode out, though they kept away from Thomas Bacon's side of Hilton. She turns from him, but there is nowhere else to go.

He stands watching the flames die away, the remains of her clothes hissing at him. And then he comes to her, takes her by the top of both arms and shakes her. 'It is done, do you understand?'

She nods, but inside she curses him for ever making her believe that love is enough.

Will acts as if nothing had happened. When he touches her, she feels as fervent a coldness as she had the heat of her former passion. And yet her body still rises to meet him, which both disgusts her and relieves her of the pretence of desire.

She thinks it will break her, this fury against the man she will marry and live with until one of them dies. And then she remembers her mother, the distance from her father for most of the time they were together, and wonders how many women must make this their task. And that settles her, to see it as a quest, a test of her mettle and fortitude. Once more, she wears a false face, feeling her way towards that which will make her life bearable. Once more, she thinks a child will soothe things between them, will help to bind her to Will in a way that is not entirely of his making. But she prays for a daughter, for Will is unlikely to be so commanding over the bringing up of a girl. Or at least she hopes not.

The night falls quickly now, their breath visible, the firewood quickly burned. She resents it, but is glad of the warmth of Will's body next to hers. She will know soon if she is with child and hopes this will bring peace. These days she mostly sits with Sarah in her chamber in the evening. She goes to bed early so as to spare the candles.

Sarah is restless and fretful these days, her face bright red despite the cold, her body prone to sweats that cause her to moan without cease. Will cannot stand her near him, leaving them alone most of the time until he can chase her away if he comes to bed before Sarah has finished undressing Fran. 'That creature should not be anywhere near you. I would find you a proper maid,' he tells her.

'I have a proper maid.' Fran is distracted, for she thinks she can feel something painful in her belly. It is a mere suspicion as yet, so she will not tell Will that she thinks her courses are coming.

The next day she and Sarah sit together in the solar. Fran reads out loud from the Bible, stumbling over the Latin but trying to keep her mind steady. Sarah is spinning, making small cries every now and then when something particularly interesting happens, the parting of the Red Sea or the bit where Abraham nearly sacrifices his son Isaac. At this, Sarah tuts. And then she rubs her hands over her face, sighing loud and long.

Fran looks up. 'Are you hot again?'

Sarah rises, a miserable look on her face. She moves away from the fire, steps through the doorway and leans over to pick up her skirts, begins to throw them up and down so that every other moment she is quite naked below the waist.

'Sarah!' Fran rushes towards the door, afraid someone might see and tell Will. But it is already too late. She didn't hear the footsteps, but there's no denying the angry voice in the passageway. And then Sarah falls backwards through the door, holding her cheek. Will follows close behind, his hand raised to her again.

Fran screams. Harry Sowerby comes in too, wringing his hands.

Will turns to Harry. 'Take her away. I want her out of this house. She can work with the flocks or the corn, but I will not have her here.'

Harry glances at Fran, but immediately puts a hand gently on Sarah's shoulder, leading her out of the door. Sarah begins to protest and Fran runs towards her.

But Will puts out an arm to hold her. 'You saw what she did. She is an ungodly creature.'

'She doesn't understand. She's not like everyone else. And where will she live, have you thought of that?'

He shrugs. 'She can stay with the widow Elliot. I'll pay her for it, so you need not complain.'

'Let her stay a little longer, so I might explain it to her.' She gets down on her knees. 'Please, I beg you.'

He frowns, pressing his mouth together. 'You have three days.' He turns on his heel without giving her another glance.

Fran waits until she can no longer hear his footsteps, flies out of the room, finds Sarah at last in the kitchen, howling in Edie's arms. She kneels down, takes Sarah's hands. 'I'm sorry, I'm so sorry.' Fran says it over and over again.

'What is tae be happening wi' her, mistress?' Edie wipes Sarah's nose with her kerchief.

'The master says she is to stay with Luke's mother. But she's been with me all my life. She won't understand what's happening to her.' Fran feels so helpless, it is intolerable. 'We cannot stay here.' The words slip out without thinking. She looks at Edie, bites her lip.

But Edie nods.

Though that does not make her any the wiser, Fran feels the relief of it. 'You will help me?'

Edie nods again.

'Then I will think of something. Keep Sarah here. She will forget soon enough what has passed this day. That is a blessing, at least.'

She has three days to decide the course of her own life and Sarah's. It does not seem enough. She goes back to the solar, kneels down before Will, takes his hand. 'I beg your forgiveness.'

'What for?' His face is like stone, his gaze far from hers.

'I disappoint you and it grieves me.'

He glances down, brows raised. 'And what has brought you to this conclusion? I am glad of it, but it seems ... unlikely.'

She nods. 'I am weary of our strife.'

He pulls her up, sits her on his knee. 'Then I rejoice.'

She buries her face in his tunic so he cannot see her

treachery. That night she tells him she fears her courses are about to begin.

'You are certain?' He pushes a strand of hair off her face, mouth heavy.

She nods. In this, she does not lie.

'But they have not yet come?'

She hesitates, for he will go to sleep in the solar while she bleeds and it is tempting to send him now, this minute. But she gives him this respite because of what was once between them, shaking her head. He reaches for her, and she kisses him fiercely, feeding her body with his sweat and his need for her. When he is finished, when he cries out and clings to her, she lets him subside and turns over. He is no longer her concern.

She whispers with Edie in the herb garden, their faces so close she can see every pore on the girl's skin. 'I would take Giles with me. It will not be long till Will sends him away anyway, and two swords are better than one.'

'But where is it you is going, mistress?'

'It's better I don't tell you, and then you won't have to lie. All I will say is that he'll never find me.'

Edie looks away.

Fran strokes her arm. 'I'm sorry, Edie. I'll miss you.'

Edie speaks quietly, but forcefully. 'I been missing you since you is coming back from Elsdon. I is not thinking I could say that. I is cursing Adam Fothergill for it, though I is not thinking he meant it.'

'No. He wasn't to know.' She thinks more kindly on

Adam for the first time in a long time, hoping he rests in peace. 'Edie, I need you to ask Giles or Willow for some clothes. For me. And if you could perhaps make them a little smaller?'

Edie nods vigorously.

'And perhaps you could speak to Giles. About coming with me. I daren't risk being caught speaking to him alone. Do you think I can trust him?'

She considers that. 'Aye, mistress. He is not liking the priest.'

'Is that enough, do you think? Would he wish to come with me?'

'You is knowing he would.'

Fran nods, but she worries all the same, for there is much about what they're about to do he will not like.

She finds it hard to conceal her anxiety and her excitement. Sometimes she catches Will looking at her with suspicion in his eyes. It's as if she's a prize he isn't sure he has truly won, which annoys and perplexes him greatly.

It troubles her too, how she will escape her room and descend the stairs without being heard. She confesses this to Edie.

'I is already thinking on this. We is needing some sort of commotion, tae draw him away.'

'I have only till the day after tomorrow, and then Sarah must leave. That reminds me. Can you give her something to send her to sleep? She's never left this house since she came as a girl. I doubt she'll leave quietly.'

Edie brings her hands to her mouth. 'What is happening tae us if we is being caught?'

Fran puts a hand to her cheek. 'He will *never* find out you had any hand in this, I swear.'

But Edie shakes her head. 'You is not knowing that.'

They cling to one another. 'I will not go.' Fran whispers it.

Edie shakes her head again. 'Look what we is doing wi' Adam, God rest 'im. We is doing this too. Giles is helping. He is thinking this is being another adventure.'

Fran smiles then. 'I'm sure he is.' But she quickly becomes serious. 'If there is to be a commotion, it must be Giles who starts it. If you or anyone else who knows come because you must have heard it, you should do it slowly, as if you rise from your beds.'

The next day they meet again, Dolfyn lying on a patch of soil warmed by a pale autumn sun. Fran paces about most distractedly, certain now they cannot devise a plan sufficient so she and Sarah and Giles might make their escape without betraying those that help them.

Edie watches her, cutting at a rosemary bush with her knife so that it might grow better next year. At last she stands up. 'Listen tae me, my lady. We is talking, Giles and me. You is having tae go to bed most early tomorrow, long before sunset. And when the priest is going tae the solar and Giles is undressing him, he will be going down the stairs and coming back soon after tae say he is seeing you running away dressed like a man again. And because the priest will not be being dressed, he will be sending him ahead tae look for you, and Giles is drawing them whichever way you is not going. And you must be hiding somewhere in your room in case the priest is going tae look for you there. But you must be telling me where you is going tae begin wi', and I'll be bringing Sarah somewhere near in the afternoon, as if we is just going for a little walk, and I is giving her summat tae mak' her sleep.'

Fran thinks this through, kneading each knuckle on her right hand. 'It's madness.'

''Tis all being madness, these days.'

'I go first up towards Murton.'

Edie nods. 'Then she is being at the chapel.'

'But how will I get Fauvel?'

'Oh, I is knowing this and is forgetting. Giles will be saddling him just before he is going up tae undress the priest so that you can get him when everything is quiet, when they are all drawn away. And then you is tae be waiting for Giles at the chapel.'

Fran blinks, working her way through the plan. She does not like that it is not of her own devising. But she cannot think of anything better, though she believes it to be of such delicate construction, one breath of wind would knock it over. 'Why would anyone believe Giles if no one sees me run? Will doesn't trust any of us.'

'You is not tae be thinking like that. You is tae be putting your faith in Giles, my lady.'

Fran strokes her brows, feeling fate gathering against her. But the die is thrown now. 'And you will not do anything that would draw suspicion upon you after you've taken Sarah?'

'You is not needing tae worry about me, I is promising you.'

'Then I will do as you say.' Fran cannot imagine it.

She feels a great lightness in her head, a nausea sweeping through her and wishes she wasn't really having her courses.

Edie puts a hand on her shoulder. 'I is bringing you some dandelion for that.'

Fran nods. They part and she feels such a melancholy that it's not difficult to convince everyone to stay away from her now her bleeding has begun.

The next morning, Edie kneels on the bare soil, tugging under her gown. Dolfyn comes to sniff beside her, but she pushes him away. At last she brings out a set of clothes tied to her waist. 'They is probably not being a good size.'

Fran nods. 'I'm sure they'll do.' She crouches down, holds up her skirts while Edie ties them on top of her chemise.

And then they must part forever. Fran holds the girl tight in her arms and lets the tears fall on Edie's neck. And Edie pulls away, walking quickly back towards the kitchen with herbs filling her hands. If her own tears overflow, Fran cannot see them.

Will sits in the hall looking through Harry's reckoning for this year. He watches her pass through and frowns. 'Come here.'

She feels the weight of the clothes about her belly. But she smiles, though only a little, and staggers as she comes close.

He rises, keeps his distance. He knows she bleeds. 'I was watching. Out there with the kitchen girl. You like her, is that not so?'

She nods, wary. 'She is teaching me more about herbs.'

He taps the side of his thigh. 'I see. I suppose that is fitting.'

'No one else knows as much as she does.'

'That will do. I have said it is fitting. But you disappeared, while you were there, crouching down. Why was that?'

Fran feels the breath leave her, swallows quickly. 'Forgive me, I am feeling most unwell. She . . .' This has an answer she has already devised, for she knows he is in the habit of watching her from the hall window. She shifts a little, holding a hand over her belly. 'She was showing me what she will plant next year, where each one will go, and what she's doing to some of the others so they will grow again abundantly. It is most interesting.'

He nods, watching her carefully. 'And you embraced.' He misses nothing.

But she has thought of this too. 'She's in love. A cowherd up at Murton. But he does not love her.'

Will grunts. He's not interested in the feelings of a kitchen girl. He takes a step towards her. 'There is something strange about you.'

Dolfyn starts forward and she fears he will bare his teeth at Will, so she holds on to his neck. Nodding, she feels her heart thud around the hall. 'I swell up sometimes. When it's really bad.'

He steps back. 'Then go to your chamber.' And he turns away, back towards the papers on the table.

She is glad of his unkindness, makes herself move slowly, painfully, though she wants to be away from him as quickly as possible. But he does not turn round again.

It is an agony, this waiting. She knows she should lie down, prepare for the long journey ahead of her, presuming she gets any distance at all. But the restlessness is full upon her now. Dolfyn yawns, lies down, and she thinks he is wiser than she is. She watches Edie depart with Sarah trundling along beside her, shrouded in a great woollen cloak. An age later, Agatha brings her supper and Fran bids the girl take Dolfyn back down to the kitchen to feed him scraps, for it would confuse matters or worse if he were left here. She does not feel like eating, but knows she must, forcing the meat into her mouth, dipping the bread into the gravy until she is in danger of vomiting it up again. She sits, hands in her lap, breathing deeply until the moment passes, a sweat upon her brow.

The sky begins to darken, clouds tinged with rose. She hears Will come upstairs, the closing of the solar door. It is time. But she is so scared, and the food will not stay down. Rushing to the garderobe next to the solar, she flings herself to her knees just as it all floods out and down the stinking hole. But then she feels better, spitting out the bile from her mouth. She must hurry now, for she hears Giles coming up the stairs, whistling cheerfully. Who would have imagined he could play such a part for her?

Tugging and tearing, she removes her clothes, shivering as the night begins to cool. Thankfully she has already found an old pair of braies that survived Will's burning and puts them on. Her new clothes are indeed most ill-fitting, the breeches so wide at the waist that the belt is useless. Throwing everything about, she finds the string Edie used to hold the clothes under their gowns. The shirt is just as huge, so that it hangs almost to her knees, and she struggles to fit the linen into her breeches.

She hears Giles go downstairs, her breath coming quickly now.

The tunic is better, and slowly she begins to feel more herself again. Throwing her gown and chemise into her bed where the rest of her clothes already lie, she seizes her cloak and puts it there too, for she must make Will believe she has fled. Pulling her cap tight upon her head, she opens her chest – empty now – and climbs in.

It seems an age until she hears footsteps again on the stairs, though in truth it cannot have been so very long. She thinks perhaps Giles is too dishonest in the noise he makes, his haste, the great knocking, his crying out that she is gone down the lower road towards Warcop. But she hears the frenzy in Will's voice, his great roar telling Giles to get after her while he dresses, the thudding back down the stairs. And she thinks that perhaps Will expected this.

She is most uncomfortable in the chest, something hard digging into her ribs. But she must not move. And, after everything, he does not come, running straight past her door and away. She opens the lid, the light outside only a glimmer in the window now. Reaching down to where she lay, her fingers find a ring, the one Adam gave her. She had not wanted to see it when she came back from Elsdon, and it must have fallen out of the pocket of her old tunic. She is glad of it now, putting it on her finger, marrying her to herself.

And then she rises, listening carefully. There is a great noise outside, the shimmer of torches. Her house lies quiet. Carefully she slips down the stairs, across the hall and hides in the shadows near the front door so she can hear when they all move away and it is safe for her to go out.

'Francis?'

She holds herself completely still, amazed to have got no further than this. Slowly she walks out of the shadows, finds Harry Sowerby standing before her.

'Harry, I—'

'Edie told me what you do and I'm glad of it. Take this. It's yours by rights anyway.' He hands her a well-worn pouch, heavy with coin.

She opens her mouth to speak, but he is already hurrying past, motioning to her to hide once more. Pulling open the front door, he walks away as fast as his aches and pains allow.

Thrusting the pouch inside her tunic, she feels weak still with the thought of discovery. But she is not yet found.

Now she listens hard. Will is gathering everyone to him outside, asking if anyone saw the mistress and which way she was going. He sends Jack the kitchen boy to look in the stables for Fauvel. Someone says they heard something, perhaps someone running, but others are not sure if it was my lady or Giles. Jack returns to say Fauvel is still there with a saddle on his back.

'And she's not there, in the stables? Did you look, you fool?' Will is shouting now, unable to make sense of it.

'No, she is not.' The voice is clear and crisp. Egidia Crackenthorpe. Fran listens even harder.

Egidia's voice comes closer. 'I saw her running down the road past my house in those ungodly garments. And later the boy riding out. You must go and fetch her back and teach her a lesson she won't forget, so these shameful things will never happen again.'

And then there is another shout. Willow. Fran hears him running towards them all. 'I think . . . she . . . is found.' He stops for a moment, unable to catch his breath.

'You saw them?' Will has stopped shouting, but his words still lie on the edge of a shriek.

'I think so, my lord. I was standing at the top of the hill and thought I saw them some way down below. It looked like Giles walking with her on the horse.'

Fran is astonished, unable to understand any of this, fearful of what it means, if she will ever know.

'God's teeth, Willow. You should have made certain before you came to me. I will fetch her myself.' Will's fury is serene now it knows where it must be directed. 'You can all go home.'

There is a murmuring, then a gradual quieting and finally silence falls. There is only one thing left to listen for. The sound of hooves, slowly at first, and finally Will gallops away. She prays most fervently this is the last she ever hears of him.

She runs to the kitchen, releases Dolfyn, who hastens to her side. Together they slip out of the front door. The star of the sea greets them with a wink, the sun still a golden line below the western sky and the moon not yet risen. They run to the stables, the grooms all lying on the straw at the back. One of them opens his eyes, sees Fran. He rises suddenly, and she is afraid, though she is expecting him to do this. Reaching into the straw, he pulls out her sword in its scabbard with its belt and she takes it with a surge of excitement. She had given it to Giles as a reward for his service more than a moon ago, not knowing what else to do with it. Now she thanks God she hadn't given it to Will. The groom wishes her God speed and settles back down to sleep.

Buckling on her sword, she goes to Fauvel, putting her hand flat on his flank to reassure him before tugging on the bridle. She and Fauvel and Dolfyn walk out, as they have done countless times before. Fran climbs on Fauvel's back, feeling at ease in the saddle, fully alive now.

Riding carefully, Fran heads away from Hilton towards the fells before turning west and descending to the beck. They move slowly but steadily, Dolfyn keeping pace. Soon they find the track up towards Murton, moving faster now.

The chapel is little more than a black shadow etched with the last of the light. Leaping off Fauvel, Fran walks carefully across the slumbering graves to say goodbye to her father, Dolfyn close by. It is fitting this should begin and end with him, even if he would cry out to know his only child is leaving Hilton. Getting down on one knee, Fran murmurs a prayer for his immortal soul and forgives him at last.

But now Dolfyn bounds away, and Fran rises with a start as figures move towards them, like ghosts or revenants in the gloom. It must be Will. It cannot be.

But it is Giles, Dolfyn leaping at his side. And behind him, another boy Fran does not recognise.

'Giles, do you know if Sarah's here?' Fran has seen nothing to suggest she is.

'Yes.'

Fran is alarmed, nonetheless. 'But who have you brought with you?'

The boy moves past Giles, bows. 'You is not knowing me?' This one smiles as if he would burst with it.

Fran gasps. 'Edie!' And it all becomes clear, how the one could be behind the door and another running down the hill. 'You should not ... Did I not say ...?' Throwing eager arms around the girl's neck, Fran is aghast all the same. 'What have I done to you!'

But Edie has already turned towards the chapel. 'Sarah is awakening, and we should be flying from here tae whereiver it is you is thinking we should be going.'

Arms linked together against the dark, they move carefully towards the ruin. A loud moaning greets them, a great creature staggering towards them.

Fran runs then. 'Sarah, come with me.'

Sarah whimpers, flings herself at Fran so they both nearly fall over. Giles pulls Sarah off, and he and Edie wrestle her arms over their shoulders.

'How in God's name will we get her on Fauvel?' Fran begins to worry again.

'Will you hold her, till I fetch Percival.' There is a tension in Giles's voice too.

'I'll try.' Fran and Edie are almost no match for Sarah, who snores now like a wild wind, but with the weight of the world encompassed within her.

Fauvel stamps his hoof, and Fran must whisper quietly

to him too. They are all eager to flee, uneasy while they remain dangerously close to home.

Giles leads Percival from the back of the chapel, tying him up next to Fauvel. 'I think you must get up, so we can push her, if she'll put her foot in the stirrup.'

Something stirs back down towards Hilton, new torches ablaze.

'Can we leave her?' Giles whispers it, but he knows the answer.

Fran leaps up into the saddle. 'Give me her hands and raise her foot up. Quickly now.'

All three of them push and pull but nothing can bring Sarah where they need her to go. Tears prick at Fran's eyes.

'Don't push me, Edie.' Giles gasps out his annoyance.

'I is not. You is pushing me.'

But it is neither.

Sarah raises her head, moans loudly at Fran.

'Come up then.' Fran holds out a hand. 'And we shall go for a ride.'

Sarah hoots like an owl, setting her foot in the stirrup. For a second, she sways, neither up nor down. But with a powerful grunt, she thrusts her other leg over, nearly pulling them both off the other side. Giles and Edie hold on to Sarah's leg with all their might. Fauvel staggers, takes a few steps. Edie gives a little yelp, but Fauvel recovers, tosses his head.

Giles unties Percival's bridle, leaps on to his back. He reaches down for Edie, and they are all away, leaping into the night, into the unknown. If there are others coming after, they do not stop to find out, for no one but Fran knows where they ride to, and this gives them courage. They pass sleeping houses. A dog barks and Dolfyn growls. 'Come.' And they go again. Fran thinks there will be a time when this moment becomes distressing, when there will be a mourning for Hilton and all those left behind, even Will. But not yet.

They steal past Dufton, the wind blowing hard across them, tugging vigorously at their cloaks. Sarah howls into the night like a demon, and, though Fran's ears are much assaulted, perhaps such wanton cries will deter anyone from coming near them. The moon is risen now, a tiny sliver of misty white cut out of the firmament. They are high up, the land a mysterious shadow beneath a veil of silver. Fran knows this is a moment always to be remembered, for beyond it there is nothing but Fauvel's warmth and strength and the colour of their breath. They ride slowly now, Sarah's head resting heavily on Fran's shoulder. 'Edie?' Fran whispers it, in case the girl sleeps.

'Mmm.' Sleepy but not asleep.

'What about your father?'

There is silence for a long moment. 'I isn't asking 'im.'

They ride on for many hours, past Melmerby where a candle lights up a window, a harbinger of the dawn to come. The path grows steep, the horses slowing, stumbling. 'Just a little further,' Fran promises. The ground rises up before them, bleak and rough and still little more than shadow. But to the east, a long cushion of cloud billows up over the horizon like a great wave, a sky of palest blue hanging modestly behind. The stars still wink, but gently now, their shine diminishing until, one by one, they slink off.

The light gathers, pushing them on. They can see the path rising slowly to the top. No one speaks, for the day is soon beginning and with it come people who will ask questions. Giles goes ahead, for Edie is a much lighter burden. Fran hums a little tune.

And suddenly Giles stops. He and Edie hang there, in the sky, until Fran catches up. Now the land stretches away from them, down the folds of the hill and reaching off towards a mist-covered land next to a dark sea.

'We will rest soon, further down the hill, so look out for somewhere to give us shelter.' Fran remembers this place, something pleasant stirring deep inside.

'Is that where we're going?' Giles does not need to point. They are all looking.

'Yes.'

'And what place is it?'

Fran turns to them both, holds them firmly with a defiant look. 'Scotland.'

Characters

Those in italics were real people, though I have certainly added to their lives and invented their characters.

Thomas Bacon

As mentioned more fully in the entry for Andrew Hilton, half of the manor of Hilton was held by Thomas Bacon, whose unfortunate name probably derives less from a pork product and more from the fact his manor's full title was Hilton Beacon.

Emma Bacon

Only child of Thomas Bacon and his wife, Egidia Crackenthorpe.

Brothers of Hexham priory

Robert, prior; Philip, cellarer; Edwin, Ralph and William, monks.

Robert Bruce

King of Scotland (1306–1329). After winning at Bannockburn, the Scottish king intensified his raiding in northern England to try to force Edward II of England to make peace on Bruce's terms.

Sir Robert Clifford

Clifford inherited large swathes of Westmorland through his mother Isabella, heiress to half of her father Robert Vieuxpont's vast estate, becoming one of the most powerful men in England. Appleby was the centre of Clifford's Westmorland possessions, which included other castles such as Brougham and Brough. A prominent player in Edward I's conquest of Scotland, he was killed serving under Edward II at the battle of Bannockburn in 1314.

Sir Roger Clifford

Son of Sir Robert Clifford; lord of Appleby. Executed in 1322, aged twenty-two, for his part in the earl of Lancaster's rebellion against Edward II.

Egidia Crackenthorpe

Wife of Thomas Bacon; mother of Emma Bacon. Mistress of Hilton manor. Medieval women generally kept their birth surname even when they married.

Jamie Dickinson

A husbandman (essentially farmer) with a few bits of land to his name and a desire to acquire more.

Rob and Wat Dickinson

Younger and elder sons of Jamie Dickinson.

Sir James Douglas

One of King Robert's most stalwart generals and scourge of northern England.

Edward II

King of England from 1307 till he was forced to abdicate in January 1327. He was murdered the following September. Generally regarded as a far more ineffectual king than his father, Edward I (understatement of the year), although it's true that he inherited an empty treasury and huge debts, thanks to his predecessor's many wars. Edward II generally failed to bring armies to Scotland because his parliaments refused to grant him the money to do so unless he agreed to noble supervision and cutbacks. He succeeded in 1314 because his new Italian banker managed to secure loans from the pope and the French king. The failure of that campaign left much of northern England at the mercy of King Robert of Scotland.

Agatha Elliot

A girl in Fran Hilton's kitchen; sister to Luke Elliot, the shepherd's boy.

Luke Elliot

Shepherd's boy. Brother of Agatha Elliot.

Adam Fothergill

A husbandman who came from Flitholme (about two miles south-east of Warcop) but married Joan Mauchell, who brought him some land at Crackenthorpe (seven miles north-west of Warcop).

Jack Fothergill

Adam Fothergill's father. A herd at Helbeck.

Sir Andrew Harclay

Originating from Hartley in Westmorland, which lies some six miles south-east of Warcop, Harclay rose to prominence through his spirited and successful defence of Carlisle during the Scottish siege of 1315. He became earl of Carlisle in 1322 after defeating Thomas, earl of Lancaster – in revolt against his cousin, King Edward – at Boroughbridge. But he was frustrated with the king's inability to protect the north and made a peace treaty with King Robert of Scotland – for which he was executed a year later.

Simon Harrison

A husbandman in Warcop; has a feud with Jamie Dickinson.

(Fletcher) Hawise

Christian Kirkbride's maid.

Giles Helbeck

Originally Andrew Hilton's squire, he is now Fran Hilton's. Son of Sir Thomas Helbeck.

Sir Thomas Helbeck

Father of Fran's squire, Giles. Helbeck lies around four miles east of Warcop. In his actual life, Sir Thomas had been a member of Sir Robert Clifford's retinue, receiving sustenance for himself, an esquire, three grooms and three horses.

Michael Hewgill

Father Will Warcop's servant.

Andrew Hilton

In 1314, an inquisition was made on the lands and properties owned by Sir Robert Clifford, who held much of Westmorland (and elsewhere) and was killed at the battle of Bannockburn. Here it was recorded that Hilton Beacon was held by 'the heirs of Andrew Hellerton' and Thomas Bacon. Andrew got his half of Hilton from his cousin Thomas Hellerton, who was still alive in 1293. Hilton itself was recorded as comprising three carucates, a carucate being the notional area of land that could be ploughed annually by a team of eight oxen, or roughly 120 acres. In modern real money, Hilton would therefore cover about 1,456,920 square metres. The manor paid thirteen shillings and four pence in cornage each year, an amount that at its lowest, equates to £482. Cornage is a tax related to the number of horned cattle held by the tenant. I have simplified Andrew's surname to Hilton.

Fran(cis) Hilton

Lord of half of the manor of Hilton Beacon; 'son' of Andrew Hilton and Christian Kirkbride.

Jack (Flitholme)

Kitchen boy.

Christian Kirkbride

A Scot, married to Andrew Hilton before the outbreak of war between Scotland and England in 1296. Mother of Fran Hilton.

Joan Mauchell

Daughter of Roger Mauchell; wife of Adam Fothergill.

Roger Mauchell

Father of Joan Mauchell, Adam Fothergill's wife; held land at Crackenthorpe.

Sir Thomas Randolph

King Robert's nephew and a talented general.

Sarah (Smith)

Effectively Fran Hilton's maid.

Aidan Simpson

Son of Edgar Simpson.

Ava Simpson

Wife of Edgar; mother of Aidan and Ralph.

Edgar Simpson

Blacksmith in Warcop; father of Aidan and Ralph.

Ralph Simpson

Son of Edgar Simpson.

Harry Sowerby

Bailiff to Andrew Hilton, then Fran, responsible for the agricultural activity on the manor; father of Simon 'Willow' Sowerby.

Willow Sowerby

Son of Harry Sowerby, Fran's bailiff; a devotee of Arthurian literature.

Edie Strickland

Daughter of Fran's cook; works in the kitchen.

Tom Strickland

Fran's cook; father of Edie.

Sim Taylor

Fran's shepherd.

Sir Henry Warcop

Though most of what Sir Henry does here is entirely made up, there are a number of things about his life that are true. His entry in *The Knights of Edward I* reads: 'Assessor, etc., of subsidy, Westmorland, 24 Oct. 1301, and 1302. Commissioner of Array to choose 500 men there, 18 Feb. 1307. Made sheriff of Westmorland 10 Jy 1314 and still so 1320. Made sheriff again and constable of Appleby castle, 6 December 1322, and of the town 25 Jan, but cedes all these 22 May 1324. Commissioner re Knights Fees in Westmorland 3 Nov 1314, and of Array 1316. Knight of the shire, Westmorland, 20 Jan 1315, and a knight perambulating forests 30 Jy 1316. Thomas Aunay and others came to his house, forcibly entered his hall and various chambers, and took away his widowed daughter Isabel and John, son and heir of John Crokkedayk, whose marriage pertained to Henry. Thomas was imprisoned at Appleby. Pardon for good service in Scotland to William Lengleys for the rape of Isabel de Warcop, for breaking into houses of Henry de Warcop, and for robbery, 8 July 1314. Henry de Warcop is custos of lands late of John Crokedayk in Cumberland 18 July, holds Warcop, a moiety [half] of Wateby, and a tenement at Hellebek, Westmorland, late of Robert Clifford, 28 July, and pays rent at Warcop to Matilda, widow of said Robert, 27 September 1314. Conservator of Peace, Westmorland 20 Nov, commissioner of gaol delivery, Appleby, 12 Nov 1321, surveyor of rebels' lands there 4 July 1322. To view Appleby Castle *re* munitions 26 May 1324.'

Isobel Warcop

Sir Henry Warcop's daughter. A widow, she was abducted and ravished from Sir Henry's own hall, probably in 1313 or early 1314. Her ravisher, William Lengleys, was pardoned on condition he went with the English army to Scotland in 1314.

Will(iam) Warcop

Vicar of Warcop. According to *The History and Antiquities of Westmorland and Cumberland*, William Warcop became vicar in 1311. Before that, he was abbot of Shap Abbey, which had the right to appoint to Warcop, a gift bestowed in the reign of Edward I (1272–1307) by Sir Robert Clifford, because 'of the poverty and ruined estate of the said abbey, occasioned by the incursions of the Scots'. Because I needed Will to be not too much older than Fran, I skipped the bit about him being abbot. I also don't know if he really was brother or, as I have it, half-brother to the sheriff, Sir Henry Warcop, but it's quite possible, given that younger sons regularly went into the church.

Glossary

All Souls – 2 November, the day on which the faithful departed are remembered by Christians

bailiff – the person appointed to manage the agricultural work on the land farmed directly by the lord

beasts – four-footed creatures, but often used to indicate livestock reared by men and not just wild animals.

beck – a northern English word for a stream

braies – medieval undergarment for men, essentially trousers

breeches – trousers to the knees

cellarer – the person responsible for provisioning and catering in a monastery

chemise – shirt or undershirt

coif – a tight-fitting linen cap tied under the chin and worn by both men and women *cotehardie* – a long-sleeved garment, usually thigh-length and belted for men and full-length for women, often made to fit tightly by buttoning or lacing

courses – archaic word for menstrual flow

coxcomb – a vain and conceited person

cur – literally a dog, but used as a term of abuse

dinner – the first proper meal of the day, usually taken between 9 a.m. and midday, by which time much work has already been completed if sunrise is sufficiently early

dowry – money, goods or lands brought by a woman to her husband in marriage

equipage – now replaced by equipment

fell – a hill or other area of high land, particularly in north-west England

felo-de-se – archaic word for a suicide, literally 'one guilty concerning himself'

garderobe – a small room, in this case a toilet, which would be built out from the exterior wall of a castle or manor house so the waste fell into moat or river. Origin of word 'wardrobe', believe it or not

gauntlet – armoured glove

gillyflower – a carnation or stock or another wallflower with a potent scent

girdle – a belt, sash or cord drawn in about the waist and fastened; worn by men and women

hauberk – a piece of chainmail originally covering only the neck and shoulders, but eventually becoming a shirt reaching to the thigh

herd – someone who looked after animals, usually either sheep or cattle. A shepherd is therefore a herd of sheep

hiccock – the old word for hiccup

hose – covering of woven cloth or leather for the lower leg, with or without feet

husbandman – a free tenant farmer or small landowner

kirtle – a man's tunic; a woman's skirt

Martinmas – the feast of St Martin, celebrated on 11 November. This was when livestock were traditionally slaughtered to be eaten over the winter

Michaelmas – St Michael's Mass, 29 September

murrain – any virulent infectious disease of livestock

palfrey – a docile horse for ordinary riding (as distinct from a warhorse)

parlour – a room off a main hall offering some privacy

privily – privately

reckoning – financial accounts

reeve – the steward or manager of a bigger estate than Fran's

rheum – a head cold

settle – long seat or bench with a high back

solar – an upper room in noble houses or castles generally used as the family's private chamber

snaggle-toothed – having crooked, projecting teeth

squire – a trainee knight from roughly age fourteen

supper – the last meal of the day, taken in the evening

tonsure – shaving of the head or part of it; monks usually had the centre part shaved

tunic – undergarment worn on the top half of the body by both men and women

unguent – ointment

unswaddled – babies in the Middle Ages were bandaged in strips of linen cloth in the belief that this would stop their limbs from becoming deformed; they were 'unswaddled' at around eight or nine months

viscera – inner organs of the body

wedder – a castrated male lamb

whelp – literally the young of a dog

Whit Sunday – seventh Sunday after Easter; marks the day when the Holy Spirit descended on Christ's disciples

wimple – head and neck covering for women

worts – root vegetables

Author's notes

Matters of gender

First of all, you might imagine – as I certainly did – that the very idea of someone whom we would describe today as transgender cannot have existed in the Middle Ages. But, as ever, there is nothing new under the sun. The book I read with much delight (it's often surprisingly humorous) was *Le Roman de Silence*,[1] where a baby girl called Silence

1   There are others. For example, *The Life of Hilaria/Hilarion* originated in Egypt sometime after AD 500 and was translated into French in the fifteenth century; *The Life of St Marinos the monk* was probably written in Greek between the early sixth century and the mid seventh century, but there were also medieval French and German versions. There was even a court case in London in the late fourteenth century, where a man called John passed himself off as a woman named Eleanor, the details indicating that John experienced what we would now call gender dysphoria (Janin Hunt, *Medieval Justice: Cases and Laws in France, England and Germany, 500–1500*, Jefferson, 2009).

is also, like Fran, raised as a boy, in this case so as to succeed to her father's earldom of Cornwall since the king has forbidden women from inheriting. Silence grew up to be the very model of an Arthurian knight. However, the fourteenth century being the fourteenth century, she was given a very conventional ending – her true gender revealed, she naturally, dear reader, marries the king.

Nevertheless, there is much about the story that remains intriguing and elusive. The main thrust of the narrative deals with 'profound questions, predicated on the primary opposition of speech and silence, concerning women's voice and men's discourse, women's place in or absence from the social contract, whether verbal, economic or political'.[2] Indeed, despite the conventional ending, one of the main arguments of *Le Roman de Silence* has been interpreted as affirming 'a very unconventional notion that women should play an active role in both governance and marriage'.[3]

And, while it's easier in the twenty-first century to contemplate a different fate for Fran than that permitted to Silence, the essential dilemma each faces is exactly the same. Indeed, Silence has to endure being fought over by Nature and Nurture, who each present their respective arguments as to why she should reassume her biological gender or why he should keep up the pretence. When

2 Sarah Roche-Mahdi, 'Introduction' in *Le Roman de Silence*, Michigan, 2007, p. xx.
3 Heather J Tanner, 'Lords, wives and vassals in the Roman de Silence', *Journal of Women's History*, volume 24, number 1, Spring 2012, p. 138.

he's heard both arguments, Silence draws his own rather obvious conclusion.

> Then he began to consider the pastimes of a woman's chamber – which he had often heard about – and weighed in his heart of hearts all female customs against his current way of life, and saw, in short, that a man's life was much better than that of a woman. 'Indeed,' he said, 'it would be too bad to step down when I'm on top. If I'm on top, why should I step down?'

But it's not easy. Like Fran, Silence experiences qualms about his deception, the narrator telling us: 'I'm not saying that he didn't go through periods of hesitation and inner conflict as might be expected in a young person who came of such good stock, but who was also a tender child who had to force herself to live that way ... for his thoughts tormented him, and he felt this and suffered from it.'[4]

The war between Scotland and England

In 1296, King Edward I of England invaded the kingdom of Scotland in a war of conquest precipitated by the untimely death a decade earlier of Edward's brother-in-law, the Scottish king Alexander III. This led to a period of sustained warfare for the best part of fifty years, though

4   *Le Roman de Silence*, p. 125.

the conflict did not truly end until both countries became Protestant in the sixteenth century.

Lies of the Flesh is set in the immediate aftermath of the spectacular and highly unusual Scottish victory at Bannockburn in 1314, led by that master tactician Robert Bruce, who normally preferred to avoid battles. However, having failed to capture the English king (Edward II), Bruce tried to force the English government to agree a final peace on Scottish terms through intensive raiding of northern England. This was a tactic he'd first tried three years earlier, but now he made it into a most efficient form of terror since most of the communities threatened by these raids soon preferred to pay off the Scots by taking a 'truce' with them. Reluctantly, Edward II then agreed they could pay less in taxes to the English treasury.

At a time of colder and wetter climatic conditions, which probably helped to precipitate the outbreak of various animal diseases, the misery and hardship visited on the northern counties of England can scarcely be exaggerated. The Scots really did burn Brough and Appleby in 1314 and besieged Carlisle a year later.

Needless to say, some of those who were supposed to help and protect these counties – from the king down – either didn't care or even took advantage of the turmoil to settle scores or commit atrocities on their neighbours. It was, in short, a very nasty and brutish period in English history, at least for the north. And while King Robert of Scotland and his generals certainly didn't have things all their own way, there was a sense in which the people on the front line, so to speak, were very much left to their own defences.

This is the world in which Fran grew up, the friendship that had begun to blossom between these two neighbouring kingdoms in the thirteenth century giving way to a bitter and enduring enmity. Though the battle of Bannockburn has gone down in the annals of Scottish history as a great and glorious enterprise, it's hard to find much in this brutal war that warrants that description. But, as ever, individuals on both sides could and did act with much honour and valour.

Languages

It's well known that, in medieval England, the nobility spoke French (the language of those who conquered the kingdom in 1066) and everyone else spoke Anglo-Saxon (the language of the pre-conquest kings and their subjects), apart from the priestly class, who used Latin. There were also pockets of previous ascendant languages, most particularly the British once spoken across the British Isles and, after the arrival of Angles, Saxons, Jutes etc., restricted to Wales and Cornwall. But you get the general picture.

However, there is some evidence to suggest that the elites could at least understand what was being said by those of lesser status. Indeed, they would have been foolish not to. I think this would have been particularly true on small estates such as Fran's Hilton Beacon, whose lords surely played a much more hands-on role in their management than larger ones. To that end, I have not attempted to distinguish between those whose first tongue might be French and those who were native English-speakers.

As for sounding 'medieval' (whatever that may have been), I wanted to have my characters speak in a way that is easily accessible to the reader without sounding too modern. I use a wonderful website called etymonline.com, which keeps me within the ballpark. In the end, however, it was more important to me to have lifelike protagonists than technically accurate language.

The sharp-eared among you will have noticed that the dialect spoken by the native English-speaking West-morlanders (as opposed to the more 'proper' English spoken by those whose first language was probably French) is very similar to Scots. I used Ann Wheeler's *The Westmorland Dialect, in three familiar dialogues*, which was published in Kendal in 1821 and has a dictionary at the back. The words there were transcribed phonetically, but the relationship to the Scots language (which isn't homogenous either) is clear. This shouldn't come as a surprise. Scots is descended from the Anglo-Saxon spoken in what became Lothian and the Borders but was once the very tip of the old Northumbrian kingdom permanently acquired by the Scottish kings more than a thousand years ago. In other words, the Anglo-Saxon spoken in Westmorland and that spoken in Scotland were once the same, though a millennium of different political circumstances and borrowings will have caused a degree of divergence.

Lastly, I really should address the use of the word 'cunt' in Chapter 15. That's not a word I'm comfortable saying, because it's used now to be extremely insulting to women. In the Middle Ages, however, it was merely the word for vagina, and everyone, from aristocratic women to peasants, had no problem with it. By the end of the fourteenth century, that was changing, perhaps because members of what was then called the middling sort (what we might call the bourgeoisie) were seeking to differentiate themselves from those below as social mobility increased after the outbreak of plague in Western Europe in the middle of the century. The obvious example is Chaucer's wife of Bath, who was certainly not afraid to speak her mind in the plainest terms. But there's also *Le Ménagier de Paris* (*The Good Wife's Guide*), essentially a 'how-to' manual for the fifteen-year old bride of an elderly middle-class Parisian. In this fascinating compendium of social mores and practical advice, he tells her not to pick up 'vulgar, lewd or ribald words' from her servants, including 'filthy' ones for her private parts. That he should need to do so speaks volumes about what was surely entirely normal, but becoming frowned upon for certain women.

Acknowledgements

As always, this book is far more than just the work of the person whose name features on the front cover. I am so grateful to the many people who have helped *Lies of the Flesh* along its way. My heartfelt thanks to Sheila Griffiths, Juliet Hancock and Rian Stubbs, who were good enough to read earlier versions and provide constructive criticism, which certainly helped to knock the plot and its characters into shape.

Then there is the fabulous team at Birlinn – Hugh Andrew, Alison Rae, Mairi Sutherland and the sales/publicity staff – who have once more shown faith in me and eased my second novel out into the wild, along with Craig Hillsley, who did another formidable editing job to improve the text beyond measure.

Finally, I want to thank my family for holding my hand and keeping me sane. To Nick, who has given me encouragement of every kind whenever it's been needed. To Finn, for listening and for helping with my research. This book is dedicated to you, and to my mum, Margaret Watson, who is loved and missed so much.